Greatcoat
Greatcoats Off!

JIM MILLER

DEDICATION

Now and always, the number one person on my list to thank is my wife, Bev. If there was a goddess of support, she would be it. Thank you, Bev.

A few years I decided to resuscitate Toby and Bowles. From that re-birth, it gathered steam, fans and friends. It is now a complete story. But it didn't get there by itself. Along this book's journey I had a tremendous amount of help and support. The book is also dedicated to all those soldiers I served with, all of you who put up with Greatcoats On! Greatcoats Off! as part of the daily routine of army life. Thanks, guys.

OTHER BOOKS BY JIM MILLER –

ACKNOWLEDGMENTS

The seed for this book was planted many years ago, while I was still serving in the infantry. It sprouted pages of ideas in notebooks, on scraps of paper and restaurant napkins. This mass of paper sat around while I did other writing. I'd re-visit the concept, scribble a page or two and drop the new material into a folder with the old. I've had the idea of a gentleman's gentleman right from the first but one day a friend said, "Sounds like Jeeves."

"Who's Jeeves," I asked. And with that came my education into P. G. Woodhouse and his marvellous stories.

Jay Currie was instrumental in getting the stalled tale off and running with his bang-on suggestions. He was the one who came up with the notion that Marvin Oxnard, aka 'Ox' was the ideal narrator. Thanks, Jay.

The Writers In Progress writing group of Oceanside on Vancouver Island continually encouraged me in all aspects of my writing.

Then there is Dominique Scott, who I am thrilled to claim as my editor. She put so much time and effort into the three different versions that I lumbered her with. As well, she patiently put up with my innate inability to place commas correctly. She salvaged many scenes where I had scattered commas like so much grass seed. While her editorial skills are excellent, it was her insight into how to transform a rambling episodic manuscript into a readable novel that saved the day. Thank you so much for everything, Dominique.

CHAPTER 1

EVERYONE MEETS
THE BOWLES FAMILY

"Bowles was promoted to lieutenant colonel yesterday."

I was in the midst of swallowing a mouthful of brandy that His Lordship had just handed me. Luckily for us both, I had been facing the wall when I spewed it back out. Not so fortunate was the portrait of Lord Haselbury the 14th. His face was now coated with a fine mist. His Lordship, or Toby as I'd always thought of him, laughed.

"Best he's ever looked," he said.

"But a lieutenant colonel?" I said. "Bowles? It boggles."

Toby said, "The Depot. Never forget that place."

He was referring to our epic adventure in Canada way back in our collective past in 1964. I stared at the flames, not hearing the roar and crackle. With the onset of memory, I too danced back to the days of the Regimental Depot of the Caledonia and Musquodoboit Scottish Regiment.

Toby nodded. "Bowles a light colonel, eh," he said, falling back into Canadian Army vernacular and adding the equally Canadian 'eh'.

"Unbelievable. I thought he'd long been released."

Toby shook his head. "This goes on, he'll be in command of the Canadian Army before he's kicked out."

He gestured toward a pair of chairs. We were in his Lordship's study, outside the rain was pelting down. Inside a blazing fire and large snifters of brandy made it all very comfortable. Even the news about Bowles was distant. Until Toby added, "It seems like only yesterday we were in Colonel Smith's office, and RSM McKindly was calling you the penguin and me the blue-blooded arse."

I shifted in my chair. "That entire episode is like something out of a bad dream, sir."

Toby sipped and swallowed. "There, that's how it's done, Ox. A gentle sip and down the proper pipe it goes."

"Yes, I understand. However, you didn't hear the news I heard as I attempted to sip."

1

"True. It would've shocked anyone."

"And Colonel Schultzberger? How do you think he's taking it?"

"Jackrabbit? If he's still around, this will more than do him in."

"He's still right side up, sir. I and J.P. correspond occasionally."

"And assuming that it's no longer top secret, what does the J.P. stand for? He never did let us filthy rabble know."

"Sergeant Jonathan Peter Clyde. And, yes, he, like the Colonel is now retired. He finished his career last year as a company sergeant major in the First Battalion."

"Good for him."

I laughed. "In his last letter he did mention that if it hadn't been for Bowles, he'd probably have retired as an RSM."

Toby nodded but made no reply. I think he had dropped back into history. His next comment showed he was moving slightly into the future. "Ox, you've got your journals, notes, etcetera, right?"

"I do indeed. At one time, my wife suggested I write a book."

Toby leaned forward with a bright smile on his face. "Brilliant. Yes, you should."

I returned that comment with what I thought was a modest smile. "I have an appointment with an editor in the city this Friday."

"You've already done it?" He didn't let me reply but went on. "Of course you would have. Always a step ahead of us all…" He stopped. "But, libel or slander? I can never remember which is which."

"It's libel, sir. Defamation by written or printed word or pictures." I shook my head. "But in this instance, it is none of them. I am hoping to publish it as a work of fiction."

"Sounds great. And the title…" he looked at me and the cheeky, young Toby showed through. "Why not call it 'An Ox Tale'?"

I nodded. "Very droll, M'lord. After all, you were always falling into the soup, weren't you?"

"In the tale of Lieutenant Bowles, yes, very much." He came over to me and slapped me on the shoulder. "But I knew you always had my back."

I stood up. "I'm sorry, sir, but I really do have to go."

Toby stood up as well. He looked at his watch. "I have to go and meet with the town council in regard to a zoning issue." He snapped his fingers. "But Friday. I'm into the city as well. Some kind of committee meeting with a bunch of windbags from the House. May I offer you a lift?"

"Yes, thank you. That would be very handy, my lord."

And so it was that Friday, at one o'clock in the afternoon I found myself in the office of Peter Warren, an editor with Willoughby Publications. He offered coffee, and I declined. It probably didn't show, due to the rigorous training I had been exposed to on the arduous road to becoming a gentleman's gentleman, but I was incredibly nervous.

He put his elbows on his desk, clasped his hands and said, "I've been led to believe you have something that might interest us."

"Yes, it's actually a true story, but because of libel, I have decided to publish it as a work of fiction."

Warren leaned back in his chair and shook his head. "No, won't do. How true is it?"

"Perfectly. And I do have witnesses and even some declaration of authenticity."

"Then, we'll see. If I like it, we'll publish it as nonfiction if it's true it can't be libel. Start it out for me, please."

"You mean tell it to you?"

"Why not?"

"It's rather longish."

He smiled. "I'm not going anywhere."

"Very well." I took a breath and plunged in. "The only reason you are even hearing about this wildly improbable tale is because of a series of huge coincidences. And if I hadn't been plunged headfirst into it, I'd never have believed it myself. The true definition of a coincidence is a remarkable concurrence of events or circumstances without apparent causal connection. And as this utterly implausible recitation will demonstrate, there is no such thing as a coincidence; the little buggers come, if you'll pardon the crude term, in batches. Let me begin at the beginning of these coincidences, not the actual saga itself."

"As I suggested a moment ago, we have all afternoon. Go ahead, and please start with how this became a book."

"My name is Marvin Eldred Oxnard. I was born to be Lord Haselbury's gentleman's gentleman, after my dear father passed on, of course. The job entailed being a unique kind of manservant: part butler, part personal servant, part companion to his Lordship and part member of the family. It had been that way for many cycles of lord and gentleman's gentleman in the Trelauney-Fitzgibboncrest family and consequently any Oxnard in the role performed many more exotic duties than that of an ordinary gentleman's gentleman and considerably less of the drudgery than that of an ordinary gentleman's gentleman.

The idea for a book began its incubation on a rainy, blustery, London afternoon, about a year ago. I'd escorted his lordship to the train station, and then I finding myself at loose ends proceeded to my old army service club to spend the remainder of the day.

"Ox, is that you?"

Imagine my surprise when looking up through the heavy drizzle, I saw, on the steps above me, sheltered from the downpour, my old comrade in arms, Charles Goodber-Frobisher, Goody, to his acquaintances. We had served in the same regiment during the war; he as my lance corporal and me as a sergeant.

The last time we had met he'd been working within some governmental red-tape manufacturing factory. We hustled inside where a hall porter immediately collared our umbrellas, raincoats, and bowlers and ushered us into the Beggar's Bar. No one knew what it had been called originally, but back on 29 January 1728, the famous "Beggar's Opera" had been first performed. Members of the club who had been at that celebrated opening had retired to the club for after-theatre drinks and began re-telling the plot and singing the songs. It had been the Beggar's Bar ever since.

Once settled in facing armchairs, hot rum toddies in our hands, the roaring fire to our flanks, I said, "Well, Goody, old Chap what have you been up to?"

"Ox, this is going to sound like something I made up while under the influence of an overly-strong Tawny Port."

"Intriguing. Air it out."

"As you know, after the war, I'd gone to work for the Foreign Office."

I nodded. Goody always needed a warm-up.

"I'd been a pretty good researcher." He stopped, smiled. "Due, most likely to you, Ox."

"Me?"

"Yes, you've always been on top of things. Always had the need to know, even as a lance corporal, you had to know everything."

I sipped, nodded. My father had called this tendency terminal curiosity because he was sure it would be the death of me.

"And so from you, I learned how to make inquiries."

I sipped and nodded again. Eventually, Goody would get to the point.

"I left the Foreign Office three years ago to branch out and became a professional researcher and historian doing freelance consultancy."

"Interesting, and you can find employment... sufficient to keep body and soul together?"

It was his turn to nod. "Usually. The jobs bounce from feast to famine."

"Maybe I should buy you dinner?" I said.

As if to show me there were other ways of communicating with his head, Goody shook his.

"Appreciated, but unnecessary. Tonight it's my treat. I'm coming off a very lucrative commission. And strangely enough, from Canada." And with that, the first of these coincidences reared its monstrous head.

"Canada, you say? I've been over there myself, with the Trelauney-Fitzgibboncrest family. We were there a number of years."

"Fascinating place, quite large, isn't it?"

"Goody, you have no idea. So you didn't have to actually go there?"

"Oh, yes, a number of times, but only to Ottawa. How about you?"

"I traveled with the family from Halifax to Winnipeg, and from there, Master Toby and I went to New Brunswick."

"How extraordinary." He stared at me. "Are you willing to carry the tale further?"

"I am, but, let's go on with you and your tale of Ottawa."

Goody went back to nodding. "Have you ever heard of the Bowles family."

I jumped as if stung. "Bowles!"

"You sound like you are familiar with them?" said Goody. Here was my deciding moment. Do I dare expose the extraordinary doings of my master, Toby and his exploits with the Canadian military? Was this fate? I had carried this tale around with me like the ancient Mariner with his albatross slung around his neck for far too long. Was this the time to seek expiation? Looking at my watch, I decided there could be no better moment. "Longish story," I said, half-hoping he'd stop me.

"Oh, no, Ox," Goody said, shaking a warning finger at me. "If this has anything to do with the Family Bowles, you've got a lot of explaining to do."

"As do you, Goody."

"Sound like we both have rather long stories to relate. Are you in a hurry?"

"Not at all. I intended a quiet afternoon here, taking a bit of supper and then making some easy money at the snooker tables."

"My wife's in Bournemouth for the next week," said Goody. "So bang goes your quiet afternoon, along with the snooker, if necessary. I'm buying you dinner, and you will tell me how you know the Bowles family."

I smiled. "I'll probably need to be kept well-hydrated as well as fed." I held up my empty glass. "But, enough of hot buttered rum. I'm going to shift to whiskey."

Goody's answer was a wave toward Jenkins, the bartender.

"Two scotches, Jenks, please."

Once our glasses were delivered, and we had advised Jenks that we would be staying on for dinner, I said, "So, you give me the background on your research, and I'll jump in where necessary, or start my story after you have finished yours."

Goody waved his glass in the air. "Cheers, and prepare yourself for a most enlightening, but alarming story of military disasters."

I waited, betting myself that my story of Bowles and military disasters would be far worse than his. I was wrong.

"My commission began with a retired General, a Canadian general, whose name I cannot mention…" he shrugged. "Part of the initial consult, but it doesn't have any bearing on the story."

To show I understood I sipped my drink.

"The General wanted a complete dossier on the Bowles family to convince himself that he was innocent of any and all military misdemeanors that occurred on his watch during the War." He waggled a thoughtful finger toward me. "My initial surmise was that the old general was a shade off his onion. And, I think the way he recited his story will bear that out."

Before we could go any further, the dining room maitre'd came and told us it was time to move our theater of operations to the dining room. Once there, we settled on a nice white wine with the fish and Goody got back to the heart of his story.

"When I told the general I needed more details to clarify the situation, he yelled out, "A Bowles fought with Boadicea!"

I chewed on a tough carrot, swallowed and said, "Startling introduction."

"Agreed, but it gripped me from the start," said Goody, who then related the following tale. If hand-me-down myth was to be believed, a Bowles had fought with Boadicea; but lost. She had arm-wrestled him for his chariot at a grand feast a few days before her war with the Romans.

Goodies' anonymous general pointed out that the clan Bowles were warriors. Not famous for deeds of derring-do. Not by any means up in the rarefied atmosphere of Roland, Caesar, or Achilles, but more on the level of Custer and Goliath and all those sorrowful others who had come in second on the fields of Mars.

Legend has it, or to be more precise, shit-house rumor has it that the most recent of these militarily-challenged Bowles' ancestors, Artie's father, had acquitted himself in true Bowles fashion during WW II. Which was the time frame the general was concerned with.

According to the Canadian War Office, Samuel "Soup" Bowles, committed no illustrious military faux pas, suffered no devastating defeats and caused his comrades in arms no friendly fire casualties. He managed to stay away from all officially recorded traces of martial infamy. It's what's whispered that gets about, not inky documents sequestered in dusty archives.

That whispery stain on his legacy came in the shape of one incident in Sicily. As a member of an Armoured Regiment, Soup Bowles had boldly and without concern for his own well-being, directed cannon fire on a headquarters. That it turned out to be an American headquarters was inconsequential as far as he was concerned. The occurrence coincided with a German counterattack, and because the Yanks were wiped out to a man, no one was around to point the finger. Because Bowles had been Johnny-on-the-spot, he received a Bronze Star for gallantry from the United States.

When Goody mentioned World War Two, I interrupted to let him know that we were closing in on the days that I had been privy to. I mentioned Arthur Bowles and Goody nodded, poured us each more wine, saying, "Arthur, usually called Artie, was the son of Soup Bowles."

By this time we were through the scalloped ham croquettes; simple fare, but being a military service club, the members didn't like highbrow grub. Ham croquettes was the club's signature dinner. As we ate, I tossed in a nod here and there, all the while thinking that Goody was talking about the Bowles family of which I was familiar. What was unfamiliar and frightening was the length of the historical trail of stupidity that comprised the Bowles' family tree.

Hasty Pudding, crackers, and cheese arrived in their turn and were devoured while Goody pushed on, but his account had now reached the part that interested me greatly; Lieutenant Arthur Victor Llewellyn Bowles.

With the war over Soup Bowles remained active in the Militia and had managed to reach the rank of colonel. This happened for two reasons. The first was simple genetics. The Bowles' clan were a long-lived family.

"In my research, I discovered that the bastards always died of natural causes," said Goody. "You would think that they would have gone the way of Tyrannosaurus Rex, but they bear charmed lives. They get everyone around them killed off, with never a scratch to themselves."

This longevity helped Samuel 'Soup' Bowles achieve his rank through the normal wear and tear of attrition. All his peers died off, retired or just quit. He hung in there until he was senior and in those days seniority was everything. In Soup's case, it was a kind of incompetence mellowed through time until he was so incompetent that he had to be a full colonel; nothing else would do.

The second reason was that the Regiment that Soup Bowles led had been raised and financed by his father-in-law, Reginald Glendenning, who for some obscure reason wanted to be called "Bob". The last thing Bob wanted to do was to bring his son-in-law into the family business, especially when Soup's sole talent consisted of being a military Typhoid Mary. To avoid such a catastrophe, Bob Glendenning initially considered an annulment to the marriage on the grounds that his daughter was an idiot. Even if this had been true, it was not something he wanted to have in the newspapers. Divorce was out of the question for the same reason. The shame of public humiliation dissuaded him.

His answer was to raise a regiment and give it to the militia on the grounds that it would keep kids out of jail. He insisted that this regiment was to be split into three battalions, each placed in a tiny hamlet far from the others. Another condition was that his son-in-law be installed as the Colonel of the Regiment. The final stipulation was that the military powers that be were to keep Soup on the road for most of his time, visiting the widely spaced armories on inspections and parades.

This also suited Deirdre Bowles, Soup's wife and Artie's mother. While at a finishing school in France she had been smitten by a wartime romance. Soup did look good in uniform; yet another example of all style and no substance. Deirdre came to what senses she possessed a few hours after the ceremony. A few dreadful hours alone with Soup quickly sank home the brutal fact that, to her everlasting dismay and regret, she had married a twit. Unkind family members had said behind her back that it takes a twit to know one. She too decided against divorce. A beautiful woman, she did not look like any other member of the Glendenning family; a family who's looks had been described as giving 'homely' a bad name. In return for this beauty, she had been short-changed in the intelligence department but had been issued a certain degree of wiliness.

Deirdre had raised Artie by herself, in an environment practically devoid of the taint of the military. Despite her cunning, this proved to be her undoing. On the road a lot, Soup's infrequent visits back home in "military splendour" simply fanned Artie's martial desires into a fierce conflagration of soldierly fervour. Naturally enough, Artie grew up a little confused. His mother nurtured him with tales of the Bowles' military calamities. On the rare occasions when his father visited home, Artie dined on a diet of no guts, no glory.

Not knowing which way to turn, Artie Bowles decided to take the Queen's shilling and see for himself. Unfortunately, history was on his mother's side. The Bowles family's track record illuminated no sterling examples of outstanding military exploits or even of exemplary role models. In civilian circles, despite their proclivity toward disaster, the Family Bowles escutcheon remained un-blotted. The same could not be said of the military world where the name Bowles struck fear into the hearts of all ranks in all arms of the Canadian military.

No history book will ever tell of that sterling British subaltern, Farquhar Bowles, who had been captured during the Indian Mutiny. During his tenure as a prisoner, he misguidedly boasted to the mutineers that there wasn't a jail that could hold them. The rebel troops countered by sequestering the captured British troops in the Black Hole of Calcutta.

Then there was the more ancient relative, a Saxon, who fought valiantly against the Conqueror in 1066. No proof exists, although there is strong circumstantial evidence that Thorvic Bowpuller was stung by a bee as he raised his bow to shoot at William's invading Norman army. In his pain and blindness, he loosed that fatal arrow that cost Harold his eye and England her freedom. To rub salt into the wound, William, now ensconced on the throne of England, rewarded Thorvic with a purse of gold. For those obsessed with the need for proof, in their home shire, there is a ragged old parchment ordering the name of Bowpuller changed to Bow-less, and a prohibition that the family of Bow-less was denied access to the village butts or target range. For eternity...

Even without that genetic toxicity, young Artie didn't have a lot going for himself. The stagnant gene pool he'd been dipped in, either proved or disproved Darwin's Theory of Natural Selection, depending on your perspective. On the one hand, the Bowles family tree had demonstrated a remarkable longevity that was a continual surprise to everyone, including the Bowles family. They were "bred for luck" as one smart-ass put it. And it did seem that the family owed its success more to serendipity than any inherited attributes such as intelligence, athletic prowess or battle-hardened aptitude.

To some, this survival of the luckiest demonstrated Darwin's theory. To others, the attendant dull-wittedness that would have doomed any normal branch of Homo sapiens to early extinction only confirmed their belief in sterilization as legitimate encouragement to Mother Nature's evolutionary aspirations.

As the latest incarnation of the Bowles' lineage, Arthur Victor Llewellyn Bowles, our Artie, was not only graced with his ancestors' over-abundance of stupidity but he had also had the misfortune to inherit from the Glendenning's side of the family, the facial expressions of a vacant playground. At the time of his enlistment, he was a tall enigma, bull-necked and carrying a large, albeit empty, head on a set of shoulders that could have graced a defensive lineman. The resemblance ended there. From the chest down, the rest of his body matched his voice. His larynx suffered from the vocal equivalent of rickets; weak, whiny and with the insistent grating quality of fingernails on a chalkboard.

But it was his uninhabited face that carried the day for those who believed that a first impression was an invaluable guide to character. In this case, Bowles' face was too blank even to house the term 'monotonous' within its boundaries. And with no signposts on Artie's mug, character was non-existent.

If a complete selection of non-features could have been assembled on one face, it was Artie's. In his case bland was an overstatement. The insipidness of his countenance was underscored by eyes devoid of wisdom, backed up by a nothing mouth and reinforced by a blob of pastry nose.

Artie's mother, while dead set against his joining the army, eventually became worn down by his sulks. To make it worse, Artie's daily tantrums were reinforced by the irregular visits from his father so that, "A hitch in the army will knock some sense into him. Look what it did to me," finally made her say, "Let it be."

Which was a far too simple a concept for what happened next. Conceived in the cosmopolitan world of post-war Paris, born in the backwater hamlet of Mustleby-on-Trent, Southern Ontario; located nowhere near the Trent River system, Artie came of age. Millions of pages have been written, huge forests destroyed in an attempt to explain teenage, baby-boomer adolescence, so no such endeavors will be made here to provide the correct explanation. This is the story of what happened, not why it happened; readers who have managed to struggle this far into Goody's illuminating history will have figured out the why without any assistance. And since Goody showed no inclination to slowing his narrative down, I sat there and let him carry on.

Bob Glendenning wielded considerable influence in Ottawa, but Deidre made no request of her father to ease Artie's way into a military career. As far as she was concerned, if he was unable to gain admission, it would be the end of all attempts to get her little boy into the army.

Soup said, "Don't worry, Son, with my connections, you'll be on a train for the Military College before you know it."

Sadly for Artie, Soup's connections only led to a train wreck. Suffice to say, Arthur Bowles arrived at the gates of one of Canada's three military colleges and was promptly shown the door before he had even set one foot on martial soil. He was rejected by the Francophone Military College the next day by telephone and the third military college, in Victoria, British Columbia, having been forewarned, sent him a registered letter denying him access even before he applied. West Point's Director of Admissions sent a telegram claiming that admission was limited to Americans. No Canadians need apply.

With nothing but a dream of glory and lacking any sense that he was not wanted by Uncle Sam or Johnny Canuck, Artie Bowles went off to the Recruiting Centre in London, Ontario. His mother went off to her analyst. His father went off to review a parade.

A Sergeant, recently demoted from the rank of WO1, Warrant Officer One, and sent to the recruiting centre as penance, interviewed Bowles. Within five minutes of their meeting, he realized that what the officer corps needed at this time was one more complete, fully-cooked, ready-to-serve idiot. He signed Bowles up. As had happened in so many of the Bowles family military blunders, luck collided with circumstance. The captain in charge of the centre, being seriously weighed down with a hangover, signed off the enrollment without reviewing it.

The Basic Officer Course in Camp Borden, just north of Toronto permitted him entrance only due to the absences of the Officer School commandant away on leave and his Deputy, away on an intelligence course. It was here that Artie had his first major opportunity to display the Bowles aptitude for ineptitude.

It was an unwritten rule that officer cadets do not, under any circumstances ever close with or come near course staff in the mess. One evening in the officers' mess, Artie's course commander, Captain Copplefield, an armoured officer who fancied himself as an old-time cavalryman, made it very clear that Bowles was destined for the infantry.

Bowles wandered over to Copplefield and said, "When I'm a tanker like you, sir, will I get a chance to join the riding troop and get my own horse?"

The Regimental Riding Troop, a ceremonial touring troupe similar to the RCMP's Musical Ride, put on displays and visited cities and towns to show off. They spent many hours charging about as if they were the Light Brigade, spearing little pieces of wood while nipping by at full gallop. The riding troop had been Captain Copplefield's previous posting, and it was a bit of a come down for him to go from training animals with horse sense to training adolescent humans with minimal intelligence.

He turned to Bowles, gave him a thousand yard stare while his cronies gaped in shock at Bowles' impertinence.

"Bowles, m'lad, there is the Cavalry, and then there is the Artillery, then there is the Cavalryman's horse."

Bowles nodded eagerly as Captain Copplefield paused to consume a dab of scotch. After an appreciative pause, he went on, "Then there is the horse's shit pile. Do you know what is under that pile of steaming horseshit?"

"Yessir, yessir, we all do. It's the Infantry." Bowles giggled.

"Well done, Bowles. We have taught you something."

Bowles beamed, looked around to see if any of his classmates had heard this note of approval. None had. Fearful of being associated with him, they had all disappeared once Bowles had crossed into the no-man's-land surrounding the instructional staff's reserved drinking table.

Captain Copplefield continued, "And, do you know what's in the infantry, Bowles?"

This stumped him. It was not part of the old joke. "No, sir."

"You, Bowles. You are in the infantry."

And that's where he went. On graduation day, although in Bowles' case, it was more a "Get him out of here and forget he ever existed" parade, there had been no offers from any of the infantry units for his services. Even Grandpa Bob Glendenning ran into difficulty getting him into a regiment. To be sure, Bowles' poor course report acted as a boat anchor to his career, but it didn't help matters that his father, Soup Bowles was notorious among the senior regular officers still serving. All infantry commanders reported that their quotas for second lieutenants were full. Sad to say, to a man, they reported no vacancies for at least fifteen years.

Goody took a break to spread some cheese on a cracker, and I looked around for our waiter. It came as a surprise to find that we had three people from the table next to us, all sitting with their chairs turned to face us.

"Danny, you like what you're hearing?" I asked one of them.

"Ox, this is more fun than beating you at snooker."

"Yes, Goody has a way with words. But, I think that if you lot are going to crowd around, you'll need to pay the price of admission."

"Buy a round, perhaps," said Nelson Morgan from behind me. I turned around to see that our table had become infested with eavesdroppers, hangers-on, and even kibitzers, as I believe the American term is called.

"Capital, a few bottles wouldn't be remiss, if this is going to become a replacement for the snooker tournament. Once we finish up the last few scraps of our dinner, we'll get back to the story."

CHAPTER 2

THE ARMY MEETS BOWLES

Dinner over, we retired to the smoking room and with Goody and myself centred on the two best chairs, about twenty or so members found themselves seats. Goody took a healthy swig of port and got back into his narrative.

Two months of having Officer Cadet Bowles hanging around the house in his uniform had finally driven his mother, Deirdre, crying to her father. Bob Glendenning, of the belief that his nitwit daughter had made her bed and that her son was a by-product of it, was initially indifferent. He was prepared to let this indifference colour his world until her husband visited him in his office. Five minutes of Soup's presence convinced him that indifference wasn't going to keep his son-in-law from occupying a chair in his office. The only way to stop Deirdre's daily telephone whining and Soup's physical visitations was to take action. Unfortunately, once the knowledge got out that the Glendenning clan had become related by marriage to the Bowles tribe, Bob's sphere of influence within the military shrank to the size of a ping pong table.

Out of desperation, Bob called his civilian friends in Ottawa demanding that an infantry battalion find a home for his grandson. He was hoping for help from lobbyists and other powerful robber barons, but they no longer saw him as one of their own. He stooped to blackmail. One of his friends was heavily involved in defence contracts and the resulting kickbacks. Bureaucratic fears of losing an untaxable financial goldmine and the scare of exposure brought that beleaguered crony onside, and he shoved the situation up to the notice of the CDS, Chief of Defence Staff, who in turn surrendered the problem to his Director of Infantry. The Director discussed quite amicably his desires with the regimental commanders of all the infantry battalions while these worthies were in Ottawa attending the annual promotion board.

Gathered together were the commanding officers of the RCR, The Royal Canadian Regiment; The QOR, Queen's Own Rifles of Canada; The PPCLI, Princess Patricia's Canadian Light Infantry; The Royal Highland Regiment, aka The Black Watch, The Royal Twenty-Second Regiment, aka Van Doos; The Canadian Guards; and The CMSR, The Caledonia and Musquodoboit

Scottish Regiment. Musquodoboit, although a fine Nova Scotian word, and unpronounceable for most people on seeing it written down, was pronounced, Musk-a-dobbit.

At this point, Goody was interrupted. "Goody, you're making this up. How on earth could you ever get this detailed a grip on this story?"

Goody grinned, waved his cigar in the air and replied, "I was in Ottawa, the capital city of Canada. I'd been there a number of times and with a bit of good luck, along with the disbursement of a few bottles number of excellent scotch and I was able to infiltrate their old boy system. You know how it goes, once you're in, nothing is kept back."

I said, "Right, Lads, let's only break in if you get lost, or we'll be here all night."

"We have nowhere else to go, Ox."

I ignored that and with a nod at our chronicler, he got back into it. I did have to admit that as a researcher, Goody was remarkable, and the intricacies, while being entertaining to the members, were enlightening to me. And they explained a lot.

There were seven full colonels, one per regiment, and in those days of post-WWII and Korean largesse with the Canadian taxpayer's money, each regiment carried three battalions. This put an additional twenty-one lieutenant colonels in the room with the colonels.

The Promotion Board was their reward for being good soldiers. Each year, they and their respective regimental sergeants major trotted off to Ottawa for a five-day conference. The conference was nothing more than five days of maligning their colleagues' top soldiers and the bragging up of their own exceptional men. They spent their days on promotion board business, their nights in the bars of the nation's capital. Career decisions were made and unmade based on the degree of hilarity of the previous evening's carousing and the magnitude of the next day's hangovers. Goody paused, held out his glass, and it was refilled.

"Hey, Goody, got any examples of this hilarity?" said a voice from across the room.

"Of, course, without anecdotal material, a researcher leans toward boredom. Here's one about the corporal promotions. I got it from the Commanding Officer of the Royal Canadian Regiment who swears the conversation actually occurred. 'No, you can't promote him to sergeant. He's got a son who had a dog who bit a captain's son in the leg.'

15

'Okay, why don't we post him, his son, and the dog to Camp Wainwright, Alberta?'

'Good idea, except the dog would never go there.'

'Besides, the captain's a jerk. He's not cut out for the infantry.'

'Well, promote the dog and let's get to the mess.'

'Doesn't matter anyway," spoke up another CO, 'I heard that the Captain shot the dog.'

'Good, that's settled, let's get on to the sergeants.'

Goody stopped there and stood up. "I need to take a break."

I joined him on my hind legs and announced, "It's going on for nine o'clock, we'll reconvene here in ten minutes. Goody needs to give his tongue a rest." I accompanied him to the men's room and said, "Your yarn seems to be slipping away on a tangent." He shook his head. "No, Ox, not at all. I'm setting the stage for something that will seize you by the throat in its intensity."

Re-settled in our pews, Goody, with a glance at me said, "Where were we?"

Someone yelled, "Canadian Promotion Board."

"Ah, yes, and what I've explained was the usual turn of events at their promotion boards, that is, until that year, when a disgruntled Director of Infantry called a conference just before the promotion board began. He'd received a call to look after a certain second lieutenant.

"Bowles!" yelled half the contingent.

Goody smiled. "Good, you're paying attention. The Director of Infantry stated that this was not anywhere near his idea of his job. The Director was incensed at the idea of going into the office in the afternoon and missing his golf game in an effort to find a worthless second lieutenant a home.

Facing his regimental and battalion commanders he got down to brass tacks immediately, "Gentlemen, with all due respect to your vast store of knowledge in regard to the Bowles family let me tell you that what's past is past. I put it to you that, while not coming from particularly valiant historical antecedents, young Bowles is not necessarily destined to bring about a Canadian version of Custer's Last Stand or the North American version of the Retreat from Moscow."

"Both of them combined would be a blessing," whispered the CO of the First Battalion Queen's Own. "Compared to what one of us is in for if we get Bowles."

"Too true. From what I've heard there has been a Bowles as a catalyst in every recorded military disaster in history," said a Guard's battalion CO.

"Yeah, a Bowles from the Mediterranean side of the family caused Hannibal to undertake that mad march over the Alps," added the CO of 3PPCLI. "Seems a certain Hasrubal Bowles had been tasked to take the bloody elephants and load them on the heavy troop transport ships. There never had been a plan to cross the Alps. The elephants got away from Bowles en route to the docks, got it into their heads that the mountains promised some fine skiing and off went a thousand elephants. Hannibal's army chased them all over the Alps."

"Yeah, they say there's even a French branch of the Bowles family. One of them was reported to be Napoleon's Meteorological Officer. When Nap asked him for a forecast for the Moscow area he had coolly replied, "Barely a flurry, Mon General."

"That's enough," interrupted the Director peevishly. "No more pessimism. You are all commanding officers because you are leaders. Well, here's a chance for one of you to make a name for yourself. Lead Bowles into a successful career. It's the Sixties. A new era. A new man. Let us put our heads together and decide who gets this golden opportunity. Better yet, I'll leave you to it. I have a meeting to attend."

"Yeah, on the first tee," came another whisper.

The Dir of Inf had one other piece of advice. "Decide today who gets Bowles. Or else decide just who it is you would like to replace you. Tomorrow morning I want the name of the regiment and the battalion that is taking Bowles. Or else I want a list of all my new regimental and battalion commanders. The choice is yours. Thank you, gentlemen."

When the door closed, the CO of the 2nd Black Watch said, "If it's such a golden opportunity, why doesn't the old bastard keep Bowles here in Ottawa as his aide?"

"It's so wonderfully golden that when a ministerial inquiry on Bowles and the poor, accursed, regiment that has the unfortunate luck to get him, lands on his desk, Direction of Inf will be able to say that the battalion commanders handled this alone."

The seven regimental commanders came to the rapid and unanimous decision that their very presence as a group would prejudice the lieutenant colonels and would prevent any opportunity for open collaboration. They deserted en masse to the Ottawa Station officers' mess to place bets on which battalion would come up the loser.

Three hours later, all civility long buried, old hatreds dug back up, all reason and logic exhausted, the commanding officers had had enough. The twenty-one battalion commanders, with a combined total of four hundred plus years of razor-sharp, rational, decision-making expertise had reached a dead end. One man was going to suffer. To solve the predicament they all signed a contract stipulating that each would contribute two percent of his military pension to the one who would doubtless be taking a disgraceful early retirement or a cashiering after being the guest of honour at a General Court Martial. Then they flipped coins, odd man out until one was left.

The winner, so to speak, was Lieutenant Colonel John "Jackrabbit" Schultzberger, commanding officer of the First Battalion, The Caledonia and Musquodoboit Scottish Regiment.

Schultzberger looked around the room. "I've only got seven years to compulsory retirement age. If I can find a safe spot for him, maybe I'll get out of this with a whole skin."

On the train back to the battalion's home station in Camp Gagetown, New Brunswick, Schultzberger spent many hours thinking just where that safe spot could be. One answer came from his wife a few days later. Not normally given to discussing battalion affairs with her, he sat surprised and a little remorseful that he had not asked her advice sooner. At first, he thought she was nuts. She wasn't, she just hated the army, but loved her husband. She enjoyed offering such a solution. It would buy her husband some time while also placing a time bomb in the regimental system. Those stupid old fogeys on the prehistoric regimental executive deserve anything they get and, knowing them, she was sure that they would buy such a short-term solution. "Well dear, why don't you promote him?"

"Promote him? Linda, have you been listening to anything I've said? The man is a menace. He will destroy this unit and me with it. Promote him! I can't believe it!"

"John, for him to be promoted what does he need?"

He wanted to say a fucking miracle, but instead answered, "First, the lieutenant's qualifying course, along with his, commanding officer's recommendation."

"Alright, John, and how long is the course?"

"Linda, you are a genius." Schultzberger saw her plan immediately; "The fool will be out of the unit for months."

"And by that time you and the RSM will have come up with another course to send him on."

"That's right. By the time my seven years are up, he'll be the most experienced course officer I've got, and I won't even have set eyes on him. And, more importantly, neither will the jocks."

His wife ignored his annoying habit of calling the soldiers 'jocks'. He had picked up the term while doing a spot of duty with a highland battalion in Scotland. The CO of the Second Battalion, Caledonia and Musquodoboit Scottish Regiment, Lieutenant Colonel Miles Jefferson had blown his top one evening in the mess when Jackrabbit had used the term once too often. "For fuck's sake, Jackrabbit, they're not jocks. They're Newfies, they're Bluenosers, they're loggers, they're even good old boys, prairie shit kickers, but they're not jocks."

"Easy, old man," replied Jackrabbit. "They wear the kilt, they've got balls of brass and most of them are hockey players, so they're jocks."

In disgust, Jefferson had flung his pewter tankard at the nearest subaltern and departed the mess.

"You mean you've never met him?" said his wife.

"Thank god, never. I spent six months with his father in Sicily. He was the catalyst for the practice of fragging."

"Fragging? Sounds disgusting."

"Depends on your point of view. The Yank enlisted man has since adopted it as his own in Vietnam. It's what you do to a superior who endangers your life for no reason, or is considered stupid. A grenade is rolled under the canvas of his tent underneath his bed at night, and that's the end of him."

"And this Bowles did that?"

"No, his troops were trying to do it to him. They almost got him twice. The first time the grenade rolled in one side of the tent and out the other and down into a ravine. Wounded three Italian civilians, killed two of their goats."

"I dread to hear what happened the second time."

Jackrabbit laughed. "The grenade went in, bounced once, landed on Soup's cot. He was standing there getting undressed. He picked it up and tossed it back out of his tent. Landed near the three fraggers. They got their asses full of shrapnel and two petrol trucks and one jeep were blown up or caught fire."

"They gave up after that?"

"Yes, but only because I ended up in his tent. The troops respected me, and since we shared the same hooch, they didn't want to do me in with him. To make sure we were not blown to bits, I got him out of the front as soon as possible."

"Maybe the son won't be like that."

"Maybe, but with that family, incompetence seems to be such a desirable genetic trait that the family passes it on in larger and larger doses with every generation."

"John. He may be a good officer."

Schultzberger wanted to agree, but he knew deep down in his sporran that Bowles was going to be worse than his father ever was. And he had no intention of finding out first hand. Using up all the favours he had accumulated with the Regiment Executive, Schultzberger got Bowles onto the next lieutenant's qualifying course. Fortunately, it started the day after Bowles' leave ended.

So at the end of September, fresh from Basic Officer Training leave, Bowles arrived at Fredericton Junction, New Brunswick, only to find that he had been booked back out on a train that very evening. He was to return to Camp Borden, just north of Toronto, where he had recently finished his BOT. He had passed it less than two days ago, en route from his home in Western Ontario.

The School commandant in Camp Borden, a good soldier who had worked his way up from the ranks had seen far too much of Bowles. On the day after Bowles graduated from Basic Officer Training, he had gone to see the Base Surgeon for a refill of his nerve medication.

The Base Surgeon tried to quell the Commandant's anxiety. "Bowles has gone now, sir. With his record, he won't be eligible for the lieutenant qualifying course for a decade. You are to take some sick leave and get him out of your mind."

The School Adjutant, Captain Peter Moore, knowing how Bowles had affected his boss and the entire camp, did not know how to go about telling the commandant that Bowles was on his way back. First, he called the School Regimental Sergeant Major. The RSM told the Adjutant to fuck off in no uncertain terms. The Adjutant, not used to being spoken to in this manner took umbrage with the RSM.

"Too bad, my apologies and all that, sir. I said it, and I meant it. I'll obey any order you give me. I've been in the army for thirty-two years, and this is the first time I've ever said that to an officer, not counting lieutenants, of course. But I mean it. I am not going to let the Commandant know that Bowles is coming back, you are. I am going to the mess to get drunk."

The Adjutant, realizing that he couldn't reprimand a man for not doing something he was afraid to do, let it go. Then he called the Base Padre. The Padre said no. He had met Bowles during Padre's hour. Bowles, that day's acting platoon leader, had marched the Protestant members of the platoon into the Roman Catholic Church, thereby disrupting Communion.

Bowles compounded his faux pas and also shocked the life out of the ladies auxiliary by screaming in his squeakiest authoritative little bellow at one of his platoons, "Take your hat off in the house of the Lord, you son of a bitch!"

The Padre finally agreed and went into the commandant's office. He left shaking his head. Two hours later the commandant resigned his commission and went to the sergeants' mess where he joined the RSM.

He took the monetary penalty for early retirement with good grace. "It's better to lose a hundred a month for the rest of my life than have to spend two hundred a month on medication, alcohol, and psychotherapy just for the privilege of spending another five months with Bowles."

His replacement as Officer Training Centre Commandant, Lieutenant Colonel Fred Hershey, came up with a plan. Having had the Bowles situation explained to him by the Adjutant, Captain Moore, he said, "Yes, I do know of him, and his father. Slam him on that course that's already in progress. It'll end a few days from the Christmas leave period. When it ends, I don't want him hanging around here. Send him home on leave. If he's got no leave coming to him, give him mine. I do not want this critter in Camp Borden any longer than necessary."

"Thank you, sir, from the bottom of my heart," said Captain Moore. Moore was a single living-in officer who dreaded the idea that Bowles would occupy the same quarters as he for the month of December. "I'll even split the leave days with you, fifty-fifty. And, if my Christmas wish comes true, Bowles will fall into the punch and drown."

"And, unfortunately, Bowles did neither," I said. "Thank you, Goody, for a very entertaining story."

"How much of that gargle is true?" yelled out a member from the back benches.

Goody smiled around at the audience. "Gentleman, every single word."

I stood up. "Yes, lads, I can account for the fact that there is such a person as Lieutenant Bowles, and he does exist in the Canadian Army."

"Nonsense, Ox, you're just trying to save Goody's face."

"For the unbelievers, there is no explanation. For those who wish to follow the further exploits of Artie Bowles, and learn how I, a former staff sergeant in the British Army became a staff sergeant serving with that very same Bowles, return here tomorrow for luncheon and the story will continue with a different narrator. Good night."

21

CHAPTER 3

TOBY MEETS SHEILA

With His Lordship and Her Ladyship off touring Paris, my days were my own, so the very next day I arrived at the club to find the place packed. As the hall porter was pulling my Macintosh off; off my arms, he wasn't wearing it, a member took control of my furled brolly, and I was permitted only moments to catch my breath before being whisked into the Beggar's Bar where a drink was slapped into my hand.

From there I was escorted into the dining room. The tables had all been moved to the monthly dining room set up in a large E-shaped design. At the head table sat Goody and a number of the more senior members. I settled in a chair next to him.

As I sat down, I said, "Good gracious, all this for Bowles?"

"No, Ox, for you. Centre stage and the opportunity to spread the word."

"Looking around at this bunch, I'd say that the word's already been spread. We don't get a turnout like this for the annual general meeting."

A voice from down the table yelled, "Get on with it, Goody!"

He yelled back, "Today it's not me, Marvin Oxnard will preside over this stage of the adventure."

With a nudge from him, I stood up. "Gentlemen, it is my great pleasure to continue the epic adventure, although in many cases, this recitation will seem more like the confessions of a gentlemen's gentleman."

I took a sip of whatever they had given me and began.

"Let us turn our backs on Lieutenant Arthur Bowles for a short time to visit with another young man, Randolph Anthony Tobias Trelauney-Fitzgibboncrest, who at the time lived in Winnipeg, Canada. When this all started, he was the son of my employer, His Lordship, the Earl of West Saxmundham and North Haselbury Plucknett. Since that was a mouthful in any language, the Earl preferred to be addressed as Lord Haselbury."

There were no questions or comments, so I carried on. Randolph Anthony Tobias Trelauney-Fitzgibboncrest, or Toby for short, was nineteen years old and he had problems. One of these problems was his name, but during a discussion with me about having a name change he changed his mind instead.

"Changing your name will probably lead to your disinheritance, sir."

"You may be right, Ox, Dad will have a fit."

"Mr. Oxnard, Master Toby," I corrected him.

But if Toby had spoken with his father about family names, he would have received a surprise. His father would have been in total agreement. All his life Lord Eustace Blenheim Cotswold Jameson Trelauney-Fitzgibboncrest had fought to have a decent name added to the already weighty list he lugged around. At school, he had fought physically and at home verbally, but it had been no use. After he had threatened a hunger strike while at home on a school break, his father had agreed to call him EB and that was how he identified himself even now. Annoyingly, that damned judge who was currently visiting insisted on calling him Lord Eustace. To make it worse, the Judge had a name the Earl would have given half his fortune for, 'Rocky'. The judge's last name was Rockingham.

"And quite likely Mother will denounce me as an anti-feminist, warmongering, whale-hating, tree-hater who is trying to destroy the efforts of all women who have fought to have their family names incorporated into history as well as into their husband's names."

"First of all, that nonsense you just spouted has no place in how the Countess would react to your name change."

Toby grinned. "But it was fun to say."

"Life is not all fun, sir, and in your case, I'd say you were long-overdue to be more serious with your life."

"No, Ox, I'm long-overdue to meet someone who can add more fun, bring more excitement into my life. I'm young and I'm fancy-free."

"And, as they say out here, 'You're riding for a fall, Pardner.'" I remember looking pleased with my attempt to speak like a cowboy.

"Oh, good one, Ox, a cowboy with a British accent. But, to get back to the subject."

"Changing your name?"

"Right. Best we don't discuss it with my Mother around."

"I have no intention of discussing it within the Countess's hearing. And, if I were you, I shouldn't be too outspoken in regard to your feelings about feminism in general."

"Oh, Ox, I know that, but you know how she is. She's caught up in the 'Hug-a-Tree and Kick-a-Man Movement'."

"Young Sir, your mother is teaching history and sociology. It just happens that one of her courses this year is The History of Women."

"Education is a wonderful thing ain't it, Ox?"

"More correctly, sir, education is a wonderful thing, isn't it, Mr. Oxnard?"

"Mr. Oxnard? Huh! You only get on your high horse when you deal with me. Mom and Dad always call you Marvin."

"They do so for two reasons sir. Firstly, they are mature individuals capable of respecting their own names and the names of others. Secondly, Marvin happens to be my name."

"Right. Thanks for the lecture. See you later, Ox."

"Yes, sir. Anytime I can be of assistance please feel free to call on me. Oh, by the way, your tie is crooked."

"Can you give it the old tug and pull to get it sorted out, please, Ox?"

I shook my head. "I taught you to tie a tie when you were six. When you reached the age of nine, I decided that I would no longer succumb to your pleadings and that if you were ever to become a man, you would do so without me helping you tie a tie." I recall aiming my eyes toward the heavens, and whispering a frustrated, "A man ties his own tie."

At that comment, a number of the group applauded. When the noise had abated, I went on, "Toby's next problem was that he was living in Canada. Manitoba to be a little more specific. Winnipeg if you wanted to be annoyingly precise. And a large mansion affair on the banks of the Assiniboine River in the more prestigious area of that fair city, if you wanted to be more than fussily accurate.

Toby, and myself for that matter, were there with his parents. The Trelauney-Fitzgibboncrests had exchanged houses with a wealthy Winnipeg grain merchant.

The exchange was reasonably fair; the Winnipeg address not quite so aristocratic as Trelauney Hall Manor on the moors, but it did include five bathrooms, for which Her Ladyship, with her chronic diarrhea, was eternally grateful.

Due to the house-swapping by his parents, Toby was attending the University of Winnipeg and was in his first year of an Arts degree. Being the pampered only child of Lord and Lady Haselbury, he had no goals, other than pursuing college girls and so he was taking the easiest courses he could find.

24

His plans for after graduation hovered around girls in their twenties, playing golf and skiing. A nice all-round boy without any aims in life other than to have fun, Toby chased amusement as if it were the holy grail. He had left England without getting any of the girls back there in trouble, but it wasn't for lack of trying. If Arthur Bowles ambition was to be an officer, Toby's was to live his life like a tourist with unlimited funds. As we shall see, their paths were due to cross in ways neither of them could fathom, but any hints on how they do converge will have to wait.

Toby's mother, Marion, A countess, as well as a professor of sociology, was teaching feminism at the University of Manitoba. His Lordship, Toby's father, stuck in Winnipeg with no real tasks to perform, gave huge parties that became the talk of the town.

It was at the party that his father had thrown for Judge Rocky that Toby indulged in a career change that would be the making or breaking of him.

After a couple of desultory attempts which left his tie still crooked, Toby was sitting on a huge black leather sofa in the corner of the huge ballroom half-heartedly discussing the semantics of feminism with a student disciple of his mother's.

Toby's stirrings were mainly directed at the bosom of his companion rather than on the worthiness of the use of the word "chairperson" as opposed to "chairman". He had decided that feminism was nothing more than a spiteful revolution of an oppressed set of second class citizens seeking revenge. Even so, pretending an interest afforded him a great opportunity to examine one of the rebel women's libbers close up.

Toby had discovered girls at age fourteen with his Irish nanny, who had been sixteen. Since then he never looked back; up or down depending upon whether it was a skirt or a blouse, but never back.

This disciple, Sheila Clements, was yapping on about the role of today's women while Toby sat and listened with one eye on her bosom and the other on her legs. She was blonde, tanned, long legged, and her tight evening gown with its long slit up one side did nothing to hide the promise of her figure. He decided that she was worth the effort of maintaining his staunch allegiance to the cause his mother so vehemently espoused.

On her part, Sheila was attracted to the cute way Toby wore his tie. As the evening wore on, Toby's and Sheila's viewpoints converged rapidly. The more they talked, the more his goal of getting a date looked surer and surer. From the sound of it, Toby had the feeling that Sheila's idea of remaining a celibate feminist martyr had become less and less appealing.

He babbled on with not a bit of understanding of the jargon he was shovelling at her. Toby kept hoping that she might at least go out with him the following Friday. Sheila, on the other hand, was becoming entranced by the load of gargle Toby spat out. She was getting more and more into the idea of ending her role as the virgin queen.

To him, his "So, maybe we should give it a try" meant that they should go out together. To her, finding out first hand exactly what men did to women was a quick route to graduation; in more ways than one.

"Oh, do you think so? It sounds interesting."

"You mean you would like to?"

"Yes, if you would."

"Of course I would." What does she think I'm trying to do, get a date for a friend?

"What about now, I mean upstairs?"

Good God, she wants it now. Why not. "Yes, let's go."

"Oh no, not together."

Not together. How else does one do it? "I don't understand?"

"Look silly, if we are going to do this right we have to set the stage."

Set the stage, who the hell are we doing this for? Is she an entertainer? Do we need to have Mummy and Daddy watch? In for a penny in for a pound. "Okay, what do you suggest."

"Okay, first I need to sneak up the stairs. I am not sure your mother would approve of me actually having a relationship with a man while I'm learning all about how badly we have been treated by men over all these years."

"Fine. Go on up, and I'll join you in a few minutes. And as far as the tyranny of men over women, I agree with you."

"You're very sweet, Toby. I knew you were sincere. Men who adopt feminism just to get women make me ill."

"Me too."

"So, I'll go up to a room and sit in the dark. You sneak in. Now remember, you're sneaking into a women's bedroom to ravish her. I'll be the poor woman at the mercy of a vile man. Go nice and slow. I want to be able to analyze each of my deepest feelings at every step of the way. But while we're doing it, no talking, okay?"

"Okay." Toby nodded thinking this girl is nuts. But this sounds like fun. Who am I to argue. She's gorgeous and if she wants to make a clinical encounter of her first time who am I to deny her. For that matter, I'll be the Doctor Kildare of the back alley. I'll be Robin Hood with a hard-on, anything. His mind came back to the party as Sheila said, "What rooms are empty?"

"Oh all of them. I don't think anyone is staying overnight."

"Good, I'll be in the first room on the right. Give me five minutes."

I can give you that, but no more, he thought, as he hurried off to the washroom.

And, as I mentioned Toby's bathroom break, I suggested to the members that we all do the same. But, before I could speak up, a comment blew in from the cheap seats.

CHAPTER 4

TOBY MEETS THE JUDGE'S WIFE

"You expect us to believe all that, Ox?" said a voice from the crowd.

"That you, Martindale?" I asked.

"Yes, it is," said Goody. "Ignore him."

"No, I'll answer," I said. I took a drink, placed my glass down on the table and looked toward where the voice had come from. "You question my veracity, Squiffy?"

"I question your sanity. You think we can accept that some kid was hoping to get laid and he actually told you about it?"

"As a matter of fact, Squiffy, what comes next is even more unbelievable. But, to answer your question. Toby gave me the whole thing the next day…" I paused. "Mind you, for a lot of this, I was an eyewitness."

"I believe you, Ox," said Goody.

"You're his pal," shouted Squiffy.

"If you don't like any of part of this, Squiffy, no one is making your stay," said someone off to my right.

Then half a dozen other members chimed in, all yelling for Martindale's scalp. Finally, the place quieted down, and Goody said, "Are you ready to carry on?"

"I am," I said. And I did. "I'll set the stage. Remember, this was a big party, over twenty guests. Two of them, Judge Rocky, Rockingham and his wife, Eleanor, were the guests of honour." I smiled inside myself in anticipation of the next phase of this affair. "Don't forget, Sheila was heading upstairs, and Toby had gone to the bathroom…

Over at the bar, Toby's father, was drinking brandy with Judge Rockingham. His Lordship, having taken up Canadian History, as a way to spend his time in Winnipeg, had offered to put the Judge and his wife up for a few nights in the hopes of pumping the Judge over the next few days. The judge was already planning to do that to his wife in the next few minutes. He had sent her up to unpack and to get ready. Whenever they were able to, they would go to a motel and live out their favourite fantasy. They pretended that they were both deaf

28

and dumb and would take turns ravishing each other. Tonight it was the Judge's turn to be the ravisher. He downed the hundred-year-old brandy in a gulp and then, after thanking His Lordship, departed for better things. Lord Eustace was left alone at the bar wondering if the Judge would be interested in trying out the cooking sherry. It tasted dreadful but was cheap. One-hundred-year-old brandy seemed a waste on the old bugger.

The Judge headed out to the car to pick up the Lone Ranger mask he had purchased at a toy store. Slipping it on, he practiced his burglar-sneak across the lawn. He skulked right into the arms of one of His Lordship's security guards. Before he knew what was happening, he was bundled into a van and whipped off to the police station.

At the same time, Toby was trotting up the stairs trying to remember which room Sheila had said she would be in. Fate was going to be as unkind to Toby as she had been to the Judge but she was going to be much kinder to Eleanor Rockingham, the Judge's wife.

First room on the right? No, first room on the left. Yes, that's right. No, it's left. Toby was so excited he almost giggled. Doesn't matter really, does it? If she's not in one, she'll be in the other. And into the room on the left he went.

In the room on the right, Sheila sat in the dark shivering with anticipation, her mind touching a niggling of doubt. Was she truly doing this in the spirit of research or to gratify her dark desires? Doubts fought assurances, shivers grew, and finally where the hell is he was replaced with where can I publish my findings?

At that minute, he was sneaking into the room on the left and up to the bed toward the naked figure he could see silhouetted in the glow of the street lamp. Covering the final few feet in a dive, he placed one hand on her shoulder and the other on a breast, pulling her down and then smothering her with his body.

Eleanor Rockingham wondered why her husband was diving at her like a lunatic, but then promptly dropped that thought the better to enjoy her ravishment. She made no noise, no sound, except the occasional tiny grunt of pleasure. Toby later told me he thought he she was too shy to admit she was enjoying herself. To Toby, whose passionate lusts battered and won the war against any going nice and slow wondered briefly, very briefly, why Sheila was not resisting.

But Sheila had resisted long enough. Getting fed up with sitting in the dark she had tossed on her dress and wandered out into the hall. She met the Judge in the hallway outside the other room. He had finally convinced the police that he was a judge, a good friend of the family and that he was only sneaking in to surprise his friend, Lord Trelauney-Fitzgibboncrest.

Meanwhile, the ravisher and the ravished were going at it full blast. Eleanor, still immersed in her mute role was trying hard not to yodel with delight at her husband's novel new techniques. Toby's silence was only maintained due to his marvelling at sexual skills more in keeping with someone from a brothel. He spared but an instant to consider that the supposedly scientific, coldly analytical student with no experience, certainly had picked it up in a hurry. As it was, neither concerned themselves overly with the night table going over and crashing the lamp to the floor.

Sheila and the Judge both reached the door at the same time. The judge automatically gave way to the lady. The lady refused to accept such chauvinistic behaviour, so they stood there each holding the door knob and looking at the other.

Toby couldn't keep quiet any longer. He let out a howl followed by, "Yes, yes…"

Eleanor yelped. "You made a noise, Rocky! I won!"

Toby's response of, "Who the hell's Rocky?" brought Sheila and the Judge to life. Rocky, on the other side of the door, knew. He also knew he had not won a thing all night. To hear his wife telling someone else, he had won was not good news as far as he was concerned. Sheila decided that Toby was after her and any other woman only for their bodies and now felt glad he hadn't had hers, at least from a feminist outlook. From a girl's eye view, she wondered what she'd missed. She decided to find out. So did the Judge. Any sign of courtesy and ladies first were left behind as he fought for the door handle.

Together they crashed through the door, the Judge slammed the light switch on. On the floor, a victorious Eleanor stared in absolute shock at her husband standing fully dressed and barely five feet from her. Toby, still partially under Eleanor and blinded by the light of love for this goddess who had taken him on the trip of his life, pulled his head out from under her buttocks and blinked blindly up at Sheila and the Judge, and then at the crowd who had gathered at the door. Toby's father pushed through and stood beside the Judge and Sheila.

At this point I paused, the crowd was laughing too hard to hear anything. I looked at Goody, who was holding his stomach, tears streaming down his face. I remembered that I had been standing directly behind his Lordship when the Judge and Sheila broke through the door but, being a professional gentleman's gentlemen, I had been well trained to show no shock or surprise. To be honest, in this situation, that was impossible. I felt a little grin slip.

As the laughter trickled down, I said, "At this point, His Lordship's breeding came through. Not a trace of a smile, no look of astonishment, no change in his even-tempered voice. It made me proud to be an Englishman, seeing the strength of his Lordship's aplomb.

One look at the bodies on the floor, then he turned and announced, "Ladies and Gentlemen, there will be another opening of that marvellous champagne we shared earlier this evening. Please make your way to the ballroom."

The Judge, not thirsty in the least, grabbed the still-naked Eleanor by the hair and pulled her to her feet. He threw a bedspread at her, and yelled, "You bitch, we're getting out of here!" As the Judge dragged a yowling Eleanor down the stairs past Lord Trelauney-Fitzgibboncrest, he said, "Lord Eustace, please thank her Ladyship." Then, with a glare at his wife he continued, "We enjoyed ourselves. Thank you, your Lordship. My wife and I must be leaving. We had a wonderful time. Goodnight."

His Lordship bowed. "Well done, Judge, that's grace under pressure… please keep the bedspread, we have plenty."

"Hey Ox, what about the girl?"

"Sheila just walked out and down to the bar where she consoled herself with His Lordship's brandy. The bartender told me later that she had been taken home by a mannish-looking female who stated that she was the girl's aunt and had to look after her."

Goody had recovered enough to say, "Talk about your tale going off on a tangent, you haven't even mentioned Bowles yet."

"It's coming. Toby and Bowles are converging."

Goodie nodded, stood up. "Five minutes to re-charge your glasses, everyone, then back in for act two."

I took advantage of the break to visit the men's room. While I was drying my hands, Squiffy Martindale came in.

"Ox, I don't care if it's true or false. You tell a great story."

I nodded and returned to my chair. Three fresh drinks were waiting for me. I picked one up and silently toasted my thanks to the crowd. As I sat down, I said to Goody, "Scheherazade didn't have it any better than this."

"Right, Ox, get on with it."

I sipped my drink then carried on.

A week later, Judge Rockingham, in an attempt to save face, notified His Lordship that he was going to take action on this outrage perpetrated on his wife. His Lordship and Her Ladyship were concerned with the publicity, especially with a Royal visit to Canada coming up shortly.

They got the Judge to meet them at the courthouse for an informal talk. The Judge was adamant that the young scoundrel was not going to hide behind diplomatic immunity and that he would pay for this terrible act he had carried out while a guest of a foreign country. It was a term in jail or nothing. His Lordship refused such a demand. It was an impasse. Her Ladyship asked if there was any other way of rehabilitating miscreants.

"Nothing short of castration."

"No Judge, that's too severe," replied His Lordship.

His wife whispered, "Especially for doing that bitch. She should be castrated, but I don't know how to do it."

"Judge, what do you do for offenders who get involved in a little mischief?" asked his Lordship.

The judge wanted to yell that screwing his wife was not just a little mischief, but contented himself with a milder reply, "If it was my kid he'd have been slapped in the army years ago. We have done that to first timers."

Her Ladyship refrained from asking the Judge if this was Toby's first time.

His Lordship said, "That's a good idea, why don't we make him enlist?"

"You're right dear, that is a good idea. Yes, we could send him home next week, and he can become an officer in the Air Force."

"No! Impossible!" shouted the Judge.

"Oh, and why not? Wouldn't that satisfy you?"

"No, it would not. He would get over there and then forget all about it. Besides, I don't want him as an officer, especially in the Air Force. He would get all the perks. I want him in the Canadian Army and as a dirty grubby private in the worst outfit we have. A place where he can learn discipline and the art of hard work. It's that or jail."

"Well, I suppose that's alright," His Lordship said.

On the steps outside the courthouse, His Lordship looked at his wife. "Come on now, Marion, it'll make a man of him."

She stared at her husband. "The Judge's wife has already done that." Then she nodded in agreement. "How will we break it to him?"

"Simple, I'll tell him he's joining the army."

As to my learning of Toby's fate, it too, was simple. I had the opportunity to be present when His Lordship broke the news to Toby.

CHAPTER 5

TOBY MEETS THE RECRUITING SERGEANT

Meanwhile, back at the ranch (as they say out here in the west), just as Toby was getting ready to leave the house, I stopped him. "That tie, young sir. It's an abomination."

Toby grinned his annoying grin at me, so I knew an insolent remark was headed my way. I wasn't disappointed.

"Ox, you're the one who taught me to tie a tie."

"That is true, unfortunately, the long hours I spent in a vain attempt to make a gentlemen out of you was a huge failure. That rope-like cord around your neck is so disgusting, it would be shameful even to be hung with it." I shook my head, leaned in, and fixed his tie. "You're going to be seen in public, which reflects on me. So, this once only."

"Thanks, Ox. Gotta look my best."

"I don't know why you are so concerned about getting all dressed up. She's only seen you naked, and that for just a minute, the rest of the time you were both in the dark. And anyway, you are not going out for dinner, just a…"

The doorbell rang, and I left his side to open the door.

"Good evening, sir. Good evening, Madam."

"Evening Marvin. Evening Tobias. Where are you going?"

"I, I'm going to uh, uh.."

"What he's trying to say is that he's got a date with Mrs. Rockingham," I said, maintaining my butleresque stone face, yet thinking it was time I got some revenge on him.

"Thanks a lot, Ox."

"What!" said his mother.

"Jesus wept," said his father. "That is one thing you are not doing. We have just come from a chat with the Judge."

"Yes, Tobias," said his mother. "You've seen the last of that bitch… pardon me, my dear."

His Lordship gave a quick tug on his tie, wiggled it a bit and then said, "The only date you have is with me."

Toby turned a terrible glare toward me. "Appreciate your assistance, Mr. Oxnard." Then looked back at his father. "Yes, sir."

"Marvin, I'd like you to be present as well."

"Very good, sir," I said.

"Come on, Dad, no fair. He's a traitor."

His Lordship ignored that comment. "Follow me, Tobias."

The three of us went the den then I closed the door.

"Sit down, son. No, not there, get off the desk and use a chair like a civilized being, even if you are not yet one."

Later that day, while Toby moped around the house in a pale imitation of his former free-wheeling self, he told me he knew by the look on his father's face that whatever he was going to hear was not going to be pleasant. "Ox, I expected maybe a couple of weeks of grounding, loss of the car. Nothing to get excited about. Then the axe fell."

I knew His Lordship better than his own son did, but even I was surprised at the retribution the Judge extracted.

"Three years in the Canadian Army? Dad, this is not funny."

"You are so right. Judge Rockingham is serious. Just between you and me, I'm sure that Mrs. Rockingham was not unduly upset since she seems amenable to a second round, but the Judge is furious. It's that or face a jail sentence. So look at this as a type of jail sentence."

"Sentence! Dad, this is not a sentence, it's a paragraph, it's a whole bloody book!"

"I'll excuse your use of profanity due to the shock this news has caused you. But let us have no more of it. Now here is what you will do…"

"It's all carefully planned out, isn't it? It's my life, but you run it. You and a judge that has to prance around in a mask to get it up. You've both charted my life for me."

"Not quite. You can go to jail. I didn't think that you would choose that option, but you are free to do so if you wish. But remember, if one of Judge Rockingham's cronies is on the bench you may get a little more than three years."

I muttered, "Aside from the disgrace to the family."

"Oh shut up, Ox," said Toby. "It ain't like it's your family."

"Toby!" his Lordship practically shouted. "As a matter of fact, it is Mr. Oxnard's family, and has been for centuries. Now apologize immediately."

There was silence. His Lordship waited. I waited. Finally, Toby said in a low voice, "My apologies, Mr. Oxnard."

"Thank you, Toby," I said.

"And we'll have no more of it," finished His Lordship. "You're in the army, the Canadian army, unless you choose incarceration."

"Oh God!" Toby sank into the overstuffed chair and put his hand over his face. "Well, I've always wanted to be a pilot."

"You are not going to go into the Air Force. The judge stipulated the meanest, dirtiest job in the army."

"What's that? A garbage collectors unit?"

"No, not quite. I've spoken with an old friend, Lieutenant Colonel Schultzberger, you will be going to the Highland Depot in New Brunswick."

"Shit..."

"Toby."

"Sorry Dad. As you said, I'm in shock. So, tell me, what was your plan? I take it that I am not to be consulted."

"Correct, but irrelevant. I'm going to send you to Toronto for three weeks. You can stay at your aunt's while all the legal paperwork is sorted out. You will sign up there. Now I suggest you go and talk to your mother."

"Alright."

"And Toby,"

"Yes, Dad?"

"Leave Mrs. Rockingham alone."

The last three weeks of his life, as Toby related to me much later when we had become warriors in arms, were wonderful. He kept thinking of the saying that knowing that one is about to die concentrates the mind most wonderfully. Toby's time in Toronto was pure, concentrated fun. But it came to an end and off he went by taxi to Number 6 Personnel Depot. About fifty other confused young men were milling around in little groups. Toby thought that there couldn't be this many criminals taking the military way out. But maybe there was, for no one in his right mind would be doing this voluntarily. He stood near the door and watched. Names were called, and people got up or were collected and taken to desks. After an hour, his name was called, and a huge clerk with three stripes on his sleeve came over and led him to a desk where he gestured for Toby to sit down.

"Fill all this out. We have most of it. For some reason, you have had special consideration. Not that it matters. You're going into the infantry. Somebody sure doesn't like you. It states that no matter what your aptitude or qualifications you are to be a ground pounder. What'd you do to deserve this?"

Oh, nothing much, wrong woman, wrong room, thought Toby. "I killed seven typists in a stenographic pool at a recruiting office in Winnipeg."

"That all?" said the clerk rolling a sheet of paper into his machine. "Try that here, and my clerks will feed their typewriters to you."

Toby went back to filling out his papers until the sergeant interrupted him again. "You have no religion listed here. What is it?"

Toby had overheard a conversation between two female clerks while waiting for his initial interview a week ago. They had been discussing a corporal who had converted to Judaism to get both Christian and Jewish holidays off. "I'm Jewish."

"Jewish? Look at you. You're blonde, blue-eyed, and your nose is too small. Prove it!"

A female corporal at the next desk laughed and said, "Go ahead boy, show him some proof."

"Why do I need to prove it? The boy before me, what did he put down?"

"Roman Catholic."

"So what was his proof? Did he have to prove it?"

"No, but you don't look Jewish."

"Did you know Jesus was Jewish?"

"Of course, everyone knows that."

The girl spoke up again, "Oh, Sergeant Lewis, I didn't think you did."

The sergeant ignored her and the other girls who were laughing now.

Toby went on, "In every picture I have ever seen, Jesus does not look Jewish. He looks like a one hundred percent WASP. In fact, he looked a lot like me except his hair was longer and he had no leather jacket."

"When The Depot barber gets a hold of you, what hair you've got will be gone too. So, let's try it again. What's your religion?"

"Jewish, go ahead put it down. If I've lied to you, won't God punish me?"

The Sergeant shook his head and after putting it down waved Toby back to the main part of the room. Toby's plan had not worked yet. He was going to be as difficult as possible, in the hope that the Canadian Army would discard him before it even got its hooks into him. Next stop was medical.

The medical corporal, a big strapping lad with "kill" tattooed on one set of knuckles and "maim" on the other just laughed when Toby said, "You're a man in a nurse's uniform?"

Any further remarks by Toby were shut down when the corporal offered to take Toby outside so they could find out quickly just who's queer, Toby saw the wisdom of shutting up and concentrated on filling the little bottle. A little later when the doctor told him to cough, Toby asked what would happen if he refused.

The doctor looked at Toby calmly. "Peter, my corporal, who you just called a queer would be more than happy to help you cough."

Toby broke into a coughing fit.

"Once is enough, young man," said the Doctor.

Toby was called to the psychologist next. "The results of these tests are terribly inconsistent, young man."

"What do you mean?"

"Well, this one with the pictures, you were supposed to draw a handle on the side of a teapot. You drew a weird kind of handle over the top like some kind of antique. You stated that you don't like your mother and that your father is dead. Is that correct?"

"Oh no. It's my mother who's dead, and I don't like the Ox."

"What Ox?"

"The Ox, He's my father's gentleman's gentleman, a fancified gentleman's gentleman. This paper had no space for me to explain."

"It's not supposed to. But this drivel does make me think a little about you."

"Maybe I'm unfit."

"Ah, ah, so that's it. I think you had better get something straight, Mr. Trelauney-Fitz… Fitzgibboncrest?"

"Yes."

"Well, Mr. Fitzgibboncrest. "

"No, not Fitzgibboncrest."

"But I thought you just said it was?"

"I did say Fitzgibboncrest."

"Well, so did I."

"But that's not my name."

"Well, what is it?"

"It's Trelauney-Fitzgibboncrest."

"See, it is Fitzgibboncrest," said the psychologist.

"No, it's not, it's Trelauney-Fitzgibboncrest."

"Well, I'm partly right, so let's get on with it. What were we talking about?"

"My name."

"No before that."

"I'm unfit for the army, and you were going to get me out."

"Not quite. I was going to tell you that you are a ward of the court. We cannot turn you down. All we can do is find you the best trade possible based on your tests. Your tests are so terrible that you qualify for only four trades, two of which the Canadian army does not and never did have. One is a galley slave, and the other is a member of a penal battalion. The remaining two trades available to you are the military police or the infantry. Since you're a ward of the court the answer is simple – you're going into the infantry."

"Well, I kind of like the idea of a galley slave, but then again the penal battalion may be the better career move. What do you think?"

"No, no, no, no! Those are the two trades we don't have. It was a joke. The real choices are the MPs or the infantry."

"Well, I thought those two were the jokes. Sounds like I'll be joining the infantry."

"Good, that will be all, Mr. Fitzgibboncrest."

"Trelauney-Fitzgibboncrest," Toby yelled as he left the recruiting centre. I finished my glass of whatever someone had placed in front of me and stood up.

CHAPTER 6

THE DEPOT MEETS BOWLES

"You going to leave us hanging there?" asked a member. Since this is his only line in the entire proceedings, he's has no name. Well, he had a name, but it wasn't worth the effort of putting it in. Besides, he was an oaf.

"Yes, I am." I looked at my watch and saw that it was getting on for half-four. This merry little tale was taking on a life of its own.

"Gentlemen, I need to take a break. A long one," I told the members. And at this point in my narrative, I was alerted to the fact that I had been going on so long at the publisher's office that all time had passed without me being aware of it.

I looked at Peter Warren, who said, "Wonderful, wonderful stuff." It was all he could do to not rub his hands together. He stood up, stretched and said, "This is top-hole. Absolutely top-hole."

I knew I was smiling but didn't bother replacing it with my stone-faced butlerine image.

"Yes, yes, yes, it's gonna be big."

"As a novel?"

"Nonsense, Marv, it's non-fiction. A tell-all about the Bowles family."

"Actually, it's Marvin."

He waved me away. "Marv, Marvin…" He stopped and looked at his watch. "I have a feeling you've barely started, am I right?"

"But can't you just read the manuscript?"

He gave another wave of disdain. "Marv…"

"Marvin."

"Right, Marvin, I need to hear it. To absorb it as an audible event. Reading a new manuscript by an unknown author usually puts me in editorial mode. I'm too busy critiquing the printout to pay attention to the story. Sitting here listening, I get the story. And story is what writing is all about."

I nodded. Seem to me that telling a story isn't about writing it all, what did I know.

He said, "Good, you agree. And me, I'm excited about this…" He stared at me. "You hungry?"

Until he had mentioned it, I hadn't been. I looked at my watch. I'd been telling my story for over four hours. "Yes."

He reached for his phone, banged out a few numbers and said, "Rosemary, Sweetie, send Jimmy to the deli. Two of everything. Ham and cheese, roast beef, chicken salad. Coffee times two…" He looked the question at me. "Black, straight up?"

"No, double-double, please."

He took the phone from his ear. "A what?"

"Double-double. It's two creams and two sugars. An expression invented in Canada."

He put the phone back up to his ear. "Two double-doubles." Then he laughed. "Come on, Rosie, it's two creams and two sugars. Gotta keep up with the lingo, Honey."

She said something and I was sure that the term 'double-double' had just become standard publishing industry jargon.

"Thanks, very much." He replaced the phone in its niche on his desk, leaned back. "Dinner in thirty minutes. Care to continue the story?"

"Certainly."

While we waited for our food I got back into my saga. At that point in the narrative, Goody and I were at the club taking a break.

I'm sure you have realized by now that I couldn't be everywhere and that I don't know everything: shocking, but true. I do know everything a genuine gentleman's gentleman needs to know about what to wear and which spoon to use, but those tricky things are unhelpful with this chronicle. Not to worry, in order to fill in the holes, I had a ton of reference material I'd collected over the years. And with that, here is one of those blank spots that was filled in direct from the various horse's mouths much later. What timing. And with that we find ourselves in Camp Gagetown, New Brunswick.

Whatever clouds had obscured the horizon in the past few months were going to seem like fluffy cotton balls compared to what was brewing for The Caledonia and Musquodoboit Scottish Regiment's First Battalion. Hurricane Bowles was in the wind and building up to make life, if not windy, at least quite drafty.

On this day, Lieutenant Colonel Schultzberger and Regimental Sergeant Major Dixon were in the Commanding Officer's office having coffee.

"It'll seem like no time at all and Bowles will be back," said the Colonel. Dixon couldn't care less since Bowles was an officer. As such the "young gentlemen" or "whistleheads" came under his beady eye only when rehearsing drill. He just grunted, his attention focused on a young soldier taking a shortcut across the parade square.

"Borrow your phone a minute, sir?" he said, picking it up before getting an answer, and not expecting or caring if he got one. Schultzberger nodded absently, but Dixon was already talking on the phone to the battalion orderly sergeant.

"BOS? Who? Sergeant Kitchin, yeah, okay, RSM here. Private Miller is sneaking across the square. Yeah, from D Company. Send the BOC over to QM to cut him off. Let his CSM know, tell him I suggest three extra duties. Yeah, something shitty. Thanks."

He hung up and smiled at the CO. "Sorry, sir, what was that?"

"I said won't be long until Bowles is back. But I suppose to you that it's no big deal, nowhere near as important as one of the jocks poaching on your personal preserve, eh, Mr. Dixon?" said Schultzberger, with a smile.

The RSM grunted back at him, two old warhorses who understood each another. "I'd say it's not like you to worry about anything, sir. Besides, Bowles is still travelling on the train, somewhere between here and Ontario heading back to Camp Borden. Maybe he'll cause a train wreck. Problem solved. At the worst, he'll be away for another ten weeks."

"Ten weeks'll go pretty fast," said Schultzberger. He looked over at his RSM. "Until then he's someone else's nightmare. Not that you're overly concerned."

"I'm not. If he's the idiot everyone around here seems to think he is, then I'll never see him. He won't be permitted on my preserve, as you call it. I'll not let him parade with the soldiers and that is that."

"Yes, that's the easy way out for you. You just tell the Adjutant to slate Bowles for orderly Officer every time we have a big parade. It's kind of dirty, though."

"Dirty? He can serve his entire career as orderly Officer for all I care, but he'll never carry the colours or march with the men."

"I didn't mean that, Mr. Dixon. What I meant was that it's kind of dirty for a Regimental Sergeant Major to get out of a bind and leave his CO in the lurch. But never mind, maybe Bowles is good at drill. He's got to be good at something."

"As sure as shit it's not a drill, sir!"

"Oh? You've heard something?"

"Yes. You know that drill at the Borden School is done bilingually, don't you?"

"Yes, I believe that the latest idiocy is that stationary drill commands are given in French, all drill on the march in English. I assume that it's still done that way?"

"Right, the usual bilingual compromise that just makes everyone uncomfortably equal. Bowles managed to dick that up nicely. During Basic Officer Training Bowles was out in front one day and he gave commands that were half and half."

"Ah, yes. I bet he had a good sound logical reason?"

"Of course. Now the current army way of doing it is stupid, I grant you. The English had no idea what was happening while at the halt, as for the frogs, it doesn't matter because none of them can march anyway. They don't know their gauche from their droit or their asses from a hole in the ground."

"Now Regimental Sergeant Major, your Francophobia is showing."

"Sorry, sir."

"No problem, get on your soapbox later. For now, get back to Bowles."

"Roger that, sir. Well, Bowles tells the staff instructors that the army was stagnant. That they needed a new military language, for tactical purposes. Using his new method, we had a military language that was nearly untranslatable. Which was an understatement. Then he said that any Russians who spoke French would know only half of what was going on. Their interpreters would use up valuable time sorting it all out."

"The instructors' response?"

"One sergeant had to be physically restrained in order to keep him from beating the shit out of Bowles. A calmer one told him he was wasting everyone's valuable time and that if he knew what was good for him, he would get back into the ranks and never ever try anything like this again."

"Incredible. This is the subaltern I am getting. For this idiot, I'm throwing my career down the toilet."

"Not necessarily, sir."

"You have a suggestion?" It was said calmly, but the Regimental Sergeant Major knew that if the CO could splutter that was as close as it came. A man who had won a battlefield commission in World War Two and then went on to call mortar fire on his own platoon during the Korean War doesn't splutter.

"It's a suggestion."

"Damn it, Regimental Sergeant Major! Spit it out. I know it's a suggestion. In this case, I'd take suggestions from the battalion mascot!"

"Okay, every three months or so we have to send one lieutenant, one sergeant and three lance corporals to The Depot..."

"The depot," breathed the CO reverentially, gazing skyward as if that's where The Depot was. "Regimental Sergeant Major Dixon, you are a genius. Pure and simple. Send him to The Depot. Perfect. I love it. Come on."

"Where? We can't go to The Depot. We have to just let him show up there. That is, if he gets through the Lieutenant's Qualifying course."

"Oh, we are not going to The Depot, Mr. Dixon. We are going to the officers' mess. And we are going to stay there."

"But, sir."

"But me no buts, RSM. I am fully aware that today is Thursday, and that it's only ten o'clock in the morning. But we deserve a break. Besides, we can get a head start on Happy Hour."

"Yeah, a head start of over thirty-six hours. But by the way, sir, in case your sudden deliverance from catastrophe has dulled your eyesight, these are galloping horses I am wearing," said the RSM, tapping his sleeves where his rank, the coat of arms of Canada, were sewn.

"Don't be silly, RSM. I'm the CO, it's my mess, just like the sergeants' mess is yours. Besides, you have just saved the battalion. I'll stop by and get the OC of A Company. He's our PMC, it can all go on his VIP chit."

"You are my Commanding officer and I must obey. I'll just let the BOS know where I'll be for the next year or so. If Major Greaves is footing the bill, I'll be there forever. As for Bowles getting through the Lieutenant's Qual, that's in God's hands."

"Too true, RSM, too true."

While the plan may have been perfect, no one notified Lieutenant Bowles, or by the sound of it, God, either. Bowles made a slight modification to the lieutenant colonel's tactics. He failed his course. He did it with a sense of Bowles-ian history that would have done Thorvic Bowpuller proud. To begin with, he failed the entrance exam. Lieutenant Colonel Schultzberger, by way of the grapevine, promised his first born and anything else to the instructor who would give Bowles a re-write. It was done. Bowles got a lower mark on the second exam, even though it was the same test. A quick-witted orderly room clerk, who knew all about Bowles, received a sudden promotion and posting to Ottawa due to his creative solution. He added both exams together to get the required fifty percent and then threw away one of them. That enabled Bowles to enter the Lieutenants' Qualifying Course and get on with his training.

A few days later, Lieutenant Colonel Schultzberger received a sharp message from the Director of Infantry to keep his nose out of the clerk trade postings. He promised never to do it again and sent a bottle of prime scotch to the clerk in Ottawa.

During the next ten weeks, Jackrabbit waited each day for a phone call to say that Bowles was being RTU'd or returned to the unit for something. And every day the feared phone call never came.

Then, with less than a week to go until graduation, the phone rang. At that exact same moment Colonel Schultzberger and RSM Dixon had been planning Bowles' new job in The Depot, he was busy failing the final written exam. This time, Schultzberger had run out of influence. Now it looked as if Bowles was on his way back to the battalion. Since he, or rather his father-in-law, had got him through Basic Officer Training, Bowles could not be drummed out. But, unfortunately, as a Second Lieutenant, he could not go to The Depot.

Salvation, at least for Schultzberger and Dixon came from Deidre, Bowles' mother. She went to her father. "Daddy, Arthur needs help. Just a little. After all, he did well on his first course. Please, Daddy."

Glendenning's first thought was that Arthur needed more than a little help. The little bastard needed to be institutionalized. But Deidre was unaware that it was her father who had gotten little Arthur through the first time. If she knew, she would raise hell. He was about to be hoisted on his own petard. Unless certain phone calls were made. The first call was to the Director of the Infantry.

"Peter, hi, Bob here."

"Who?'

"Bob, Bob Glendenning."

"Don't know a Bob Glendenning. Know a Reg Glendenning"

"For God's sake! Reg… Reginald Glendenning. But I go by the name of Bob."

"Why?"

"Why what?"

"Why do you go by the name of Bob, if your name's Reginald?"

"Never mind that now. Just accept that it's Bob, okay?"

"Okay, Bob," he said cautiously. "What can I do for you?"

"You can get that stupid son of a bitch through his course."

"Not me. I've done enough for that idiot. No disrespect to your side of the family, Bob."

"None taken." Although he was quite sure that the stupidity his grandson displayed could not have come solely from one family. After all, his own wife had to have passed on some degree of lunacy from her idiot family through to her daughter.

His fierce threats and promises of personal gain fell on cement-plugged ears. Peter cooperated instantly when Bob said that he'd be pleased to show Mrs. Peter the secret apartment Peter kept for his equally secret lady friend.

Word went back to OCS, Officer Candidate School, Camp Borden: Pass Bowles! Promote every instructor. But only if they unanimously gave Bowles a free ride. One or two of them balked at this, but when it was explained that Bowles will never be promoted again, that he would die a full Lieutenant, and as the kicker in the pot, they were all given an absolute guarantee that Bowles would never hold command over any of them, they agreed. Oaths were sworn that even if war was declared and Canada's Officer Corps wiped out to a man-that man being Bowles, he would not be promoted. Bowles is grudgingly given a low passing grade. A minute after the conclusion of the graduation parade, Lieutenant Bowles was bundled into a staff car, along with his belongings and was transported from Camp Borden to Toronto's Union Station on his way to sunny Camp Gagetown.

Already present at Union Station on this momentous occasion was Toby. He had been delivered there by his Aunt Mary's chauffeur, Digby Sutcliffe. Digs, as Toby called him, having been a soldier in World War II, had some interesting stories to tell Toby about the army. But it was his last few tips as they drove to the station that Toby was grateful to hear.

"Recruit means everyone will want a piece of you. If it's another recruit, ignore him. If it's got pips, hooks, or stripes on its shoulders or arms, stand to attention and say nothing unless spoken to."

"Okay."

"Your job is simple, eat three squares a day, keep a clean rifle and draw your pay. Simple, eh?"

"Three squares?"

"Three square meals a day."

"Okay."

As the two of them were unloading Toby's mountain of luggage, Digby said, "Work hard, follow orders and help your fellow recruits. Do that, and you will get through it with only a little pain. Act like a know-it-all you're going to be friendless and helpless."

He held out his hand. "Good luck, Toby and remember, it's a big army."

They shook hands. "Thanks, Digs, take care." Toby said, reaching into his pocket. "Can I offer you a tip?"

"No, you can't. Your Aunt employs me at a good wage. This job, I volunteered for because we're friends. You never tip friends, unless it's on a horse." He put his fingers to his mouth and blasted out a piercing whistle. Next thing you know, three red caps were hovering around his luggage. Toby turned to the three porters and said, "Train to Fredericton, track nine, I think."

"Yes, son, track nine. Leaves here every other day at 3 o'clock."

"No worries, lad, we'll get you there." And they did.

"Hey, Ox, this about Bowles?" yelled a heckler.

"Or is it about that Toby kid?" another added.

"A couple of good questions. And, I'll answer them right now."

"No, Ox, give us a few minutes. My back teeth are floating."

The membership, en masse, gladly took a break. And as I took a break, there came a timely knock on Peter's door. A voice said, "Dinner is served, Peter." And in came a young man I guessed was Jimmy. He was bearing two large paper sacks.

"Thanks, Jimmy. We're starving." He got up and relieved Jimmy of one bag, and brought it over to the coffee table in front of me. "Eat what you like, leave the rest."

"And, please, sir, don't eat too much," said Jimmy, a roly-poly youth who looked like he hadn't missed too many suppers.

"Why is that?" I asked.

"Because, whatever you don't eat, I gets as my wages. Terrible place to work this is." He placed the remaining bag on Peter's desk, and pointed a finger at the now re-seated Peter. "An' he's the worst. Why, I'll bet he takes the cost of these sandwiches out of my pay."

Peter laughed, pulled open a desk drawer and took out a large, pink eraser. He threw it at Jimmy, who caught it neatly and put it in his pocket. "Only tip, I'll ever get from him. And, there's guys on the third floor, who'll buy this eraser from me."

Jimmy left and we dug in. I was grateful for the break in talking. Peter took over the speaking role. He chattered away as he gobbled, telling me how great this story was going to be. "Sorry, Jimmy," I said as I packed up my sandwich wrappers. I'd eaten the lot. And as I swilled the last of my coffee, I said, "Peter, that was delicious. However, I'm afraid that I'm done for the day as far as reciting the story. Are you sure you wouldn't rather just read the manuscript?"

"You're not enjoying this re-telling?"

"In a way, it's been helpful, as I can now see some holes in the original story."

"There you go, now you can go home and fix it up."

I stood up.

Peter said, "No, I didn't mean now. I mean after you've told me the whole thing."

I sat down again as he looked at his watch. "Just past seven. I suppose I'm good for at least another hour." I sighed, took a moment to remember where I had been in the story, then went on. "Right, we were back in an evening session of the club and I was telling them about the train trip."

CHAPTER 7

TOBY MEETS BOWLES ON A TRAIN

"If a train traveling east at an average speed of forty-five miles an hour has a first class section and a coach section separated by the club car, a dining car, and an observation car how long will it take for Toby and Bowles to meet?" To get us back into the right frame of mind and to follow through on those earlier questions, that was how I returned to the story.

The correct answer is as soon as Bowles figured out how to open his compartment door and as long as it took Toby to find a conductor and upgrade the coach class ticket he had been issued by the army. For Toby, it took thirty-five seconds and a ten dollar bill. Bowles took twenty minutes.

They met as Bowles was trying to get back into his compartment and Toby was obsequiously being ushered into the one beside it. Toby nodded at his neighbour, whose face reminded him of an empty pie plate and squeezed on by. The conductor, in passing, reached for Bowles' door handle, gave it a quick twist and, as if by magic, the door swung open. He then set Toby up in his first class compartment.

At breakfast the next morning, Toby kept to himself, partly because of what he considered his traditional British reserve while visiting the colonials, but mainly because he felt like a criminal being shipped to Devil's Island and had no wish to discuss the trip with anyone. As far as Toby was concerned, life was over.

This didn't deter Bowles for a moment. Seeing Toby at a table for four without a soul to keep him company, Bowles made for it like a herring gull on a discarded hot dog bun. With a similar squawk, he dove to a seat. Toby pretended Bowles was invisible. All his life, Artie Bowles had been ignored or overlooked. This was now so commonplace for him he found it if not comfortable, at least normal.

Toby looked over the top of his menu, said, "Good morning." And then dove back in behind his menu.

Bowl said, "Right fine day, eh?"

Toby nodded.

Bowles, the sparkling conversationalist, said, "By the way, where are you from? I know it's somewhere in England, but I can't quite place the accent. Are you Scottish?"

"Winnipeg."

"Winnipeg? You mean you have one in England, too?"

"No, from Winnipeg, Canada. It's just north and west of Toronto."

Toby's understanding of the immensity of Canada matched Bowles' knowledge of regional accents.

"But you sound so English. I could have sworn that you weren't a Canadian."

"I'm not. I am British. My father and mother are spending a few years here, and I have been condemned to share the experience with them."

"Oh, I say, that is putting it rather strongly," said Bowles, attempting to sound more English than Toby.

At that moment the waiter appeared beside their table and with an attempt to show that he had taken no offense Bowles said, "Please, order first,"

"Thanks." Toby looked up at the waiter and said, "I see there is something here that says breakfast special. I'll have that, please."

"Very good, sir, and how would you like your eggs?"

A glance at Bowles showed Toby that his breakfast companion was hanging onto every word. He thought that he would have some fun with this colonial yokel. Looking back at the waiter, whose name tag read, 'Robert' Toby said, "Well, Robert, to date, the service in the dining room has been superb. Shall I test your chef's capabilities to the limit?"

Robert, who personally thought that the unreliable cook couldn't parboil shit for a Hudson's Bay trapper and who hated him with a passion larger than Lake Superior, grinned at Toby. "An excellent idea, sir. It's been my experience that Cheffy, as we call him, will relish the challenge."

Robert, who normally addressed the cook by the uncomplimentary term of 'Welder' because he usually burned hamburgers solidly to the grill added, "Just try and stump our cook, sir. He's back in the kitchen giving those pots and pans a good going over as we speak."

Robert was telling the truth, but the pans were receiving such unbridled attention because the Welder was tearing the kitchen apart trying to find some cooking sherry so that he could drown the remains of last night's hangover.

"Okay, then here we go. This is one of my favourite egg breakfasts."

Robert took out his pad and pencil and readied to write.

"To begin we'll need a cup of red wine, a Chardonnay or a Burgundy, a clove of garlic, a bit of minced onion, and a sprinkle of pepper. Now simmer that all together until near boiling point. Take two eggs and break them into two separate small cups. When the liquid comes to a rolling boil, reduce heat and bring the edge of each cup to the surface level. Slide the eggs gently from the cups into the liquid. Simmer for four minutes and twenty seconds, then lift the eggs out and place them on hot buttered garlic toast. Sprinkle with basil and serve with five rashers of crisp bacon."

Robert had stopped writing at the mention of chardonnay and stood open mouthed as Toby dictated the recipe. Toby thought Robert was just paying close attention. Robert was wondering if there was any wine left in the kitchen and hadn't heard a word Toby said. Bowles, on the other hand, was mesmerized. He thought this was an enchantment.

Toby brought the both of them back to the dining car from wherever their minds were traveling. "Got all that, Robert?"

"Uh, uh, er...No."

"Gosh, I have," said Bowles. And he repeated the entire process without missing a beat. Robert, this time, copied it all down.

"Very good, sir." And he turned to face Bowles. "Your selection will be, sir?"

"My good man, I'll have the same thing, only I would like mine simmered for four minutes and nineteen seconds."

Robert wrote on his pad, 'Same as the Brit.' "Gentleman, it has been a pleasure serving you both. I'll get this order to Cheffy immediately and return with fresh coffee."

On entering the kitchen, Robert gave the cook's chair a kick. "Wake up, Wally, time to go to work. Here's a recipe for some kind of eggs. Make it snappy."

He ripped the order from his pad and left it on the counter top. Picking up a carafe of coffee three hours old, he returned to the dining car.

Wally the Welder shook himself, took a swig of the contents of a bottle he had found in the back of the fridge and reached for the note.

Wally had been a short order cook in a Bar and Grill in Sioux Lookout, Northern Ontario, who had indulged himself one too many times of the bar stock. When the train pulled in, Wally had been sleeping on the station bench. He had a ticket purchased for him by the local constabulary and was waiting under the watchful eye of a determined cop for a train, any train. The one heading toward Halifax was good enough for Wally's custodian, and he flung him aboard.

At the same time, at the other end of the train, the regular cook was off-loaded on a stretcher with a bad case of food poisoning, caused by eating a half-raw hamburger at the station in Winnipeg. As Wally was climbing on, he heard Robert and the conductor talking about the cook crisis and offered his services. Robert, not one to overestimate the potential in the wretched creature being pushed on board said no when Wally volunteered to cook for the duration. The conductor, who was getting off in Sudbury where his replacement would be getting on, cared less about the quality of the help, and more about the complaints that would hit head office if there was no one to cook, said yes. Wally was hired.

Staggering over to the grill Wally read the note. With a contemptuous sniff, he crumpled the note and said, "Fancy eggs, eh. They're poached eggs, and that's what they'll get. He fried up some bacon, boiled some water and broke four eggs into it.

After five minutes, during which he had made some toast, had a few more swallows from the wine bottle, he fished the eggs from the water, flipped them onto the toast, laid the bacon beside the toast on the plate and muttered, "Wall-a." As a finishing touch to his artistry, he sprinkled the remaining few drops from his wine bottle onto each set of eggs and rang the waiter's bell.

Robert came on the double, looked at the two plates and said, "Where's the basil?"

"We ain't got any. Here, this'll do," said, Wally as he took a few sprigs of parsley and crunched them over the eggs. "There, deliver these to your royal highnesses."

Back in the dining room, Toby and Bowles ate the eggs with enthusiasm. Toby had only heard of this recipe from his father, who had learned it while up in Scotland as a boy visiting some distant relative, so he had no idea what it was going to taste like. He wasn't even sure that he had gotten it right. He admitted to himself that the eggs were pretty good, even if the charred sticks he took for bacon were inedible. Bowles gobbled the whole thing down with exhilaration. He was eating a unique British upper-class meal.

As soon as he could, Toby left the table and Bowles. That evening, he was seated in the dining car at the last dinner setting in the hopes that he would miss Bowles.

"Good evening, your worship."

It was Bowles, who had visited the previous two dinner settings and sat through them without eating just hoping that Toby would arrive. "Jolly good that we're both dining at this time, eh?"

"Yes, quite...Although you don't need to sit here just because I'm a visitor."

"Not at all, I would love to hear all about your trip over here. Get better acquainted, so to speak."

Toby's desire to remain solitary had increased, and he was even more determined not to talk to anyone.

He soon discovered that Bowles was not just anyone. According to Bowles, after two meals at the same table they were practically blood brothers. With such contrary perceptions, dinner was, to say the least, interesting.

"So at lunch did I hear you say that you were going on a business trip?" inquired Bowles.

"Sort of," mumbled Toby. A none-of-your-business trip.

"I'm off to Camp Gagetown, myself. Can't really discuss it, you know. All kind of hush-hush. I can tell you that I am an Officer in the Canadian Army. Just finished some special training at Camp Borden. That's all I can let out at this stage of our relationship."

"Don't worry I won't pry," said Toby. Oh God, I hope he's not Infantry. He's probably some son of a friend of the Judge sent to ensure I suffer sufficiently.

Bowles had attempted to imitate Toby's accent and then went on to use what he thought was the correct slang to impress such an obvious, although quite young, gentleman.

"Oh, jolly good. Loose lips sink ships, eh? Better dead than red. Number, rank, and name. That's all we'll give 'em, number, rank, and name. Right?"

"Oh, yes, although I am not too sure about better dead than red."

Bowles looked at him suspiciously. "Pardon me?"

"I mean, what do your Indians think about that? After all, I'm sure that they would much rather be red than dead, don't you think?"

Bowles didn't think too much of it and was beginning to get the idea that his companion was putting him on.

Toby, looking around for an escape, spied the club car sign. "Well, it was nice talking with you. I'm off now to have a beer and to sit for a while in the club car."

"Jolly good idea. If you don't mind, I'll join you. I am in the mood for a sniffer or two of brandy, say what?"

Toby did mind. He minded that sniffers were attached to the head of dogs and were used to track down escapees from military institutions, and he did not need such images right now. He minded that Bowles used such affected language, and in a silly manner. And he minded that Bowles was going to be with him still longer. One beer and then back to my little dungeon on wheels, he thought.

The club or bar car was nearly empty. At the end farthest from the bar, three tables were occupied by a group of noisy young men and some very tall, muscular young ladies. He took a seat at a table nearest the bar and waited for the waitress and Bowles to join him. Bowles didn't.

He stood at the doorway and in his most irritating manner yelled, "Garçon, a bottle of your cheap wine for my cheap friend and I."

The garçon, who happened to be a jeune fille, and a very pretty one at that, had just reached Toby at his table. She looked at Bowles then said to Toby, "He with you?"

"I'm afraid so," replied Toby. "But I'll do my best to keep him under control. He is harmless, I assure you."

"Fine, but what about you? Unless I miss my guess, you're a bit too young to be looking after anybody in a licensed club car. So, quickly, before I have to ask for ID, tell me you're twenty-one."

"I'm twenty-one. He's twenty-three. How old are you?"

The Club car waitress smiled and said, "I'm old enough to work here. But this guy, are you sure he's alright? Looks quite ill to me."

Toby was about to find out just how harmless a descendent of Thorvic Bowpuller had become. Bowles came over and sat down, smiling up at the waitress in what he thought was his most appealing and seductive smile.

"I can bring you an Alka-Seltzer, sir, if you have indigestion," she said.

"Don't bother, Miss. He always looks like that. That's his sexy smile. He used it on the dining car waitress earlier, and she wanted to fetch a doctor," explained Toby.

Bowles stopped his idiot grin and said, "Can we get some service, without all this gossiping?"

"Certainly sir, what would you like?" she said. Then turning to Toby. "You were here first, so I'll take your order first. What will it be?"

"I would like to know your name. So I can converse with you in a friendly manner, and I'll have a beer, please."

"My name is Cynthia. Will a Labatt's be okay?"

"Fine. My acquaintance will have a snifter of brandy. The best you have."

Bowles, who had never even tasted brandy, and had been known as two beer Bowles all through training, coughed slightly and said, "Yes, sounds excellent. Hit the spot won't it?"

Cynthia looked at Toby, who rolled his eyes and shrugged. She returned his shrug with a smile and went back to the bar. When she came back, she sat with them and every so often went down to the other tables, filled their orders and then rejoined Toby and Bowles. Toby, enjoying Cynthia's company as he made every effort to ignore the babbling from Bowles, had three beers. Bowles had washed down two double brandies, choked down one scotch, each accompanied by a beer; this on Toby's recommendation that it would help digest his dinner. He was now working on his third Rusty Nail. He felt wonderful. He had never been so filled with goodwill toward men and women. He was flushed with a euphoria so overwhelming he had to do something other than sit and watch Toby and Cynthia make calves eyes at each other.

"Calves eyes, or is it calf's eyes?" he giggled aloud.

The other two just looked at him and went back into their own world. Bowles, secure and confident enough to make a speech in Parliament stood up and wandered, with a bit of a wobble, over to the other tables. Anyone not familiar with Bowles would be impressed with his bearing, and the well-cut, tailored-suit his mother had selected. His manner, and his clothing, which his mother had picked out for him, belied his personality and, for that matter, his intelligence. He made it to the other side and pulled a chair from another table shoved it in beside a tall, statuesque blonde, pushed an ardent admirer aside, causing said admirer considerable dismay.

The men at the table grudgingly gave him space and liberal issues of glares, then returned their attentions to the respective apples of their eyes. The tall blonde was well matched by her twin sister and by two brunettes and a redhead. They were scattered like tall, gorgeous flowers among the crude, pimply faced, long haired weeds that appeared to be all that the garden contained. It turned into a jungle with the arrival of Venus Fly Trap Bowles.

CHAPTER 8

BOWLES MEETS THE GIRLS' VOLLEYBALL TEAM

The five girls, first string members of a semi-professional traveling volleyball team, were en route to Halifax. The six young men, now seven with the arrival of Bowles, were just ordinary travellers on the great Canadian railroad. Two were draft dodgers from south of the border, getting out while the getting was good. Two were good friends taking a summer vacation together to find out if they were gay; one hoping, in the presence of such female delights that he wasn't. The last two were college dropouts on their way to India to find truth and themselves.

While merely incidental to Bowles and Toby's story, all of them did have lives after getting off the train. One of the Americans, after six months in Quebec City, got homesick and went home. He found himself doing two years in Vietnam, still homesick, but now busy dodging incoming mortars and syphilitic whores. The other married a French-Canadian girl, settled in the hills and was never heard from again. The gender undecided pair discovered one was and the other wasn't, but were never sure if that was what they wanted. The searchers after truth found it. They also found themselves doing ten years hard labour for attempted drug smuggling. The truth, for them, was that crime doesn't pay.

But enough of the far distant future. Back in the club car, Toby examined his immediate future and found it extremely promising. Cynthia had already decided on her future, at least for the duration of the trip.

Nestled queasily in a maelstrom of intestinal upheaval, Bowles was trying his best to keep from just plain ordinary heaving. He was drunk. At least he thought so. Things were spinning around, and the engineer had found a downhill slope and was doing his level best to get a speeding ticket. The combination of drink, speed, and the nearness of the ladies had gotten the better of Bowles. Trying to get up, he spilled drinks on everyone. His little attempt at humour did nothing to endear him to those drenched in beer, wine, and liqueurs.

One of the blondes, Virginia, her T-shirt now soaked and displaying her charms, gave vent to her feelings by shoving Bowles across the table where he landed in her sister's lap. Samantha, who'd had her eye on Bowles all evening, loved it. She gave him a hug and, ignoring the wet table and chairs, hung on tight. Snuggled like a foetus and smothering under her breasts Bowles was unable to appreciate his position or the situation. The boys all wanted to get a shot at him and the girls all wanted to protect him. Matt, a tough guy in his own mind, gave Florence, the redhead, a shove. She gave him a hard right cross that knocked him into the wall. As the crowd milled around, Bowles and Samantha, still sitting pretty, were flung over backward. Bowles screamed and in doing so accidentally bit deep into the left breast of his protectress. Distressed by landing heavily on her backside and at the same time receiving a bite on the bosom, she heaved Bowles from her and jumped up.

"You son of a bitch. I'm gonna plough you one right in the face. Now get up!"

Bowles looked up stupidly from the floor, unaware even now that he had precipitated such an uproar. He staggered to his feet not entirely sure just why his recent pillow raged at him. "I don't understand."

"You don't have to understand. No one bites my tits and gets away with it," shouted Samantha, waving one fist and massaging her breast with the other hand.

"It wasn't both of them," he replied, quite puzzled by now.

"Wasn't both of them? You idiot, I don't care if it was half of one. No one bites them!"

Virginia, now trying to talk while bending over with huge belly quaking laughs said, "That's not what you said the other night behind the stadium bleachers with that basketball coach."

"Shut up, Virginia. I decide who bites me. And for that matter, I decide when and where they bite me. Here is not now and he is not who."

"You didn't say if where he bit you was okay," said Virginia.

"Shut up, Virginia.

Cynthia had gotten up at the start of it all, but had been pulled back down by Toby. "Wait until it's all over and then you can go and clean up. If you go now, you may get hit by one of those amazons."

"I suppose you're right," she replied, not really noticing that Toby had pulled her down onto his lap. A few spectators had gathered in the doorway. One, a blue-haired lady, who could have passed for a retired transvestite wrestler, held a yapping poodle who added his bark to the general uproar.

Bowles and Samantha had started to square off, Bowles shifting gradually toward the door.

Samantha finally lost her temper. "You had better put up your hands because I am gonna give it to you right here!"

"But I'd never fight a woman," he wailed. "I can't hit a lady!"

"Too bad. I can hit a man." And she smacked him. Blood exploded from his nose as he was launched onto the blue haired woman and her dog. The poodle, never suspecting that he would get his chance to engage the enemy was flung out of her arms and landed on the sprawling Bowles. Agamemnon, as brave as his name, and standing staunchly on Bowles' chest, cheerfully bit him on the ear. Bowles went berserk. Mentally wasted from the alcohol, physically in pain, and totally confused by all that was going on, he snatched the pygmy warrior from his chest and hurled it at Samantha. She ducked. The dog flew, yapping as he went, and sailed through an open window out into the night. Blue Rinse shoved Samantha aside. She screamed as her dog vanished, then looked around at everyone in the suddenly silent club car.

Then she reached for Bowles just as he was getting to one knee. "You little bastard! That dog was worth seven hundred dollars." And she gave him a slap that deafened him.

Samantha, conveniently forgetting that she had been beating Bowles, yelled, "No one beats up on my man!" and hurled herself at Blue Rinse.

"And no one beats up on my sister!" yelled Virginia, now an enraged mother bear, who dived at Blue Rinse to protect her sister. They both arrived on top of Blue Rinse as she continued to slap Bowles across the face rhythmically. Bowles' only reaction was to let his head flop back and forth in time to the blows.

Blue Rinse discontinued her attack when she found herself flying through the air in the general direction of her dog. She was prevented from joining Agamemnon by a quick-witted Toby, who grabbed one leg as she flew past.

With her out of the way, and all violence satisfactorily purged from their souls, the two girls tenderly carried their trophy out of the car and down to their compartment. Bowles, only knowing that his head was no longer whipping to and fro as if he were a spectator at a tennis match in hell didn't utter a sound.

Cynthia closed the club car temporarily and with Toby's help got most of the mess cleaned up just as her relief arrived. She told him the story and then she and Toby departed for his sleeper. The next two days and nights were blissful lust for them both.

Which, in a general way of speaking, could have described Bowles' remaining time on the train. After carting him off to their compartment, they were joined by Florence, the redhead. The girls used lots of tender loving care and compassion to tidy him up. Then they used all of their considerable feminine wiles to arouse the passionate nature that Samantha steadfastly maintained lay buried within him.

Virginia had argued that while he may have been cute, even cuddly, he was not much in the way of passion. It was not totally Bowles' fault. He had lain for hours in a semi-drunken stupor and then lapsed into a semi-coma caused by the hands of Blue Rinse. Upon recovery from that state he slipped into a bruised, aching, hangover. The sad physical condition he was in was matched by his sexual experience or lack of it.

All of Artie's sex education had come from secret masturbation parties he had held in his father's study when that worthy was away on his many trips. The parties were held in that room because it was the only place where he could safely lock the doors and be alone. That, plus the fact that his father kept the dirty magazines stuffed in a shoebox under his desk, away from his wife's prying eyes.

It came as a surprise to Bowles that he had become a sex object to be used in a kind of Olympic marathon competition whose sole objective was to be the girl who could first assist Bowles into reaching orgasm. Samantha won. It took approximately eight and a half hours. From then on there was no holding Bowles back. He exhausted all three of them, and they had to call in the reserves.

At a small stop somewhere in New Brunswick the sexual Frankenstein that they had created broke loose from the compartment. He chased a nearly-naked Jessica, one of the not-so-willing-any-more-reserves, down the corridor. She had been given the mission of keeping him quiet until they came to a big enough station where the entire team could de-train. Their plan was to wait in peace and quiet for something less monstrous, such as a gang-raping by the Hell's Angels. She failed. Screaming her way through car after car, with Bowles hot on her trail, she was stopped only by running out of train. Taking shelter in the caboose, she met the conductor and a Mounted Policeman, who was handcuffed to a prisoner he was escorting to a cell in eastern New Brunswick.

Clad in a towel, Jessica complemented the deranged Bowles who stormed into the caboose wearing nothing but Virginia's volleyball shorts. The shorts were a conservative crimson, with the legend "ALL GIRLS" nicely embroidered on the seat. Bowles' face was just as crimson as he tried to explain that the slogan did not apply to him. The Conductor just nodded, the handcuffed prisoner said that it was a nice touch and that when he had completed his twenty-five-year term, he would get some made for himself. The Mountie removed another set of cuffs from his belt. Bowles was then placed in custody for the remainder of the trip. During the day he slept cuffed to the other prisoner but ignored him by sleeping. He was fed a dried out sandwich or two and some muddy coffee. That night he was kept secured in the caboose and for the duration was not permitted to bathe, although he was escorted to the washroom three times a day. It didn't matter to Bowles, he was in some kind of alcoholic, sexually sated fog.

"And, since I'm rapidly approaching a similar state of inebriated-ness, without the satiation, I must bring this latest episode of Toby and Bowles to its conclusion."

CHAPTER 9

THE ADJUTANT MEETS THE TRAIN

Toby and Bowles both left the train early the next morning at a dreadfully dreary place known as Fredericton Junction. According to my research, the junction was a mail stop fifteen miles away from Fredericton, the capital city of New Brunswick.

The Junction, not the Province, although there seems to be a debate here, served no valuable purpose. It had been originally designed, with such foresight by the Provincial Nabobs, as the future site of downtown Fredericton, so that in a hundred or so years it would be right in the middle of the teeming capital.

Unfortunately for those land barons and merchants who had used conflict of interest as a kind of Droit de Seigneur and had bought up all the surrounding wilderness, that did not happen. From the start of the railroad through until the army moved into Camp Gagetown from Aldershot around the late fifties, early sixties for those who got lost on the move from Nova Scotia to New Brunswick, no use was made of the Junction other than as a mail drop.

For most trains passing through it wasn't even a stop. The mail was delivered by the human arm of an equally contemptuous conductor, who not caring for accuracy simply hurled the bag from the train as the sign post came into view. This often led to the mailbag ending up in the vicinity of an area sixty feet wide but three miles long.

The good Fredericton Burghers, having missed their chance of a land grab, successfully lobbied for the construction of a large army camp sixteen miles from the city. And as was expected, along with the camp came hordes of young soldiers all heading in their off-duty hours to ravage the city. The Fredericton City Council, wanting the money, but not the aggravation decided to make the junction the stopping place for the military. The reasoning here was that the troops would then only be in town on payday. A fine plan. But the only time a soldier really causes problems is when he is out of camp on a payday with his pockets filled with what he called beer coupons.

When the train carrying Toby, Bowles, and the girls arrived at the Junction, there was already a crowd gathered on the tiny platform. In the interests of

Military and Mounted Police cooperation, the Mountie had decided to unload Bowles on the Military Police and had called ahead for them to meet him. To fulfil that requirement there was a jeep, complete with two burly Military Police corporals.

As was customary, a two and a half ton truck, known as a deuce and a half, was waiting for its load of recruits. What was new and unusual was a staff car containing a driver, Lance Corporal Jenkins, as well as Colonel Schultzberger's Adjutant, Captain Jack Wavell.

The Adjutant was there to take Bowles by the hand and inform him of his new position as a squad commander in The Depot. Standing on the platform with the Adjutant and Jenkins was Lance Corporal Townsend, in a walk-on role as the driver of the deuce and a half. A few paces behind them stood the two MPs. Both groups observed two departures from the train. At the first class end, Toby, clad in the latest style from London, was wrapped tightly in the loving embrace of Cynthia. His baggage was manhandled off by three porters and reverently piled neatly and carefully. Cynthia, like Sheila, had been attracted by the cute way Toby wore his tie, although, unlike myself, she did not think that a man ties his own tie. Just before they stepped down from the railway car, she gave it a tug and pull. "There, now you look ready to meet the army."

Bowles, still confused from his alcoholic and sexual depredations and shackled to the Mountie, was dragged off the back end of the train wearing nothing but a sheet. And not ready for anything. His companion, the Mountie's first prisoner, wearing only Virginia's shorts was unable to disembark. His farewell was limited due to the constricting embrace of being handcuffed to a stanchion inside the caboose. He was only able to wave and blow kisses.

On this particularly bright, shiny, new morning, there was an understandable mix-up where the Adjutant and Jenkins met Toby, and the MPs claimed Bowles. Once the mistake came to light, the Adjutant went into a kind of seizure that required Lance Corporal Jenkins to pound him between his shoulder blades. Recovered slightly, it still took him some time to get over the shock of seeing an officer in a state that resembled that of a homeless man who had been dipped in shit, dragged through a knothole and left for the vultures.

"According to this guy here, who says he's a recruit," said one of the MPs. "The one in the sheet's an officer."

"Corporal Graham, you may be an MP, but if you don't wipe that fucking insolent smile off your fucking face, you'll spend the rest of your fucking career in your own fucking jail."

"Yes, sir, sorry, sir," said a deflated Corporal Graham, knowing full well the danger of upsetting the Adjutant.

Seeing himself inches from a cell he was only too glad to hand Bowles over into the Adjutant's custody. Without a prisoner, the MPs were now only along for the ride.

Toby, who happened to be the only recruit, loaded his belongings into the back of the deuce and a half. After an invitation from the driver, he climbed into the front seat.

With Captain Wavell, Jenkins, and Bowles loaded into the staff car the convoy set off, staff car leading, then the jeep, with the deuce and a half bringing up the rear. The three vehicles turned their noses toward Camp Gagetown; Bowles destined for the officers' mess and Toby to building P-47, which was the barracks of The Caledonia and Musquodoboit Scottish Regiment's Regimental Depot.

The Adjutant instructed Jenkins to take the back roads and off they went, heading toward yet another disaster. On such a beautiful Saturday morning the Adjutant sat in the rear silently anticipating the afternoon's bridge game in the mess, along with a few double scotches to clear away last night's hangover.

Jenkins drove in that same silence, trying to figure out why the Adjutant was up so early in the morning, especially after a wicked Happy Hour, and for what – to deliver a whistlehead to his quarters? Knowing the Adjutant's normal predisposition to junior officers at the best of times, Jenkins couldn't figure it. Bowles felt much the same way. Neither had been privy to Lieutenant Colonel Schultzberger's direct order Friday night to his Adjutant that he would collect Lieutenant Bowles from the train and personally deliver him to the officers' mess. He was also to explain clearly and authoritatively that Bowles was now a member of The Depot and to stay away from the battalion.

Bowles' hangover duplicated the Adjutant's and his incomprehension at least matched Jenkins'. Unaware of his reputation as a dangerous sex offender he could not fathom why the Adjutant had met him at the train station. As the three of them sat in the quiet hum of the vehicle, the aroma from the now rancid Bowles began to make its way over to where Jenkins sat and, from there, floated poisonously into the back seat.

A few miles down the road and coming doggedly toward them was Farmer Josiah Appleby, using for his taxi a massive combine harvester. Not yet aware of any hangover, he was still three-quarters pissed from last night's pub party.

He was mournfully aware of the mountains of sausage, french fries, buckets of beer, and the odd quart of scotch he had gobbled or swilled earlier.

Appleby's guts were in much the same state as Bowles', so he was barely paying attention to the road ahead as he pointed his combine harvester toward the farm. He had hoped that it would make it there before his bowels and bladder found it necessary to relieve themselves of his load of beer, sausage, fries and scotch.

Accompanying Appleby's over-full sense of excess was the knowledge that it was his youngest daughter, Tuesday, who was totally responsible for the state that he was in. Tuesday, on Thursday, had announced that Long Robin Devant had proposed to her. Appleby had long believed that no one would ever ask for her hand, let alone the rest of her and had come to the conclusion that she would be his misery for the rest of his life. Not that there was anything wrong with her.

Tuesday was a bright girl, fairly attractive, and everyone knew she would come bearing a large dowry. It was just that she put the boys off. No one reason, just a lot of little things. She was always right. She was always kind and considerate. She was always on time, and she was always dressed appropriately to the occasion. She was annoying; not like her older sister, Melanie, who was married right after she graduated from high school and headed off to Ottawa with her well-connected husband. But the boys never took Tuesday on a second date.

Appleby had put it down to her being too perfect. It came from her mother he supposed, who had been totally perfect in everything she did, except for choosing him as her mate. Juana had passed away giving birth to Tuesday and Appleby felt that somehow Tuesday had taken on many of his wife's most disconcerting virtues.

Be that as it may, someone had finally popped the question, and there was no question in Appleby's mind that Tuesday would accept. He did have a wrinkle of doubt about Long Robin, a mild-mannered blacksmith from over by Oromocto. The rumours about Long Robin's nickname had never matched. Some said it was the length of his neck, which was very long, some said that one of his legs was longer than the other, although he appeared to walk with a normal gait. Finally, there was the story about the length of his whatsit, which at the best of times, Appleby didn't want to hear about.

On Friday, Appleby left Tuesday to look after things and made his way to the pub to celebrate. Standing rounds at eight and going on until well after four that morning, Appleby had felt compelled to have a drink at every round. This was why he was proceeding home, accompanied by a couple of bottles of good whisky, in time to be on the wrong road at the wrong time as Bowles.

The odour in the staff car creeping toward the Adjutant forced him steadily backward in the rear seat. Jenkins, unable to escape, leaned toward his door to keep the distance between him and Bowles as great as possible.

"Soldier, stop the car!" said Bowles. He had learned that officer talk directed toward enlisted men was done imperiously, no matter how horrid you felt.

"Why?" said the Adjutant and Jenkins.

Bowles ignored the driver and turned to the Adjutant. "I need to relieve myself, sir. You know, Number one and number two," he said, as he pointed at Jenkins and nodded as if the two of them were in a conspiracy.

The Adjutant ignored the pantomime. "Tough shit. The answer's no. Let your number two bake and tie a knot in number one. We're not stopping for anything short of a log-jam of rampaging elephants, and you're not leaving this vehicle until I get you to the back door of the officers' mess, you filthy, little animal."

A comment that, coming from the Adjutant, caused Jenkins to smile because the Adjutant was a weaselly-looking, five-foot, six midget, while Bowles was well over six foot. Jenkins said nothing.

"Shut up, Jenkins," said the Adjutant, affably.

As the vehicle sped on its merry way, Bowles bowels began to rebel. The first sign of this uprising was a substantial, silent but deadly, aroma wafting through the compartment.

Jenkins, now feeling overpowered by Bowles' foulness said, "I think we'd better pull over, sir. He's dropping roses all over the place, sir. It stinks up here."

"Never mind, Jenkins, just open your mouth wider and breathe deeper, it'll go away faster. But for the record, Jenkins, you are one hundred percent correct, the man stinks."

"With all due respect, sir, I am not a man, I'm an officer."

"You're neither. What you are is a pig. Be quiet."

Feeling that this was not the time or the place to discuss his biological make-up in front of the troops, Bowles decided to concentrate on being a container that did not leak from any orifice. The fullness of his bladder, eruptions emanating from his nether regions, and now car sickness set in on Bowles. Hangover nausea and hairpin turns, which Jenkins made little or no effort to pilot through, all came together in one unhappy, heaving soul. Jenkins stepped on the gas to get out of this nightmare as soon as he could. The staff car soon outdistanced the MPs in their jeep and the deuce and a half. What else could happen?

Jenkins entered a tight curve too fast, just as Bowles began a series of dry heaves.

Jenkins took his eyes off the road long enough to eyeball Bowles. "Jesus, he's gonna puke. We gotta stop, sir."

"Ignore his pathetic attempt at getting your attention, Jenkins, drive on."

At that moment, through the other end of the curve and on their side of the road came the Canadian equivalent of a log-jam of rampaging elephants in the guise of Josiah Appleby.

Jenkins, shifted his eyes from the ghastly lieutenant, back on the road only to see that a gargantuan monstrosity had appeared in front of him.

With a very unsoldierly, "Eek!" He swung the steering wheel, and the tires lost contact with the gravel. As he regained control, Bowles fell against his shoulder. Bowles barfed the load of partially digested steaming chunks of hamburger, fries, and pickles that had been marinating in his gullet along with the alcoholic dregs onto Jenkins's lap.

Jenkins reacted as any sensible person about to be engulfed in a horrific avalanche would act, he tried to jump out of the way. This was not a good tactic when sitting behind the wheel of a staff car throttling along at better than sixty miles an hour on a nasty, gravelled road. It's a recipe for disaster when said staff car is hurtling toward a huge combine harvester that was occupying the centre of the road.

Jenkins was too busy doing a seated version of the twist as the car slammed into the rock solid combine. At the moment of impact, Josiah Appleby, in the same state as Bowles, had been busy with an alternate remedy. Steering with one hand and holding a quart of whisky in the other, he had been actively removing an aluminium screw cap with his teeth from a bottle of whiskey. At the last minute, he saw the car rocketing toward him.

He made a frantic swerve to get out of the way, but it only served to point a flimsy but pointy part of the harvester at the windshield of the car. The windshield promptly dissolved in a shower of gem-like particles. The farm implement snapped off, but this act probably saved the Adjutant's life.

On impact, Bowles had nearly been on Jenkins' lap, but the force of the crash wedged him sideways under the dash. Jenkins was brought up smartly against the steering wheel, the wind knocked out of him, then collapsed unconscious over the wheel.

The Adjutant, just as Bowles had fallen onto Jenkins, had made the mistake of rising from his seat to a vain attempt to pull Bowles away from the driver. As the staff car rammed the combine, the Adjutant was in a half-crouch leaning forward over the front seat. His words of rebuke frozen on his lips he watched the combine smack into them, then he saw the windshield magically disappear. The staff car suddenly stopped proceeding rapidly forward, while the Adjutant kept on moving upward over the seat.

The impact stopped the car rather quickly but did nothing for the Adjutant's peace of mind, nor his velocity. The force tossed him like the proverbial rag doll or skinny soldier; as in this case, either description was appropriate. As the skinny soldier was launched out the now open windshield, he bounced like a rag doll onto the hood of the smoking pile of rubble that had once been the CO's favourite and only staff car. He lay there stunned and immobile.

Farmer Appleby fared no better. His sudden panic attack at seeing the staff car up close and rapid caused him to gulp. Appleby learned that gulping is not the recommended methodology of soothing anxiety attacks when holding the aluminium screw cap of a whiskey bottle in one's mouth. He inhaled the cap as far as it would go and that was the last breath that Appleby took. The cap jammed itself in an air-tight seal down his windpipe, sending the amazed farmer on his way to asphyxiation. As his oxygen-starved brain went to sleep, so did the rest of him and there he sat, slumped forward with two broken arms, three broken ribs, and a concussion larger than Mount Olympus.

CHAPTER 10

THE ASSISTANT ADJUTANT MEETS BOWLES

I stopped the story there and looked around the club. I had been going strong since right after lunch. Goody had told me he'd been hearing some complaints about this story-telling séance I had been conducting.

"I'm a full member and I'm breaking no rules," I said.

"No, no. Not that at all."

"What do you mean then? Complaints?"

"There's been grumblings around that you come in and tell a chunk of the story at any time of the day that you feel like it and not everyone knows that you've started. As well, some of them just can't come and stay the same hours as you."

"Oh. So they like it..." I paused. "Even the Committee?"

"Especially the Committee. Harvey tells me he's had eleven defections from St. Orange's Club because of you and Bowles. Another dozen have joined even though they belong to other clubs already."

"Will they reduce my annual subscription?"

Goody shook his head. "I'd say no. They're not that thrilled with you."

"All right. So what do we do? About the time and days?"

Goody shrugged. "No idea."

"Very well, here's what I'll do. I'll hold these briefings every Saturday and Sunday from one o'clock until four o'clock, until the entire tale is finished."

I already had a plan. My wife had seeded the idea quite some time ago, and it, plus the members getting me three fifths of the way to being sozzled gave it a larger sense of life. I had walked home that evening as well. That time, as I toddled along a little unsteadily, I realized that I had quite a story here of Toby and Bowles. I said out loud, "If I wrote a book the members could read it themselves."

"Pardon me, Mr. Oxnard?" a voice had said right beside me. I hadn't realized I'd spoken aloud. Neither had I recognized that the local representative of law and order, on his nightly beat, was walking alongside of me.

"Oh, hello, Constable McQuarrie. Sorry, just had a great idea."

"Better tell me what it is then, Mr. Oxnard. I'd say from the state you're in, you'll wake up tomorrow without a memory of any of it. Tell me and I'll make sure your idea doesn't vanish along with your hangover."

"I'm going to write a book, about Lord Toby and Lieutenant Bowles."

"That's it?"

"That's it, and here's my stop," I said as I reached the wide open gates of Toby's estates.

"Right then, Mr. Oxnard. I'll drop by tomorrow and tell you you're going to write a book."

For the record, the Constable was perfectly correct. I woke up without any memory of our meeting of the night before. At about 10 o'clock the next day, he came by and reminded me that I was going to write a book.

And that's when I started writing it all down. I'd come home from the club and then scribble out what I'd told them. I was already almost caught up to where I had been telling the tale. Very soon, especially if we were going to be meeting only on weekends, I'd get ahead of the talks and use the manuscript for my notes and as a review of the tale.

Once I had the story written, I handed it over to Toby's secretary, Roger Evans. He gladly typed it up, making editorial changes as he went.

***

So, to carry on, of the four men who minutes earlier had been, in varying degrees, enjoying the delights of an early morning summer cruise, three had exchanged that state for varying degrees of unconsciousness. The fourth struggled up from below the dash, his bed sheet in disarray. Opening the passenger door, which promptly fell to the ground, Bowles dismounted the wreck. He left half of his once pristine robe, now bile-covered, snagged on the broken door frame reducing its dimensions measurably.

Bowles staggered around, backside bare to the wind as the two vehicles settled gently on what was left of their springs. Bowles had a quick barf and then decided to perform his own concept of triage on his companions. He turned and surveyed the scene; Adjutant on the hood, Jenkins across the steering wheel, and Farmer Appleby hanging from his seat by one of his broken arms as he lay jammed inside the combine's cab.

Bowles' knowledge of First Aid was limited since that part of his training had been completed after only one lesson. During his attempt at playing Florence Nightingale, he had reduced a splinting and bandaging exercise into eight miles of unwrapped bandages and thirty splints into kindling. The Instructor, an Army nurse wearing the rank of Major, kicked him out of the class. That was unfortunate because a later class on first aid priorities on multiple injuries to a number of victims at the scene of an accident would have been useful.

Bowles opted to offer succour based on rank. The Adjutant, a captain, outranked Jenkins, a corporal, and one look at the farmer and he was instantly rated as a civilian and therefore almost a non-entity. But before that, some vague thought about saving himself first, so that he would be able to render aid more comfortably, entered his head.

Bowles agreed with this assessment and nipped into a hedgerow to ease the pain in his bladder and bowels. The removal of a bit more of his toga solved the toilet paper problem, and he returned to the scene of the accident ready to perform battlefield surgery.

His nonchalant re-appearance greeted the Adjutant, who by this time was sitting dazedly on the hood, shaking his head. Spotting the uninjured, but filthy Bowles, who was whistling the regimental march as he approached, the Adjutant gave in to his desire to commit murder.

With a cry of rage, he threw himself off the hood. Bleeding from a number of minor facial cuts, none of which were capable of causing his immediate demise, he looked a gory mess. The blood-soaked apparition leaping from the hood startled Bowles who was busy rummaging through his limited first aid memory bank. He yelped and scrambled away from his attacker.

Bowles ran around the wrecked vehicles, the Adjutant hot on his bare ass. As they lapped the driver's side for the third time, Jenkins came to. He thought he saw a half-naked man being pursued by a raving, bloody, maniac. Still groggy, Jenkins sensed instinctively that this was an unorthodox first aid procedure and promptly fell back into a semi-coma.

As the rampaging pair headed into the back straight, Farmer Appleby's body gave a frenzied last-chance jump and then toppled from the combine's cab straight into the path of the fleeing Bowles. Bowles, seeing this as one more attacker, jumped with both feet over the stretched out carcass of Appleby. Underestimating the distance to the other side of the plump farmer, Bowles landed feet first on Appleby's tummy. This action initiated a primitive but effective Heimlich manoeuvre. Bowles couldn't care less; he made it over the objective and continued on.

The bottle cap flew into the air and Appleby's windpipe, suddenly clear, was engulfed in the fresh air, and he began to revive. He lay on the ground gulping in precious oxygen.

Jenkins, watching the tableaux, saw the Adjutant finally catch up with Bowles and fling his arms around him in a death grip. Since Bowles was nearly a foot taller, the Adjutant's arms did not reach Bowles' throat, but only contained him in a bear hug. Bowles panicked and with a mighty heave, flung the Adjutant through the air where he crashed head first into a large boulder. Once again, the Adjutant slept the sleep of the innocent.

The Military Police, long out-distanced by Jenkins's attempt to get home before Bowles committed some foul act in the car, finally arrived on the scene.

Not so Toby and his chauffeur. Once the two smaller vehicles had charged out of sight, Lance Corporal Townsend suggested that they forget following the jeep and staff car and get onto a real highway, one with a decent diner on it. Toby, thinking that was an excellent idea, even offered to pay. In doing that, they missed all the excitement but did receive excellent breakfasts.

They also missed the MPs doing their peculiar form of military triage by calling in for an ambulance on their jeep radio. That done, they loaded up the still unconscious Adjutant in their jeep and headed off to the camp hospital.

Jenkins, now up and about, assisted the farmer to a grassy hummock. Bowles, wrapped in a blanket given him by the MPs, wondering if he would ever wear clothes again, joined them.

The ambulance crew arrived to find the three of them drunk on the second bottle of whiskey that Farmer Appleby had stashed inside a bale of hay on the back of the combine. During their Happy Hour, Jenkins had explained how Bowles had saved Appleby's life, and all were quite euphoric. So much so that Jenkins had tossed his filthy pants and shirt in the underbrush and was sitting in his underwear. Appleby, sitting drunkenly with two half-naked soldiers, happily stripped to his long-johns in order to match the dress code of his companions. To him, Bowles was a hero.

The ambulance crew checked the two inebriated soldiers and the similarly smashed civilian and declared them fit for duty, but unfit to travel in a military ambulance. They radioed in and the hospital dispatcher, seeing that it was no longer a medical emergency, handed the problem off to the First Battalion duty officer, who promptly slung it toward the Adjutant, who of course could not be reached. Lieutenant Donald Karlsen, the Assistant Adjutant ended up taking the call and once he discovered the Adjutant still sleeping peacefully in the camp hospital, had to deal with Bowles himself. He rounded up a staff car and a driver and off they went to find the missing Lieutenant Bowles.

On arrival at the scene of the crime, Karlsen got out of the car and with the driver in tow, marched up to where Bowles, Jenkins, and Appleby were now fast asleep. Jenkins was stretched out on the ground with his head on a boulder. A few feet away, Bowles and Appleby were snuggled up in a warm, but rather disconcerting embrace.

Once Karlsen got the two of them untangled, he led Bowles back to the staff car. His driver, Lance Corporal Swadley, did the same with Jenkins. The two officers stood beside the vehicle with Jenkins propped up against it. Corporal Swadley retrieved the baggage from the wreckage and placed it in the trunk. While they waited, the Assistant Adjutant looked Bowles over as if he were a bitter taste in his mouth. To break the ice, he congratulated Bowles on his recent promotion, thinking that that promotion was soon to be rescinded. "Hard lines, there, eh, Bowles? Coming fiftieth out of fifty. And to top it off, getting promoted out of it. Must have made a couple of instructors a little annoyed."

"Yes, sir, that it did." Bowles was still not clear on who his benefactor was and didn't realize that they both held the rank of Lieutenant. He went on, "I was quite unhappy to find I'd done so poorly. During Basic Officers, I finished much higher. I was number thirty that time. Hope I haven't let the Old Man down."

Knowing that Bowles' class during that course numbered thirty souls, Karlsen failed to understand how coming last out of thirty was any better than coming last out of fifty said nothing. His fondest desire at that moment was to snatch the keys from the driver, leap into the car and commit a particularly bloody case of vehicular homicide on the dolt standing beside him. Seeing the carnage littering the roadside, he gathered that had already been attempted and had failed.

Karlsen also knew that Captain Wavell had done a tour with the Brits ten years ago and he was always using the term 'Old Man'. As far as Karlsen was concerned, it was fine for the Limeys to use such terms because it was their language but these days, no self-respecting subbie modelled himself on Monty and his gang, even if ninety percent of the senior officers in the regiment still thought they were part of the British Empire. Didn't this idiot know that the new role models for the younger officers were the Special Forces of JFK and their exploits in the jungles of Southeast Asia? He was pretty sure that the CO, even though an ancient, doddering lieutenant colonel at the age of thirty-eight wouldn't appreciate being described as the 'Old Man'. He ignored his desire;

desires are just wishes that can be overcome, he thought as he told Bowles and Jenkins to both get in the back; he sat in the passenger seat beside Corporal Swadley.

The trip back began with Bowles and Jenkins both going back to dreamland. As they neared the camp, Bowles woke up and asked if the Assistant Adjutant knew what his job was going to be in the battalion.

"Oh, my, haven't you heard? You're not going to the battalion. You're cross-posted to The Depot. I was instructed by the Adjutant to ensure that come Monday, you were off to clear into The Depot. I had all your paperwork in my room and had planned to give it to you when you arrived. I didn't know that I would end up coming to get you."

"But what about clearing into the battalion, getting fitted for my kilt? I need to get down to Scully's to buy my accoutrements. I was also planning to meet the other subbies. They play a crazy game on the pool table called 'crud'. Sounds like a real laugh."

"It is," said Karlsen who was known as one of the best crud players the battalion had ever seen. "You'll live in the Transient Officers mess, so you won't get to meet the lads for a while. As for being fitted for your kilt, you'll get a chance to do that when your squad gets theirs. Meeting the subbies and playing crud…" Karlsen shook his head. "Not possible. You won't have time. You'll be so busy with your squad for the next nineteen weeks that you'll only see the inside of the mess at bedtime. When your squad graduates, you'll be cross-posted back to the battalion. Then you can move into the battalion mess."

The car pulled up outside a building way off from the other messes. A large sign indicated this was the Transient Junior Officers mess. Hearing Bowles groan at the idea of being sent to such a horrible place, the Assistant Adjutant did have a fleeting flood of sympathy for him. Bowles drove that away when he said, "Oh, I say! That is really spiffing."

"What is?"

"You putting me up with those officers who are just passing through. I'll be kind of the block senior, right?"

"I suppose so. Anyway, Swadley will unload your bags and see you to the accommodation office." Karlsen turned to look at Swadley. "Thanks for coming out, Corps. I'll just leg it over to the mess and get into the bar for a picker-upper."

"No problem, sir. I'll see you tomorrow."

With that, Karlsen left them to it, speeding off, he told me later, to get a couple of whiskies inside of himself to get the horrid taste of the idiot lieutenant out of his mouth and mind.

CHAPTER 11

TOBY MEETS MAD DOG

Toby's arrival at The Depot opened up a brand-new, shocking world that he and thousands of civilians could scarcely comprehend. I understood, I'd undergone a similar upheaval in my own military basic training. But Toby's experience was doubly shocking because when the deuce and a half arrived at The Depot, Toby was asleep in the cab. He was awakened by the smash of a swagger stick against the truck's door. He looked around, not quite ready to enter enthusiastically into the army world. Fortuitously for Toby, the Lance corporal was there with his sharp tongue and nasty swagger stick to tell him in no uncertain terms what his parentage was and where his ass was going to be if he didn't get it off the truck a little quicker.

Toby had formally arrived at The Caledonia and Musquodoboit Scottish Regimental Recruit Depot. This was hell for most Canadian young men, but for an upper-class British kid, it was the kind of hell that is only dreamt of in hell.

The lance corporal announced that he was Lance Corporal Anderson. With a variety of orchestral flourishes of his swagger stick, he persuaded Toby to lug his trunks, suitcases, and travel bags into the building. Inside the lobby, Toby nearly tripped over a man on his hands and knees shining a brass plate in the middle of the floor. Shaved head, clad in coveralls, he resembled a prisoner of war.

In stunned shock, Toby made three more trips into The Depot. The lance corporal kindly held the door, but other than that, offered no assistance. His silence made the scenario more melodramatic, and as Toby wondered what was next, he was ushered back out into the grey early morning. The truck disappeared, and moments later another deuce and a half pulled up. The same routine was repeated by another immaculately clad lance corporal who herded his charges into the building with their luggage. This lance corporal accompanied his instructions with curses and death-dealing promises centreing around someone he referred to as "Mad Dog".

When the boys had shifted their belongings inside and had returned back out onto the sidewalk, the mouthy lance corporal nodded at Lance Corporal Anderson and with a last, "Mad Dog'll see to you lot." vanished.

A few minutes later the door opened and out stepped the duty Sergeant. He stood on top of the steps looking down at the group of bewildered recruits. He stood five feet eight and one-quarter inches, the one-quarter existing only in his imagination when clad in his highland hose and his double-soled ammunition boots. Today those boots, gleaming-black lacquered, toe-capped inspirations were working hard at keeping Sergeant Gallagher upright as he introduced himself to this latest batch of recruits.

They stood shivering, scared, and hungry in the, for them, still-early morning, as Sergeant Gallagher moved to the edge of the steps. In Toby's mind, he was a nightmare from a misty highland moor, taking this morning off from slaughtering Sassenachs to talk at a handful of recruits. Such a spectre would have been nicer, much nicer.

Being duty Sergeant had had him up at 0600 hours, and since he had only landed in his bunk at four, this left him with a combination hangover and drunken stupor of such epic misery that he felt it only fair to share it with every recruit in The Depot. The new arrivals were about to get their quota.

The twenty-four vibrating souls nervously scuffing, coughing, and muttering at his feet were looking everywhere but at the kilt-clad Sergeant. They did not know that he always closed out Happy Hour. They were not to know that his Saturdays belonged to him. After the Friday night Happy Hour at the sergeants' mess, Gallagher was in no mood to be up and around before noon.

"Gentlemen."

Excluding Toby, they were anything but, and Gallagher knew it. They didn't. A few even thought, "Hey, this is a nice guy."

"Gentlemen."

This time the sound was accompanied by a sense of grim foreboding that even the most naive recognized. Opinions on Gallagher changed swiftly, but the consensus was 'This guy is freakin' evil.'

"My name is Sergeant Gallagher. I am not a nice guy. It's not that I couldn't be, it's just that I don't want to be."

"Probably didn't get laid last night," whispered a tall red-haired boy behind Toby.

He was right. Gallagher was unmarried and lived in the sergeants' quarters. He did not get laid very often; which likely contributed to his not being a nice man. But being right did not make the unfortunate boy popular with Gallagher.

"You! You horrible little man!"

75

No one seemed to notice or care that the 'horrible little man' towered over everyone there.

"You are a disgusting piece of filth. If you ever interrupt me again, I'll have your guts for garters. Do you understand?"

Sergeant Gallagher came the down steps to the roadway and marched slowly toward the group as he spoke. The crowd parted. Gallagher advanced. The redhead retreated. The dance ended with Gallagher and the boy in the centre of a semi-circle of recruits, the lad with his back to The Depot wall. Gallagher's face was inches from the skinny boy's chest, his eyes, two piss-holes in snow, burned upwards.

"Yes," whimpered Red.

"Yes, what?"

"Yes, I understand."

"Understand what?"

"I understand that you'll have my garters, whatever they are."

"No, you idiot. I'll have your guts for garters. And if you ever speak to me again without saying Sergeant, I'll rip out your heart. Now do you understand?"

"Yes, Sergeant, yes, Sergeant."

"Shut up." He pivoted slowly in his boots, the noise of his metal horseshoe cleats grinding the pavement into crumbs made every recruit feel as if it were his bones being ground to dust.

"And that goes for the rest of you. You answer 'Sergeant' when I speak, and you stand as close to the position of attention as your ignorance permits. Got it?'

No one spoke. Gallagher raised his drill cane at one of them. "Well, speak up. Have you got it?"

Toby put his feet together, looked around at the rest of them before saying, "You just told us to shut up, Sergeant."

Gallagher advanced on Toby. "Then why in the fuck are you speaking, boy?"

Toby didn't have the faintest. Then, from some dim memory of martial adventures as told by Ox, he gave the right answer, "When faced with two conflicting orders the soldier will obey the last order given. Your last order was for us to speak up, so I did...Sergeant."

Gallagher was impressed, not sufficiently to become any nicer, but enough to say, "Good answer, Twerp, even if you sound like some kinda fucking limey."

"I am not a twerp, Sergeant. My name is Randolph Anthony Tobias Trelauney-Fitzgibboncrest, and yes, I am some kind of limey, I am the English kind, and I would appreciate it if you would desist in your sneering at my background. Furthermore, I insist that you apologize for the insulting name you just called me. I may be in the Canadian Army, and I may be a private, and you may be a Sergeant, but that is no excuse for bad manners."

Gallagher laughed. Lance Corporal Anderson jumped down from the steps and moved toward Toby. "Shall I throw the twerp in jail, Sarge?"

Gallagher whirled around to face Lance Corporal Anderson. "Lance Corporal, if you want to be wearing that stripe by the end of the day, I would suggest that you never, ever again address me as Sarge. This is not the Marine Corps. I am not Sergeant fucking Rock, and you are hopefully not a fucking, gum-chewing, you-all, dratted Yankee. Got it?"

"Yes, Sergeant." Lance Corporal Anderson, in fear of his life, decided not to point out that a you–all and a Yankee were two different species of American. He swallowed hard, turned about and returned to where he had been standing. Then he began imitating his previously silent self.

Gallagher rotated back to face Toby. "So, you're a little upset that the big bad Sergeant is calling you names, eh, Limey? Well, I've got news for you. I'll address you as twerp, idiot, or asshole if I so desire. And that goes for the rest of you. When you graduate from here, maybe, just maybe, I'll call you by your name. Your last name."

Toby was not to be denied. "Just a moment, Sergeant. I insist on an apology. If I do not receive one right here, right now, I'll seek redress from your Commanding Officer."

Gallagher was amazed. The kid has guts, he thought, but I'll be goddamned if he's getting an apology from me. His eyes sought the redhead. "Redtop!"

The red-haired boy bounced to what he thought was the position of attention. "Yes, Sergeant?"

"Red, I have neither the time nor the inclination to discuss this further with. ..." He turned back to Toby. "What'd you say your name was?"

Toby thought he should do it right. "Private Randolph Anthony Tobias Trelauney-Fitzgibboncrest, Sergeant."

"Fine." Over his shoulder, Gallagher said, "Red, Private Randy Toby Treelawn Something Fitzsomething else wants an apology. Give him one."

"You want me to apologize for you, Sergeant?"

"Sure, if someone's gotta do it, it may as well be a shithead like you."

"Yes, Sergeant." He started to speak to Toby.

"No, Red, go over and stand in front of him."

Red went over and said, "On behalf of Sergeant Gallagher, he's sorry."

Gallagher screamed, "For fuck's sake, asshole, I'm not sorry, you are. Say it again."

Red went white. He tried again, "The Sergeant says I'm sorry for him calling you names."

Gallagher slammed his drill cane down on the ground. It split in two. Lance Corporal Anderson went over and picked up one piece. Gallagher stepped on the other piece, crunching it beyond repair and reminding the lads that their bones were a bit too close to those wicked boots.

"Red, you gotta be the dumbest recruit I ever laid my poor eyes on. Now, Limey, that's the closest I'd say we're gonna get with an apology from Red. Take it and shut the fuck up...Lance Corporal, get 'em sorted out. Sergeant Clyde'll be here shortly. I'll be at the mess if there's any trouble."

Fortunately for Toby and his squad-mates, Sergeant Gallagher's time in connection with 1313 Squad was short-lived. My meeting with Sergeant Gallagher went a lot more smoothly, but that's another story.

CHAPTER 12

TOBY MEETS HIS ROOMIES

"Look, Marv… in, we need a bit more of Toby's experience with the Canucks. Most of our readers are not going to know how a soldier lived and for that matter where they lived."

"Understood, Peter, and here's a short piece where the life of a recruit in today's Canadian Army is explained," I said.

I then proceeded to explain the Canadian Depot to him. The depot was housed in the typical Canadian Army barrack block, two wings down, two up, with a common area in the middle of an "E" shaped building, but instead of a middle leg, it was shaped like a python with a cow halfway digested through its length. That was the common room, and in any unit in the army, other than a recruit barracks, it had a TV set, some games, and a lounge area. In The Depot, the lounge was closed off. No one had any time to spend relaxing.

The lance corporal took the boys into the building to meet the other recruits who would make up Recruit Squad 1313. For thirty-two civvy kids, the long process of socialization into the military mystique that had begun with the paperwork processing reached its culmination with their entry into the dreaded depot. Anderson led them down the corridor and into the end of the hallway where a Sergeant and three other lance corporals were waiting with the rest of the Squad. They were lounging around, leaning against the walls or sitting on the floor. A few enterprising young recruits had brought chairs and were the most comfortable. After the new ones had mingled in, the Sergeant came to stand a pace in front of the nearest kneeling boy.

"Welcome to The Caledonia and Musquodoboit Scottish Regimental Depot, lads. Or as we know it, The Depot. My name is Sergeant Clyde. The lance corporal who brought you down the hallway and is now standing behind you so that you don't try and make a break for it is Lance Corporal Donald Anderson. Beside him is Lance Corporal Rene Duguay. To my right is Lance Corporal Peter Caruthers. And to my left is Lance Corporal Jason Steele. We are the training cadre for your Squad, Squad 1313. There are one or two more of you still to come, but for now, you're it."

A bright-looking lad with the bald-chimp hair style that was awaiting the new guys, put up his hand and asked, "Excuse me, Sergeant, but don't we have a squad officer?"

The cadre had had a meeting in their office in regards to the squad commander. Rumours were flowing that he had been arrested while on the train. Until they got confirmation, Clyde had decided that they would keep mum. "Later, lad, right now we're talking about the squad staff who work for a living."

"Each one of the lance corporals will have one section of eight recruits. The rooms hold eight bed spaces. You can sort out who gets a top bunk or a lower on your own time. You will be divided into your sections at the end of this little session. For now, we'll cover the ground rules on how to survive depot and the army in general. This camp has over five thousand soldiers and over a dozen units of various sizes and trades. What you need to know for now is that we belong to the CMSR, The Caledonia and Musquodoboit Scottish Regiment. There are three battalions of CMSR, the first and Second Battalion are stationed here in camp with us. The Third battalion is over in Germany on a NATO posting. Officially we are The Caledonia and Musquodoboit Scottish Regimental Depot. But as I said earlier, to us it's The Depot. You are to stay away from all other unit areas, especially the First and Second battalion's lines. Got that?"

A few voices knew the correct answer and replied lustily, "Yes, Sergeant!"

Others nodded, some said 'yep', some 'yeah', and some answered, 'okay'.

Lance Corporal Anderson startled those unready types by bellowing, "The correct answer is, 'Yes, Sergeant.' Don't forget that."

Toby and the lads who had been welcomed to The Depot by the cordial Sergeant Gallagher were among those who had answered accurately.

Sergeant Clyde nodded and said, "Shall we try it again?" This time the chorus of correct replies showed that this was a bright group. "Better, lads, better. Now Lance Corporal Steele will call the roll. You will answer, 'Here, Sergeant!' and that's all. Got it?"

This time they all got it, and the required reply satisfied the training cadre. Lance Corporal Steele stood up from the wall he had been supporting and looked down at his clipboard. Things went well until he got to Toby's name.

"Trelooncydashfitzsomething?"

"Trelauney-Fitzgibboncrest, Sergeant," spoke up Toby.

"No lad, it's only sergeant when you answer a roll call, and a sergeant is the highest rank present. When you talk to an individual, you use his rank. In this case, that would be Lance Corporal Steele, alright?"

"Yes, Sergeant," said Toby, not understanding a word of what Clyde had said. "So if I speak to him, I say lance corporal, but if I speak to you it's sergeant, correct?"

"Correct," said Sergeant Clyde.

"Thank you, Sergeant," Toby turned to the lance corporal and said, "That's Trelauney-Fitzgibboncrest, Lance Corporal."

"Yeah, I heard you tell the Sergeant. What is it, some kinda limey name?"

"No, Lance Corporal, it is actually a Scottish name."

"We've been through this with Sergeant Gallagher, so I suggest that you learn his name or we'll still be sorting this out at Graduation Day," said Lance Corporal Anderson.

"Ah, so you've met the famous Sergeant Gallagher, eh, lad?" asked Sergeant Clyde.

"If that's that rude boor who met us at the door, yes, Sergeant, I have met Sergeant Gallagher, and I would like to know who I report him to?"

"See me later, son, we'll talk."

"Yes, Sergeant."

And with that, Toby found himself, along with thirty-one other puzzled recruits, in the unique socialization program that the Canadian Army decreed would change civilian boys to military men. That was not his aim. His plan was to leave the army as soon as possible, and without making that terrible transition.

Once the roll call had been called, and all were declared present, they were taken down the long hallway to their series of rooms, where they were placed eight to a room in circumstances no one but a homeless man living in a cardboard box would consider palatial.

These rooms, a suitable size for four soldiers, were quite crowded when a platoon of recruits was jammed into them, eight to a room. In each corner of the room were lockers that ran from the floor to the ceiling. Inside each locker was a rifle rack, a set of four drawers and a crossbar for the hanging articles. Above that, the locker had a small cupboard where suitcases or cases of illegally purchased beer could be stored. In place of four beds, there were four sets of bunks so that two recruits shared the space normally occupied by one soldier.

In the crowded situation that the recruits found themselves, each single locker was now shared. Two rifles would shortly occupy the rifle rack, each soldier had two of the four drawers, and they shared the bar with their hanging items. Under each bed would go two olive drab, fibreglass barrack boxes, and two fat, khaki coloured kit bags. During the day, each mattress was rolled up to form a giant jelly roll; on top of this were carefully placed the blankets and sheets in a blanket roll. This sandwich affair of blankets and sheets neatly folded and ironed was twelve inches high, three feet long, and one bayonet length wide.

Below this, on the bed springs were the two soldiers' sets of webbing. Webbing consisted of a series of straps and a belt from which dangled two ammo pouches, a pair of cross straps, one bayonet in a canvas frog, a mess tin carrier with mess tins, a canteen, and carrier. All this in the olive drab canvas material that looked so good on parade, but was the very devil to clean and maintain.

The uniform was battledress in the winter or bush clothing in the summer. The only difference for the recruits was which one to wear. Upkeep was the same. All uniforms were pressed every evening, six days a week in order to develop permanent creases in everything. Both pairs of boots and shoes were shone nightly, and all drawer layout items were either pressed, shone, or polished during those same evening hours. Shoe polish and brass shining solvent cans had the paint scraped off them, and they were then shone themselves.

After learning from the more senior platoons, the new boys soon learned that the bed was rarely slept in. Only the outer blanket was ever used. It was placed on the barrack box as an ironing board cover. The rest of the bedroll stayed intact until Tuesday evening, then the sheets could be used, for Wednesday was sheet exchange. From day one until the recruit completed training, he did not sleep in a normal bed. The outer blanket and the mattress were the only items unrolled at the end of the day.

In Toby's room, there was a Newfoundland lad named Paul McGuffin who slept in the bunk above him and with whom he shared a locker. Along with McGuffin, there were two other lads from Belle Isle, a fishing village in Newfoundland. They all came complete with unintelligible dialects, and not one of these dialects was the same, even though they had been born and raised within sight of each other. Two more were from Nova Scotia, one a rich kid from Halifax, the other, came from a family of butchers and meat packers and was from Dartmouth, the twin city tied to Halifax by a bridge and little else. Next, there was a lumberjack from the interior of British Columbia and a Jewish boy from the heart of Cabbagetown, the Toronto slum, who made up the roster for the eight man room.

Now the stage was set. Bowles was stashed safely in The Depot, hidden from all eyes, excepting those of the commandant of The Depot, who in the grand scheme of things was not destined to be a major player, at least not for long.

Bowles had been sorted out smartly by The Depot Adjutant in regard to his amorous exploits on the train and given three weeks of Depot duty officer. The rumours ran contrary to fact, as rumours so often do, and his seduction by an all-girls basketball team had been twisted so that he had single-handedly serviced a railroad car load of beauty pageant contestants. To the single living-in officers, all lieutenants, and second lieutenants, he was a hero. The married officers, who knew better, accurately put him down as an idiot.

None of it bothered Bowles. He was filled with the pride of the ignorant. His three weeks of duty officer he viewed not as punishment, but as the keys to the kingdom. He, after all the officers had gone home, was in total command of The Depot and all its inhabitants.

Bowles had never made the connection between the well-dressed toff who had shared the dining car with him and the shaven headed private soldier who was now in his platoon. In fact, he had never even thought about his soldiers as individuals or bothered to learn their names. They were his platoon, a lump, a group, a single entity that jumped when he spoke, that rushed the barricades at his command, that charged blindly after him as he galloped forward on the blood-soaked ground of Gallipoli. They were nothing more than a stepping stone to the command of a company, a battalion, a brigade, and then a division; who knew, maybe that marshal's baton was indeed in his knapsack.

CHAPTER 13

THE SENIOR SQUAD MEETS TOBY

"That's good, Marvin, and you'll also tell us about the instructors, were they all like Sergeant Gallagher?"

"No. He was actually a rare one. But instructors are a different breed of animal from school teachers. For the most part they treated the recruits fairly, but very firmly. To them, training civilians to be soldiers required a degree of destruction of the civilian ego. Once they had reduced these egos to broken eggs and shattered their self-images as if they were glass, it was time to build them up into images of themselves – images they saw as being warriors.

Of course, at the beginning Toby and his buddies didn't see it that way. He had never been so fed up in his life. He had been in The Depot for two weeks and for him these fourteen days felt as if they had been going on since he had left the cradle. As far as he was concerned, the entire depot staff was comprised of sadistic, bellowing, moronic, Neanderthals. They were on the recruits from reveille to lights out and then they, in their inhuman way, cunningly permitted the senior squad to take over during the hours of darkness.

From the first night, the senior squad, once the duty corporal had turned out his own light and dropped off to dreamland, climbed up the stairs at their end of the corridor and came across the empty top floor, then descended from above Toby's squad's rooms to inflict their own kind of hell on the new guys. Fire hoses were unrolled, and dragged by senior recruits, trying hard to stifle their giggles in their anticipation of the fun to follow, along the corridor to be positioned at the exteriors of the new recruits' doors.

On a signal, the low vents in the doors of the new boys' rooms were kicked in, and the fire hoses were thrust through the openings and turned on; soaking everything that the squad owned. Ten seconds of deluge, withdraw hoses, move to the next pair of rooms where the process was repeated. Initiation it was called. The first night came as a real shock. Toby, on a lower bunk to the right of the door as you entered, received the brunt of that blast. Drenched and stunned he awoke from a dream of London, screaming that London bridge had fallen down and he had been on it at the time.

On the second night they were ambushed again, but this time, they were not so shocked. They weren't as horrified. They had not been expecting it, saw the first night's ordeal as a one-time effort. By the fourth night in a row, they had enough. Toby had managed to gather about half the squad to lie in wait in the shower room. Hidden behind the door with wet mops and buckets of water the brave little band of new recruits charged out at the first sound of a vent being kicked in. They routed the senior lads who had been as surprised by this offensive manoeuvre as Toby's squad had been on night number one.

After supper the next day, a delegation arrived in the junior squad area and held a summit conference to announce that as the senior squad they were the hazers and were permitted to indulge in hazing without any fear of retaliation from the hazees. Squad 1313 demurred, and a more vigorous form of discussion led to an escalation that threatened the peaceful calm of The Depot.

The duty corporal, this time one of the senior squad's own staff, refereed the conflict down to the junior participants doing a few hundred turns around the outside of the building at a gallop. Toby and McGuffin objected. To which the Corporal replied, "Sorry lads, this is a tradition in The Depot. You'll just have to bear it until the next squad behind yours arrives on the ground."

"No, Corporal, with all due respect, that's not what is going to happen. We have been initiated, and we are declaring our end of The Depot lines to be out of bounds after lights out to all recruits not in 1313. We will hospitalize them if necessary."

"That's right, Corporal. We have had the bun. Any them fellas cross to our end, we're puttin' them in body casts," added McGuffin, waving a broom handle.

Emboldened by Toby and McGuffin's response, the squad agreed. Only a few of the more chicken-like members remained silent. The near-open rebellion put Corporal Sheldon's back up.

"Hey, I ain't telling you lot again. I'm in charge here, and there's to be no comebacks on the senior squad from you lotta chumps. Anyone I catch pulling any fancy stuff will find themselves getting air pumped into them at the guardroom. Got it?"

The threat of going to jail did not work on Toby who thought that the worst that could happen would be a dry night's sleep. It might be an even better place to live than the one he was inhabiting now. "Pardon me, Corporal, but what we have just said, stands. You can put us all in jail right now. We'll have a dry roof over our heads, and you can answer to our squad sergeant as to why we were absent from his parade tomorrow morning."

The idea of answering to an enraged Sergeant that his entire squad had been incarcerated for insubordination did not appeal to Corporal Sheldon. "You some kinda limey, kid?"

"I'm the kind that will not put up with being treated unfairly, Corporal. Those guys have been soaking us for a week now, and we are through with it. Do what you have to do, we're going to do what we have to do." Toby turned to McGuffin and the rest of them. "Right, lads?"

"That's a fact, Squire. We're wit ya all the way!"

"No, not quite, Trelauney-Fitzgibboncrest," said a large, lumpy looking boy standing off to the rear of the crowd.

"Yeah, Stuffy's right, Squire. We can't go against the whole depot," said another lad.

Seeing the division among the lads and breathing a sigh of relief from not having his bluff called any further, the Corporal said, "Sort this out tomorrow, among yourselves. For now, get to bed. There'll be no further horseplay in the halls tonight." With that, Corporal Sheldon beat a hasty retreat and hoped the senior squad would stay where they belonged. The senior squad decided that the fun was over and that ended 1313's initiation.

As for the squad calling him Squire, that had started as a form of self-defence on both the squad and the squad staff's part. Toby's name had played havoc with the culture of the Canadian military. In an environment where profanity was an art form and nicknames the rule, the name Trelauney-Fitzgibboncrest was not to be accepted. For the lance corporals in charge of Toby's socialization process, yelling his name out prior to issuing the obligatory blast of shit, the name was just too, too long.

"Private Trelauney-Fitzgibboncrest, if you don't get those disgusting boots out of my sight this instant, I'll have your bloody balls for bookends."

The impact was lost long before the entire statement was out of their lungs. A care package addressed to Randolph Tobias Trelauney-Fitzgibboncrest, Esquire, sent by his worried mother gave the lads something to work on. It was easier for all concerned to call him "Squire". The care package containing jars of caviar, a wheel of Brie, plum puddings, tins of ham, and lobster pate soon won the hearts and stomachs of his bunkmates.

As you can see, creating warriors out of students, fishermen, lumberjacks, coal miners, shopkeepers, farmers, bank tellers, and even the unemployed was a tough job. Moulding them into their own image took time, effort, and skill. Luckily, most instructors in The Depot were prepared to spend that time ensuring that come graduation day, their squad 'Passed Out' proudly.

CHAPTER 14

THE ADJUTANT MEETS APPLEBY'S LAWYERS

If you think Toby and his squad were the only ones whose visions of Camp Gagetown were mirrored on hell, I'll take a moment to let you hear how Captain Wavell, Lieutenant Colonel Schultzberger's Adjutant, who endured Bowles and Appleby in the same car crash was seeing the world at that moment.

"The Sunnavabitch is suing us!"

"Who and why is he a Son of a Bitch?" asked Lieutenant Karlsen, the Assistant Adjutant.

"Give your head shake–anyone who sues us has got to a son of a bitch."

"Yeah, okay, sir. Fine, he's a son of a bitch because he suing us. So who is he?"

"Appleby, that bumble-brained farmer who practically killed me and Jenkins."

"Oh, and wasn't Bowles there too?"

"Now there's a real sunnavabitch. And if he'd been killed, then the story would've had a happy ending."

Lieutenant Karlsen thought that if both the Adjutant and Bowles had gone off together to that Big Home Station in the Sky, the entire Army would have been better off.

Karlsen was a bright, fairly young officer who, during his initial interview, had made a mistake of letting the DCO know he held a degree in business administration.

"That's the ticket. Sounds like you'd be perfect as the Assistant Adjutant, young Karlsen. With all that education, you'll have the place in top hole precision before we know it. Capital. It's set then."

"But, sir, what about a rifle platoon?"

"What, egad, Chappie, you'd give Assistant Adjutant a miss? Most young officers would give their right arm for such a job, you know."

None of the young officers who had arrived at the battalion with Karlsen would have given a toenail off their left foot for the job. They were all panting at the thought of getting their own platoons; of leading men into battle, of being in command, of winning the annual skill-at-arms competition, of just being able to play with a bunch of real soldiers instead of the plastic ones they had grown up with. How would it look in the mess tonight when they're excited about their platoons, and all Mrs. Karlsen's little boy can say is, "I'm the Assistant Adjutant."

But Karlsen had no say in the matter. Off he went to report to the Adjutant. The Adjutant was a complete and unequivocal snob, a petty bureaucrat, and a bully. Karlsen hated every minute of his new job. Therefore, he was secretly pleased to hear the Adjutant bemoan his fate as the two of them sat among the ruins of a coffee break. Crusts and crumbs littered the tables. Coffee cups and ashtrays and some used as both completed the scene.

"So what happens now if we're being sued? And by we, I am assuming it's you and the regiment that's being sued and not the rest of us, sir?"

"Well Karlsen, I'm so glad to hear of your strong support. If you're so damn eager, I'll ask the legal beagles if they'd mind adding your name to the suit."

"Not necessary, sir. I was only asking because me and the rest of the battalion were not in the vehicle when you ran Appleby off the road."

The Adjutant spluttered in his coffee. "Off the road? There was no fucking road! Nobody with an ounce of grey matter would call that fucking shit-stain of a topographical fucking cow-path a road! That drunken son of a bitch planted his fucking tractor right smack in the middle of a gravel trail."

"I believe it was a combine harvester, sir."

"Do I give a fuck, Karlsen? A tractor, a combine harvester; it could have been a fucking Centurion tank for all the difference it would have made to the Colonel's staff car. Why...Why...I..."

"Yes, quite. Point taken, Adjutant." Karlsen spoke quickly.

The Adjutant was about to lose it again. He hadn't been a pretty sight the morning Karlsen had visited the hospital. After receiving a medical once over, the Adjutant had vented his feelings on Karlsen, then on a medical orderly who stopped in to see how he was doing and on farmers the world over.

Karlsen preferred not to experience another of the battalion-famous blowouts the Adjutant favoured the subbies with.

As the Adjutant resumed breathing, a second lieutenant came into the room. "Excuse me, sir, the CO wants to see you right away. The DCO sent me to find you."

Karlsen, not thinking, said, "Thanks, Jerry. I'll be there immediately."

"Not you," said the Adjutant adding, "You idiot!"

Second Lieutenant Watkins threw in his two cents. "I don't call Lieutenants, sir, Donnie, my boy."

He also didn't say to the Adjutant exactly what the DCO had really said, which was, "Mr. Watkins, see if the Adjutant is still in the mess. If he is, tell him to get his fucking face out of the trough and to get his skinny ass over to the CO's office, toot sweet."

While it was perfectly acceptable, though a bit rude for a major to speak thus of a captain, Watkins knew it was not militarily correct for a second lieutenant to address said captain in the same manner, not if the second lieutenant ever wanted to command a platoon or wear the two pips of a full Lieutenant.

The Adjutant, face whiter than a winter camouflage jacket, rose and with an unseeing hand reached for his last sip of coffee. The cup his frozen fingers corralled was not his, so the Adjutant blindly swallowed two soggy cigarette butts, an equally soggy, but more appetizing crust of toast. He spat these remnants of the morning feast across the room where the piece of toast came to rest on the picture of Lady Matilda de Brisbane, the Honorary Colonel of their Allied regiment.

Karlsen, ever mindful on the Adjutant's bad temper remarked in an approving tone, "Nice shot, sir. And I even think that moustache you added gives Lady Matilda a more feminine look."

Choking up coffee, butts, and oaths, the Adjutant departed, pausing only to grab a full silver creamer from the serving tray. As he crossed the road to battalion headquarters, he swilled some cream into his mouth to dispel the ugly taste, gargled, spat, and then flung the creamer into a nearby bush.

At the CO's door, he was met by the DCO who took one look at him and said, "Get your arse in here and wipe that cream off your face. You look like Al Jolson with heartburn."

The Adjutant wiped his face on his arm and presented himself in front of Colonel Schultzberger's desk. Jackrabbit looked up from the pile of papers and said, "Good morning, Adjutant, have you ever studied for the bar?"

"No, sir."

"Too bad, because it looks like we're gonna need some legal advice. You are aware, of course, that we are being sued?"

The Adjutant's face actually brightened. "We, sir? You mean not just me, but us?"

"Unfortunately, yes, it is us. You were on duty, as was Jenkins. As for Bowles, God only knows what he was on. But, yes, it's us...Besides, you should be aware that an officer looks after his men—in this case, that includes you."

The DCO coughed. Jackrabbit looked up at him and remembered the Adjutant's arrival in the battalion. Wavell hadn't always been the Adjutant; years ago he had arrived in the battalion as a platoon commander.

Captain Jack Wavell, Adjutant of The First Battalion of The Caledonia and Musquodoboit Scottish Regiment was not the most well-liked officer in the Unit. Aside from being a snob and a bully, he was generally regarded as a troublemaking fool. Which in some ways was the reason for the battalion placing him in the position of Adjutant. The job was important, quite important, but Colonel Schultzberger knew that Wavell's influence on people could be kept to a minimum if his main point of contact was the DCO.

From day one, he had created dissension among his peers and as a lieutenant running a platoon had his platoon sergeant, a reasonable NCO by the name of Dave Horsmann, locked up in jail for being ten minutes late for parade. The Sergeant had been battalion orderly sergeant the night before and at the time of his alleged absence had been giving his after duty report to the QMSI, the Quartermaster Senior Instructor. Leaving the Q's office, he had been quite surprised to find himself being hauled off to jail by two burly regiment policeman. On release from custody, Sergeant Horsmann had immediately tracked Lieutenant Wavell to the platoon office and dragged him over the desk by his lapels.

The Army being what it was, Sergeant Horsmann found himself back in the cell he had so recently vacated. In the end, Horsmann was cross-posted to Mortar platoon and had to serve twenty-one extra duties. Fifteen of his colleagues, who had been victimized by Wavell, offered to do a duty each and so his punishment was significantly reduced.

Lieutenant Wavell's questionable assets of a fanatical devotion to minutiae, his compulsive, by-the-book-mentality, and his utter disdain for the troops did not offer too many places for the CO to hide him. He was shifted to Assistant Adjutant where his skill at mishandling soldiers was not so noticeable, and to be fair, where his dealings with paperwork would be appreciated; by everyone in the battalion but those in headquarters. The then Adjutant, Captain Terry O'Sullivan, hated him, but because Jackrabbit hated paperwork and his DCO loved it, Wavell and the DCO got along like an incendiary grenade in a lint factory. Then the DCO retired, and Captain O'Sullivan accepted a posting to Camp Borden. Major Colin Bradshaw, the incoming DCO hated paperwork and also hated Wavell. On more than one occasion he had begged Jackrabbit to give him a more personable Adjutant.

"Sorry, Colin, you have my deepest sympathy. But look at it this way, in giving the little bastard a place to work, in a job mind you, that in many ways he is more than competent to do, you are taking a bullet for the battalion. Better you than a platoon of Jocks, eh?"

Now, with the Adjutant in front of him and despite the DCO having urged him to cut his losses and toss the Adjutant to the wolves, he asked the DCO to bring them all up to date.

"Roger, sir," said the DCO with a look at Captain Wavell. "Pay attention, Adjutant. You're in deep shit. If it were any deeper, we'd see nothing but your hackle. And, by association, so are we. By we, I mean both the regiment and One Bun."

One Bun had been the soldiers' term for the first battalion. Two bun was, of course, the second battalion. The third battalion was known as 'The Third', because everyone knew you only had two buns. Once the term 'bun' had been adopted by the officers, the men dropped it like a bad habit.

The DCO, Major Colin Bradshaw, was a soldier's soldier who looked like the offspring of a mismatched meeting between a low-rent prize fighter and a prize hog. And you could pick either to be the father. Tougher than three sergeants, he was more loyal to the regiment and to Jackrabbit than bark is to a tree. Jackrabbit had saved Bradshaw's life in Korea. As the DCO he was responsible for the battalion's funds, and you could get money out of Ebenezer Scrooge easier than you could gather shekels from Bradshaw. On top of that, he was smarter than all the brass on the Regimental Executive put together.

On more than one occasion it was Bradshaw who was responsible for keeping Jackrabbit on the visitor's side of a cell door, especially in the areas of fiscal accountability.

The DCO went on. "Yes. Judge Advocate's office informed. Rocket came down yesterday." He looked at the Adjutant. "Aimed at the Colonel."

Jackrabbit shrugged it off as if rockets and other missiles were daily occurrences. He took over from the Deputy Commanding Officer. "As you know, Major Bradshaw took a statement from you and the RSM took one from Jenkins. Since the stories didn't match, the DCO immediately dispatched Jenkins to the Third Battalion in Germany. He had done nothing wrong, and his statement seemed to be the most comprehensive and logical. He gets a three year posting to Germany."

As if performing a duet, the DCO stepped back in. "Jenkins' statement was then massaged to exclude any mention of Bowles appearance, flatulence, and your murderous assault."

"Assault?"

"Leave it be, Adjutant. It's as apt a term as any other," said Jackrabbit.

Major Bradshaw took his turn. "That Farmer, Appleby. Son-in-law's a lawyer who has an uncle in Ottawa, a Vice Air Marshall or some damn thing. The Minister of National Defence has put his Chief of Staff on this one. Colonel St. Claire wants answers. We want answers. Appleby wants money. Roger, so far, Adj?"

"Yes, sir."

"We don't have money. We do have Bowles. We had Jenkins. And… We have you. Jenkins has given his statement. So has Bowles."

Jackrabbit jumped in. "Bowles' statement is barely good enough as raw material for Appleby's pig sty. Nothing in it for either the defence or the prosecution; which is in itself a change for the better in regard to Bowles. And a relief."

"Quite," said the DCO. "And we still have you. Accepting Jenkins' statement at face value…"

Again Jackrabbit butted in. "I've known Jenkins for fifteen years, so that's a given."

The Adjutant's head swivelled back to face the DCO, who went on, "Roger that, sir. Understood. So we toss you, Captain Wavell, to the wolves."

"They're lawyers, Colin, more like sharks."

"Yes, sir," said Bradshaw as he waved a hand in Jackrabbit's direction. "But, luckily for you the CO won't consider that an option."

"Damn right, DCO, look after the troops!"

"Yes, sir. And, from that point of view, right and proper. Comments from you, Adjutant?"

The Adjutant took in a bushel of air. "Well, sir, I'd like to think that all I did was insist that Jenkins do his job."

"While preventing Bowles from doing a non-specified job or two of his own," cut in Jackrabbit.

"Those jobs, according to Jenkins, he did in a ditch beside the road," said the DCO.

"But, sir," said the Adjutant. "In a court of law surely that drunken oaf would be found to be in the wrong. I believe that the tractor's license had expired..."

"Combine harvester," said the DCO. The Adjutant didn't use the same words he had used on Karlsen when he had corrected his use of the word 'tractor' but instead continued as if no interruption had occurred. "If we fight this in court, we're sure to win."

"You're probably right, Adjutant and in most cases, I'd agree. We should tell Appleby to go to the devil. But word has come down from the top. There is to be no display of the Big, Bad, Army ganging up on a poor helpless farmer."

"So we pay?" said the DCO, who had a vision of battalion funds disappearing just to save Wavell's worthless hide. In his mind, the best route was to convene a court martial for the Adjutant, fight Appleby until he was broke, charge Jenkins with negligence and finalize it all by charging Bowles with leaving the scene of an accident, being drunk and disorderly, and refusing to fight. He would do his part to achieve all this, but if he failed, then he would follow faithfully down whatever road Jackrabbit led them.

"So we pay, Colin."

"But, if there's enough pressure put on Colonel St. Claire by the regiment couldn't we get the Director of Infantry to foot the bill. Especially if we..."

"If what, sir?"

"If we produce a scapegoat."

The Adjutant's knees gave out, and he nearly fell. He was the only goat worthy of scaping. Jenkins was not even in the running. Bowles was not of sufficient stature to carry the can. It was him. The CO had been playing with him. He was for the high jump.

"Court martial me, sir?" he squeaked.

"Yes," said the DCO.

"No," said the CO. "And, I'm doubtful that Director Infantry will cough up a bean." He looked at his DCO, shrugged. "Sorry, Colin, all costs will come from us. But, I also know you'll come up with a plan to recoup them down the road." Colin sighed but said nothing. Silent loyalty was the only way to support his boss.

"Oh, God," said the Adjutant, but to which answer, only God knew.

As luck would have it, with Appleby's oldest daughter married to the son of a political heavyweight and the CO not wanting the publicity, the matter was settled out of court. No publicity, a fifty thousand dollar new combine, damages of a quarter of a million dollars and a public apology. A demand for heads to roll was also part of the deal. But it was to exclude Bowles. With Jenkins long gone, there was only one person left, Captain Wavell. The Adjutant was given a 'severe reprimand', as a notation on his personnel file. This effectively ensured he would not be promoted for five years, if ever.

The Brigadier didn't agree with Bowles escaping and over Jackrabbit's objections reduced Bowles to the rank of Second Lieutenant, fined him and placed him on duty officer for life or longer. Josiah Appleby got wind of this plan to punish his knight in shining armour and pretending ignorance asked that the public apology be done in the officers' mess.

Jackrabbit reluctantly assented. Three days after Appleby's plaster casts were removed he arrived at the mess. After the apology, in an attempt to smooth everything over, the DCO offered Appleby an associate membership in the mess. He accepted and then made a speech praising Bowles for his life-saving gesture. Laying a thousand dollars on the bar, Appleby bought a few rounds, then asked for Bowles. After some difficulty, since he was the duty officer at The Depot, Bowles was produced. Appleby's threat to go public ended when the Colonel reinstated Bowles to Lieutenant.

One reason Colonel Schultzberger hadn't fought Appleby's demand, was that as a second lieutenant, Bowles wouldn't be permitted to remain in The Depot. The only place for him would be back in his battalion. Accordingly, he handled the re-promotion ceremony himself and then the party began.

But not for the Adjutant. He attended Happy Hour only because of a direct order from Colonel Schultzberger. He sat gloomily in a corner while he drank up Appleby's largesse. He put away as much scotch as he could guzzle and thought that if Bowles had landed a few inches lower on Appleby, he would have castrated him. He swallowed the last of his whiskey and as he headed to his room, sighed softly. "Life is a game of inches."

CHAPTER 15

BOWLES MEETS THE DEATH SLIDE

But enough about Captain Wavell. As interesting a person as he is, he cannot displace Lieutenant Bowles for feats of derring-do. In The Depot the following Monday, Bowles took his squad to the obstacle course, which included the death slide. Bowles couldn't wait to demonstrate this. "Out of the way, Sergeant, I'll show the lads this one."

"But, sir, this is dangerous," said Sergeant Clyde. "Besides, I've got Lance Corporal Anderson doing a demonstration."

Bowles shook his head. "No, Sergeant. This type of training can be extremely time consuming. We need to get started on it right away. The lance corporals could be gone for hours."

"That's true, but, it's still dangerous."

"Nonsense, You give it the once over while I explain it to the troops. I've done this thing in officer training."

"Well, okay, sir. Give the boys a demo," Clyde shrugged. It was no skin off his nose, he thought. Besides, it would be a novelty to finally see Bowles do something right.

But, once again, Clyde was doomed to disappointment. Any novelty that caught Bowles doing something right would have to occur on another day, perhaps in another dimension.

The death slide was a long stretch of cable strung from the top of a large hill down to the bottom and tied off between two large pine trees. It was like a giant clothesline, except that the clothing was a soldier who dangled from a pulley as he traversed downward at a dizzy speed to the bottom. Those that fell off hopefully landed in the deep pond, strategically placed below to prevent fatal injuries.

At the top was a sturdy, wooden platform, fifteen feet square. Open at both ends, it had wooden railings on either side. The end facing the gravel parking lot was the entrance. The end that led to the wide open spaces was the exit. It was here that the troops were launched down the slide. To accommodate this operation, at the opening hung a pulley system with well-worn, sweat stained handles on either side of it. Grabbing the handles, the unfortunate victim would walk to the edge of the platform and kick off, hoping that he would have the strength to hold on until he crashed into the pile of loose, soft, sand seventy-five lower down and five hundred feet away.

Sergeant Clyde couldn't refrain from one last word of advice. "Make sure that you let go immediately that your feet hit the sand pile, sir, or you'll smack into the tree."

"Yes, yes, don't be a mother hen, Sergeant Clyde. Go give that thing a once over. I'll give the lads a bit of a quick overview."

Overview? Yeah, you go over, and we get the view, thought Clyde as he checked out the pulleys and placed them neatly where Bowles could reach them.

Bowles stood in front of the three ranks of nervous boys. "Now then, the best thing to do if you're the slightest bit nervous, I've always found, is to take a run at the pulley, grab it with both hands and before you realize what's going on, you're halfway down. Then you just hang around and enjoy the view as you sail through the air."

With that, Bowles waved the three ranks of recruits apart so that he was standing about ten yards from the platform, with the squad of recruits forming a gauntlet he was to run through.

"All right, here I go."

Bowles broke into a jog that rapidly expanded into a gallop. Five yards from the hanging pulley, Bowles gave a yell that sounded like the beginning of 'Geronimo'. His cry shifted quickly into a yelp of "Gerroonneeee—oh, oh, ohhhhh…." as he realized that his yell had startled his Sergeant. Moving too fast to stop, Bowles gave a tremendous forward dive, arms outstretched to grasp the life-saving pulley handles.

But, they had magically disappeared. Sergeant Clyde, in carefully following Bowles' orders to give it the once over, had his back to the platoon and had been busy checking the cable and pulley. Bowles' sudden bellow caused Clyde to lose his balance. In desperation, as he plunged over the edge of the platform, Clyde somehow managed to find one of the pulley handles. Fingers locked onto it. Unbalanced, the pulley swung him out over the edge and back to the other side in a half moon swing. This put him in an excellent position, high above the ravine, to watch his squad commander fly past in what he described later in the sergeants' mess as a suicide plunge.

With the pulley handles drawn off to one side by his attempt at saving himself, Sergeant Clyde quite selfishly, although unknowingly, denied the use of them to his platoon Commander at a critical moment.

All the recruits saw was Sergeant Clyde hanging by one arm out in mid-air as their illustrious Commander dove head first off the platform, shrieking in dismay as he realized that the pulley was no longer available to him.

The yells got quieter the further Bowles fell, and when they finally stopped, the recruits hauled Sergeant Clyde back to safety and then they all peeked over the edge.

Clyde yelled down, "Are you okay, sir?"

A tiny voice came back up, "Yes, no problem, I'm doing fine."

And then Sergeant Clyde turned to the men and looking at Toby and Offside said, "Go get that sonofabitch...I mean, go and get your squad commander and make sure he's not dead."

"Right, Sarge," said Toby.

"And don't call me Sarge."

Ten minutes later Toby and Offside hauled a bedraggled Bowles to the platform where a number of helping hands hauled him aboard. His uniform was torn, he had numerous cuts and bruises on his face, and one leg of his bush trousers was ripped from the knee to the boot. One puttee had draped itself around a tenacious, small, branch that had been dragged up with him.

After a few minutes of rest, the platoon was formed up again in three ranks, and Bowles once again stood in front of them.

"Okay, chaps, that's the one way I do not, repeat: do not, want you to do it. It's been my experience that when you've seen it done the wrong way, you never forget that lesson. And you make sure that you never ever do it that way yourselves. I hope you've learned something here today."

"I have," said Offside.

"What's that, McGuffin?" said Clyde.

"To make sure I never get near that fucking death slide as long as I live."

"Well, we'll see. You can go last if you like," replied Bowles, turning to Toby. "And did you have something to say?"

"Yes, sir. I was wondering if you were now going to show us the correct way to go down the death slide?"

"No, he's not," snarled Clyde. "And don't you go stirring it up, Squire."

"Okay, Sarge, just thought Lieutenant Bowles wouldn't want to leave his troops hanging, so to speak, as you just were."

Bowles interrupted what looked like Sergeant Clyde making for Toby's throat. "That's enough, Sergeant. In this instance, I believe the soldier is correct. I've recovered from the trip up the hill and will now give it another shot."

"But, sir..."

"No buts, Sergeant. Get the lads into a good position, and I'll make sure the pulley is properly placed."

Clyde shook his head but moved the boys to a place where they could all see the platform, the slide and the landing zone which was looking like it was miles down the ravine.

This time, Bowles grabbed tightly onto both handles. He then turned and walked back from the edge to as far as they would travel.

From his vantage point, Clyde said, "Squire, you've done it now. He's going to try the Flying Leap."

"What's that, Sarge?" asked McGuffin.

"Don't call me Sarge. It's something only a rappel master would attempt. You go back as far from the ledge as you can and then charge, just before you get there you fling yourself up into the air and then...All being well, we see you down at the bottom of the slide. It can be spectacular when done correctly."

Which is not what we are about to witness here, Clyde thought.

With a yowl that scared himself, Bowles took off at full speed toward the precipice.

"What happens if it's not done properly, Sarge?" asked Toby.

"Because you provoked him," said Clyde glaring at Toby. "You and the rest of us are about to see a perfect example of it not being done properly. And don't call me Sarge."

Bowles catapulted himself into the wild blue and Clyde almost closed his eyes. He kept them open, not because he thought there was a ghost of a chance that Bowles could pull it off, but rather, to be able to relate the disaster accurately that evening in the sergeants' mess.

The impetus of Bowles' fling put him way out in front of the handles and the pulley apparatus. He was off and flying. The pulley, not used to traveling second on this downward swing, was caught napping. It jumped and bounced along the main cable, setting up an oscillation that made it leap up and down like a hooked marlin. This up and down motion caused the pulley to lock in place, jump forward, lock again, and surge up again. Caught on one of these upswings, Bowles' forward motion suddenly metamorphosed into the round the world yo-yo trick with him as the yo-yo. Aside from the twanging noise from the vibrating main cable all was silent but for the howling emanating from the centre of a gift-wrapped Bowles tied in by the pulley ropes which were strung tight around the main cable.

From their lookout, the boys stared. Clyde said in awe, "I was fucking wrong! Bowles made it spectacular, bloody spectacular."

Moving the squad back up to the launch area, Sergeant Clyde wondered what to do next when Toby said, "I can get him down, Sarge."

"Yeah, so can I, just hacksaw the main cable."

"Nothing so drastic. I can go up there and untangle him."

Looking at Toby as if he had supped from the same cup of insanity as Bowles, Clyde shook his head. "No chance, Son, not a chance." He smiled and added, "Nope, we'll just have to cut our losses, so to speak."

Toby gazed intently at his squad sergeant. "Come on, Sarge, I've been climbing and rappelling all over the Alps. At the age of eight, I was climbing the lower face of Mount Eiger." Which was only a little lie. He was in the Alps, but the lower face he was climbing was a replica that a hotel owner had erected to look after the babysitting needs of his wealthy guests who were off busily breaking their necks on the real thing.

Sergeant Clyde thought it over and then said, "Okay, c'mon over here." He raised his voice, "The rest of you relax and behave. Davis, every few minutes, yell out to Lieutenant Bowles that we're getting a rescue party ready. Keep him calm, if possible. Lomax, trot off to the vehicle park and keep anyone from coming up here unless it's one of our lance corporals."

He led Toby out of hearing distance which. "Look, Squire, he got himself up there. And if it was anyone else, I'd say it was his job to get himself down. But, this will reflect badly on me. I should have never let him do it. And, fuck me gently with a wire brush, I should never have let him do it a second time."

"Well, I did egg him on to that second attempt, Sarge, so I am partly responsible."

"No, no, you're a recruit. Recruits are supposed to cause trouble. You were just doing your job."

"I can get him down, though."

"Without killing yourself?"

"Definitely. Worst case scenario, he falls into the lake."

"Squire, you untangle him, get yourself down safe. He falls into the lake…" Clyde paused and then looked at Toby. "Then you're talking best case scenario."

And so it began. First, Toby took out his army pocketknife, opened the blade and by means of some string from McGuffin's pack, tied the knife to a belt loop on his combat pants. Next, he took a six foot length of rope and wrapped himself into it using a technique called a 'Swiss seat'. He attached that to another length of rope by means of a carabineer and hooked himself to the main cable. Then he swung himself up onto the cable and went hand over hand out to where Bowles was bundled. Once there, he reassured his whimpering squad commander that all would soon be well.

Swinging up so that he was balanced on the cable, Toby cut what he could find of the pulley assembly. He then shifted around, manoeuvred himself into a new position by means of draping his legs over the cable and with one hand pulled himself up and across Bowles' trussed carcass. This put him on the downward side of Lieutenant Bowles. Toby was now first in line for the decent. Using the knife, he sawed Bowles into freedom. Reminding himself that Sergeant Clyde's best case scenario was Bowles tumbling into the drink, he said, "Sir, I can only cut you loose. Once you get a hand free, you need to reach up and grab onto the cable. Then get the other hand loose and grab with it. Once you are free, you will have to go hand over hand to the bottom."

"Yes, fine, yes, I think that will be acceptable under these conditions."

Toby had a moment of guilt thinking that Bowles could have hitched a ride with him down the rest of the way, then shrugged that off. After all that his squad sergeant had gone through with his incompetent superior, Toby thought that Clyde deserved a bit of revenge.

Bowles got a hand free, then another. The rope remains of the pulley fell away. Toby attached the pulley to his Swiss seat. Carefully taking up the strain, he let himself hang, gave a pull on the cable that started the pulley down on its journey, although with a different passenger, and enjoyed the ride down.

Toby hit the sandy landing area, got himself turned around just in time to watch a screaming Bowles plummet into the lake. And let me tell you, that's just the start of Bowles shenanigans.

CHAPTER 16

BOWLES MEETS A ROCKET LAUNCHER

After Bowles' death slide demonstration, he kept a low profile and the squad trained for two weeks without seeing him. Sergeant Clyde and the lance corporals, once over their initial surprise, arrived at The Depot every morning with fingers crossed. But Clyde was convinced they hadn't seen the last of their squad commander. "He's still in The Depot. He can spring out on us at any time."

No one in The Depot knew how he spent his time, but the best guess came from Lance Corporal Duguay. "I'll bet the sunnavabitch is sitting in his room, getting shitfaced."

"Good. And if necessary, I'm prepared to keep him there by supplying him with a case of whisky," said Lance Corporal Steele.

"No, Jason, a good idea, but we're gonna have to have him with us for the range work," said Clyde. "All rifle and small arms live fire ranges had to have an RSO, a Range Safety officer."

"You're shittin' us, Sarge," said Lance Corporal Peter Caruthers. "Can't you do it?"

Clyde shook his head. "In theory, yes, I'm qualified. But The Depot wants its Lieutenants to train as RSOs. The Commandant insists we train our squad commander while training our recruits."

Bowles got through the first few rifle practices and the lance corporals and the recruits breathed easier; so far, no casualties. Clyde was hoping for their luck to continue when the squad went out to the Rocket Launcher Range. He should have known better.

Bowles said, "I'd better do a demo on these babies." He looked around. "Right, Sergeant Clyde, you'll be my number two."

"Sir, I have Lance Corporal Anderson and Lance Corporal Steele ready to do a dry run and then a demonstration using live rounds."

"Oh, pooh, Sergeant Clyde. No need of a dry run. Waste of time. What's to run? You pick it up." As he said that, Bowles picked up the rocket launcher and turned it on end, then peered down the hollow tube. "Anyone home?" he boomed through the tube, then looked around to see if everyone got the joke.

The 3.5 rocket launcher had been used in WW11 and in Korea, where it was not that effective against North Korean tanks. It was still in use in the Canadian Army when Toby showed up. It was often called a "bazooka" after the funny instrument that a musician made for television. Optimally fired from the kneeling position, it could be fired from the standing, prone, or sitting positions. It was called a crew served weapon because it was handled by two men, a loader and a firer.

Bowles carried on his babbling as he picked up the rocket launcher held it out and down range and peered into the back end. His hollow, echo-chambered voice reverberated across the range, "You get the number two to pop a rocket in, check that the safety is off, line up an enemy tank, and Kablooey!"

"Now, sir, we have a proper training routine here," said Sergeant Clyde. "The depot has a range procedure that we must follow."

"Nonsense, Sergeant Clyde. The depot is flexible. Remember the Principles of War, Sergeant. One of them is flexibility and flexibility means be prepared to alter plans, have agility of mind, and rapid decision-making. That's officer-speak, but it means initiative, rapid-thinking, and originality. And even if it is officer-speak, we can still teach it to the troops through example. Flexibility – that's what's needed, not some two hundred year old method of training soldiers. After all, we're not still climbing the heights to the Plains of Abraham, eh?"

And those highlanders who did never had to lug rocket launchers up those heights. And they didn't bloody well have Bowles leading them, thought Clyde, but said, "Yes, sir."

"Remember that, Sergeant Clyde." Bowles was so impressed with his words that he repeated them, "Flexibility, initiative, rapid-thinking, and originality. And, after all, I am the Range Safety Officer. Correct?"

"Correct, sir, you are the RSO. And as RSO, you need to be ensuring all is safe on the range. We cannot afford your expertise and authority to be wasted in acting as a part of a demonstration team." Clyde gave himself a mental pat on the back as he finally figured out how to deal with Bowles.

"Oh… Yes, of course. Please carry on as you had planned, then, Sergeant Clyde."

Clyde gathered the squad around Lance Corporal Anderson, who held a rocket launcher on his shoulder and Lance Corporal Steele who stood on Anderson's right side. At his feet was a dummy rocket. With a nod in their direction, Clyde gave a fire order and the lance corporals went through the drill. Once the practical demo was completed, Lance Corporal Caruthers yelled for the squad to come over to him. He was standing behind a four foot table that had on it a number of plastic models of armoured fighting vehicles. He picked up a model of a Russian T-55 tank, and said, "This is a Russian T-55 tank." He used an unsharpened pencil and pointed it at the centre of the tank and at the tracks. "You want to hit a T-55 on its tracks. It's too well armoured for you to do much else. So stand in there, and let it turn to give you a clear shot."

Toby nudged Offside. "If something like that appears on my horizon, I'm not waiting for a clear shot. I'm clearing off."

"Quiet," came an order from behind the lads.

"Any questions?" said Caruthers.

"It's kind of small," said Morgan.

One of the unkinder comments from a lance corporal about Morgan was that he could have passed in a dim light for Bowles' little brother.

"Wouldn't need to be a dim light," said Toby to Offside. "Morgan'd be just as thick as Bowles at high noon."

"Well done, Morgan," said Bowles. "He's right, Sergeant Clyde. And the range these lads will be firing the bazookas?"

"Rocket launchers, sir. And the range will be between 75 and 100 yards."

"Yes. Of course! And you expect him to hit that little tank in its tracks from over 100 yards away? Impossible" he gave his donkey bray and carried on. "Morgan's got you there, Sergeant Clyde."

Clyde sighed, shrugged his shoulders. "Morgan, these are plastic models. The real thing is as big as a bus, weighs around forty tons. But this is just an example of where to aim at the targets we have out on the range."

"Oh, thank you, Sergeant," said Morgan.

Clyde and the three lance corporals got through the demonstration without further mishap, and then the squad started to settle into the routine. Broken into four-man relays, soon there were four recruits firing, four loading, four unpacking ammo, four doing dry training and the rest reviewing marksmanship techniques. According to that plan, after the four firers had finished, they would be sent off to smoke and joke near the coffee table area and the rest of the four man groups would all move up to the next job in the line. But today the squad had missed lunch due to Lieutenant Bowles losing his copy of Range Safety Orders. The squad had to wait until a new copy was brought back from the Range Control Office. Today they ate in shifts, down in a gully out of sight of the range.

Sergeant Clyde took over from Bowles as the RSO while Bowles went off to eat. A few relays later, there was a misfire. The unfortunate firer was one of Toby's roommates, Stuffy Stouffer. He correctly carried out misfire drills and kept the rocket launcher pointed down range while he maintained a proper fire position. The entire squad waited the required five minutes, then Stuffy re-cocked the weapon and took up another sight picture. On command from Clyde, Stuffy's number two, Butch Vincent, looked to the rear to see that no one had wandered into the backblast area, slapped Stuffy on the shoulder, yelled "Backblast area clear!" then snuggled in close to Stuffy to avoid the concussion that would spread out from the weapon's rear end as the rocket launched. Stuffy squeezed the trigger. Once again the rocket failed to launch.

Stuffy carefully walked down to the far end of the firing point, all the time ensuring that he kept the launcher pointed down range because the rocket could suddenly flash to life and head off toward whatever it was aimed at. Stuffy laid the launcher gently down. It was theoretically possible that once left to its own devices, a slow-burning fuse would need but a sharp bang to remind it that it had a job to do. Once the fuse got back to work, it would ignite the main charge and off the rocket would go. For the moment, this rocket launcher and it's comatose rocket lay quiet. If it did ignite without human assistance, there was no chance of injury or damage. That was the game plan according to the safety manual, 'Explosives, Ordnance, Mark II, Safe Destruction Of'.

With the excitement over, Clyde was taking a break and waiting for a new relay when he noticed Bowles wandering around over in the latrine area. He realized that Bowles had not been in sight when the misfire had occurred. Lance Corporal Anderson wandered over to chat with Clyde, and for the time being, Bowles had no adult-eyes on him.

Bowles had not been present when the safety manual had been written, nor had he been available to participate in the Range Safety Officer's orientation programme held during his Basic Officer's Training Course. He had been lost with his instructor and four other candidates on a map and compass exercise he had been leading. Now Sergeant Clyde was not a genius, but he was a fast learner. These last few weeks with Bowles had made Clyde realize that Bowles was living proof of Murphy's law, and it was only a matter of hours before

Clyde had paraphrased it to be "If there's more than one possible outcome of a job or task, and one of those outcomes will result in disaster or an undesirable consequence, then Bowles will do it that way."

In order to keep the squad and the range from going up in smoke, Clyde had tried to circumvent Murphy and Bowles by posting a sentry in the ammunition area, one more on the road down to the range and then posted another sentry a few yards off to a flank of the dud rocket launcher. All in all, you could say he had taken reasonable precautions to protect his squad and himself from their squad commander. But Clyde was unaware of the propensity for a Bowles to mix it up with Fate. The sentry on the dud, our hero, Toby Trelauney-Fitzgibboncrest, had been instructed to keep everyone away from the rocket launcher as it lay in its dormant state. Everyone to him included his squad commander, Lieutenant Bowles.

Bowles, seeing this one soldier off to the flank, immediately identified him as a malingerer who had dodged Sergeant Clyde's eye.

"Lad, you! You there! Why are you way over here?"

"I'm standing guard on this rocket launcher, sir."

"Ha, ha, yes, very good, Trelauney-Fitzgibboncrest, isn't it? Yes indeed, Trelauney-Fitzgibboncrest, a very good wheeze. Now hop along and rejoin the squad. Anyone can see that there's no one around here who's going to steal it. There's no one here but us."

"I can't, sir. I have to guard this dud rocket launcher, sir. I'm to keep everyone away."

"Nonsense, waste of good manpower. You sitting out here when you could be doing something useful. A good soldier never misses an opportunity to hone his fighting skills, lad. Off you go and tear into that training."

"But, sir…"

"No buts, lad. Off you go. I'll be here, and I'll make sure no one sneaks up to steal the rocket launcher."

"Yes, sir. But it's a dud."

"Carry on, I won't tell you again."

"Yes, sir," said Toby and off he went. But he didn't go far.

Bowles, feeling very pleased with himself began humming a bagpipe tune and walking around enjoying his sense of command and his overwhelming mastery of Toby. His tour of that piece of ground brought him to the rocket launcher.

"Well," he said out loud. "A dud, eh?" Going over closer he picked it up. To one of Bowles' rather loose mindset, a dud was something that was not working. "So this is a dud, eh? It certainly looks fine to me."

Bowles was on top of the world because he had jacked up Toby and sent him back into play. The rest of the world was about to be less pleased. For Bowles down range only existed as an abstraction. For everyone else, down range is not an essential direction when one is toying with devices capable of taking lives, destroying tanks and building, it is the only direction.

Holding the rocket launcher in both hands, he gave it an exploratory shake. "Maybe there is something wrong with it. Seems heavier than the one I used earlier. Wonder what's stuck in it?" he turned it tail to the earth and gave it a sharp bang on the ground. Lifting it up a few inches clear of the ground, he peered into the muzzle end of the tube. He shook his head and laughed in an all-knowing manner. "Of course it isn't working. Those silly enlisted men have stuck something in it. Good thing I'm here." And with that pronouncement, Bowles lifted it up a couple of feet and slammed it back down.

Meanwhile, Toby, who had only drifted off toward the rest of the squad, stepped a bit further away from Bowles. The rocket had never been designed to emerge from the tube the way it went in. As far as rockets go, they only want to come out the other end. Bowles, standing silently with the rocket launcher in his hands came to a similar conclusion. Reversing the tube he then slammed the muzzle onto the hard packed soil.

"A good, solid jolt will get that thing moving."

The rocket, after all previous attempts to resuscitate it, sent a message to its fuse that Bowles' revivifying actions had done the job. Burning a bit slower the so-called dud did indeed get moving.

All Bowles heard was a faint hissing noise coming from the sporadically sparking fuse. Realizing that something was up and that it was unlikely to be pleasant, Bowles looked around for anybody. As he turned this way and that, the rocket launcher swung toward from Toby's direction around and toward the ammo dump. It then shifted to the recruits all smoking and joking in a group safely out of harm's way. Spotting the wayward Toby, Bowles yelled, "Soldier, get over here and take this thing from me."

Toby gave a rearward glance toward the squad and decided that closer to the muzzle might be safer than trying to outrun a rocket. He charged at Bowles, hoping to get the rocket launcher pointed down range before it had a chance to fulfil its destiny. But today, Destiny was in a playful mood. Toby grabbed Bowles and tried to swing him around so that the muzzle was pointed down range. As they banged together, the fuse ignited the main charge, and the rocket exploded out of the tube. It headed off, not down range which would have been too serendipitous, and thankfully not off to Bowles' right where Sergeant Clyde and the boys where unconcernedly going about their business of destroying tanks. Nope, the rocket launcher's muzzle, nudged sufficiently by Toby's diving lunge at Bowles, shifted its point of aim off to the left a bit towards the most densely populated section of Camp Gagetown.

Fortunately, the squad's three-quarter ton truck prevented the rocket launcher from getting a clear shot at camp headquarters, the officers' messes, and the Hospital.

Just as Bowles and Toby collided, the launcher ended up between them, muzzle pointing at the prescribed angle to take out a Russian T-55. At that instant, Sergeant Clyde and Anderson were still awaiting the next relay. Clyde had removed his ear plugs a few seconds too soon. But the break in training presented him with the opportunity to watch his truck disappear in a flash of light, a whoosh of smoke and a hearty hail of shrapnel. Minutes before he had congratulated himself and Lance Corporal Anderson on their placement of sentries all round. The truck, now a ball of fire, burned fiercely for a bit and then as Clyde's retinas resumed communications with his brain, his ears had partially regained their ability to recognize auditory signals he was able to observe and register the scene of his squad commander and his sentry engaged in a weird kind of polka with a rocket launcher between them.

Clyde reached the dancing pair. "I suggest you release the Lieutenant, Squire, and you, Mr. Bowles, put down the rocket launcher."

Toby let go his squad commander and stepped back. Bowles let the now empty rocket launcher drop as he too took a step away from Toby. He said, "I'm glad you're here, Sergeant Clyde."

Yeah, me too, thought Clyde. As if I would be allowed to be any-bloody-where else. Outwardly he showed the stuff sergeants are made of. "Why would that be, sir? All it means is that I'll be the star witness at your court martial."

Bowles took another step backwards and tripped over a range stake. From the ground, he said, "My court martial? For what? Didn't you see this rabid dog of a recruit attack me?"

Toby, not caring to be described as a rabid dog said, "Pardon me, sir. All I did was attempt to get the rocket launcher pointed down range. I wasn't the one who banged it on the ground and set off the fuse. I was the one who warned you it was a dud."

Bowles scrambled to his feet, face red, and pointed a fat finger at Toby. "Dud? You call that thing a dud? It was live, you idiot boy. Look!" He shifted his finger over toward the still burning truck, where a number of recruits under Lance Corporal Anderson's command were shovelling sand and dirt onto it. "You call what I did to the Sergeant's truck a dud?"

"I suggest, sir," said Clyde. "That you stop this discussion right now, sir. We'll all take a breather and settle ourselves down."

He turned, looked over the crowd until he spotted Lance Corporal Duguay. "Rene, go to the range phone up the road and called Range control. I know, we've got a radio, but I don't want this thing plastered all over the airwaves. Tell them to send out a recovery vehicle from the maintenance shop. Although, there's not a fuck of a lot to recover. Then have the operator call the military police."

"MPs? Good show, Sergeant," said Bowles. "We'll slap this mutinous, know-it-all Lord in irons ASAP. Rapid thinking. I can see where you've taken my little quote to heart. Flexibility, initiative, rapid thinking, originality. F. I. R. O. Good show."

"Easy, Squire," said Clyde as he noticed Toby getting ready to go on the offensive. He turned to Bowles. "No, sir, the MPs are not going to lock anyone up. They are required because we've got a training accident."

"Accident? Accident, my Granny's Fanny, this is the second time he's tried to do me in."

"When was the first time, sir?" asked Lance Corporal Caruthers.

"Why, the death slide, Ninny."

"That's enough, Lieutenant. You need to apologize to Lance Corporal Caruthers," said Clyde, with a bayonet of threat in his tone of voice."

Bowles caught on quickly and apologized. The Sergeant gave the lance corporals their marching orders and soon all that was left of 1313 squad on the rocket launcher range was the smoking remains of Sergeant Clyde's three-quarter ton truck.

As Clyde and Lance Corporal Anderson drove off, Anderson said, "The shit's gonna hit the fan tomorrow."

"No," disagreed Clyde. "The shit'll be flying tonight. My guess is that Bowles, probably me, and the RSM will all be sharing space in the commandant's office before twenty-one hundred hours this evening."

Both were partly right. The shit did hit the fan. They were a bit off on the timings. The Commandant ordered Bowles, Clyde, and Toby to attend a meeting in his office at seventeen thirty hours that day.

CHAPTER 17

TOBY MEETS THE DEPUTY COMMANDANT

I have to admit that I came away from my own first meeting with Major Ascot-Gray quite impressed. As for Toby, however, he might have seen his first meeting with the Major quite differently.

"You the lad from 1313, the Commandant wants to see?" said a voice behind Toby. He turned to see the Deputy Commandant, Major Phil Ascot-Gray standing in the doorway of his office.

"Yes, sir." Toby slammed to attention and saluted.

"Stand at ease, son, and relax. As I understand it, you're here to give us a wee picture of what actually happened out there this afternoon." The Deputy Commandant looked at his watch. "You're a bit early. The meeting is at seventeen thirty. It's only just ten after."

"Yes, sir, I wanted to be on time."

"Good, gives you and me a chance for a chat. Come on in."

Toby sat, told his side of things and was quite astonished to find out that the Deputy Commandant was human. When he finished his tale, the Major grunted then said, "Kill him, eh? Where did that lunatic ever get that idea?"

"On the death slide, sir. We had problems with the Lieutenant."

"Yes. The Adjutant had been told a bit of that. How a recruit rescued the Lieutenant. That was you?"

"Yes, sir."

"And now that's become an attempt on the idiot's life?" he paused. "And you never heard me say that."

"Right, sir."

The Major looked at his watch again and stood up. "Right, let's go see how the next phase of this circus plays out."

As they left his office, a lance corporal appeared, saluted and said, "Sir, the RSM is not available. He left just this evening for a meeting in Camp Borden. He won't be back for a week."

"Very well, thank you, Lance Corporal Dawkins. We'll see if we can get through this without him. Dismissed."

The lance corporal saluted and left. Toby and the Deputy Commandant continued on to the Commandant's office. The Commandant, Bowles, and Sergeant Clyde were already there. The Major knocked on the door frame, saluted, and said, "Here's Recruit Trelauney-Fitzgibboncrest and we missed the RSM. Off on another swan to Borden, sir."

"Fine, we'll make do without him. Take a seat over there, Phil." Dillingham looked at Toby. "You, stand over there. Beside Sergeant Clyde."

Bowles and Clyde were standing along the left wall. Toby said, "Yes, sir," and moved over to stand at ease beside his squad sergeant. The Major settled himself in a Naugahyde chair over on the right and, knowing what he knew of the Bowles business, prepared to enjoy himself.

Dillingham blew out a gust of air, looked around at each face, grimaced as his eyes came to rest on Bowles' empty-plate of a flat-face, and finally said, "Lieutenant Bowles, as I understand it, this... this, unmitigated disaster, it occurred on your watch, correct?"

"Not exactly, sir, I wasn't on watch. I was on lunch."

"On lunch. What the... explain yourself, were you or were you not RSO at the range?"

"Yes, sir, I was. But I had handed the reins to Sergeant Clyde and then went off to have my lunch."

"You cannot be such a shit-headed nincompoop to think you can hand off that responsibility to Sergeant Clyde."

"Why not, sir? He told me he was a small arms instructor at the beginning of our training, and I know that ... that..." Bowles looked around at his squad sergeant and then back to the Commandant. "You mean he lied about being a small arms instructor? Never! Sergeant Clyde would never do such a thing. I don't believe it."

"I don't either. And what's more, I don't believe I'm having this conversation. Are you a complete idiot, Lieutenant Bowles?"

"I don't follow, sir."

Dillingham leaned over his desk toward his squad commander. "You don't follow, eh? Well, let me tell you something. Sergeant Clyde is a fully qualified small arms instructor. Just as you are an out and out fully qualified shit-headed nincompoop. You are listed in Range Standing Orders as the RSO. Unless you drop dead, which might have been a good idea, you are the RSO until the end of the range practice."

The room was silent.

"So, we're clear on that. You were the RSO."

"Yes, sir."

"Fine. Go on."

There was silence. And more silence. After an eon or two, Phil spoke to Bowles, "Lieutenant Bowles, I believe the Commandant wants you to carry on."

"With what, sir? He asked me if I was the RSO and after we got a couple of quibbles sorted out, we reached a conclusion that I was indeed the RSO. I…"

"And you still are!" snarled Dillingham.

"I'm still the RSO? I don't follow, sir."

"I'll spell it out for you, Bowles. You are an R.S.O. – in this instance, it means, Really, Stupid, Officer."

"Oh. I say, sir. A bit harsh, don't you think?"

"Never mind. Tell us what you did after Sergeant Clyde relieved you."

"I had lunch. And then…" Bowles gave out with what he thought was his witty laugh, but which to others came out as a simpleton's simper. "And then," he went on. "I relieved myself."

There was no sound but a muffled cough from the Deputy Commandant. Dillingham shot him a glare. "Major Ascot-Grey, if you find this amusing, I suggest you depart for elsewhere."

"Pardon me, sir," Phil said, still smiling broadly.

"And after relieving yourself, Lieutenant?" said the Commandant.

"I wandered over toward a recruit. That recruit." He leaned out past Clyde's ample tummy and pointed at Toby.

"Why did he attract your interest?"

"He was away over on his own, just standing around. Miles from everyone else. Just standing there. As I watched him, he turned and faced a new direction every few minutes. I thought he was on the lookout for any of our staff coming to jack him up."

"I suppose that it never occurred to you that he had been stationed there as a sentry?"

"No, sir, I thought he was goofing off. I went over to put the fear of God into him."

"And?"

"And he had the gall to tell me I couldn't touch the rocket launcher." Bowles stopped, pointed a finger at his own chest and said, "Imagine him saying that to me. Why, I'm his squad commander, and he's telling me what to do. Can you believe it? A recruit. A foreign-born one at that, telling a Lieutenant what to do. Unbelievable."

"Yes, Lieutenant, unbelievable, but can you imagine what we would all be doing at this very moment if you have done what he had asked?"

This had Bowles baffled. He pondered. Using the world-renowned ponder movement of the finger to the corner of the mouth, he completed the gesture by adding a layer of puzzlement to his face. Finally, he said, "My guess is we'd all be in here staring at each other wondering why you had called this meeting, sir."

"Not quite, Bowles, the right answer I suspect is on the lips of the recruit, even though foreign-born. What would your guess be, Trelauney-Fitzgibboncrest?"

Toby looked around and then said slowly, "I'd say none of us would even be here, sir."

"Yes, exactly. But, we are here, and we need to all stop being here."

"Should we go, then, sir? Are we done here?" asked Bowles.

"No, Lieutenant, not yet, as painful as this meeting is, we still need to get to some level of understanding in regards to the destruction of one three-quarter ton truck, two radios, one first aid kit, one stretcher and a variety of miscellaneous range stores." Dillingham looked over at Clyde. "Did I leave anything out, Sergeant?"

"Yes," interrupted Bowles. "There was one haybox of coffee, a container of sugar, one sleeve of paper cups, and one tray of cookies, sir."

The Commandant lost his power of speech. Phil stepped in for him. "So, a tray of cookies, Mr. Bowles? What kind?"

"Chocolate chip, I believe, sir," said Toby.

"No, you silly assed-recruit, they were peanut butter. I know. I had some for lunch."

"What does it bloody matter what kind of bloody cookies they were?" said Dillingham in a near-scream of frustration.

At his post by the door, Sergeant Clyde muttered, "Fucking cinders now. Who cares what kind of cookies they were?"

"I just wanted to set the young soldier straight, sir," said Bowles.

"Don't bother, he's just winding you up," said Major Ascot-Grey. With an eye in Toby's direction, he then said, "But he stopped doing that as of right now."

"I concur, Major Ascot-Grey. A waste of winding in my opinion. Let's move on."

"Winding me up, sir? I don't follow," he leaned out past Clyde again and said, "I'll have you know that I'm sufficiently wound up, thank you very much, Recruit. And I realize this meeting is important. We are listing everything that was destroyed because you tackled me…"

He stopped, a dim light seemed to glow in his eyes, a Frankenstein monster coming to life, Lieutenant Arthur Bowles giving birth to a thought. "That's right! He assaulted me! That's why we're really here, isn't it, sir?" He looked at the Commandant. "Yes, very wily, sir. All this is a smoke-screen, you're using that little truck fire to get my recruit to confess to the assault on a superior officer. Well done… but I hope I haven't spilled the beans, sir?"

The Commandant had no reply. He looked over at his second-in-command. Phil looked as stunned as his boss. Toby had maintained his power of speech and he used it, "Assaulted you? Confess? I blew up the truck?"

Clyde moved closer to Toby and put a hand on his arm, he whispered, "No. Be calm. He's an idiot." And then louder he said, "Don't say or do anything you might regret or that the Commandant would have to act on."

"Excellent advice, Sergeant," said Phil, who had recovered the use of his tongue.

The Commandant said, "Lieutenant Bowles, I agree with what Sergeant Clyde tried to whisper to Trelauney-Fitzgibboncrest. Any fool, no let me re-phrase that since you are The Depot's own fool…aaaaaarrrgggghhhh"

Phil stepped in. "Lieutenant., this meeting is about trying to sort out your actions and yours alone. From the statement of one of the squad lance corporals, it is quite likely that if Trelauney-Fitzgibboncrest had not tackled you, we might be attending a mass funeral for the majority of your squad. There are no grounds for Recruit Trelauney-Fitzgibboncrest to worry about any disciplinary proceedings at all."

"Correction, Major Ascot-Grey, no disciplinary proceedings against him. He may be involved in Lieutenant Bowles court-martial, though."

"Roger that, sir, I stand corrected."

"My… my… court… court-martial, sir? All I did was…"

"All you did was destroy a truck…" he stopped. "Bah! It's hopeless. We'll be here until the Last Trump… Enough!" the Commandant slammed the desk. "This has gone far enough. Major Ascot-Grey?"

"Yes, sir?"

"You will conduct a summary investigation into what happened. Get a couple of clerks on the financial loss of the truck, radios, first aid kit, stretcher, and…" he stopped to think.

Bowles seeing the hesitation decided to be helpful one last time. "Don't forget the haybox of coffee, a container of sugar, one sleeve of paper cups, and one tray of cookies, sir." and with a glance at Toby added, "Peanut butter…"

"Shut up, Bowles. Sergeant Clyde, get him out of here. Now! Major Ascot-Grey, you know what to do."

***

The outcome of the summary investigation proved to be very disappointing to the Commandant, to Major Ascot-Grey, and even Jackrabbit, or especially Jackrabbit, sitting over in his First Battalion lines.

RSM Dixon came into Jackrabbit's office late one afternoon after the battalion had dismissed for the day. Dixon said, "Heard the latest, sir, on your protégé, Lieutenant Bowles?"

"RSM, we have had a long, sometimes irritating, sometimes enjoyable, always interesting, and until now, a highly satisfactory relationship. But, if you ever refer to that imbecile as my protégé again, I'll personally shoot you with the ball of your own shit."

"Well said, sir, but we both know your marksmanship is not what it was. But, as I expect to backstop you in the battalion for a while longer, I'll desist. Now, the latest?"

"Very well, go on, Mr. Dixon."

"The Depot Commandant had Major Ascot-Grey do a summary investigation that proved conclusively that Lieutenant Bowles was the perpetrator in the incident."

"We knew that going in. But will this get rid of him?" asked Jackrabbit.

"Not according to RSM McKindly. Seems Bowles may have saved his squad from being blown up."

"How on earth? The man had picked up a dud, was banging it around. It came to life and was headed at the troops when that Brit kid intervened."

"Quite, sir. That seems to be what happened."

"Seems, RSM?"

"Yes, sir, Bowles maintained that if the recruit hadn't attacked him, he'd have had the rocket launcher pointed downrange and no harm would have occurred to anyone. Furthermore, if the lieutenant had had the opportunity to finish his act, the truck would not have been destroyed either."

"Bullshit!" said Jackrabbit, sitting upright in his chair. "That is pure, one hundred percent, unfiltered bullshit!"

"Be that as it may, sir, it has introduced enough reasonable doubt that Bowles got off."

"But that truck cost thousands!"

"Yes, sir, but the Brit lad shits money. Because his squad was short one truck, he covered the damages. Out of his own pocket."

"Did he realize that Bowles could have been gone if he had left well enough alone?"

"He didn't until after he paid up, sir. By then Ottawa lost all desire for justice and its attendant publicity."

"Shit!"

"Yes, sir. No argument from me."

"And so he's back in training?"

"Yes, and blaming the recruit for attacking him on the rocket launcher range and on the death slide."

CHAPTER 18

THE OX MEETS THE NEW EARL

As the RSM had said, Toby had bags of money, and buying a new truck for his squad seemed like a good way to spend some of it. He didn't actually go out and buy a truck, he signed the papers to get the old one written off and then the squad was issued a one. Toby's lawyers in London handled the rest. So that was that until the word got out to the squad that if Toby had kept his money in the vault, then their dopey squad commander would have disappeared. He took a lot of ribbing over it, even from Sergeant Clyde.

And then things got back to as near as normal for Squad 1313. As for Toby, slogging it out below decks as it were, the fates were going to be unkind to him yet again; if the affair with the Judge's wife were to be seen as an unkindness. And on that note, Dear Reader, it is time for me to take the podium once again. When we last had met, I was eating lunch with Peter Warren in his office. We were still there, and it was well past five o'clock. We had had a couple of coffee breaks, both of us having double-doubles and taken a couple of bathroom breaks. I was feeling exhausted. Warren was jubilant, and I hoped he was tiring.

"Marv…in, this is gonna be big. I can see my Canadian publisher slavering over this story. It's a winner."

"That may be, Peter, but I think it's time for me to go home for the day."

He nodded, looked at his watch, picked up the phone, dialled and waited with the phone to his ear. "Margo? Peter, sorry to call so late. Are you up for a dinner date with an author?"

I assumed he meant me, but I didn't think I was up for it. He looked over at me, winked and nodded. "Okay, but it's bigger than that." He put the phone in the cradle, gestured toward it. "That was Margo Dundee, our Editor in chief. She's on her way down. Said she couldn't go to dinner with us, got some posh dinner with some other editors."

I was glad to hear it. I didn't mind the idea of coming back tomorrow and taking up where we left off, but my tongue was on its last legs, so to speak. I drained the last of my cold coffee. "Oh."

The door swung open, and her voice leapt into the room. "Before you tell me this is a goldmine, the budget won't stand it."

I think some part of my brain was relieved. I could go home.

"Now, Margo…"

"Sorry Peter," she said without a trace of sorrow in her voice. She came into the room and stopped. We stared at one another.

"Mrs. Crampton?" I said, my legs propelling me and my chair straight back into the wall so rapidly, I think I got whiplash.

The six-foot, six Amazon pointed at me. "I know you."

I nodded. She knew me well.

"Well, who are you?"

"Marvin K Oxnard, ma'am."

"Don't call me ma'am. I had it for twenty years. Call me Margo."

Every ounce of butler valet training stepped up, and I was back in command of myself. Still, it had been a very great shock.

"Very well. Margo. It's nice to see you again."

"No, it's not. You were one of the Ox brothers, weren't you?"

"Correct. I still am, as a matter of fact. I'm the oldest brother."

She gave a quick glance toward Peter. "Marvin and Adam Oxnard. Both pills, I recall."

"We did leave school rather early."

"Left? No." She waved a finger at me. "Expelled. I expelled you both myself."

She advanced further into the room, finger still aimed in my general direction. The former Mrs. Margret Crampton, currently Margo Dundee, dominated the room as she had always done. But her grey curls had been replaced by raven's wing black hair that hung down her head, bangs in front, Cleopatra-style around the rest of her head. Gone too, were her tweeds and brogues.

"You no longer carry a cane," I said.

She shook her head. "No need to. No bothersome children here." She stopped in front of Peter's desk, the aim finger shifted toward him. "Although, it might be a good idea to bring it back just for him."

Peter said, "I'm the best you've got, and you know it."

"Bah. You're the biggest irritant to my well-being and so-called restful retirement."

Mrs. Crampton was now dressed in the finest black silk suit I had ever seen. She definitely had a bespoke tailor from deep in London's tailoring and haberdashery district. I had glimpsed stark, black patent high heels as she had crossed the open space. A ruffled black blouse peeked out at the lapels. Bright red lipstick on lips that I recalled had never used the stuff.

"So, Oxnard." She shifted her eyes back to me. Those eyes that shot steel-tipped glares at any schoolboy who dared step out of line had never changed, unless they'd been sharpened. "What piece of deviltry have you brought us?"

Peter said, "An Earl, Margo, sit and listen to Marvin's story."

I didn't like the sound of that. There was no way I was going to re-tell this thing yet another time. "Peter…"

"It's okay. Margo can listen in from where you ended."

"No, I can't, Peter." She looked at her watch. "I'm already late. Mr. Oxnard, can you tell me, briefly, what the book is about? Give it to me and what we call a pitch."

I nodded. I'd heard the term pitch before, and I had been ready to pitch to Peter, but due to his needing to hear it, my pitch had gone unpitched.

"It's nineteen sixty-four, Canada, mostly Camp Gagetown, where British Earl has been forced to join the army against his will.

"You mean press-ganged?" She interrupted.

"Press-gained by circumstances," I answered.

Margo held up a hand, looked at Peter.

"Take Mr. Oxnard to Barribeault's, give him a feed and get the rest of this story. Report to me tomorrow and if you think it's a go, sign him to a contract right away."

She whirled around, headed for the door. Once she had closed it behind her, Peter's office settled like the aftermath of a cyclone. I sighed and sat back.

Peter said, "A whirlwind, right?"

"Very much so. Even worse now than she was when she was my teacher."

Peter smiled. "Another story there, but save it. We had better do as she says. I get a lot of leeway in how to do my job, but when she gives direct orders, I obey." Tired as I was, I was aware enough to see that going home was out of the question. This could lead to a contract which is what I had been after. Subsequently, I found myself seated at Barribeault's being wined and dined like a celebrity author.

While we ate, Peter had me get back on track with the story.

You may recall that Goody and I had left the club's membership hanging, according to one unnamed member. Toby had been sent off to Toronto and then to the Recruit Depot, and as I've related had been involved in a series of adventures.

Meanwhile, I had been enjoying the sights and wonders of Winnipeg. With only His Lordship to look after and an eye to assisting Her Ladyship, I was given plenty of free time.

Then my world stopped. Granted, my experience was nowhere near as extreme as His Lordship's. Lord Haselbury dropped off the twig on the thirteenth hole of the Glendale Golf and Country Club where he was a visiting member. He had just putted for par and was reaching into the hole when a massive heart attack laid him flat out on his back on the green. I had been caddying for him. While wiping off his putter, prior to shoving it into his golf bag, I was possibly five yards from him when he keeled over. He gave out a huge sigh, pulled his knees up and struggled to speak. "Easy, your Lordship, easy. Help will be here momentarily," I said, not knowing where to go for help, but knowing that even if I did, it was not going to arrive in time. I hadn't fooled him. He gave me a weak grin, then groaned in pain. "Two...th..."

"Your..."

He waved lifted a hand, but it fell. I waited.

"Two things, Marvin..." his eyes closed and I thought I wasn't going to know. Then his eyes opened. "First, tell Marion that I loved her the first time I ever saw her and love her even more now." He stopped again, this time with his eyes staring straight up into the heavens.

"Yes, I'll tell her."

"And, Toby. I've written a letter for him. See that he gets it." And this time, when His Lordship's eyes closed they didn't open again.

While a sad occasion for all the family and friends, it was a gigantic blow to me. A death in the family meant that as the personal attendant of the Earl, my services would pass on to the new Earl. That had been decreed over two hundred years ago in a joint death-pact between the then-Earl and the then-Ox. These two had been Toby's Father's and my respective great, great, great, great, with maybe even a few more greats thrown in, grandfathers.

High in the Himalayas, the then-Earl and the then-Ox had become separated from a British cavalry patrol the Earl had been leading. The pair of them had been set upon by rebel tribesmen and had taken refuge in an abandoned hill fort. Two days later, when the patrol located the bodies, they discovered the will that the Earl had written out. Among other things, the will stated that Ox's descendants would always have a job with the Fitzgibboncrest family, and that every first-born, male Oxnard would continue to be the gentleman's gentleman to the Earl.

I may not have had a high regard for Toby, but my sense of duty and my integrity left me no option. With Toby's mother's blessing, I boarded a train to join my new master.

On the evening that I arrived at The Depot, the duty lance corporal was out of his office at the main door having a smoke, so I marched in unchallenged. I found Toby by asking a shaven headed, coverall-clad, recruit, who was walking the corridor eating a tub of ice cream. The recruit did not know Toby by name, but when I told him that Toby's platoon number was 1313, the recruit knew where they were.

I moved off down the hallway in the direction the recruit pointed with his wooden ice cream spoon. I was not at all shocked to find that everyone was dressed in the same dreary black coveralls and all sported the same lack of hirsuteness. Having accompanied the previous Earl overseas in World War Two, as a staff sergeant, I was familiar with training barracks.

Both sides of the hall were littered with recruits sitting on the floor, their backs to the wall, tins of boot polish and the lids of the polish filled with water at their sides. On their laps was a boot or a shoe, already glistening as far as I could see; and I was a spit-shine expert. Burnt shoe polish was the aroma of choice, but now and again my nostrils became full of the odours of Old Spice, Brut, or Hai Karate. I had no idea why they were all smelling so nice but put it down to their primitive attempts to hide the smell of burnt shoe polish. Transistor radios belted out horrifying music. Everyone was talking at once or swearing about the day's activities or the treatment they had received at the hands of this sonofabitch or that dirty bastard. It was so welcoming an atmosphere that it made me homesick.

Stepping over legs and asking for Master Toby got me strange looks and scattered insults. I finally found Toby in what I later learned was the webbo room. This was a white tiled, long, narrow room with two white tiled counter tops running the length on each side. The counters were interrupted at regular intervals by two sinks. Toby stood at one of these sinks busy scrubbing at some kind of metal rod.

"Excuse me, Lord Haselbury?" I said to the new Earl's back.

A recruit perched on the counter to Ox's left gave Toby a kick with a sneaker and said, "Hey, Squire, there's some guy here in a tux. He thinks he's talking to you."

Toby turned. "Why, it's Ox...Hello Ox, and what the hell are you doing here? Have I been granted a reprieve?"

"No, Lord Haselbury, and please, be careful with your language. As for me, I am the bearer of sad tidings."

"Lord Haselbury?"

Toby's body sagged against the sink. The polite form of address sank home. "You mean? Yes, you do. It's Dad, isn't it?"

I nodded.

"Come with me, Ox."

Toby led me out and down the corridor in the opposite direction from which I had come. We went through a set of fire doors and then to a stairwell and outside to a large boulder on the grass.

For me, this was probably the first time since Toby had been three that I had ever felt anything other than a steep disaffection for the boy. Once Toby had full use of his legs, hands, and mouth, we two had been at various levels of escalations in conflict. Later, mulling the scene over in my room, I thought that Toby handled the news of his father's death like a gentleman. The few sniffles that escaped from Toby while he had his back to me were perfectly acceptable, as far as my persona as a gruff, old gentleman's gentleman was concerned. I'd had a good old cry himself when my father passed on, and we hadn't spoken to each other for years.

After Toby had composed himself, I made my state of the union address.

"Lord Haselbury, I had the luxury of grieving for your father while I made my travels to this benighted place on that unmitigated cattle train..." I paused, looked at Toby. He looked back at me, nodded and I went on. "I understand that you will need a bit more time, but it is important that we get our relationship sorted out right now."

"Our relationship?"

"Yes, sir. According to custom you have not only inherited your father's title but, as distasteful as it may sound to both of us, you have inherited his gentleman's gentleman, namely me."

"Ah. Yes, I see. Could be a problem for both of us in this arrangement, eh? What are our options, then Ox, my boy?"

"To begin with, sir, to address each other as befits our stations. I'll address you as Lord Haselbury or your Lordship, as it pleases you. You, on the other hand, will address me as Mr. Oxnard, or, as unpalatable as it is for me to answer to someone of your tender years, you may call me Marvin, as your parents did."

Toby looked at Ox. "Have I ever called you Marvin?"

"Yes, on your fifth birthday, behind the stable as I was leading you and your new pony back from a celebratory ride."

"Well, that wasn't so bad was it?"

"It was ghastly. It was appalling; I was devastated. I took to my quarters for three days with six bottles of your father's best scotch."

"That's all?"

"No, sir, before I went, I boxed your ears for you. I am still not sure if I hid away because of the sheer unmitigated gall of such a pipsqueak calling me Marvin, or because I had actually walloped a young Earl."

Toby smiled, and surprisingly, so did I.

"Well, as far as I am concerned you are free to leave and to find another employer, especially since I am now a soldier."

"Yes, sir, I understand, and I probably would, except for two diminutive considerations, and it's something that through benign neglect neither your father nor I ever explained to your mother."

"Oh, come on, Ox.....I mean, Mr. Oxnard, spill it. What's so bloody secret that you can't tell me?"

"The first one is not a secret, it is a letter from your father to you. He dictated it; I wrote it. Here."

Toby opened the letter and read the contents.

Dear Toby;

You're reading this because you are now the Earl of West Saxmundham and North Haselbury, effectively, Lord Haselbury. I would appreciate it if you would do this one thing for yourself. I ask that you remain in the Canadian Army until your three years are up.

Your stint in the Canadian Army may seem rough on you, but it is no longer just about you and the Judge. In order to save you and our family some embarrassment, I gave my word that you would serve in the Canadian Army. I was wrong to do that. My word is not binding on you. You can go absent, cause any amount of trouble to get yourself thrown out on your rear end – but is that the right way to go? If you can, I'd like you to serve the complete enlistment not for the family's honour, nor mine, which is now nothing important, but for your own. I believe you can do that. I only hope that you will.

I have been very proud of you, and I know that I can rest peacefully knowing that you will continue to make your Mother proud. Goodbye, Son.

Toby looked up at me with a tear in his eye. He sniffed and said, "Ox, this Army thing, it's what one of my Canuck buddies calls a 'bum rap' or a 'dirty beef', but it's done. I'll pay the piper."

He flashed his widest smile. "After all, the look on the Judge's wife's face; that's probably worth three years in the army, anyone's Army. I'll be the best soldier I can be, and I'll do the three. My promise to you and to my Father."

I drew myself up; the stately gentleman's gentleman, and smiled back. "Well done, Toby."

After a pause while both of us gathered our thoughts, I spoke, "Next we have a bit of what might become a sticky situation. Your father, well aware of the rancour that you and I held toward one another, asked me specifically that should harm ever befall him, I would remain as your gentleman's gentleman until you reached the age of twenty-five."

"And you agreed?"

"His Lordship was very compelling."

"Oh, he offered you money, big bucks as they say over here?"

I sniffed. "You dishonour both His Lordship and myself, sir. In fact, I hope you are joking, because I never would have thought you would stoop so low."

Toby smiled. "Ox, I do apologize. Yes, I was pulling your pisser. I have long ago realized that your loyalty was never for sale." Toby looked thoughtful. "It's probably that realization, on some subconscious level, that has made me give you such a hard time. Now that I think of it, it seems that I was taking advantage of the situation, and for that I am sorry."

"Thank you, sir, that admission means the world to me. As for your father's request, he made it on his death bed. Death bed requests, and favours, seem to run in our families and I could not turn him down. So you see, I am committed to this relationship, and unless you are adamantly against it, I am your gentleman's gentleman."

"Well, I'm not sure how this is going to work out, but I'm game. Here's my hand on it, Mr. Oxnard. And I shall address you by whatever name you are the most comfortable with."

Marvin reached out and shook Toby's hand. "Thank you, Lord Haselbury, and now that I have had a few moments to consider it, I believe that Ox will do just fine."

Toby laughed, remembered the situation, and then said, "I recall an earlier death in our family that seemed to bring us together, even though it was only for a short period of time."

"Yes, Lady Victoria's passing; but that truce held for you for about three hours, if I recollect accurately."

When Toby was twelve years old, his Father and Mother had gone off to Switzerland to ski and get some sun. It turned out to be a very expensive tanning session. Toby had been left with his father's mother, the Lady Victoria, a grand dame of the old school, and wealthy in her own right. Lady Victoria fell ill and was hospitalized, insisting that Toby stay with her. The private hospital suite was re-designed to accommodate two in the decadent splendour reminiscent of Lady Victoria's own home. A telegram was sent to Switzerland. Lady Victoria ill. Hospitalized. Suggest return at once.

Lord Eustace, normally the most caring of men, had been the victim of similar telegrams in the past.

"No Marion, honey, it's just a ploy. We've only got three days left. Let the old dragon stew. As the Yanks say, 'Let's hit the slopes!'"

Meanwhile back in England...

"What do you mean there's no reply?"

"Exactly what I said Madam, no reply, no response, no rejoinder, no rebuttal, no reaction, in short, no answer from the snowy hills of Europe," I replied.

"Never mind the vocabulary lesson, Oxnard. That's ridiculous. Did you get a telegram sent out or not? And stop calling me 'Madam'. I am not the keeper of a brothel. Although from the activity going on around here in the nights I wouldn't be surprised."

"What's a brothel, Grandmother?" said Toby from behind a comic.

"Never mind, read your book."

"It's not a book, it's a comic. Oxnard is a brothel a whorehouse?"

"Toby!"

"I shall explain it in due time, Master Tobias," I said.

"He probably learned it from you, Oxnard."

"Madam, I am a gentleman's gentleman. If I were to use such a term, which I wouldn't, then it would be more delicate. Can I get you a drink, Madam?"

"No, Toby can do that. You can get Applecrumble and Mudcastle, Get 'em pronto, as my dear departed husband would say. And listen Oxnard, I want them standing at the foot of this bed in less than two hours. No excuses, rejoinders, rebuttals, and no replies. Tell them it's be here or be fired. If it comes to that, once you have fired them, get me two more lawyers, then fire yourself for incompetence."

"Yes, Madam." I left the room, but in keeping with a butler's duty to keep abreast of everything that went on in the household, I glued an ear to the keyhole.

"Oh Grandmother, you can't fire Ox."

"Toby, I have hired hundreds of housekeeping staff. I've fired nearly as many, and I can fire him. He's an idle layabout. Not as idle as your father, but almost. And don't call him Ox, it's Mr. Oxnard to you."

"Yes, Grandmother. But I call him Ox because he hates it."

Two hours later, I had Lady Victoria's chauffeur, Ferdie, take Toby to the zoo while the lawyers were ushered into Lady Victoria's room. I remained with Lady Victoria.

"Take this down, I, Lady Victoria blah, blah, blah, you know how it's done."

"We ought to," whispered Abercrombie to Maardcasell. "We've only done it about ten times in the past two years."

"Never mind, Applecrumble. If you want to remain my solicitors, you'll do as I say. Now listen."

They stood open-mouthed in amazement as the old woman they secretly called the "Iron Bitch" announced that henceforth Toby was to be her heir. He would inherit everything if only he remained unmarried until after he was twenty-four.

"And furthermore, Toby is not to learn of this will, ever."

"Twenty-four?" said Maardcasell.

"You heard me. Twenty-four. My son married while he was twenty-three and now he leaves me to die among strangers."

Another whisper, this time from Maardcasell, "Die? The Iron bitch will outlive us all."

"Thank you, Maardcasell. I hope I do, but no, this time it's for keeps. And since I am really dying this time, I'll let you know a secret. I've known about that awful nickname for over twenty years. It's one of the reasons I call the pair of you Applecrumble and Mudcastle. Your nickname for me, I find quite complimentary, thank you both. I christened the pair of your that way because you are both incompetent boobs, but the brightest, incompetent boobs in your profession. Anyway, if Toby does marry before he's twenty-four, then my son will inherit, and Toby will have to wait until his father dies to get his share of my money."

Three hours after the evening meal Lady Victoria passed away in her sleep. I kissed her cheek and silently led a sobbing Toby from the room. It was the first time that Toby had ever had brandy. As I sent him off to bed he told me he quite liked it.

CHAPTER 19

THE ARMY MEETS THE OX

We chatted a bit, brought one another up to speed, as Toby put it, and after a few more sniffles, he took me back to his room to meet his roommates. Lord Toby Haselbury, the new Earl of West Saxmundham and North Haselbury, who had left the room as Squire Randolph Anthony Tobias Trelauney-Fitzgibboncrest, led me, his gentleman's gentleman into his cramped quarters. The sight of a British gentleman's gentleman in his working clothes must have been a strange sight to the seven boys who were tumbled everywhere. One lad, seated on the floor, had one big black boot shoved over one hand and held a yellow chamois in the other. Periodically, he would rub at the boot, spit onto the rag, and then dip the rag into a giant can of black shoe polish. He looked up as I stepped over him to stand in between the four sets of bunks.

"Squire, is this the guy you talked about?"

"Yes, this is Mister Marvin Oxnard." Toby turned to face me. "And these miserable examples of humanity are my roommates. Some of the worst soldiers the army ever recruited."

"Speak for yourself," said a chubby, black haired boy who was sitting on the springs of his bed, a large bag of potato chips in one hand and a bottle of Coca-Cola in the other. On his lap was his rubberized groundsheet and in it were crumbs and slivers of broken chips that had escaped his mouth. Normally, I would have referred to them as 'crisps', but this is Canada.

"Mr. Oxnard, my name is Arnold Stouffer, but the rabble, unable to enunciate clearly, call me Stuffy."

"Not quite," said another boy from under a bed. He was busy waxing the already glistening floor. "It's because you're such a stuffed shirt that we call you Stuffy, that and because you're always stuffing your face."

I nodded politely at the boy on the bed, turned to nod at the form scrubbing away under a bed and remained silent.

Toby spoke up, "Over there, ironing his uniform on a barrack box is Offside. He's a Newf."

I bowed in his direction. "Pleased to meet you, Mr. Offside."

"No, Ox, His names McGuffin, but he's got a dimple. Look at him."

The boy turned his face toward me and grinned. Sure enough, there was a large dimple in his chin. It was not in the centre of his chin, but off to the left side. "See, the dimple is off side. So that's his name."

Toby quickly went around the room with his introductions of his bunkmates.

I, Marvin K. Oxnard, late of his Lordship's service in Winnipeg, the British Isles and parts foreign had arrived at Camp Gagetown, New Brunswick. Accustomed as I was to making myself at home wherever his Lordship might reside, this primitive locale did not upset me. Unfortunately, the same could not be said of the members of The Caledonia and Musquodoboit Scottish Regimental Depot. My appearance put the cat among the pigeons. That the Earl was a private soldier in the Canadian Army, I considered an inconsequential item on the agenda. I promptly moved into the quarters and took up residence in an empty room on the second floor.

It was to become not so inconsequential to the lance corporal who had held the duty shift of The Depot orderly corporal on the evening of my arrival. Since he had been out smoking on the back steps of The Depot building when I made my way in through the front door, he was blithely unaware that a born and bred, British, gentleman's gentleman, had taken up residence in the barracks.

He became aware of it early the next morning. He was obviously surprised to see a man dressed in what appeared to be a tuxedo marching confidently down the main corridor, with a wash basin full of hot water. He saw me halt, balance the basin in one hand then knock quietly on the door of one of the rooms and say, "Good morning, Lord Haselbury, I believe it is but ten minutes to reveille."

Toby and his roommates were just as surprised. Normally, reveille had meant the playing of a recording of the massed bands of three highland units at high volume over the public address system. The thunderous racket of the bass drums, snare drums and the howling and wailing of two hundred sets of bagpipes tumbled the boys from their beds to begin their day. Not content, or not sure if the recording had done its job, the duty corporal then roamed the corridor banging and kicking doors and yelling, "Grab your socks and drop your cocks, it's daylight in the swamp. Get up you miserable rabble. Get those feet on the floor and the rest of you vertical."

Not this morning. Lance Corporal Laurel, who bore an unfortunate resemblance to Oliver Hardy, and was unmercifully known as "Ollie" to the recruits, followed his curiosity down the corridor to Toby's room.

There, he nearly swallowed the toothpick he had been chewing on. Seated in front of the window, his shoulders swathed in a white, army-issue towel, looking for all the world like a king, was Toby. I was preparing to give Toby a shave. Ollie propped himself against the door frame, his free hand clenching and unclenching the swagger stick all corporals in The Depot carried as a symbol of their authority.

The only other occupant of the room who was awake was "Offside". He was an early riser and was always finished washing and shaving ahead of the other hundred recruits who battled for the thirty six sinks and six showers. Ollie's hand began a slow, steady slap, slap, slap of the stick against his highly starched Bush trouser leg.

"And a very good morning to you, Squire. Please be so kind as to explain why a fucking penguin is readying to give you a shave in the comfort of your own room?"

Busy scrubbing up a lather in a shaving mug, I answered for Toby. "Not at this moment, Lance Corporal. Yes, I realize this is the army, but as I understand it, reveille is not for a few more minutes, so please excuse us. As you have no doubt observed, we are busy with gentlemen's ablutions. Lord Haselbury will be unavailable for the next half hour. And, as you go, would you close the door behind you?"

It was all too much for him. The swagger stick slid from numbed, unfeeling fingers, clattering to the highly-polished floor and shattering the shocked silence. His other hand grabbed wildly at the door frame in an attempt to keep him from falling over backwards. He staggered, eyes blinking rapidly as he tried to process this astounding piece of information. But the lance corporal was a professional soldier. Shaking his entire body like a rain-soaked retriever, he came back to life. His tongue and brain finally meshed. "Not available?"

He stormed into the room. "Squire," he bellowed. "I suggest that you get your limey-arse out of that chair and get your heels together, now!"

The harsh tones brought the remainder of the lads wide awake. They sat up in their beds and stared. I had finished lathering up the brush, so turned toward the lance corporal with the wash basin in my hands. We didn't know it, but the stage was set for disaster. Toby, attempting to carry out the last order given, obligingly complied. the lance corporal was moving forward, hob-nails and horseshoe cleats tearing up the gleaming floor. Offside, scurrying out from under his bed where he had been searching for stray dust balls, backed on

131

his hands and knees into Ollie's path. Ollie pitched forward, heels leaving the ground.

At the same time, Toby sprang out of the chair, snatching the towel from around his neck and heaving it away from himself. The towel caught me full in the face as I was turning around. I tried to dodge it and swung away blind. Toby, still in the middle of leaping to attention pitched into me, causing the washbasin to head off toward the doorway. This was the direction the lance corporal had been coming from. The lance corporal's face met the wall of water. Blinded, off-balance and skittering across the polished floor like an elephant on roller skates, he hit the chair Toby had just vacated. The chair's legs had been resting on woolly scarves, normally used in winter. In the Recruit depot, they were used as pads for chair legs and recruit feet and were known as 'scuffies'. Ollie became a one-man bobsled as he landed on the chair on his knees, eyes shut tight against the pain of the hot water and soap. The chair, as slick as if it had been launched from a cannon rammed backwards until it slammed to a stop against the radiator below the window. All two-hundred pounds of screaming lance corporal catapulted through the plate glass window to crash on the rock hard sod ten feet below.

Toby and Offside dashed through the broken glass to the window and looked at their lance corporal. Toby turned slowly toward me. As befitted a gentleman's gentleman, I played a statue calmly standing by the bed, the towel now neatly draped over one arm.

"I told him you were not available, Lord Haselbury. May I suggest we retire to my room to finish your ablutions? Room 213, if you please, sir. I'll join you after I refill the basin." I turned and walked out of the room.

The sun came up as it always did. Life continued on in The Depot, although it was a different life for some of the featured players. Toby was placed under close arrest in the Regimental guardroom, the lance corporal was placed in intensive care, and the Commandant spilled his tea.

The Commandant, Lieutenant Colonel Travis Dillingham, slammed an open hand down on his teak desk, rattling his bone china teacup and saucer, spilling tea over his rare copy of Julius Caesar's Commentaries and startling his blue-eyed Persian cat, who, until that moment, had been sleeping comfortably in the Commandant's in basket.

In an icy clear, glacially calm voice he said to Bowles, "I don't care if Private Trelauney-Fitzgibboncrest is a peer of the realm, nor do I consider your assessment that he is a deucedly nice chap any kind of a recommendation.

What I want, Lieutenant Bowles, is for you to get that bastard's civilian batman out of my depot and then get on with your job. Which, in case you may have forgotten, is to turn civilians into soldiers. It is not your job to hold tea parties with recruits, no matter what their pedigree. And furthermore, wasn't it this same recruit who you raved was trying to kill you? Don't even answer that, Lieutenant. Just get out of my office, or I'll kill you."

Next door, The depot RSM, Gerald Ulysses Franklin McKindly was treating Sergeant Clyde to a similar discussion. Of course, since neither of them were officers and by implication, gentlemen, the talk was of a more visceral nature. The RSM, whose initials were GUF had been nicknamed "Goddamn Un-Fucking Kindly" needs no further introduction.

As the lieutenant colonel was slamming his cultured palm on his expensive desk, the RSM was hammering with his pace stick on the scarred and stained six foot table he called a desk. The crushing blows were conducted with military precision. RSM McKindly was nothing if not a methodical, military man. His stick crashed down upon the table top with the menacing authority of a frozen metronome; one hundred and twelve paces to the minute, the speed that a Highland unit marched in quick time.

Keeping cadence with his pace stick, his words pummelled Bowles' poor Sergeant Clyde.

"Put…that…fucking…idiot…Lance…Corporal…on…three…weeks… extra…duties. Charge…the…recruit…with…assault, throw in mutiny and offering violence to a superior." He paused for breath, but the banging kept on. "And if necessary, man-handle the bloody royal servant off camp property. And, Clyde, have it all done by coffee-break."

He stopped banging and shouting, glared at the Sergeant for what seemed like a year and a half, then said, "And if it's not done by then, march yourself to the guardroom and lock yourself in a cell."

Sergeant Clyde could only nod.

"Good. Dismissed."

Sergeant Clyde slammed to attention, executed a sharp right turn, executed the standard military pause of "one, two" and then marched to the door and opened it. As he stepped out, the RSM added a final word, "And, Clyde, lock the keys to your cell in with you, because if I get in to you, I'll rip your head off and shit down your neck. Get out."

Sergeant Clyde closed the door behind him and found himself face to face with Lieutenant Bowles who had just left the Commandant's office. Clyde saluted.

Bowles returned the salute and said, "There, that wasn't so bad was it?"

The Sergeant, contemplating suicide, thought once again, as he did three or four times a day, that Bowles was a fucking idiot.

CHAPTER 20

JACKIE MEETS THE OX

When Toby had been marched off to jail in a pair of baggy coveralls, carrying his small pack, which contained his shaving gear, change of underwear and wearing his web belt and accoutrements, I sat stunned on one of the beds of the lower four bunks in the room I had commandeered in the upstairs wing of The Depot.

Usually, an infantry rifle company was housed on each floor. At this time in Canadian history, with there being no shortage of work out on the civilian economy and a veritable drought of juvenile delinquents being offered a jail term or a stint in Her Majesty's Canadian Army, there was only the need for the lower floor to house the recruits of The Caledonia and Musquodoboit Scottish Regiment.

Descended deeply into my misery over the jailing of his Lordship, I barely aware of the door bursting open. Finally, I noticed two burly lance corporals, each wearing the armbands of the battalion Regimental Police, striding into the room.

"You Ox?" said the bigger one. There was only an inch or so of difference between the two of them; they looked like a pair of walk-in refrigerators with heads. They were clad in the Garrison dress of the day, Other Ranks, Non-Commissioned Officers, Moderate Climate, Summer Order, otherwise known as Bush Ones. Bush Ones was starched razor-creased bush trousers, complete with trouser weights, puttees, garrison boots, and balmoral and an olive drab short sleeve shirt, complete with armband denoting rank and regimental shoulder flashes. The RP staff wore an additional armband that said "RP" on the other arm.

"Not to you, Lance Corporal," I said, as I stood up to my full six foot-two inch height in an attempt to make them appear smaller. Didn't work. There were giants among policemen. "To you, I am Mr. Marvin Oxnard."

"To me, you're a pain in the ass. Get your shit together and let's go. You're evicted."

"My 'shit', Lance Corporal, as you call it, is together. Since I have already completed my morning toilet. You may want to check, by now it should be well on its way to your house."

The littler green monster chuckled. Biggie turned to him and said, "Shut it, Turner, this guy ain't funny."

"He's funnier than you, Jackie."

"Shut up and gimme a hand with the penguin, he's goin' outa here horizontal."

I moved back from the bed to the space in the centre of the room and removed my jacket, folded it carefully then laid it on a spare mattress. I turned and faced the two RPs and said, "I should warn you that after such a threatening statement, any movement directed toward my person shall henceforth be construed to be offensive. I shall have no choice but to retaliate in kind."

"What the fuck does that mean?"

"Since you lack the rudiments of understanding the Queen's English, I shall put it into words that I used when I was a professional combatant myself, although those years are long past. So, my barbarian friend, succinctly put, it means that I shall kick the living shit out of you and your partner if you take one more step in my direction."

Jackie laughed.

Turner said, "We can't get into a fight with a guy his age, Jackie, he's probably eighty if he's a day."

"Not quite, Lance Corporal, I am fifty-two years of age. I joined the British Army in 1943 and attained the rank of staff sergeant in the infantry. I am fit enough to handle both of you and a couple more louts just like you, so let's get this over with."

"Louts. The sonofabitch called us Louts, Turner. I don't care if he's Methuselah's Grandpa, I'm gonna kick his ass. Pay attention, you might learn something."

Jackie spat on his hands, rubbed them together and stepped toward me.

I said, "Yes, indeed, Lance Corporal Turner, pay extremely close attention, it may mean the difference between you walking out of this room or being carried out."

Jackie laughed, and tested the air with a couple of swings of his fists. "Yep, school's in, Turner, my boy. You and the Penguin are gonna learn a lot."

"Now, Jackie, go easy."

"Yes, Jackie, please go easy. After all, someone who is transporting all that lard around his middle may trip and fall and land on some unfortunate," I said.

"Lard. First lout and now lard. Pop, you're the one who's gonna be unfortunate."

Jackie closed in to where I stood waiting, hands at my sides. Jackie gave a tremendous swing toward my head. He missed. By a large margin. To them, I may have looked like an overdressed penguin out on his first date. I may have sounded like a refugee from a dictionary factory. And to the youthful eyes of the twenty-three year old RPs, I may have appeared to be outrageously ancient. But this so-called harmless old man in front of them still ran a yearly marathon, jogged three miles a day, three times a week, and bench pressed my own weight. It was an unlucky Jackie who failed to ask me for my martial resume. Even Toby could have told him that I had been an unarmed combat instructor in my infantry battalion and the holder of a third degree black belt in Judo. This oversight on Jackie's part proved to be a tad unwise.

"Huh?" He swung again. Missed again.

I said, "You're quite fast for someone so fat, but I'm not in the mood to play games with you." I put up my hands and squared off.

Jackie, now a maddened porker, rushed at me making a grab for my left hand. I stepped smoothly back, reached out and grasped Jackie's hand and wrist. With a swift move, I twisted the arm, and Jackie dropped to his knees as if hit with a rocket. He screamed, and the now dislocated arm hung awkwardly at his side. I dusted off my hands and said, "Corporal Turner, it would appear that school is now out."

Jackie's response was a howl. Turner said, "Hey, we're RP staff, you can't do that." But he didn't come any closer.

"Then you should be aware that to lay your hands on a person is a form of assault and can be defended against by the person being assaulted."

"We got orders to get you off the camp. And we got an hour to do it."

"Very well, that was all that was needed. If you get this cry-baby out of my room, I'll pack up and meet you downstairs in five minutes. Then you, and you alone, may escort me to the extremities of military jurisdiction."

"Yeah, right, sure, five minutes. I'll take Jackie to the UAS. Thanks for being so cooperative."

He stooped to pull Jackie up, grabbing him by his dislocated shoulder. Jackie was able to shout curses and fling feeble punches with his good arm as the two of them left the room.

An hour later I was standing on the sidewalk outside the main gate of the camp. I had used the phone at the main gate to call for a taxi. As I stood there in my finery, a pair of motorcycle dispatch riders pressed into service as vehicle escorts, lights flashing, pulled up and were waved through by the sentry on duty. Right behind them came a string of five, shiny, black staff cars. The first four passed on in the wake of the dispatch riders, the last car stopped a few yards past me. Out of the back door came another penguin, who could have been my twin. Although, I must admit the new arrival was shorter, slimmer, and greyer of face and hair. Point of fact, he was not as handsome.

"Marvin? It really is you?"

"Cleeves, you here? And yes, it is I."

"What are you doing in this godforsaken place?"

"I might ask you the same question. I have just been removed from the camp due to a slight misunderstanding."

"Yes, fine, but why are you even here?"

I gave Cleeves a short version of the death of his Lordship's passing and my re-assignment, so to speak, to Toby.

"So that's why I was standing at the front gate. Now tell, me, Cleeves, why are you here?"

"Well, I'm still in the employ of His Lordship, The Baron of Sanda Island Two. Sir Richard Norbury, The Third. He's now the Titular Designate Colonel-in-Chief of The Caledonia and Musquodoboit Scottish Regiment. He is presenting them with their new Colours. There's going to be plenty of work for me. Why don't you stay and give me a hand? That way, you will be in the know about your young master and maybe His Lordship will be able to do something for him, after all, they are related in some obscure fashion, aren't they?"

"Yes, I believe they are. From his mother's side, I think. The McWhinnies have some obscure branch of theirs, probably Campbells, residing in the Isle of Man who trace their ancestry through the Stanleys of the Isle of Man. And, Toby's father and Your Master went to school together."

"Righto," said Cleeves. "Bang on! Wonderful memory you have there, Marvin. They were chums. One summer break, Lord Eustace even spent a fortnight on Sanda Two. I remember that he used to tease Sir Richard about the way he liked his breakfast eggs cooked...Chardonnay Specials or something. But never mind that, what about you? Staying on to help?"

"Thank you, Cleeves, as long as I am not intruding...."

"Not at all, my dear fellow. It will be like old times. Like the time we were under footmen at Bicester Bottoms. Although, here we will be giving the orders."

Later on, while Cleeves and I were sitting in a spare room behind the bar in the Caledonia and Musquodoboit Scottish officers' mess, His Lordship came seeking his gentleman's gentleman.

"There you are, Cleeves, and sipping the mess scotch if I'm not mistaken."

Both of us stood, stiff penguins on parade, His Lordship waved us back into our seats. We both ignored him and remained at attention.

"Can I be of service, sir?" said Cleeves.

"Yes. Begin by telling me why you picked up another gentleman's gentleman at the main gate of this military establishment, why there was a gentleman's gentleman at the main gate in the first place, and, since this looks like the gentleman's gentleman who was at the main gate, perhaps an introduction might be in order. Humph?"

"Quite, Sir Richard. This is Marvin Oxnard, the gentleman's gentleman of the late Earl of West Saxmundham and North Haselbury …"

"The late, did you say?"

"Yes, M'lord. Unfortunately, Lord Eustace passed away recently in Winnipeg," I said.

Cleeves went on. "And now Oxnard is gentleman's gentleman to Lord Haselbury, or as we knew him when he was little, Randolph Tobias Trelauney-Fitzgibboncrest, his late lordship's son."

I said, "Lord Haselbury, as he is now formally known, is a member of the Canadian Army and is stationed here at this camp."

"Goodness gracious. EB passed on. I hadn't seen, nor heard from him in years…We're related, you know." Sir Richard sat down, and there was silence in the room for a few minutes, then he looked at Cleeves.

"EB was a fine man. Even though we lost touch, I know that we will miss him. But, it's not him we need be concerned with now, is it? Mr. Oxnard, can you give me the address of where her ladyship is staying. EB's wife, I mean."

"Yes, sir. She's in Winnipeg. I have only recently arrived from there to take up my duties with Lord Haselbury, but…"

"Yes, quite. And you say that he's a member of the Canadian Army? Extraordinary. There would appear to be a story here. Sit down both of you, no, Cleeves, before you do, top up Mr. Oxnard's glass, get me one and then sit."

Cleeves looked his master straight in the eye.

"Oh, botheration, Cleeves, yes, get one for yourself, then sit."

"Very good, sir."

CHAPTER 21

THE TOP DOG MEETS THE CALEDONIA MUSQUODOBOIT SCOTTISH REGIMENT

If I may digress for a bit here, I'd like to give you a bit of background on British royalty, the Canadian Army and colonels of regiments. As was the custom, regiments frequently offered the position of colonel-in-chief to members of British royalty, and while there was no legal compunction to do so, the disadvantages of having an eminent personage hanging about were more than offset by the publicity and prestige they often brought with them. So it was that The Caledonia and Musquodoboit Scottish Regiment, formed originally for service in the Great War, cast about for a patron and since they were a Canadian highland regiment it was only proper that they have a Scottish Colonel-in-Chief. Unfortunately, all the Royals of such lineage were taken. With no Royals available, a dilemma appeared.

The Colonel of the Regiment at the time, Colonel "Soapy" McGrath wouldn't have it. "It's not on, we have to have a Colonel-in-Chief, and he or she has to be of Scottish descent. I don't care about what the Canadian Army has stated about colonels-in-chief as only coming from the Royals. We need one, and we'll get one. And, that's that."

The higher-ups in Ottawa did not agree, but Soapy had a few friends, and soon an amendment had been made to regulations. Historically, a colonel-in-chief was a Royal. There was no getting around that, but as a compromise, a new designation was created for regiments that were unable to snag a true-blue blood: the Titular Designated Colonel-in-Chief or the TDCINC. This was shortened to TTD, The Titular Designate. From there it was only a short hop to the current name, "The Top Dog", a designation not used around the personage bearing the title. This satisfied Soapy and so his "Dog Team" went off to Scotland to find their own Top Dog and finally located Sir Richard's family.

The Island of Sanda Two is a tiny island that during very low tides becomes part of the main island known only as Sanda Island, a small island due south of the peninsula of Kintyre in the north of Scotland. Sanda Two is so small that it does not appear on any map. There was one road, and it led from the ferry dock to the main entrance of the castle, a distance as the crow flies of a mile and a half. If the crow is driving an old Bentley and coping with the myriad turns and twists that mirror the landscape of Sanda Two, it is five and a half miles.

Sir Richard Norbury was the third Richard of the family and the third Titular Designate, following in the footsteps of Sir James, his father who had been preceded by his father, Sir Archibald.

Sir Richard, on his appointment as The Top Dog, had little or no knowledge of the military, Canadian or otherwise. What little he had, had been gleaned from watching movies such as 'The Bridge on the River Kwai', 'Rorke's Drift', and 'Tunes of Glory'. The family had only recently become re-involved in public service after a long absence.

The Norburys were not even true Scots. Their enemies referred to them as the Nobodies. They were descended from Sir Hotspur Marmaduke Norbury, a very brave and fearless lieutenant of Charles I. The source of Sir Hotspur's undaunted courage came from his being hard of hearing. Too many times he had interpreted the call to retreat as advance. On a number of occasions, that resulted in one or two battles being turned from defeat into victory. That he was responsible for ten or fifteen routs of his own regiment brought about by his deafness was overlooked. While his military blunders arose from his auditory handicap, it is not inappropriate to note that the regiment that acquired him also was the one under duress, that offered a place within its ranks to Lieutenant Bowles.

After one such disaster, Sir Hotspur was honoured by some worthy of Charles I by being granted the title of colonel-in-chief of his own regiment. This dismayed his decimated troops so much that they deserted en mass to Cromwell's side. Sir Hotspur was left with a choice; should he follow them or remain with Charles I and be colonel-in-chief of a one man regiment? He chose to stay and waged a one man campaign in Cornwall where he attacked and burned out a small Cornish farmer on a tiny island. He held it loyally for the duration of the war. It had been of no consequence to either Sir Hotspur or to Charles I, that the farmer until that time had been a loyal follower of the King.

When Charles I was captured and locked up, Sir Hotspur arrived to serve as his aide de camp. There exists a small group of historians today who deeply believe that Cromwell and his Parliament, reluctant to kill their monarch, decided to give Charles I another chance at ruling England. Sir Hotspur was instructed to escort Charles I to the Parliament hall to discuss matters.

At this time, Parliament was meeting in an old school, and the Long Parliament met in the Headmaster's Hall. Sir Hotspur was directed to, "Escort His Majesty to the Headmaster's." His ears heard the message as "Escort His Majesty to the Headman."

These historians claim that Sir Hotspur was responsible for the end of a Monarchy and the execution of the British King.

Cromwell and his Puritans, far from finding this to their liking, nonetheless covered it up by not explaining anything to Sir Hotspur or anyone else. They got Sir Hotspur out of London by rewarding him for his loyalty to Charles I and by giving him an Earldom and Sanda Island Two.

Sir Hotspur put down roots there and concentrated on raising rare, three-horned sheep. The family remained in obscurity, never again venturing into politics or the military, until the Boer War. Sir Ganglion Norbury, then the current Earl, volunteered a regiment, 'The Sanda Two Scottish' or the S2S for service in South Africa. This sudden outbreak of patriotism shook the family tree, and one of his sons joined up as a subaltern in the 'Sandies'. Unfortunately for him, his atrocious Scottish accent got him mistaken for a Boer, and he was executed. That left such a sour taste on the tongues of the family that they again withdrew from service.

In Canada, when war was declared a number of wealthy or influential persons started up their own regiments. The Caledonia and Musquodoboit Scottish Regiment had been one of them. Shortly after, along came Colonel Soapy McGrath's Dog Team, scouring the ends of Scotland for a Top Dog. Sir Archibald Norbury, Richard's Grandfather, on hearing that some colonials were mucking about near the Mull of Kintyre, and misunderstanding what it was about, jumped at the chance to go to London for the ceremony.

It was not until he reached Southampton and was being escorted aboard a ship destined for Halifax, Nova Scotia and from there to Fredericton, New Brunswick, that he balked. He was mollified by the Dog Team Chief, Major Gilbert Distante, also known as, 'Major Disaster'. Major Disaster sweetened the deal by throwing in the mascot's position to one of Sir Archibald's sheep, free room and board in perpetuity for the sheep and its subsequent sons or daughters and one gold embroidered parade blanket for ceremonial occasions.

The family agreed and so the Top Dog was established, and through the years it became a tradition for the current Top Dog to periodically visit his overseas regiment and be fawned over by colonial troops. And now it was Richard's turn, having inherited the lands, the title as well as a fair bit of the ready, to meet the regiment that had come along with all the other goodies.

After I had explained the story, Cleeves left to prepare His Lordship's wardrobe for the evening's activities. With nothing better to do, His Lordship and I had a few more scotches.

"I can't believe that EB is no longer with us. He was still in the prime of life, eh? And to top it off, young Tobias in jail. Tommyrot. Can't have that. Just won't do."

"No, sir."

"Well, for the time being, you will remain here. Can't have Tobias's gentleman's gentleman wandering the streets of this horrific city."

"Very good, sir. Thank you, sir. And you'll get Lord Haselbury out of jail?"

"Damn right. That's nonsense. He'll be out this evening. That good enough for you?"

CHAPTER 22

THE TOP DOG DOESN'T MEET THE EARL

Cleeves found me a job assisting him in the officers' mess, fetching drinks for the assembled hangers-on that travelled with His Lordship, Sir Richard Norbury. I positioned myself close to His Lordship in case he found out more about Lord Haselbury, or Toby, as he thought of him. My duties were not onerous, Cleeves saw to that. I was free to wander, but did have a tray close at hand in case I was pressed into an emergency role of acquiring drinks.

That evening his Lordship was surrounded by a group consisting mostly of gold braid, bristle-brush moustaches, and hairy legs in kilts. Among the more notable officers surrounding The Top Dog was Colonel Posadieukiewicz, the honorary colonel of the regiment. Not to confuse the issue but with a Canadian regiment there was the ceremonial hierarchy consisting of the Top Dog as colonel-in-chief, then came the honorary colonel, usually a retired battalion commander. To further complicate things, the three battalions, as well as their regimental depots each had a lieutenant colonel as their respective commanding officers. To make things even stickier, each of these COs was entitled to be called colonel.

A red-faced, tubby, civilian was harassing the honorary colonel. "Can't for the life of me, understand these prehistoric customs of yours, and begging your pardon..." He fingered the Colonel's name plate. "With a name like yours, Colonel Poss-I'd-die-ookie-wick-zee, I'd have never have taken you for a Highlander."

"Not a problem, sir, happens all the time. And it's pronounced Posa-ad-joo-kee-wits. But my mother was a MacGregor, and when I decided to join the army, there was only one unit for me. But what customs bother you, sir?"

"The kilts and the trews business. If I understand it, you wear kilts, with nothing underneath when there are ladies present in the mess, but trews when they are absent. I've always thought it should be the other way around, just in case you get each other mixed up, heh, heh, heh. A little joke. My lawyer told it to me."

"Yes, hilarious, sir, lawyers can be very funny, can't they?"

"Speaking of funny and lawyers, Colonel," interrupted Sir Richard of Norbury: who in case you had forgotten, was the Top Dog.

"I understand that from his gentleman's gentleman that an Earl is present in this camp. He's a good friend of mine."

"The gentleman's gentleman is a good friend of yours?"

"No, of course not, the Earl, the man who the butler works for."

"Oh, sorry? An Earl, very impressive and he's here in this camp? But how does this relate to the legal profession?" said the Honorary Colonel. In order to keep this missive moving, so to speak, let's call The Top Dog by his name, Sir Richard, and the honorary colonel, we'll call 'The Honorary Colonel'.

"I'm not sure at the moment, but it could relate to a lawsuit. According to his gentleman's gentleman, a funny thing's happened to him, it'll slay you," said the Top Dog.

"To be sure. So, tell me all about this funny thing that happened to your friend's gentleman's gentleman, and by the way, why didn't you bring him along?" asked The Honorary Colonel.

"He's here, in fact, he's standing behind you with a tray of drinks."

The Honorary Colonel turned around to see me standing at his elbow, holding a silver tray of cocktails.

"Good God, why are you holding that tray, this is outrageous. Let me get someone to take that tray from you, I'm terribly sorry, your Lordship."

The Top Dog put a hand on the Honorary Colonel's arm. "No, Colonel, no, no, no. This is insane."

"It sure is, your worship, and as soon as I find out why someone gave the Earl a tray to hold, I'll have him shot."

"I don't want the Earl shot."

"Not the Earl, the guy who gave him a tray."

"He doesn't have a tray. He's in jail," said the Top Dog.

"Well, it sure looks like he's out on bail or something, because he's here passing out drinks."

"No, he's not the Earl, he's the gentleman's gentleman ."

The Honorary Colonel turned purple. "Why in the hell is he trying to get rid of that tray for, then. He's supposed to carry a tray."

He moved his head so that he was eyeball to eyeball with me. "You should be ashamed of yourself, my man. You're a gentleman's gentleman, stop fooling around and deliver drinks."

"Yes, sir, would you care for a drink?"

"Thank you, I don't mind if I do."

Taking a drink from the tray, he turned to Sir Richard and said, "Now where were we?"

"I was telling you about my friend the Earl, he's here in your camp."

"Another Earl, that is interesting and a funny thing too, what? I can't believe we've got two Earls running around here."

"There's only one Earl," said a frustrated Sir Richard.

"Of course, silly of me, that one carrying drinks is not an Earl, he's a gentleman's gentleman, right."

"Oh never mind him. I'm trying to tell you about the other Earl."

"Oh, so there is more than one. I thought you said there was only one Earl."

"There is only one Earl," said Sir Richard slowly, through clenched teeth.

"Well, pardon me, Your Worthiness, but you distinctly said 'I'm trying to tell you about the other Earl. That, even to us colonials indicates that there is more than one. But if you wish I'll go along with this," said The Honorary Colonel.

"Thank you, now, as I was telling you, this Earl is here in your camp."

"Tell me his name, Your Worthiness, and I'll ensure that he is invited to the remainder of the ceremonies, unless...He's not here this evening is he?"

"No. Actually, that's part of the funny side of things. And that's where the lawyers may come in."

"Oh, really. Well, let me in on the little joke, just a sec, let me find my aide. I'll see that he's invited to tomorrow's show."

As the Honorary Colonel of the Regiment sipped his drink, he looked about for his aide.

Sir Richard said, "Quite a good joke and one I'm sure you will enjoy, Colonel. You see, my friend, the one who's an Earl, I may have mentioned this earlier, but he's languishing in your jail."

With his glass at his lips, his mouth opened to receive another delivery of scotch, The Honorary Colonel's ears were unprepared to hear about an Earl languishing in jail. A gush of ice cubes and scotch sluiced out from his glass creating a blockage in his esophagus and sending a hammer blow to his brain.

He spat ice and liquor on the man next to him. Luckily he was only a Major. He didn't stay to hear the apology, which was a good thing, as there was none forthcoming. The Honorary Colonel's mind was too far gone into a world where an Earl could languish in a Canadian military jail.

He gathered his wits, spat a final ice cube to the floor and said, "Did you say jail?"

"Yes, Colonel, I did. His Lordship, Lord Haselbury, otherwise known as Tobias Trelauney-Fitzgibboncrest is in a Canadian military prison. But, not to worry, I've booked my confidential secretary on a flight to Ottawa to pay a call on the British ambassador first thing in the morning."

"To Ottawa?"

Visions of headlines, rockets from on high, and the end of his plum job danced through The Honorary Colonel's head. "The Ambassador? Is that wise? Is it really necessary? Do you think I could do something?"

"That's a lot of questions, Colonel, the last one's important. Yes, I do think you could do something. You could get the poor sod out of jail and find out why he's in there?"

"Yes, of course, sir. Right away. What's his name? Never mind. Patrick? Patrick? Damn that man, as an aide, he's a waste of rations. Patrick?"

Out of nowhere came Captain Patrick Dawson, the colonel's aide. "Yessir, right here, sir."

"Bloody hell, man, an aide is supposed to be handy at all times, where the devil have you been?"

"You sent me with your driver to pick up your wife, sir."

"Well, dammit, what took you so long? Never mind, she wasn't ready was she?" He turned to His Lordship and said, "Sir Richard, tell Patrick the name of this Earl friend of yours and he'll get him released immediately."

"We always called him Toby. His full name is Randolph Anthony Tobias Trelauney-Fitzgibboncrest. His father passed away recently. So Toby is now the Eighteenth Earl of West Saxmundham and North Haselbury."

"There, Patrick, get that down and get hold of whoever's responsible, I'll have his guts for garters. Tell the ass that I'll see him not right now, but right fucking now."

"Yessir, who is it you want to see?"

"Pay attention, Patrick. Whoever's responsible for putting the Earl in jail, you nitwit."

"I understand, sir, but just who might that be?"

"I haven't the foggiest, Patrick. That's what I'm paying you for, get on with it."

"And if there's more than one, sir?"

"I don't care if it's a platoon. When I get my hands on them, they're fucked, fucked in order of appearance. You got me, Patrick, m'boy?"

"Yessir."

Patrick moved off, not sure what he was doing and ran into a fellow Captain. "Hey, Jonesy, heard anything about some Earl being put in jail?"

Captain Evan Jones was well on his way to having a very large hangover in the morning and was in no condition to get involved in any intellect-heavy discussions.

"Earl's in jail? Earl Taylor of B Company? What'd he do?"

"Earl's not in jail, you idiot. There's an Earl in jail, put in for nothing."

"First you say Earl's not in jail, then you say he's in jail for nothing. If Earl's not in jail, why do you say he is? This aide thing is getting to you, Patty, my boy. If I were you I'd ask to come back to the battalion, at least there we don't put Earl in jail for nothing."

Another Captain turned around. "You may not put Earls in jail, but we put Brits in jail. The Commandant fired a Brit into the pisscan this morning. He'd been storing a butler in his room. Destroyed a room, from what I hear. Sounds like your man, Pat."

Patrick grabbed him by the arm. "Mac, are you sure. A Brit and a Butler? That'll be my guy. But what's he doing in depot?"

"He joined up. Doing his bit for Queen and country, although why our country I'll never know."

"Oh, god, no, not Dilly-dally. He put him in jail? The Honorary Colonel is not going to be pleased. Where is he, Mac?"

"The Honorary Colonel? We don't know, that's your job. Rule number one," said Jonesy, who had not really followed any of the conversation. "Rule number one, always know where your aide is, right, Mac?"

"No, Jonesy, wrong, dead wrong. Pat is the aide, he's supposed to know where his boss is at all times. And, Pat, he is right about that, you should know where the Honorary Colonel is, but not to worry, I see him over there with some dopey looking guy in a moth-eaten kilt and all kinds of gold and braid."

"That, you Arses, is Sir Richard Norbury, The Top Dog of the Regiment, and he's not happy that someone from the regiment has bunged an Earl into the battalion's dungeon. And it looks like you depot boys are responsible.

"Not all of us. The Commandant and Lieutenant Bowles. The Brit was in Bowles' platoon, God help him. 'Course, you've probably not heard of Bowles yet. Sounds like you're about to, though."

"You're right, I haven't heard of him. Who's Bowles?" said Dawson.

Jonesy, finally catching up with the conversation, swallowed the last of his drink and with a drunk's care and concern, gingerly lifted the lid of the mess piano and placed the glass inside. He wagged a finger at the glass, said, "Stay," added a genteel burp, then closed the lid. He turned with the same infinite concern back to Dawson and MacDougal. "Doesn't know Bowles, eh, Mac? Ol' Patrick better watch out, Bowles will be snatching up his job."

"Never mind my job, just give me the dope on Bowles."

Jonesy, another drink in his fist, laughed. "The dope on Bowles. Hilarious, my aide de camp buddy, absolutely fucking hilarious."

Dawson stared.

Mac said, "You've got it, Pat, Bowles is a dope."

"Then why is he in The Depot?"

"They've run out of places to put him. He's bombed out of pretty well everything from Officer Candidate School to that simpleton course they send the worst subaltern in the battalion. The Welfare Officer program. He lasted two days on it."

"Why don't they punt him?"

"Can't. Too well connected. But, our drunken comrade here may be right. Bowles is gonna fuck it up, if he hasn't already, and they're gonna need another hidey-hole for him. He just may end up on the Honorary Colonel's staff. That's him over there. The subbie with the face like a vacant lot. And believe me, a vacant lot is absolutely overcrowded compared to the activity in his brain case."

Dawson turned, saw Bowles and couldn't have agreed more. Bowles normal expression suggested a deep lack of intelligence; with a few drinks in him, his features turned positively Neanderthal. At the same time Dawson saw Lieutenant Colonel Dillingham. "Can't stay boys, if you're right, there's my target, Dilly-dally, over there, brown-nosing the battalion CO's. Save a drink for me, Jonesy. Look after him, Mac."

As he moved through the throng, he shrugged and said to himself, "Well, I guess I'd better go and give him the bad news. After all, it's not my ass in the sling, it's his."

He went over to the group of battalion commanders and tapped Lieutenant Colonel Travis Dillingham on the shoulder. "Excuse me, sir."

Lieutenant Colonel Dillingham turned. "What? Oh, it's you, Dawson. Still as rude as ever, I see."

"No, sir. Not rude. I have a message for you. The…"

"Dawson," said his former boss. "You need to remember that just because you have a message, it's not so important as to interrupt Mr. Logan, here. He's the president of the local bank."

"Sorry, sir, but it is necessary for me to interrupt…"

"No, it's not! Damnit man, I'm busy."

Patrick ignored him. "I'm here to tell you that the Honorary Colonel of the Regiment would like a word with you."

"With, me, whatever for? Why didn't you say so?"

Having hated the tyrannical commandant since he'd taken his turn as a squad commander in The Depot three years ago, Captain Dawson took a lot of pleasure in answering, "Something about you putting an Earl in jail. Seems The Top Dog, Sir Richard Norbury, is quite upset about this and the Honorary Colonel is trying to find out who did it."

"An Earl?"

"Yes, sir, he's a private in The Depot at the moment, but it seems he's a real live Earl from England." Dawson couldn't help himself and stirred the pot a bit. "Colonel's talking court martial for the idiot who put him in the slammer. That's why he sent for you, thought you might know who did it. Best we move along, sir, don't want to keep him waiting, do we?"

Lieutenant Colonel Dillingham went white and swallowed. He made no reference to Dawson's implication that he was the idiot. "No, no, of course not. Right, Dawson, lead on."

As they passed by the rowdy group of foolish subbies that made up Bowles' group, Dawson snagged him by the arm and pulled him along. "Mr. Bowles, the Honorary Colonel's in a bit of a tizzy over the recruit you put in jail. If you don't mind, he'd like an explanation."

Lieutenant Colonel Dillingham had been moving ahead of Dawson and as he heard those words he couldn't have stopped faster if he'd run into a tank. "No, no, no, Dawson, there's no need for Bowles to accompany us. I'm sure I'll satisfy the Honorary Colonel with my story." He turned to Bowles and said through gritted teeth, "Bowles, get lost. And I do mean now!"

Dawson saw this as his chance and embroidered the instructions his Boss had given him. "The Honorary Colonel said he wanted all responsible to see him, sir. I think Bowles should be present."

As he talked, he dragged Bowles along, with Dillingham backing up and trying to keep Bowles from getting in range of the Honorary Colonel and Sir Richard. Dawson had no intention of that happening, he ignored Dillingham, tugged Bowles and then made eye contact with the Honorary Colonel.

CHAPTER 23

THE TOP DOG MEETS THE DEPOT COMMANDANT

Dawson sang out, "Here they are, sir. Commandant of The Depot, Lieutenant Colonel Dillingham and one of his squad commanders, Lieutenant Bowles."

Dillingham sagged visibly and muttered to Bowles, "Say nothing, I'll do the talking."

Bowles, still not present in the new environment he found himself, nodded. The train trip had been his first experience with liquor, and since then he had refrained from touching it until this evening when his fellow lieutenants explained social drinking. To them, social drinking was drinking until someone sociably knocked your head off. Then you quit. So Bowles was giving hard liquor another try. It was too bad that those buddies of his, more clearly aligned on the wrong side of any average IQ score, were feeding him doubles. Standing a foot or two from Bowles, well clear of the group itself, I could see the poor lad was near to being legless with intoxication.

"Ah, good, very good, Patrick," said the Honorary Colonel. He turned to Dillingham and said, "Ah, Dillingham, may I present the Titular Designate Colonel-in-Chief, His Lordship, Sir Richard. Your Lordship, the Commandant of The Caledonia and Musquodoboit Scottish Regimental Depot, Lieutenant Colonel Travis Dillingham. I'm sure that Colonel Dillingham will be able to shed some light on how soon Lord Haselbury's incarceration will be ended. Ah, I see a look of confusion here. Would it be preferable for me address him as Private Trelauney-Fitzgibboncrest? No matter, all I want to know is how soon he can be released, right, Colonel?"

Bowles stood chewing on an ice cube and nodding. It was obvious that he was not too sure of the events that had brought him out of his peer group to stand in front of forty miles of braid and arrogance. But, he didn't let that ignorance stop him. He said, "Out of jail? Not a chance, sir, not a chance. Commandant's seen to that. I admit I was wrong, but it's all very clear to me now."

He waved his arms expansively in Lieutenant Colonel Dillingham's direction, causing the Honorary Colonel and Sir Richard to duck and to pull back. "And I owe it all to this man here, the Commandant of The Depot. Yes, Lieutenant Colonel Dillingham, very graciously put me straight. Just this afternoon we were discussing that wretched recruit."

Lieutenant Colonel Dillingham's eyes rolled back into his head, he shook himself and stayed upright. Dawson, two paces to the rear of the Honorary Colonel, congratulated himself on his audacity. By the sound of things, Bowles was about to dig a very deep sewage pit for the Commandant. Hoping to hear Bowles destruct Dilly-Dally's career, Patrick moved closer. Bowles didn't disappoint him.

"The Commandant's advice to me was to steer clear of that bloody Brit. He's a troublemaker, he said, mark my words, Bowles, that limey-shit-disturber means trouble. Damn bluebloods wander over here and think they own the place. Well, I'm not going to stand for it, he said. Right out front the Commandant is."

Yeah, right out in front of a firing squad, thought Dawson. And, now that they've got Bowles babbling, they'll soon see that he isn't shut down, not by a long shot.

"Told me, Lock him up, Bowles, my boy. Slam that son of a bitch so far in cells that they have to pump daylight into that damn blueblood arse-hole."

The damn blueblood arse-hole beside the Honorary Colonel blanched. Too shocked to comment, and hardly believing his ears, Sir Richard, wondered how Toby's mother, Lady Marion, would take this description of her family. He hoped to see the day when the Commandant and Lady Marion were together in the same room.

The Honorary Colonel, seeing that the shit wagon was on a roll, didn't try slowing it down. "Let me get this correct, Mr....Er...Mr... Blows, is it?"

"Bowles, sir, Lieutenant Arthur Victor Llewellyn Bowles, sir, of The Caledonia and Musquodoboit Scottish Regiment, presently serving as a squad commander in The Depot, sir."

"Yes, quite. Now Mr. Bowles, all of that little speech you just made, you know, dammed bluebloods, limeys, etcetera...."

"Limey-shit-disturber, sir, to be accurate."

The Honorary Colonel grimaced and cast an apologetic glance at His Lordship then went on, "Accuracy is vital, Bowles."

"Yessir, which is why I corrected you, if you'll pardon me as a green lieutenant correcting someone as old as you, sir. Not that you're over the hill by any means, sir."

154

"Thank you, Bowles. Now let me finish."

"Yes, sir, please go ahead."

"If you will shut up, I intend to do so. I.."

"Roger that, sir, you have the floor."

Dawson, seeing that this was going nowhere, pushed his upper body in between the Honorary Colonel and His Lordship and barked, "Mr. Bowles, attention!"

Bowles jumped to attention, lips jammed tight, heels together, eyes straight ahead; locked on nothing.

Dawson said, "I believe you may proceed, sir."

With a sigh of relief, the Honorary Colonel said, "Thank you, Patrick. Now, Mr. Bowles,"

"Yes, sir?"

The Honorary Colonel lost his composure. "Don't start that again, just stand still, keep your trap shut and wait until I ask you something. And don't, on pain of an excruciatingly slow death, say another word. Just nod."

Bowles nodded.

"Good. Now we're getting somewhere."

Bowles nodded, the Honorary Colonel sighed, but being a survivor of Dunkirk, he was not about to let a simple-minded subaltern get the better of him. "That list of words, limey, shit-disturber, damn blueblood, Are they your words, Bowles? … Remember, just nod."

Lieutenant Colonel Dillingham willed himself invisible. Bowles just stood there, moon-faced and silent. The group waited. He stood, at full attention.

"Well, man, go ahead and nod. Are those your words?"

Bowles soldiered on, a silent statue.

The Honorary Colonel exhaled in a blast. "Fuck me gently! And with a rod of cold steel. What the fuck is wrong with you?"

An elderly woman a few feet behind prodded him with an ivory and silk fan. "Watch your language. There are ladies present."

The Honorary Colonel turned, his anger pushing him past all pretence of civility. "Fuck off!"

Dawson took her arm as she fell a step backward. "He's a bit upset, Ma'am. Here, let me escort you to another, more congenial part of the room."

"Yes, please. That creature is an abomination." As Dawson led her away, she said, "That big-mouthed asshole needs his mouth washed out with lye and battery acid."

155

"Yes, Ma'am. I'll let his wife know."

"Married? That rotten prick of a mother-fucker is married?"

Dawson refrained from pointing out that most mother-fuckers were. He also ignored pointing out to her that she had complained about the use of profanity in the mess.

"Yes, Madam, to a long-suffering woman of great virtue. Here you are, Ma'am. And if you don't mind, I'll just get back to that rotten prick. After all, someone's got to look after him. Good evening."

Dawson arrived back to see that the stalemate had been sorted out. Bowles was speaking again. "No, sir, I cannot take credit for any of that. That's why I couldn't nod. A nod would have meant yes, and a yes would have meant I'd said the words and that's a fib. I'd also be attempting to hog the Commandant's credit. Wish I could, but can't. This man here, my Commandant."

Bowles actually simpered. Dillingham stood his ground praying for a flash flood to sweep through the mess, drowning everyone, including himself, but especially Bowles.

"This man, Lieutenant Colonel Dillingham, Commandant of The Caledonia and Musquodoboit Scottish Regimental Depot, that's the man. We owe him a lot. Man's a champ. Sterling. Can't go wrong following the Commandant." Bowles gave the Commandant a gentle nudge in the ribs. Lieutenant Colonel Dillingham stunned, nearly tumbled into a potted plant, and eyed it as if hoping it contained a bunker he could dive into. He steadied himself, physically readying himself for the worst. He was not to be dissatisfied.

Dawson was enjoying himself as he listened to Bowles lead the Commandant into a military gulag.

"Sorry to build you up like this, sir, know you're a modest man, and all that, but facts are facts. You put me right about that limey-shit-disturber, your words, Commandant, no one else's. No credit to me, please. Limey slammed in the Digger. Job well done."

Finally breathless, Bowles beamed at the Honorary Colonel and Sir Richard, still unaware of the shit that was about to be disturbed by that damned blue-blooded limey-shit-disturber, standing right in front of him.

Sir Richard turned to the Honorary. "Comments, please, Colonel?"

The Honorary Colonel, now pink with embarrassment, managed a few words. "My apologies to you, my lord and I think that what I have to say to these two may lower your desire to pack up, go home and declare war on Canada."

Sir Richard found no humour in that comment. He was still in glare-mode. Catching that, the Honorary Colonel turned on weaker prey. "Lieutenant Colonel Dillingham, I do not want to hear anything from you except a "Yes, sir," when I dismiss you. Nothing else." He shifted his eyes to Bowles. "Mr. Bowles, you will not speak again in front of me. Go back to your quarters immediately, you are dismissed. No, don't speak, just go."

Bowles stood gaping. Dawson grabbed one of his arms and dragged him away, gave him a shove toward the exit and said, "Fuck off, now. You're getting a break. Lucky for you the Honorary Colonel's got bigger fish to fry." Then, not wanting to miss the ending, Dawson dashed back to hear the Honorary Colonel.

"Lieutenant Colonel Dillingham, go yourself and immediately get Lord Haselbury out of jail and install him in the best hotel in town. Arrange for a vehicle to pick him up and bring him to my office tomorrow at thirteen hundred. Secondly, when I arrive at my office at that time, I wish to find your full and final resignation on my desk. If it is there, you will be permitted to retire on a full pension as of this date. If it is not there or you have chosen to appeal it, I'll ensure that you are court-martialled, stripped of all ranks and honours, figuratively and literally fucked in the ass, career-wise for eternity and publicly dismissed from Her Majesty's Canadian Army. I hope that is clear because there will be no questions, now or ever. You are dismissed."

He turned his back on the Commandant, took Sir Richard by the arm and in a calm voice over his shoulder to Dawson said, "Snifters of brandy for the three of us, please, Patrick."

Minutes after Lieutenant Colonel Dillingham's departure from the mess, an undercurrent swept through the vaulted ceilings in the officers' mess Bar, skipped through the sergeants' mess, dashed across the parade square and then rattled around the corners of the mens' mess, to bang through the corporals' club and crash land in the mens' mess. The corporals' club, littered with those who had been given extra duties for little or no reason gave three cheers. The PMC, the president of the mess Committee, bought a round for the house. He and Dilly-Dally received another plateful of applause.

In the men's mess, where dozens of former recruits had been subjected to Dillingham's reign of terror, free beer flowed until closing.

The Sergeants and staff sergeants ignored the fuss, after all, as one company quartermaster Sergeant put it, "What's one officer more or less?"

In the officers' mess the feeling was restated a bit differently by the DCO of the First Battalion, when he said, "Heard the news about Dillingham, Colonel?"

"Yes, Colin," agreed Jackrabbit. "A shame he didn't take Bowles with him."

CHAPTER 24

THE TOP DOG AND BOWLES MEET AGAIN AT BRUNCH

The next morning was a Saturday, and the battalion, as well as The Depot, had been stood down. Being a weekend, that meant that it was brunch at ten or later instead of the zero-dark-thirty of the regular breakfast. Sir Richard had given his staff the day off, and Cleeves was sleeping in. Toby had spent the night in a hotel and just after eleven o'clock a staff car and a driver returned him to The Depot. I was sitting in the cook's dining area at the officers' mess awaiting word that Toby was alright and had been re-united with his squad. Chef Jeff, as he was known, was a staff sergeant cook who ran the officers' mess kitchen. He had spent a year at a Canadian base in England and once Cleeves and I introduced ourselves, he gave us the run of the place. We couldn't venture out into the officers' area, but the kitchen and its environs were ours to come and go as we saw fit. I had been on my third coffee when I heard Lieutenant Bowles yelling for the steward. Then shortly after that he was yelling again, some kind of VIP had entered the dining room.

Turns out that it was Sir Richard coming in from his VIP suite to the officers' mess Dining room. Entering the posh establishment, he found only one person sitting at a large table, face buried in a newspaper.

As he moved toward him, a mess steward broke cover and scurried over to assist him. He said, "Coffee, please," and made his way to the occupied table. "May I join you?" he inquired of the paper.

It was lowered, and the face behind it said, "Why. Certainly, sir, I'd be honoured."

As he pulled out the chair, Sir Richard recognized the face. It had assumed a bit more of an intelligent facade, but still looked as if the owner were a few books short of a library. He looked around, but the room was still empty. Good breeding prevented a move to another table, so he pulled out a chair and sat across from Bowles.

Bowles was thrilled. In his blissful ignorance, last night's events were simply that he had met The Top Dog and had a drink with him and the Honorary Colonel and then been courteously escorted out of the mess by an aide. The incident with Dillingham had not been too heavily embossed on his brain and a night's sleep had erased whatever had gotten through. For Bowles, Dillingham had vanished, and Bowles' career had not even suffered a glancing blow. Proof of this, at least by Bowles' reckoning was The Top Dog's request to join him at breakfast.

Sir Richard, on the other hand, would have, if given the chance, gladly fasted in his room for the weekend if it meant staying clear of Bowles. But it was too late now.

The steward reappeared with a silver coffee pot and hovered beside the table as The Top Dog passed his coffee cup.

"What can I get you this morning, sir?"

Sir Richard had been looking forward to a whopping meal of eggs, bacon, potatoes and hot cakes with toast, but knowing that would prolong the agony of enduring Bowles said glumly, "Just toast, please."

The mess steward disappeared and Bowles, ever eager to toady to a superior, broke into what he thought was his best British accent, "Luverly day, Wot, sir."

Sir Richard still sopping from the two-second dash from his building to the mess took a sip of coffee and said, "I've seen better. It's raining a bloody downpour, you know."

"Yes, but since you're from England, I thought you liked this kind of weather."

"Not exactly. I enjoy sunshine. But never mind that, tell me, have you seen the Earl since he was released from jail? He has been released, hasn't he?"

"Oh yes, sir. It was very strange. One of my lance corporals was the duty NCO last night. He called me a little while ago. That's the only reason I'm up at the moment. If he'd left me alone, I'd be snoring the walls down."

And I'd be enjoying a decent meal, Sir Richard thought.

Bowles, given his head, babbled on, "Strange doings that. I couldn't understand for the life of me why he'd been let out. The Commandant led me to believe that he'd be getting daylight pumped into him." Bowles shrugged. "Oh well, that's the army for you, Greatcoats on, Greatcoats off."

Sir Richard not wanting a second round of the shit-eating limey routine nodded and Bowles, lungs reloaded, gave him another burst, "It seems the Earl arrived back in The Depot just this morning. I learned from the duty NCO that the lad had the audacity to spend the night in a hotel. Not bad, eh? From jail to a five star hotel."

Sir Richard nodded, thinking that if this miserable village had a one star hotel it had one more star than it deserved. Bowles took the nod for approval and carried on, "Yes, that's the army for you. One day a dog, the next day a prince."

Sir Richard nodded again.

"His butler joined him." Bowles laughed. "Imagine, me a lieutenant and one of my privates is an Earl and to top it off, he's got his own butler."

"Yes, rather amusing," said Sir Richard, not in the least amused. And certainly in no mood to correct Bowles on the distinction between a butler and a gentleman's gentleman.

The arrival of Bowles' breakfast filled in the granite silence. The Top Dog looked on in jealous awe as a large platter was placed in front of Bowles. This steward, Private Proctor, a man who had worked in the mess for most of his military career, said, "Oh, it's so good to see someone with a healthy appetite, Mr. Bowles."

The platter was heaped with scrambled eggs, bacon, ham, fried potatoes, and sliced tomatoes. He put another, smaller plate beside the platter. "And here is your sausage, I put an extra couple of links on, just for you. It's that special farmer's sausage you like so much."

He looked over at Sir Richard, whose eyes had locked onto Bowles' meal. "Your toast will be along in a moment, sir."

"Yes, thank you. And while I wait, may I have some more coffee, please?"

Proctor topped up Sir Richard's cup and then said, "If you want seconds, Mr. Bowles, just give me a shout."

"Thank you, Proctor. I surely will," he replied as he smothered the mountain of food with ketchup. Bowles turned to Sir Richard. "Toast, not good on its own, sir. You need a good solid breakfast, especially after last night."

"After last night?"

"Yes, you know, Happy Hour and all that. My bet is that you were treated to every drink under the sun. I'm surprised that you're up this time of day. I know I wouldn't be up and around now if I had stayed late. Too bad I had to leave or right now I'd be suffering through the world's largest headache and hangover, if you know what I mean."

"Yes, too be sure, and generally I do enjoy a robust breakfast." Said Sir Richard.

Bowles, taking time out from wolfing his food said, "Well, let's get you some." He turned and yelled, "Proctor, front and centre, on the double, there's a lad."

This despite the fact that Proctor was in his forties.

"Oh, I say, it's not necessary, luncheon is not far off," Sir Richard said, eyeing Bowles' plate and wishing he was at home with his own cook or at the least that he had ordered something a bit tastier than plain old toast.

"Nonsense, sir, if it's alright for a mere lieutenant to tell a lord nonsense. It's his job, and it's the cook's job, and since you're a guest of the mess, it's now my job. After all, you are The Top Dog."

Proctor scurried in to answer the call. "Yes, sir?"

"Proctor, are you ready to take another order?"

"But, you've scarcely touched it? Is there something wrong?"

"Not at all, Steward," began Sir Richard.

"Quite, Proc, old chap. Nothing wrong, but our guest here has changed his mind."

"Yes, sir, what can I get for you?"

While Sir Richard hesitated, Bowles' mind bridged a gap in time and space. He recalled the last time he had breakfasted with a British gentleman. Unaware that Toby's egg dish was not the national meal of England he yelped, "Please, sir, let me. I know what you'd like. Please, sir, may I, oh, may I?"

More to shut the fool up than anything else, Sir Richard nodded. Out of Bowles' mouth came word for word, the same recipe that had been handed down out of the mists of Scotland that Toby's father had learned on a bet so many summers ago.

"To begin with, Proc. we'll need a cup of red wine, a chardonnay or a burgundy, a clove of garlic, a bit of minced onion, a sprinkle of pepper all simmered together until near boiling point. Take two eggs and break them into two separate small cups. When the liquid comes to a rolling boil, reduce heat and bring the edge of each cup to the surface level. Slide the eggs gently from the cups into the liquid. Simmer for four minutes and twenty seconds, then lift the eggs out and place them on hot buttered garlic toast. Sprinkle with basil and serve with five rashers of crisp bacon."

Mouth agape, Proctor scrambled to keep up with Bowles as he recited the recipe. Sir Richard, mouth even wider, stared in disbelief as Bowles recounted instructions for his favourite breakfast, Poached Eggs Chardonnay, on a bed of garlic toast and served with a side of blackened bacon. It nearly brought Sir Richard to tears just hearing of it.

But it didn't mean he missed the reference to The Top Dog.

"The Top Dog, is that some kind of reference to me, Lieutenant?"

"Yes, sir. That's what we all call the position you hold. It's got some other name, but according to regimental history, there was a "dog team" that went out in search of the Titular Designate."

"Oh. Quite uncomplimentary. Most distressing."

"You don't like it, sir?"

"Not at all."

"Then we'll do something about it. I'll mention it to the duty officer ."

"No need to do that...Ah, ha," said peeved The Top Dog as his eggs arrived and any further canine nomenclature was forgotten. At least by The Top Dog. Bowles reported it, but nothing else occurred. The duty officer didn't even enter it in the log book, although it did get mentioned at the mess bar.

Luckily for Sir Richard, Wally the Welder, who had created the counterfeit poached eggs and the burnt bacon on the train, was hundreds of miles away. The duty cook in the officers' mess was a sergeant and making a meal like this was nothing for him. It was the world to Sir Richard. He raved about it and while marvelling later at Bowles' knowledge of his likes and dislikes requested Bowles as his aide de camp for the duration of his visit.

As he put it to Captain Dawson. "Yes, the young fool may have overstepped the line a bit, but he needs to learn about us Brits. He may have been a bit drunk, but, remember, 'in vino veritas'. He was honest, and he spoke up. I'll give him a try. After all, he's got a lot of enthusiasm, and if he's willing, he'll do fine. Hire for attitude, train for skill, I always say. It's self-evident."

Later in the mess, Dawson repeated that to Lieutenant Colonel Schultzberger. Jackrabbit replied, "What's self-evident is that the pair of them are a perfect match. As for attitude and skill, that's what the bugger's got, Patrick, an attitude, and Bowles sure as hell, lacks the skills. According to The Top Dog's employee prerequisites, Bowles is the perfect candidate."

"And something else, sir,...I've a feeling that Bowles has dropped us into it again."

"Good, I'll be glad to have you all join me in it. But what is it this time?"

"It's The Top Dog, sir. Bowles told him about it?"

"About what, Pat? Don't be obtuse, boy. You've been hanging around Bowles too much. Spit it out."

Yes, sir, I mean, no sir. What I do mean is that Bowles has let him know that we call the Colonel in Chief of the Regiment, 'The Top Dog'."

"Ah, so the cat or the dog as the case may be, is out of the bag, so to speak?"

Dawson, as the Honorary Colonel of the Regiment's aide, was pleased about Bowles appointment. Since some cock-up had meant that The Top Dog had no aide assigned, the Honorary Colonel had offered Dawson as a stand in. Which was kind of him, but he kept Dawson as his own aide, giving poor Patrick twice the duties. Dawson was glad to have someone take over the duties of the Top Dog's aide; anyone but that is, Bowles. Even though it saved him some work, he knew that disaster would be the consequence.

CHAPTER 25

JACKRABBIT MEETS MILES IN THE MESS

Monday morning arrived at The Depot to find the commandant's seat empty. Later that afternoon, Major David Smith, a senior major from the second battalion was installed as the new commandant. He would be promoted as soon as Dillingham's resignation registered on the Regimental Executive. Smith was an older major, well-liked by the troops; who he ensured were well looked after. Consequently, because he refused to see the regimental system as a series of stepping stones to the rank of brigadier, with the soldiers' heads as the stones, he had been left for dead in his current rank.

It's been said that you can have a successful military career in one of two ways. The first invariably led you up the rank structure where you ended up as a public success. Success in the second way was not usually that obvious and often the only recognition came from the men who said, "He was a good soldier."

Method number one meant look after yourself, get the courses you need, do the time, get the rank and never, ever, ever rock the regimental boat; especially if it was for one of the men.

Option number two was to be as good a soldier as the men who followed you, be firm, be fair, but all costs look after the men. Major Smith had chosen number two and had never regretted it. He had refused to play the promotion game, and it had cost him, but he was still able to look himself in the eye every morning as he shaved.

His cross-posting from support company of the second battalion as a company commander to commandant of The Depot was a surprise to everyone including himself. To discover the reason we have to go into the officers' mess just after coffee break on Tuesday and listen in on Colonel Schultzberger of the First Battalion and his counterpart, Colonel Miles Jefferson, Commanding Officer of the Second Battalion.

Schultzberger was one of the few good officers to surmount the huge obstacle of getting past the rank of major and he had been observing Major Smith's career. In fact, they had been through officer training as subalterns together. "Smitty" had all the right moves, intelligent, tough, big and strong; John Wayne in a kilt was how one officer described him.

"Smitty, as commandant? Are you mad, Jackrabbit?" said Colonel Jefferson.

"Miles, he's perfect. And he deserves a shot."

"He'll never get past the Regimental Executive."

"Regimental Mafia, you mean. Well, he will if we support him and if we put a man in before they nominate some weasel."

Colonel Jefferson started to object, but Schultzberger cut him off, "I know he's had his copy book blotted but tell me truly, isn't he the best officer in your battalion?"

He stared at Jackrabbit. "I couldn't support him. He's been bounced to many times and Colonel Sanderson's got it in for him."

"Sand Pebbles had it in for him because Smitty stood up to him over the court martial of Lance Corporal Murray....And Smitty was right. The lancejack was innocent."

"But...But..."

"But me no buts, Miles. Let me tell you something about Sand Pebbles. He's not just pissed off because of that, he's also pissed off because Smitty married his daughter. He had told her she'd marry someone with a career in front of him. She defied her father. Smitty and Joanne eloped. Now Smitty suffers. Is that fair?"

"No..."

"Look, Miles, here's what we'll do. I'll formally ask you for a major because it's my turn to supply the commandant to The Depot. That will leave me one major short. When word gets out that Smitty has been shifted laterally to another battalion, Sanderson will be ecstatic. He'll think Smitty's done for."

"Well..."

"Miles, it's perfect. You get to promote a deserving captain. The regimental executive will think I'm sending a major of mine to The Depot. But I'll send Smitty. You'll be in the clear. I've already got the Honorary Colonel on my side. That's all there is to it."

"Risky. But what about you? You'll bring down the wrath of Sand Pebbles on your head."

"No problem, I've got Bowles to take care of my career. Whatever Sanderson does to me will be a vacation compared to what Lieutenant Arthur Victor Llewellyn Bowles is going to be doing to my battalion. So, all alright? Good, it's settled. Cross-post Smitty to me effective yesterday. I'll take care of the rest."

"Yesterday?"

"Yeah, that way I can get him on strength today and posted to The Depot tomorrow."

"But he's on leave, he won't be back until the end of the month. The depot can't run for that long without a commandant."

"Wrong, Miles. Smitty's already in The Depot. I called him off leave Sunday and had him report to The Depot yesterday afternoon."

"You what? But...But...But..."

"Miles, you're right, The Depot, especially with all this fuss and the Top Dog and the Honorary Colonel being here, The Depot can't afford to be without a head at this time. And....You are agreed, right. Thanks. See you later, Miles."

Jefferson had a last comment, "Jackrabbit, if you were any more devious, you'd be Prime Minister.

Colonel Schultzberger drained his coffee, said, "Thank you, Miles."

He stood up, shook the crumbs from his kilt, adjusted his sporran and left the mess whistling "Highland Laddie". A sergeant he passed on his way to his office tossed him a salute. Jackrabbit waved his ash plant walking stick, said, "Good day, Sergeant," and continued on with his whistling. The sergeant dared not tell him that the tune he was joyfully, but tonelessly whistling was a regimental march of their hated rivals, The Black Watch.

CHAPTER 26

COLONEL ST. CLAIRE MEETS HIS MATCH

Meanwhile, unbeknownst to me at the time, back in The Depot, Toby had become a hero. To these young lads, from all over Canada and new to the army and its ways, having an Earl as an acquaintance was a very big deal. To have that Earl, as a private soldier sleeping in the lower bunk in your room was a bigger deal. When said Earl has done time in the "digger" it was the ultimate big deal. And they were a part of it.

As Offside put it when Toby returned to quarters. "Squire, you were a novelty just cause none of us could pronounce your name. Now, I reckon you've turned this camp on its head."

Which was a bit of an understatement, but was entirely on the right track.

Only thirty-six hours after Jackrabbit and Miles had finished their little chat, the General in charge of the army had been in his office in Ottawa, having a quick one with his aide, Colonel Malcolm St. Claire, when word of Toby's exploits reached him. His comments echoed McGuffin's. "Why that little bastard's turned the entire military on its arse!"

"Pardon, sir, but it's little Honourable Bastard or words to that effect," said St. Claire.

"Who gives a shit, Malcolm? Get a rocket off to whoever is his CO and have the right Honourable son of a bitch released this minute!"

"He's got no CO, sir. He's in the CMSR Depot. Word is that The Depot commandant just resigned."

The Colonel, an infantryman by background, seconded from one of the western battalions had kept up on the infantry gossip through his many contacts.

"I'd bet my bottom dollar that their Honorary Colonel, the one with the name no one can pronounce is at the bottom of that."

The Colonel nodded. "Colonel Posadieukiewicz." The General glared at him. "No one likes a smart ass, Malcolm."

The Colonel smiled. "I worked with him many years ago. Trick is to not try and see the name in your mind when you pronounce it. Posadieukiewicz."

"Never mind. I'll be he had something to do with that."

"I'd say so as well, sir."

The General went on, "No matter, who do you know down there who's reliable?"

"There's Jackrabbit, sir. Lieutenant Colonel Schultzberger of the First CMSR."

"Excellent, Malcolm, excellent. Tell Jackrabbit, personally from you to him, with him knowing full well we'll support him in his decision… tell him to find a replacement for the commandant."

"Right."

"And then as his first job as the commandant have the guy, I don't care who he is, have him promoted to lieutenant colonel and have him kick that fucking limey the hell out of camp, the hell out of my Army, and if possible, have the little prick deported the hell out of Canada!"

"Roger that, sir," said Colonel St. Claire, who only intended to get the Earl released from the army.

It would seem that Lieutenant Colonel 'Jackrabbit' Schultzberger was not only blessed with common sense, but he also seemed to have the gift of prophecy. Colonel St. Claire called him right away. He was even prepared for Jackrabbit's response.

"Hello, Jackrabbit, it's Malcolm St. Claire. How are you?"

"Malcolm, don't even talk to me. You've called me three times in the last year. Not once was it good news. You're the military version of the Grim Reaper. Usually, it's been Bowles, but he's been quiet or at least relatively quiet. Or maybe I should say that he's been no bother to me since I sent him to The Depot. This call is for me to promote him, right? And then put him in as my own second in command?"

"Jackrabbit, Jackrabbit, don't be so suspicious. I'm actually calling with some good news."

"Malcolm, unless you're calling to tell me you're retiring, there is no good news."

St. Claire laughed, just to show he was one of the boys. "Not yet, but when I do, I'll recommend you as my replacement."

"Just try it, Malcolm. You'll be dead before your resignation letter hits the General's desk."

"Go easy, Jackrabbit, the General's a good guy. He wants what's good for the army. But never mind, I've news that won't keep. We've heard Dillingham's gone, that true?"

"Malcolm, you amaze me. That news is barely out of the mess. How do you do it? Never mind, you'll only lie to me. Let me tell you how your intelligence system works. You got it from the RSM of the army, Foxworth, who got it from RSM McKindly, correct?"

"No names, no pack drill, Jackrabbit. But, Dilly-Dally's gone, and that's a roger?"

"It's a roger, Malcolm."

"Good. Good for us. Good for the army. And good for the CMSR and finally, good for all those recruits he's been tyrannizing."

"Spit it out, Malcolm, don't spin it out. And for a change, give me the catch first."

"No catch, Jackrabbit, the General wants a commandant in The Depot right away."

"No catch? Since when does the General of the Army begin interfering with the command and control of the Infantry recruit depots? I thought that was reserved for lowly clerks."

"Yeah, usually, but we are also aware that you have got your Colonel-in-Chief over for a visit, as well as having Posadieukiewicz wandering around the place offering unwanted advice to all ranks. The General's concerned with you lot keeping all the command positions in place while a visiting dignitary is in town, so he's offered to help."

"How?'

"He'll let whoever I suggest in the CMSR pick the new commandant. I suggested you, and he went along with it."

Jackrabbit coughed. He took a sip of cold coffee, choked again and said, "You're offering to let me pick the next depot commandant? No strings?"

In Ottawa, Colonel St. Claire cleared his throat, took a sip of cold coffee, choked and went on, "Can't you think of anyone?"

"Sure I can, but this is the job of the regimental executive. They'll be on me with the muzzle velocity of a rabid cobra if I select someone."

"Nope. You pick the man. I'll promote him effectively today to lieutenant colonel. The General will send an order to the president of your regimental executive backing it up. End of story. You like?"

"I love it. But, just so I understand, I pick the man?"

"Jackrabbit, you pick the man. I promote the man, and the General approves the man. Over and out."

"You're on, Malcolm. Give me two hours, and I'll call you back."

"Roger, but Jackrabbit, that's all I can give you. The General wants this done by the end of the day, Ottawa time. Goodbye." He hung up.

Less than an hour later, Lieutenant Colonel Schultzberger was still doing a jig of delight when the phone rang.

"You sneaky, no-good, low-down, doubling-dealing, skirt-wearing Polack!"

"Malcolm, you sound a mite distressed."

"Distressed? Foxworth just met me in the hall. He tells me that you've already put Major Smith in The Depot as commandant. Tells me you've been wheeling and dealing with Miles Jefferson, without any authorization. Who do you think you are? The Career Manager?"

"Whoa, slow up, Malcolm. All I've done was do exactly as you wanted me to do. I just did it a bit before you knew what it was you wanted to do."

"Oh...Yeah, I guess so." St. Claire began laughing. "Jackrabbit, my boy, you are one tricky son of a gun."

"It takes one to know one, Malcolm."

"What's that supposed to mean?"

"Your little explanation about the General's overwhelming concern about the CMSR. Now all I want to hear is the other shoe dropping. I know it's up there, hanging. Remember, Malcolm, never shit a shitter."

St. Claire laughed. "Fine, there is one small task that the General wants taken care of..."

"In our depot?"

"Yes, but it's harmless."

Jackrabbit immediately thought of Bowles and suspected a trap. The real thing was an anti-climax.

"The General wants that kid, the British Earl, released."

"The Earl? Fits-something. Yeah, he's the one who precipitated all this. Your boss wants him out, eh?"

"Yes. Feels that with his title he's a potential publicity problem. Could lead to all kinds of newspaper nonsense."

Schultzberger, already aware from Captain Patrick Dawson, the Top Dog's aide, that it was rumoured Toby wanted out, decided to play this for all it was worth.

"Look, Malcolm, this could be a problem in itself."

"Jackrabbit, we had a deal."

"Nope, no deal. I was to pick my man. And I'm not saying that it can't be done, just that it might be difficult. If this kid joined up to serve his Queen and we toss him out, it could do the very thing you say the General wants to avoid – become a publicity nightmare. It has to be handled carefully. I'm going to do the best I can, but I need your support."

"Sounds like Jackrabbit's setting me up for more favours. And after I've just done you the biggest favour of your career. I'm letting you pick the commandant."

"No, that's already been done. All I'm getting out of this is you and your Boss's influence to make the promotion stick. There was a good chance that I would have gotten the regiment's approval on my own."

More like a fat chance, Jackrabbit thought. This backing by St. Claire and the General was a godsend, but I'm damned if I'll let them know that.

"Jackrabbit, remember your own words a while ago? Never shit a shitter. What's the catch?"

"Well, I don't need a favour right now, but if I do, you'll come through for me if I help Smitty get the Earl out of the army, Okay?"

"Roger. But only a little favour."

Then St. Claire let Jackrabbit know that he knew just how slim Jackrabbit's chance of getting regimental approval for Smitty was. "By the way, how's Sanderson going to take Smitty's promotion?"

Jackrabbit recognized the ploy but ignored it. "Not well, but, but he'll toe the line once the regimental executive gets the General's message. That's all we need now, Malcolm, a message from the General, a fully classified message promoting Smitty, substantiated, on my desk tomorrow?"

"That's the favour? Jackrabbit, that's a bit of a rush. Gonna need at least a week."

"A week…" Jackrabbit paused. "Very well, Malcolm. Me and Smitty should have the limey kid released in about six weeks."

"Blackmail…"

"You said something, Malcolm?"

"Okay, okay, promotion message tomorrow, Kid out in a week, deal?"

"Deal. Thanks, Malcolm."

Both of them hung up.

CHAPTER 27

THE COMMANDANT MEETS AN EARL

Almost instantly the entire depot knew of Lieutenant Colonel Dillingham's departure and of Lieutenant Colonel Smith taking the helm. And aside from all the rumours, they knew very little of the whole truth.

Toby's squad was undergoing bayonet training when he was called to the commandant's office. Until that moment Toby heard nothing regarding how the army was reacting to his being an Earl, being in jail, or anything else to do with Lance Corporal Ollie.

Ollie had been released from the hospital and been sent on leave wearing a neck brace. Along with his leave pass, he was carrying a posting message. Once he recovered from his injuries, he was to report to a military installation on the Dew Line, at Cambridge Bay, in the Northwest Territories in Canada's high arctic.

The summons came as Toby and Stuffy were paired off and sparring with each other. Stuffy held his FNC1 rifle, ten pounds with a fully loaded magazine, and attached bayonet. Toby held a broom handle that had a wire loop at one end and a padded boxing glove-like apparatus on the other end. When the two combatants came together, they would stand at the alert position facing one another. At a whistle blast from one of the lance corporals, the trainer, in this case, Toby, would feint with the padded end, smash up against Stuffy's rifle and then quickly twist the broom handle to bring the looped end around and offer it to one side of his body for Stuffy to try and spear with his bayonet.

If he missed, as Stuffy always did, the trainer would swiftly twist the broom again and give the unfortunate Stuffy a sharp jab with the glove. After a number of minutes of this, the combatants would change around. Toby being naturally quick was able to spear the loop or recover quickly enough to fend off Stuffy's blow.

In fact, while Toby was showing excellent potential as a bayonet fighter, he was also letting his natural abilities take over. As he had told me, "I'm kind of glad that I can drop this bad attitude that I had been lugging around. It was hard playing dumb or doing dopey things to try and get thrown out of the army ."

"I agree, young, sir. And from what I've seen you have the making of a real squaddie."

"Squaddie?"

"A member of an infantry battalion rifle squad, sir."

"Ah, a rifle section. We call them infanteers or riflemen, Ox."

"Just so, sir, infanteers it is then."

As Sergeant Clyde ambled over to where Toby and Stuffy were sparring he too noticed how in a few short days the once useless British recruit had blossomed. He was already shaping up as one of his best recruits.

"Squire, hold up a sec. Give him a break. Stuffy's already sweated ten pounds off, and he's yet to even see the loop."

The boys stopped, Stuffy grateful for the break.

"Drop the stick, Squire, sort yourself out and then head up to The Depot orderly room. You're wanted by the commandant. Leave your rifle, helmet, and webbing here. Put on your balmoral and hurry it up."

"Yes, Sergeant, any idea why?"

"Nope, maybe the Queen wants you to go home and take over the British army, now that we've shown you how to do it. Nip along, lad. It's not a good plan to keep the commandant waiting."

Toby made his way smartly along the road, enjoying the freedom of not marching in a group, and of not having to hear, 'eft, right, 'eft, right.'

The sun was out, the sky was blue, the birds were twittering, and Toby was feeling pretty good about the world in general. He had never realized how much fun it was being a soldier. Sure, there was a ton of things not to like; such as shining boots, floors, and brass incessantly. Getting up at zero dark thirty was becoming easier, and with the busy, challenging schedule, even the food was tasting better. The chaps, or rather, the guys, he ran with were splendid or cool depending on one's background. Even the non-stop raving by anyone with a stripe or two had taken on the air of a joke. Life was good. As he, marched along, arms swinging breast pocket high, Toby realized he loved the army. Keeping his word to his father was going to be a piece of cake.

On his arrival at headquarters, Toby was escorted to a spot opposite two closed doors in the long, dim, hallway. He stood at ease and while he wondered what was going on stared at the door across the corridor. Its door showed off a brass plate that read, WO 1 G.U.F. McKindly, RSM.

Other than one parade, where the RSM had halted in front of him to tell him his boots needed work, Toby had never seen RSM McKindly before. Toby knew that the senior recruits called him Un-Fucking Kindly, but whether that was due to some sinister, well-deserved reputation or just because they liked the name, he never knew.

He was about to find out. The other door had a dusty, blank space that he guessed had once held Colonel Travis Dillingham's nameplate. As a loud stamp of cleated-boots, and an even louder, "Yes sir," rang out, the unmarked door flew open.

Out came McKindly, all arms, legs, and swirling kilt. Deep blue eyes, sharper even than my own, razor-pierced Toby and impaled him on the wall. McKindly's blonde, heavily waxed moustache quivered as he screamed at Toby, "Get your heels together, Laddie! Look sharp. The commandant's waiting on your Lordship's pleasure."

Toby snapped to attention, eyes front and waited. With a "Quick march, left, right, left," Toby and the RSM performed the usual dance steps. The performance ended with Toby at attention on one side of the desk, acting Lieutenant Colonel Smith seated on the other and the RSM three paces to Toby's right rear.

"RSM, you may leave us. Have the clerk bring in two coffees. That will be all, thank you."

Toby was sure that the next sound he heard was the RSM's mouth dropping open and his chin hitting his glossy toe-caps.

"Beg pardon, sir?"

"You heard me, RSM, carry on."

Like all RSMs, some gene they carried or from some skill developed in RSM school, McKindly was pretty much unflappable. Even in this case, where he had been caught napping, he made a snappy recovery. "Cream and sugar in both, sir? Won't be but a moment, sir."

Toby heard the crackle of a starched shirt, a pause, 2, 3...more crackle...2, 3...Turn, 2, 3...Stomp, door opening. Door shutting. Toby and the Commandant were alone.

"Please be seated, Private Trelauney-Fitzgibboncrest."

"Yes, sir."

Toby glanced around the small office and saw his choice lay in the usual army issue imitation Naugahyde arm chair, of which there were two, one red, the other green. The only other chair in the room was an upright wooden-style interrogation chair.

He chose the red armchair and sat on the edge, as close to attention as he could.

"Private Trelauney-Fitzgibboncrest, while I recognize that you are a peer, I am also cognizant of the equal fact that you are also doing service for Her Majesty in the uniform of a private in Her Canadian Army. So I'll address you as that. Any problem?"

"No, sir, I accept that as a logical solution."

"Good. And why do you think I asked to see you?"

"I thought it was because of my performance to date, sir.. ..But now, being invited to sit and..."

A knock on the door stopped him. "Williams, here, sir."

"Enter."

A lance corporal came in bearing a tray with two coffee mugs, an opened tin of canned milk and what looked like a smoke grenade canister, which turned out to be just that, although it had been astoundingly transformed into a sugar bowl. Williams placed the tray on the Major's desk, saluted and left.

"Help yourself, Trelauney-Fitzgibboncrest," said Major Smith as he reached for a cup himself. "And do go on."

"Well, sir," Toby said as he fixed his coffee up and returned to his seat. "This does not appear to be a situation where I am about to receive a reprimand."

"No, son, you're right, it isn't. I'm the one who has to tell you that we are releasing you from the army. By next Thursday you'll have achieved your aim— you'll be a civvy again. Although why you ever volunteered to join, I'll never figure out."

"My aim, sir?"

"Yes, I'm well aware of your dislike of the military and your avid desire to get kicked out." Smitty picked up a file folder. "It's all in here, lad. Even the times where inexplicably you shone...And of course, your bad attitude and low marks."

Toby gulped. This was not in the plan. "But my marks have been good these last two weeks."

"Good? Your last four tests were perfect. Four straight 100's. Not bad for someone who scored twelve out of a hundred on map symbols three weeks ago." Smitty paused, sipped coffee and said, "I find it hard to believe you cheated; do you care to tell me what's going on?"

"Cheated? Not a chance, sir. Those tests are all simple. It's just that I wanted to do poorly, to get punted."

"So why the sudden change?"

Toby stared at the Commandant for a long time. "I've changed my mind. I want to be a soldier." He swallowed again. "At least for the next three years."

"Really, why's that then?"

"I can't say. I can tell you that I have to stay. I have to complete. Don't just look at my marks, sir. Check the weekly write-ups by my Lance Corporal. Ask the platoon sergeant, all the lancejacks. They'll tell you I've straightened out." Toby sat up straighter. "I'm a soldier now."

"Yes, well, that may be, but the fact remains, you've a nasty record and based on that I don't see you as being fit for the army."

Smitty realized that while not actually lying, he was not being totally accurate. And, he noted, not being true to himself. Yes, Trelauney-Fitzgibboncrest's record was dismal until about two or three weeks ago, and Smitty guessed that this miraculous change must have occurred about the time I had arrived on the scene.

"Trelauney-Fitzgibboncrest, is it my imagination that your turn around from being the most rotten soldier in the world to suddenly becoming the new Montgomery had something to do with the arrival of your civilian batman?"

"My what, sir? Oh, Ox? He's my gentleman's gentleman." Toby went into stare mode again, then said slowly, "I suppose so, although through it all I did rather like this life. The chaps are splendid. I mean, the guys are pretty neat. And I do so much need to stay in the army, sir."

Smitty looked over at his filing cabinet. It offered no assistance, so he shifted his gaze back to the mournful young man in the large ugly chair. He let out a huge gush of air and made his decision. "Okay, here's how it is. You come clean with me all the way. No holding back and I'll give it to you straight from my end. Deal?"

Toby thought it over. After all, there had been no oaths of silence, no deathbed promises, least ways not from him in regard to how he got here or why he needed to stay.

"Righto, sir. I'll give you the lot." And he did. When he was done, Smitty said, "Thanks, son. I appreciate your honesty, and I would guess that you have emptied the bag." He grinned at Toby. "No one makes up a story about a Judge and his wife playing the Lone Ranger meets the Silent Lady."

Toby nodded and smiled back, then Smitty said, "Now it's my turn and what you've told me makes it that much harder for me to come clean with you. Your story explains a lot. But it looks like it's a bit too late."

Toby's face lost its smile, and his shoulders dropped. He knew he was not going to get good news.

"Private Trelauney-Fitzgibboncrest, what do the soldiers call you?"

"My chums and even the Squad staff call me Squire, but my family calls me Toby."

"Well, Squire I can understand, but if it's alright with you, I'll call you Toby. Toby nodded.

"Okay, Toby, no holds barred. The Army wants you out. You, your gentleman's gentleman, and your title are an embarrassment to the brass in Ottawa. One of the conditions under which I was put in this job was that I get rid of you. When I saw your personnel file, I figured it was going to be an easy job."

"But now?"

"No change really. But since we are being honest, even with your lousy marks, bad attitude, and intense desire to get out, had all that belonged to an average, everyday Canadian kid, we would have at worst only back-squadded him. We'd see it as a challenge to get him through The Depot." Smitty stopped then went on, "You do know what back-squadding is, don't you?'

"Yes. We have a guy who was back-squadded from two platoons in front of us."

Smitty went on, "So…What do we do with you? There's got to be something."

"You mean I'm not going to be kicked out?"

"Well, it is my job or one of them. But I've never yet let my career stand in the way of looking after my men." Smitty shrugged. "And when I inherited The Depot, I inherited you. So, I'm stuck with you, and you're stuck with me."

"Thank you, sir."

"Don't thank me yet. All that may happen is that I get kicked out alongside you." Smitty grinned again. "Got any openings for another gentleman's gentleman?"

Toby laughed at the idea of Smitty trying to do Ox's job. "No, sir, but maybe, if you've any experience in coaching volleyball, I do know a team that needs help."

And then Toby told him of the train trip.

Smitty listened intently, and his only reaction was both a tightening of his eyes and his sphincter whenever Bowles' name was mentioned. They enjoyed the story together and then Smitty said, "I may have an out for us. Report back to your Squad and tell Sergeant Clyde I want Lieutenant Bowles here at sixteen hundred hours this afternoon. As for you, be back here tomorrow at ten hundred...And bring that gentleman's gentleman of yours. Got it?"

Toby, seeing the interview was over, stood up. "Yes, sir, got it. Squad commander here sixteen hundred, Ox and I here tomorrow, ten hundred. And thank you, sir."

He saluted, Smitty rose and came over and held out his hand. "It's not over yet, Private Trelauney-Fitzgibboncrest, now off you go."

CHAPTER 28

BOWLES MEETS TOBY AGAIN

Toby left the commandant's office a trifle upset. He headed back to the parade square to join the squad in what was left of a drill period. As he marched along, preoccupied with this new problem, but arms still breast pocket high to the front and no bend in the elbows, he didn't notice his squad commander and his driver going past him in the duty officer's jeep.

Toby barely registered on Bowles' mind, but then he realized that he had allowed a private soldier to pass him by without saluting. "Can't allow that, eh, old son," he muttered to himself. "Driver, halt."

The jeep slowed, stopped. Bowles hopped out onto the sidewalk and bellowed at the retreating uniform, "You, Soldier! Come here this minute."

Toby surfaced, shook his head and turned around to see his squad commander yelling at him. He tucked his elbows in, pulled his fists up to his pockets and smartly, in the correct manner, double timed up to Bowles. Halting the required two paces in front of him, Toby saluted.

"Yes, sir?"

"You didn't salute me."

"Yes I did, sir. But you haven't returned it."

"No, no, I mean while I was driving by."

"That's alright, sir, the driver of a motor vehicle is not required to salute, it's part of our General Service Knowledge, sir. But since you are no longer driving, you can return my salute."

This stumped Bowles. "I wasn't driving. What the blazes are you on about?"

"Well, sir, I just saluted you, and you haven't returned my salute. That's against regulations."

"No, no, no. You didn't salute me first. You're supposed to salute me."

"I just did, sir. And you still haven't saluted me. I'm afraid that I'll have to put in a report to The Depot sergeant-major."

"You can't put in a report on me, I'm an officer. And anyway, I'm putting in a report on you for not saluting me."

"But I just saluted you. As an officer you are supposed to set an example, isn't that right?"

"Yes, of course. And I am also supposed to correct young recruits who don't do things they are supposed to do."

"Yes, sir, I understand, and that's why I want to ask you a question."

"Very well, go ahead."

"When a private comes up to an officer and salutes that officer, isn't the officer supposed to salute the private in return?"

"Yes."

"And officers are not supposed to tell lies are they?"

"No, of course not."

"Then I'll ask you another question. When I ran over to you did you see me salute you?"

"Yes, you're supposed to salute me, I'm an officer."

"Then if I saluted you how can you put me on report for not saluting you when you just admitted that I did salute you?"

"That's a good question. Hey, don't I know you?"

"Yes, I'm Trelauney-Fitzgibboncrest. I'm in your Squad."

Toby did not want to remind Bowles of their mutual acquaintanceship aboard the train.

"Ah, ah. I thought I recognized you. Yes, of course, you're the one impersonating a duke. Good God! How could I have not recognized you? The rocket launcher range, right?"

"Yes, sir and the death slide."

"Oh, yes, how silly of me. I should know my own men, shouldn't I?"

"Yes, sir."

"And you were the one responsible for the firing of Lieutenant Colonel Dillingham."

"I had nothing to do with that, sir."

"Fine, let's get back to why we are here…" Bowles looked lost then a spark struck and he said, "It's to do with you pretending to be a Duke, right?"

"An Earl, sir."

"Alright, impersonating an Earl. Doesn't matter, one impersonation is as good as another. But then again, I guess that's why the impersonation worked, isn't it? It was better than any other. And that fake manservant you got? Is he an Earl, too?"

"No, he's a gentleman's gentleman."

"He's a gentleman's gentleman impersonating a manservant. Not very imaginative of him was it? At least you're impersonating some high-priced nobleman." Bowles laughed. "Imagine that, a manservant impersonating a butler."

"A gentleman's gentleman, sir. Ox is a gentleman's gentleman."

"Ox?"

"Ox, actually, Marvin Oxnard. That's his name. He really is a gentleman's gentleman, and I really am an Earl. Now can we go back to the matter at hand, sir? Are you going to salute me?"

Bowles stepped back as if slapped. "What? An officer returns salutes he doesn't give them. This time you've gone too far. I don't care if you are the Queen of England, as an officer I'm not giving you a salute, even if you are some kind of fake baron."

"I'm an Earl, sir. And I'm not fake. I inherited my father's title, and because of that I'm leaving."

"You can't leave until I dismiss you."

"No, sir, I mean I'm leaving The Depot."

"You can't leave. You haven't finished your training yet."

Bowles leaned forward and wagged a large, skinny finger under Toby's nose in what he must have thought was a menacing manner. To Toby, he looked more like a peevish school marm with a bad case of indigestion.

"Leaving without permission is desertion. If you think that you can desert just to get out of saluting me, you'll be in bigger trouble than you are now."

"I'm not deserting. And I already saluted you, and now I'm going home. The Commandant just told me."

"The Commandant's just new on the job, so don't try dragging his name into this. I happen to know because I'm off to his O group this very minute. In fact, if I don't hurry, I'll be late. Good day."

"But, sir, we have been talking about saluting, and I'm the only one who has saluted. You said you're in a hurry, but so am I and I have to go now, so I'm saluting you now, and I am carrying on." Again he gave a salute, this time putting more drive into it.

"Well, is that so? I'm an officer! I say when you can carry on! I say that you will be standing here until I give the word. Do I make myself clear?"

"Clear as glass, sir. Ever so clear. But I do have one request?"

"What is it?" asked Bowles.

"I would like you to write out and give me a note stating that you kept me here, making me late for Nuclear, Biological, and Chemical and gas mask training because you hauled me over and then refused to salute me."

Bowles glared at Toby. "Mister High and Mighty, some kind of Earl, you remind me of that arrogant British guy I met on the train. Well, I guess you think you're some kind of smart-ass, don't you, eh, private? Well, go on, get out of here. And we call it NBC training."

"Yes, sir, thank you, sir." Toby made as if to go then said, "One more thing, sir?"

"What now?"

"The Commandant wants to see you at 1600 hrs, sir."

"Baloney, I'm off to his O Group. He can see me there. Now, let's look at you. Why aren't you in training?"

"I was on my way when you stopped me. But, sir...You still haven't returned my salute. Should I do it one more time, sir?"

"Don't bother. Here's your salute," Bowles said as his hand went up and down. "Now carry on. But don't think I'm going to forget you."

"Yes, sir," said Toby.

And with that, Bowles saluted.

Toby said, "Carry on."

Bowles nodded, turned and re-turned to his vehicle.

It's so easy, Toby thought as he headed for the parade square.

CHAPTER 29

THE RSM MEETS A PENGUIN

After that day's training, Toby was given leave to find me. He showed up at the back door of the officers' mess while I was at dinner with Cleeves and Chef Jeff. The other cooks had left for the day, the dining room staff had cleaned up and departed, so there was only the three of us drinking coffee, well-laced with brandy. Toby came in and once Cleeves saw who it was, they had a bit of a reunion. with that out of the way, Toby gave me the message and returned to training.

The next morning when Toby arrived at depot headquarters with me in tow, we were ordered to stand outside Lieutenant Colonel Smith's office as Toby had done the day before. Moments later the door opened, and RSM McKindly stuck his head out around the door.

"Right. Get in here, both of you. No, not the penguin first, you, your Majesty, get yer blue-blooded arse in here, then the waiter."

We moved in, Toby saluted, and as his right arm came down, he realized that a crowd had gathered.

"Okay, Smitty, we're all here, let's get this lunacy over with," said a voice from the back corner. Toby turned. Leaning up against the filing cabinet in all his parade finery was Lieutenant Colonel "Jackrabbit" Schultzberger. Quivering beside him and looking about as comfortable as a salmon at a Siamese cat convention, was Lieutenant Bowles. Next to him was The Top Dog, also known as Sir Richard Norbury. When Toby's eyes came to rest on the face of Sir Richard, his Lordship slowly closed one eye in a welcoming wink.

"Gentlemen, please be seated," said Lieutenant Colonel Smith. Once the rustle and scuffle of the seating process had been accomplished, there were two men left standing and two empty chairs. Both the RSM and I remained on our feet.

Toby and Smitty looked at each other. Toby nodded at me and then at a chair. I gave a tiny head shake of refusal. At the same time, Smitty gestured at the other chair, and the RSM grunted his reply. Toby looked at Smitty, Smitty shrugged his shoulders and cleared his throat.

Jackrabbit, seeing the by-play spoke up, "Never mind, Smitty, if those two stiff-necked old warhorses won't sit, hell with them. Get on with the rest of it."

"Yes, sir. As you all know we are here to...What is it, Mr. Bowles?"

"Sir, I guess you had better go over it once again. I think that for me, the penny hasn't dropped yet."

Jackrabbit snorted. "Forget it, Bowles. If a dump truck full of pennies hit you between the eyes, you still wouldn't get it. Sit there and listen. I don't care if you even pay attention. You're only here because when Colonel Smith's brilliant plan is unleashed, I want to be able to blame it on you. Now belt up."

Bowles nodded and turned white.

Toby and Sir Richard appeared shocked, Smitty, well used to Jackrabbit, ignored him. "Here we go, then. First, the army wants Private Trelauney-Fitzgibboncrest released." Smitty stopped and then started again, "In order to save time and me a ton of oxygen, I'll refer to the private in question as 'Toby'. And it is Toby that the army wants done with. Ottawa cannot see us having a member of the British peerage running around Camp Gagetown disguised as a private. Fair enough, except that Toby joined us legitimately, is performing well and is a British citizen. None of which is grounds for giving him the boot. Roger so far?"

"Yep," said Jackrabbit.

"Seems to nicely sum it all up, Colonel Smith," said Sir Richard.

"Roger that," said Toby, wanting to display his knowledge of military jargon.

"Harrumph," said the RSM.

"Correct and succinct," I said.

"I, er..." Bowles, catching Jackrabbit's glare, subsided.

"However," Smitty went on. "We have been ordered to release him. My question to you all, is what do we do now?"

"Does that mean me, too, sir?" said Bowles.

"No, it does not," replied Jackrabbit. "And as to what do we do now, Smitty, I thought that's what this little charade was all about. I thought you already had a solution?"

"Kind of, sir. Plan 'A' was to get you to come over here, get the big picture and go back to Ottawa and tell them it's all off. That a terrible mistake has been made."

Jackrabbit snorted again. "Not a fucking snowball's, Smitty. They want him out and out he's going. That doesn't seem to be an option. What needs to be decided is not if he goes, but how many of us does he take with him." Jackrabbit pointed a finger at Smitty. "You, me, Bowles. That's what we need to decide."

"That's true, Colonel Schultzberger, and I have decided. I am committed to doing everything in my power to ensure that Toby is permitted to serve his three years."

"You may find yourself serving three years with him in the detention barracks in Valcartier. And it's now Toby, eh?"

"An expedient only, sir. As I described earlier, beats the hell out of saying, Recruit Trelauney-Fitzgibboncrest and saves wear and tear on the tongue."

Jackrabbit nodded. "I'd be smart just to bite mine. But you're serious, Smitty, right?"

Without waiting for an answer, Jackrabbit rose up from his chair, drew in a kitbag's worth of air and then slowly and deliberately pounded a huge fist on the corner of Smitty's desk. "I knew you'd be a pain in the ass, Smitty. You always have been. I must have been crazy to get you in here. We've got a solution. We've got things about to get all straightened out. We've got a chance to get out of this entire nightmare without doing anything illegal, time-consuming or frustrating." He stomped over to the filing cabinet and stared at it. Smitty just looked at everyone and grinned. He seemed oblivious to the rage and the remarks, in fact, Toby guessed, Smitty was actually enjoying the Colonel's outburst and discomfort.

Jackrabbit kept his eyes glued to the same filing cabinet that Smitty had stared at yesterday. Getting the same amount of help from it, he snorted again. With his back to the rest of them, he began again. "All sorted out, except that I had to get involved and try to run my own battalion and The Depot as well. I had to go and put in as the new commandant one of the most bothersome, irritating, pig-headed, …."

"Inflexible?" offered Smitty.

"That works," said Jackrabbit. Turning to face the seated men, he said, "Any other suggestions?"

"Mulish?" said Smitty again.

"Obdurate?" I suggested.

"Excellent, any more?"

"Not quite sure what we're doing, sir?" came from Bowles' corner, where he was cowed by Jackrabbit's glare.

"If I may, sir?" said the RSM.

"Go ahead, RSM," said Jackrabbit.

"What about loyalty downwards, sir, or looking after the troops? With all due respect, sir."

Jackrabbit looked at the RSM, then to Smitty, gave a rueful smile and said, "Point taken, RSM. Point taken. And exactly what I would expect from you. And, that's exactly why I'm so pissed off. Because, until you spoke up, no one in authority has been looking after Private Toby here." He pointed with a long arm over at Smitty and said, "Except the RSM and you, too, Smitty. It is, I admit, why I wanted you in here as Commandant. I can't complain when you do what I expected of you, can I?" By this time, Jackrabbit was grinning along with Smitty. "So...It's settled then."

"'Fraid so, sir," said Smitty through his smile.

"Quit sirring me. You may not be wearing three pips and a crown yet, but we're the same rank."

"Right...Colonel," said Smitty.

"Obvious that it needs to be done. Pathetic that it's us who need to do it," Jackrabbit said. "Yes, you son of a bitch, grin at me. Well, I'll be damned if some maverick light colonel's gonna set me an example. And a rookie light colonel at that."

He directed his glare at Toby. "Son, you're gonna remain a jock for at least three years or else there's gonna be two pairs of feet marching alongside yours out that gate to civvy street." He pointed at a wall in the direction of the main gate.

"Jolly good, sir, except for one thing," said Bowles.

The Colonel looked at him. "Well, what is it? Don't tell me you're gonna resign your commission along with us?"

"Oh, no, sir, I couldn't do that. If you and Colonel Smith get kicked out with his Lordship, I'll be needed here. With you both gone there's at least two promotions. What I wanted to say is that the main gate is behind you, not in the direction that you pointed."

Jackrabbit drew an evil breath, expelled it with a loud whoosh. "Thank you, Bowles. Your never-ending assault on stupidity never ceases to amaze me."

"Thank you, sir."

Sir Richard spoke up, "Lieutenant Colonel Schultzberger, if I may?"

"Certainly, your Lordship."

"Thank you. Now the crux of the matter lies in the embarrassing circumstance of the Canadian Army in general and The Caledonia and Musquodoboit Scottish Regiment in particular; in that having within its bastions as a soldier, a private, an untrained recruit at that, who is actually an Earl in Britain. Is that the gist of the problem?"

"That about sums it up. But that's the army's problem. Our problem is that we've been ordered to get rid of the embarrassment."

"Truly. And based on what's been said here today, you and Colonel Smith are having a devil of a time, with your own perception of integrity, or sense of fair play, interfering on a personal level with your complying with that order?"

Jackrabbit answered a bit gruffly, "Not my sense of fair play. I just can't stand to see Colonel Smith make an ass of himself all on his own."

"Yes, quite. Commendable. We understand, Colonel Schultzberger. Be that as it may. Would the solution be rectified if the chappies in Ottawa were to rescind that order?"

"Rescind the order? Not a hope in hell."

"Well, possibly, but in that case, I have a suggestion put to me by Mr. Oxnard that..."

"Mr. Who?" said Jackrabbit.

"Mr. Oxnard, Ox, sir, that's him in the corner. My gentleman's gentleman, sir," said Toby.

"A gentleman's gentleman?" Jackrabbit, Smitty, and the RSM stared at me, and I calmly nodded at no one in general.

"You mean to tell me that Canadian Army policy is about to be dictated by a fucking gentleman's gentleman?. ...No offence, Mr. Oxtail."

"None taken, Colonel, but it's Oxnard."

"Yeah. Oh, hell, what else can happen...Never mind, Bowles, don't even think of answering. Let's hear it, Mr. Oxen."

Toby interrupted, "He answers to Ox, sir, makes it easier."

"Yeah, okay, Ox, give."

"Certainly sir, well it occurred to me that Lord Haselbury's title is a hereditary title and that he is indeed a peer of the realm and also a British citizen."

Schultzberger was getting a bit tired of everyone giving him the entire story every time they had something to say, but held his tongue.

I went on, "As such, he can enlist in the British Army with no limitations, embarrassments, or mortification on the part of Her Majesty."

"I guess it's a bit late to ask why the fuck he didn't do that in the first place," said Jackrabbit.

Smitty, knowing why Toby had enlisted in the Canadian Army said, "Way too late, Colonel. But let's give Ox a shot at this."

Jackrabbit nodded. Smitty said, "Go on, Ox."

A snigger came from Bowles. All eyes turned to him as he giggled and said, "Ox. The Ox and the Earl– great title for a book."

He stopped as everyone stared at him. "Bowles, how does, 'Duty Officer For Life' sound as a book title?" said Smitty.

"Or 'I Was Killed By A Colonel'?" added Jackrabbit.

"Oops."

I mentally shook my head at the antics of the Canadian officers, cleared my throat and continued, "To carry on, gentlemen. If Lord Haselbury had indeed joined the British Army it would have been seen to be meritorious service, and completely and socially acceptable by all members of society."

Bowles couldn't contain himself. "Great. Not only do you want to get him kicked out of the Canadian Army, now you want him to get kicked out of the British Army as well. No wonder they call you Ox. Maybe donkey would be a better name."

Bowles tittered at his own wit. That was it. Jackrabbit had had enough. He moved toward Bowles. Smitty, having seen Jackrabbit hammer two or three subaltern's heads together in a friendly game of touch football, jumped up and stepped between them.

"Mr. Bowles, I'd like to thank you for your contribution this morning. I'm sure we could all benefit from your assistance, but I remember that you have a squad in training. I suggest that you go and locate them. Now."

Smitty turned to the RSM. "Mr. McKindly, escort Lieutenant Bowles out of my office."

With Bowles gone, Sir Richard, shaking his head said, "Remarkable fellow. I rather suppose that your one hope is that he'll mature into a good officer eventually."

"It won't be maturity, with any luck at all we'll get a cross between manure and dry rot as that idiot gets older," said Jackrabbit.

I spoke up, "If I may continue, sir. If Lord Haselbury were to voluntarily leave the Canadian Army…

Toby leaped to his feet, I held up a hand. "A moment, young sir."

Toby sank back into his seat.

"If Lord Haselbury took a voluntary discharge, joined the British Army and was then ordered to Canada as an exchange soldier." I paused. "I believe that policy is still in place?"

"Yes, it is, usually an officer or a senior NCO, but that's not a large obstacle," said Smitty as he looked at Jackrabbit.

"Sounds like a plan. He's released, joins the British Army, arrives here on exchange, completes his training in The Depot, serves his three years on a posting to Canada, and it's all over. And once he's released voluntarily, I doubt if the brass in Ottawa much care what happens to him."

I nodded. "Yes, and it can all be done without him leaving Canada or Camp Gagetown for that matter."

"Correct," broke in Sir Richard. "I have already called our Ambassador in Ottawa. He is prepared to underwrite the whole scheme on one condition."

"I knew there'd be a catch," said Jackrabbit. "What's this bird want us to do? Promote Bowles to Captain?"

"Nothing so expensive or foolhardy. All that is required is that within six months of completion of Lord Haselbury's basic training that he be placed on a Junior NCO course. If he places in the top three candidates, then he can be selected for officer training. He could then return to England as a Lieutenant."

Smitty said, "It just might work."

Toby stared at the Top Dog. Nothing had been said to him in regards to the Junior NCO course or officer training.

Jackrabbit laughed. "Ox, you're a genius. You gotta meet my wife. And, I take it all back, maybe we should have a gentleman's gentleman running the Canadian Army." He turned to Smitty. "Well, Commandant, what the hell are you standing around for? Get this man released immediately, he needs to be an exchange soldier by supper time."

And so it was done. Not that quickly, but a week later Toby's release documents had been sent to Ottawa, and as far as Colonel St. Claire and the rest of the brass was concerned, the Earl was out.

Jackrabbit did neglect to inform him that that 'Limey Bastard' was at the very time of their telephone call engaged in marksmanship training on one of the many rifle ranges in Camp Gagetown. No one bothered to tell Toby that as a member of the British Army he was expected to dress in their uniforms. And no one bothered to tell the British Army where Toby was, just that he had enlisted and that his pay was to be sent to a bank in London.

Once this had been sorted out, Sir Richard visited the newly-promoted Commandant of The Caledonia and Musquodoboit Scottish Regiment Depot in the fond hopes of being assigned another, very different, aide. Smitty tried to be helpful. First, he requested that Bowles be returned to his battalion.

Jackrabbit replied that while Smitty may be a lieutenant colonel now, there are some requests that beg to be refused, this being one of them. As well, Jackrabbit stated very firmly that until there was a way of returning the stupid bastard to the womb, he was staying where he was. At least until he had completed training the squad of recruits he had been assigned to look after.

Smitty, figuring half a Bowles was better than a whole, went back to Sir Richard and told him that the best he could do, since no one else was available was to share Bowles with him. Smitty would get him during the day time, Sir Richard in the evenings.

Sir Richard protested that he couldn't bear to have that "remarkable young man" around him for that length of time as he had just extended his stay until September.

Smitty said so sorry, and that September was when Bowles' squad was scheduled to graduate so both he and Sir Richard would suffer together until then. Smitty was determined that on Bowles' completion of his tour as a depot squad commander, he would be shipped back to Jackrabbit, forever.

CHAPTER 30

THE DEPOT OFFICERS MEET SMITTY

With the Earl's situation sorted out, Lieutenant Colonel David Smith turned his attention to running The Depot. No one mentioned what I was to do, or where I was to reside, so I promptly shifted bag and baggage back upstairs in The Depot.

Lieutenant Colonel David Smith to celebrate, held an Orders Group or O Group of all his officers. These worthies, all surprised at Smitty's appointment, included the Deputy Commandant, Major Phil Ascot-Gray, who had not expected to get the nod as the new Commandant. He had been around as long as had Smitty, and in fact, they were the best of friends. Along with him, there was The Depot Adjutant; the Training Officer; a Supply Officer and the eight lieutenants who were temporarily posted in to command the recruit platoons. The meeting was short and to the point.

"Welcome, Gentleman, I won't keep you. As you all know, I am the new Commandant appointed by Colonel Schultzberger. I was posted from the Second Battalion to the First Battalion and then from there to here. My promotion may be confirmed by the regimental executive, or I'll be replaced. Until that happens, I am the Commandant."

He looked around the room at all the faces staring back him then continued, "The first matter is for all of you to get back to into your routines as soon as possible. I'll be spending a week or so getting reacquainted with The Depot. Keep doing what you've been doing or if it's illegal, immoral, or unfair to the soldiers stop it immediately. Train them hard, but be fair."

He looked around again, stopping to stare at one or two Lieutenants he knew from hearsay who had been shirking or taking advantage. He then shifted his gaze until it rested on the vast wasteland that was the face of Lieutenant Bowles. "Mr. Bowles."

"Sir."

"In regard to your squad's particular situation, here is what will happen. Private Trelauney-Fitzgibboncrest will remain with your squad until I tell you differently. As for his gentleman's gentleman, he'll remain upstairs in The Depot quarters. I have already spoken to him. He'll also limit his gentleman's gentleman duties to those that he and I both think Private Trelauney-Fitzgibboncrest as an Earl is entitled to. That and nothing more."

Smitty looked around, took a sip of his coffee and began again, "With all that out of the way, let's get on with the job...Let's get these lads trained." Half turning to the Deputy Commandant, Major Ascot-Grey, he said, "Phil, am I correct in thinking that The Depot will send a squad or two to the First Battalion to participate in the brigade concentration?"

Major Ascot-Grey nodded. "Yes, sir, we're expected to send three squads, generally those close to graduating, but they have to have had some training in basic tactics and section battle drills."

"Okay, so looking at the training schedule, we'll have Squads 1311, 1312 and....." He stopped, realizing that the third Squad, 1313 would be the one commanded by Lieutenant Bowles.

Bowles didn't hesitate. "And Squad 1313, sir, my squad."

"Yes..." Smitty said very slowly, thinking hard of how to avoid what he saw as a replay of a military catastrophe combining Custer's Last Stand, Napoleon's Retreat from Moscow and an afternoon with the Three Stooges. Then again, he thought, the silver lining in this will be handing Bowles back to Jackrabbit for two to three weeks. That was worth it. But he needed to be sure the squad would be ready.

"Yes, Mr. Bowles, yes. But will they be ready? Perhaps we should send only two Squads."

"Oh, no, sir, my Squad will be ready. We'll be in Week Thirteen by then, all section tactics will have been covered."

"Week Thirteen? Sounds too soon to me, what sayest thou, Phil?"

The Deputy Commandant saw an opportunity to give Smitty a bit of a hard time. They had golfed together this past weekend, and Smitty had taken a few bucks from him. This was a chance to gently nudge the new commandant. He knew from talk in the mess that no matter what Bowles did, no one else would be held accountable for his actions and there would be no repercussions. Knowing that Smitty would not be tarred with the same brush as Bowles he grinned and said, "Week Thirteen's usually very good, sir. We've sent Squads with only nine weeks under their belts. We've given them a crash course in section battle drills and off they went. Accounted for themselves quite admirably. Lieutenant Bowles has some very good instructors with him. I'll bet they do just fine, sir."

Smitty knew exactly what Ascot-Grey was up to and he smiled back at his mischief-making pal. "Very well, Major Ascot-Grey, since both you and Mr. Bowles feel the Squad will not shower The Depot with disgrace, they shall attend."

"Yippee! My chance at last," yelled Bowles.

"Calm yourself, Lieutenant. And Major Ascot-Grey, because you hold this particular squad in such high regard, I'm holding you personally responsible for all their actions," he paused. "Not Lieutenant Bowles, his sense of their level of proficiency may be a bit jaundiced."

Ascot-Grey's smile vanished from his face to re-appear on Smitty's. A wink from Smitty let Ascot-Grey know he was on to him. But Ascot-Grey was made of sterner stuff, and he was not about to surrender so easily. "Roger, sir, I accept the challenge. However, since the honour of The Depot is at stake, I'll need to spend a lot of time with the squad. I'm sure you won't mind if I hand the task of the change of command audit over to you?"

Smitty nearly fell for it. "Ah, ha, so now you're telling me they will not be ready, after all; that is, without your able hand to guide them? Really, Major, the squad will be ready, or it won't be. You'll just have to hope that they come through without your extra assistance because you'll be tied up with that audit. The squad fails, you and Lieutenant Bowles carry the can."

Smitty beamed around at the group in front of him, then stood up. "Thank you for your time, gentlemen. That will be all. Dismissed."

A voice from well the back in the bunch suggested that it would not be all.

"There is one slight problem, sir..."

Smitty looked around and saw, half buried behind the desolate plateau of Bowles' face, a short Michelin-man-like Lieutenant.

"I cannot read your name tag from here, Lieutenant?"

Ascot-Grey spoke up, "Won't matter in the least, sir. The name on the tag bears no resemblance to what he's called."

Smitty turned to Ascot-Grey. "Surely not, Phil, no name calling here is there?"

"None at all." Ascot-Grey gestured for the little lieutenant to come forward. "Here's the name tag, sir."

Smitty looked at down at the small man in front of him. Plastered across most of the right side of his shirt was a strange collection of letters.

"Feather… Stone… Arghh?"

"Well, sir that's the way it looks, but it's pronounced. Fanshaw, sir."

Smitty looked amazed. "It's pronounced, 'Fanshawsir?"

"No, sir, just "Fanshaw, sir."

"Isn't that what I just said? It sounded the same to me, Fanshawsir."

"No, sir, Fanshaw. He's only adding a sir there to indicate that he is talking to you," Major Ascot-Grey explained.

"Oh, I thought he was adding it to confuse me. Not that Featherstoneaugh doesn't do the job on its own. Alright, let's skip the name lesson for now. You said there was a problem? Does it affect your platoon going on the Brigade concentration?"

"Yes, sir, we're to attend a shopping centre opening. We're on display for Friday, Saturday, and Sunday afternoon."

"A shopping centre opening? And your soldiers are attending?"

"Yes, sir, seems one of my lads is the Mayor's son. The Mayor is an ex member of the Regiment who served with Lieutenant Colonel Dillingham."

"Ex member, Featherstonehaugh? Was he the CO?"

"No, sir," Featherstonehaugh was trembling visibly. "He was the Colonel's batman, sir."

Smitty stared, then looked at Ascot-Grey for repudiation of such an unbelievable fact. Ascot-Grey nodded grimly and shrugged. "We expressed our concerns to Colonel Dillingham. Denied, sir. The RSM was threatened by a court martial if he didn't shut up. The platoon was going, and that was that."

Bowles simpered at Featherstonehaugh. "Should be a jolly good wheeze, eh, Feathers?"

The RSM grunted, Feathers shoved an elbow into Bowles midsection, and he grunted. Smitty threw his hands up in the air. "Well for God's sake, is there any squad in The Depot not in training to become sales clerks or store keepers? Am I missing something here? I was under the impression that this training facility was created to turn out infantrymen…" Then it dawned on him. "Well, what's done is done. So be it. Lieutenant Bowles, your squad will open the shopping centre. Featherstonehaugh, yours will go on the brigade concentration. End of story, end of meeting. Thank you all."

Everyone came to attention, replaced their headdress, saluted and then filed out of the new commandant's office. Bowles spluttering in the rear as he tried to put on his balmoral, salute and still contain himself at the injustice of his squad opening a shopping centre instead of going out to do battle under his command.

CHAPTER 31

SERGEANT CLYDE MEETS A FAMOUS GROUSE

"Excuse me?" said a voice from the hallway. I looked up from my imported week old London Times newspaper, considered by many to be the newspaper for the upper echelon of the civil service.

"Yes, Sergeant, can I be of service?"

"May I come in? I'd like a little chat," said Sergeant Clyde.

"By all means, here, take this chair." As Sergeant Clyde came into the room, he looked around. I had managed to make the barrack room quite homey by shifting all the bunk beds into the next room, moving three dressers, one officer's bed, a card table, and a pair of straight back chairs in. Clyde heard a chugging noise somewhere behind him and looked around. Over in a corner set an old beaten-up fridge with '1st CMSR Corporal's Mess' stencilled on the door.

Clyde gestured toward the fridge. "All the comforts of home, eh, Mr. Oxnard?"

"Quite, Sergeant, if home is a field tent or a barrack room." We smiled at one another in that way that old soldiers do when they realize that they are in the presence of other old soldiers; as if the world's their kingdom and they don't get fooled by anything thrown at them.

"My name is Clyde, Jonathan Peter Clyde. I'm the Squire's squad sergeant." He held out his hand as he crossed the threshold and walked up to halt a pace in front of me. "My friends call me J.P.."

"I'm honoured, J.P., and very pleased to meet you," I said as I shook the Sergeant's hand. "His Lordship has spoken highly of you on most occasions. Although I must admit that he is less than effusive with his praise after those sneak inspections you put the boys through."

"I'm sure. And that's partly why I'm here."

"Partly?" I asked and then added, "Forgive me, Sergeant, for being a wretched host. My manners are deteriorating to the level of those young savages below stairs. Please take a seat. Sorry, I forgot to introduce myself, my name is Marvin. And might I offer you a libation?"

Clyde moved over and sat on one of the straight back chairs and removed his balmoral. He was dressed in clean but rumpled combat clothing. I was dressed in my own uniform of a black tuxedo with all the accoutrements of my office, but I had removed my jacket. My crisp white shirt shone in the light from the windows, and my sleeves were held in place by a pair of black sleeve garters.

Clyde looked at his watch, and then nodded. "Why not?" he motioned with his head toward the chattering old fridge. "That thing hold any cold beer? And how did you scrounge it anyway?"

"Ah, Sergeant Clyde, I mean J.P., no names, no pack drill, as we used to say."

"Yeah, we use the same term."

"I can tell you that the loan of it cost me a couple of bottles of excellent scotch. Famous Grouse."

"Never heard of it. My tastes in hooch runs to dark rum and CC, Canadian Club rye whisky. I tried scotch while posted to Germany, but found it awful."

"A poor brand no doubt. Do you remember the name?"

"Black Unicorn I think it was called. Tasted like battery acid laced with cat shit. Burned going down. Burned coming back up the next morning and in between it felt like I was pissing liquid lava."

I shuddered. "Exactly. That's because Black Unicorn, while famous the world over, is not considered scotch – it is battery acid, and well done in guessing the cat shit, but to be accurate, it's distilled from highland sheep shit."

I walked over to one of the dressers and said, "Why don't I introduce you to real scotch? After all, you are in a Highland battalion."

Before Clyde could reply, I poured out two glasses of water from a glass pitcher, then pulled open a drawer and hauled out a cut-glass decanter, turned to face Clyde and held it up. "Famous Grouse. So smooth that you'll think you are sipping liquid gold."

After pouring three fingers of scotch into two more glasses, I carried a glass of water and one of scotch over and handed them to Sergeant Clyde.

I returned to the dresser and picked up my own glass and held it high. "To your Regiment."

"The Regiment!" replied Clyde and each of them took a sip. Clyde's face had been screwed up in anticipation of the fire he was about to swallow. As he sipped and then swallowed, his facial muscles relaxed and a smile grew and grew. After another sip and a small swallow of water, he said, "Magic, Mr. Oxnard. Magic. That almost puts Canadian Club in the Black Unicorn category."

"Yes, it is excellent isn't it?" I said returning to my easy chair. "And the nature of your visit, now that the niceties have been taken care off, J.P.?"

"Yes, well. I'm about to lose a lance corporal for a couple of weeks. He's off with a broken leg and won't be able to even supervise for least ten days. I assume that the Squire debriefed you on the shopping centre opening, right?"

As he said that, Clyde held up his now empty glass and added, "Chance of seconds on this, Mr. Oxnard?"

"Of course. You've enough water left, I presume?" I finished with the refills and resumed his seat.

"Cheers," said Clyde. He took another sip and added, "I think I'm a scotch convert from now on. And, as I was saying, Lance Corporal Caruthers is out of it with a bum Leg. If I try and get a replacement for that short a time, the RSM will have a fit. My squad commander, Lieutenant Bowles has already suggested that he fill in for Caruthers on the morning inspections. It's bad enough when he…" Clyde paused, looked over at Ox and went on again, "We can treat this as the sergeants' mess, okay?"

"You mean what's said in here stays in here?"

"Exactly. Bang on, Marv…"

"You have my word, J.P.."

"Good, let's face it," he gave a sigh and went on, "My squad commander is a dope. A first class idiot dressed as an officer. I dare not let him near the troops, except when it's unavoidable."

"Such as the Death Slide?"

Sergeant Clyde laughed and said, "Yep. A perfect example, and one where the Squire demonstrated guts."

I bowed my head in acknowledgement as if that side of my master's character was beyond question.

"So how do you think I can help? Assassination?"

"That'd work. But no, I have a far more, but less interesting task for you. There's a rumour going around that you were a Sergeant in WWII. That a fact?"

"A staff sergeant, actually. His Lordship, Toby's father, and I served in a Highland battalion for a bit and then did a bit of a stint behind the lines in France in 1944."

"You jumped in to join the Resistance?"

"Well, yes," I said hoping for modesty.

"Ever do any recruit training or any instructional experience?"

"Some. I did take a platoon of Sandhurst officers through some training, route marches, hand-to-hand combat, obstacle courses and marksmanship."

"Terrific," said Clyde as he finished up his drink. "So, I need a favour. If I can dig you up a uniform, will you take over the morning inspection for one of the sections? I'll make sure that it's not the Squire's section."

Ox thought it over and then nodded slowly. "Yes, yes, J.P., Top hole."

"Good stuff… And just for the record, you'll be quartered in the sergeants' mess." Ox started and gave Clyde a look. Clyde went on, "I know, you have to stay here to look after the Squire. No problem. You'll be listed on ration strength at the mess and have a room there. Store your scotch there if you want. And if you go up there this evening, you'll meet Staff Sergeant John Yorath with the Engineers. He's an exchange Sergeant from Britain. Interesting sort of a guy once you get past his accent. He's from North Wales. He was sent here from 33 Engineer Regiment as an EOD specialist, Explosive Ordnance Disposal. Our Field Engineers requested a bilingual exchange staff sergeant, and they sent John."

"He's Welsh, and he speaks French? Amazing. From what I know of the Taffy's they are lucky to speak English," I said smiling at Clyde.

"No, not French, John is bilingual, but it's English and Welsh. No one knew until he got over here."

"And he's got a uniform that will fit me and that he is willing to loan?"

"Yes, pay him a visit this evening. I'll be there for a while."

"And my role will be to assist you, correct?"

"Roger that. You'll be a kind of shadow squad sergeant," he shrugged his shoulders. "After all, the Commandant did say you could stay, and he'd be the first to agree that you would be of use to The Depot." Clyde stood up. As he did so, they heard low voices from out in the Hallway, one voice not so low that the occupants could not hear. "It's Clyde, and he's in there with Jeeves."

"Not loud, you idiot. They'll hear you," said a voice that I recognized as His Lordship's.

Clyde moved toward the door when in a whisper, I stopped him. "Just a second, J.P., I believe that it is time for me to earn my pay. Besides, it'll be my pleasure." Clyde nodded and sat back down, made himself comfortable and prepared to watch his new instructor demonstrate his skills.

I pulled myself up to full height, drew in a breath and then bellowed like an RSM on parade at Buckingham Palace, "Attn-shuunnn!"

Feet in the hallway slammed together as the boys responded. Clyde told me later that my parade square voice would have intimidated even salty old captains and so let me carry on.

"Get in here, you horrible shower and make it quick!"

Four sets of feet marched in bringing with them four bodies. In single file into my room, Toby, McGuffin, Stouffer and Tremaine marched up to where I was standing and came to a halt in file.

I said, "Recruit Trelauney-Fitzgibboncrest, you have been counselled in the past in regards to that term. I had expected that you would have made an effort not to pass it on to the other primitives occupying the rooms in this building."

Not being aware of what my new role was, Toby gave me an amused glance and relaxed out of the position of attention. He was unprepared for my reaction.

"No one told you to move, Recruit Trelauney-Fitzgibboncrest. Get up to attention. Now!"

Toby jumped and stood there in bewilderment. McGuffin made the unfortunate mistake of looking around to see what his squad sergeant was doing. Clyde was doing just fine. He was smiling as he nodded at McGuffin. "Best face front, Recruit McGuffin, else Staff Sergeant Oxnard will have you for breakfast."

Toby tried again, "But… I don't…"

"Silence in the ranks!" I spoke with firmness, but not as a scream or a yell. However, silence did prevail. Then after I had achieved my aim, said, "Stand at ease. Stand easy. No talking."

I walked around the four confused lads and the addressed Toby. "Recruit Trelauney-Fitzgibboncrest, as I was saying, in reference to that word that you pass off as my nickname…"

Toby said, "You mean…"

"Do not say it, Master Toby. I warn you do not say it. I am not Jeeves. I have never intended to be Jeeves." I spoke slowly and with such cold determination that everyone in the room knew that I was serious.

"Furthermore," I added, "While I think that Jeeves does do credit to the butlers and gentleman's gentlemen of the world, he is a caricature. Something put together by that fiendish Wodehouse. And I…" he paused to draw in a bathtub full of air then continued. "I. Am. Not. Jeeves. Thank you."

There was no response from the four recruits. Sergeant Clyde came around to the front of the file and stood beside me. "Gents, I'd like you to meet your new squad instructor, Staff Sergeant Oxnard. You will address him as Staff Sergeant or Staff." He took time to look at each young soldier to let that announcement sink in. "Any questions?"

He was met by four closely spaced shouts of, "No, Sergeant!"

"Good. Dismissed." The four boys turned and marched out.

Letting them get down the hall, Clyde turned to me, replaced his balmoral on his head, checked out his uniform, gave a pull here and there to get it sorted out. "Thanks for the scotch, Staff Sergeant Ox." He marched out of the room. At the door he half turned, gave a casual salute and said, "You'll do."

CHAPTER 32

MEET MELTON MOWBRAY

This next part came to me as a strange kind of coincidence. I got the story from Corporal Rodney Smathers-Hughes eight years after the events here in Gagetown took place. By this time he was a staff sergeant working in London running an orderly room for one of the London militia units. We had met at some kind of official bash that Toby had been invited to in his role as Lord Haselbury. It had been held in an armouries and the former corporal, now Staff Sergeant Smathers-Hughes, had been there in his finery because his unit was hosting the event. Toby recognized Smathers-Hughes and then introduced me. The three of us settled in a corner and bought one another up to date. On their trip back to England, Urquhart and Rodney, both sitting in second class on the plane while Masterson sat in first, gave each other their tales of the big event. Rod, as he now called himself, had spent the entire flight home swapping stories with Urquhart and scribbling the entire story into his journal. Which was how Smathers-Hughes was able to fill in the blanks in this tale of incompetence.

Mind you, as a lover of fine British cooking, he didn't need to tell me about Melton Mowbray. Every schoolboy worth his salt knew that it was a town renowned for its pork pies, its thousand year old weekly market and where its equally ancient and smelly cheese known as Stilton was sold; but thankfully, not produced.

Smelly was also the distinguishing characteristic of the offices of the UARB or Unexplained Absences Review Board. Housed in what was once the prime quarters of the mules, pack horses, and re-mounts of the RAVC, Royal Army Veterinarian Corps, UARB was not a place where you would willingly volunteer to serve. None of the present incumbents had volunteered either. When you start with accommodations designed for horses, add antiquated army-issue furniture, then accessorize the place with remnants of field equipment retrieved from Waterloo, you cannot expect too much in the way of luxury. It would be nice to say that you could salvage out of the catastrophe an ambient atmosphere but that disappeared under the aroma of equine flatulence that had been marinating in the wooden beams, walls and floors for over three hundred years. Staff Sergeant Todd described the tang in the air on his first day at UARB as, "A bloody ripe barnyard pong, eh?"

The Commanding Officer, Major Rupert Masterson a member of the Ordnance Corps, occupied the large room at the end of the building farthest from the main entrance way. On meeting him in those early days, you would have said that he was flushed with excitement over his first real command. The truth was that within hours of taking up residency in his office he developed dripping sinuses, watery-eyes, and a furry-coated tongue. This was not surprising when you learned that one corner of his office had been created by adding two walls and enclosing what had once been a manure pile started by Richard the Lion-Hearted's knights. Plywooding over the pile had added twenty feet to the end of the building and increased the stench levels fifty fold. White-washed walls, indifferently re-painted khaki, surrounded Masterton's battle-scarred desk and his four wheeled, only three working, ancient chair. The rest of the office had been tastefully decorated with a battered, First World War vintage four drawer wooden filing cabinet of which only two opened, a wooden chair that resembled an unfinished do-it-yourself garden-style guillotine and a carpet that had been trampled by every single member of Napoleon's Army on its retreat from Moscow. One window, identified by the weak glow that it emitted, provided no view and only served as an excuse not to hang pictures on that wall.

Further down the building from Masterton's office in another horse stall that served as his office, a gargantuan captain sat looking at the weekly reports of unauthorized absences and other attendance irregularities within the British Army system. These reports were culled from each unit headquarters across the crumbling British empire, reviewed by the appropriate platoon sergeants, company second-in-commands and their sergeants-major, then tossed forward to the unit RSMs who then passed them upward to the unit adjutants who handed them off to a headquarters clerk who tossed them into his 'awaiting further disposition' basket. In the majority of the units, there was no further action necessary. All required action was signed off as completed if the subject member had been apprehended or turned himself in or otherwise explained himself. If the absentee was still on the loose, the report showed that the military police were on the job and outlined the steps they were taking in the capture of the runaway.

There really was no need for these reports to go any further than their unit headquarters, but in the interests of organizational overkill, regimental redundancy, and bureaucratic empire building, the UARB office had been established way off in Borden, Hampshire. The Army Emergency Reserve was headquartered there as well as the Infantry Driver Training Wing where they tried to teach soldiers to drive armoured personnel carriers.

Neither the AER or the Driving Unit wanted anything to do with UARB, and it was only under duress that the General Officer Commanding even permitted them office space. Although designating a horse barn, a granary and a small barrack block where drovers and muleskinners had lived, as office space was pushing the definition toward the absurd.

UARB was staffed by five individuals, three of who were officers who had been listed as D-SAFE at their home units and had been sent off to the UARB, there to wait out the days or years to retirement. Carrying a notation of D-SAFE or 'Declared Supernumerary, Awaiting Further Employment' on your personnel file was the military equivalent of ringing a bell, wearing monk's robes and wandering the streets bellowing, "Unclean! Unclean!"

There was a school of thought that UARB stood for 'Useless Arses Retirement Bungalow' and for all the productivity that had come out of it; they were more accurate in their judgment than those who annually refilled the UARB coffers.

The other two members were a staff sergeant who had been convicted of fraud in regards to the NAAFI canteen system and his one subordinate, a corporal clerk. The corporal, Rodney Smathers-Hughes by name, was also the best bridge player at the UARB and was essential to the afternoon game held every Friday in the refurbished granary that served as their lunchroom, canteen, gymnasium and lounge. Obviously, the bridge game could not have proceeded without the corporal, so he was never sent anywhere. He was also the only one who could shuffle the deck thoroughly.

On this particular Thursday, Major Masterton was away on the trip to London. One of the three officers travelled up to London once a week to deliver any analysis of the unexplained absence reports, and to receive any bumf that their civilian overlord, Mr. Cordell Kennecott, deemed of sufficient non-importance to be unloaded on them.

Masterson was a tall, slender soldier who had risen through the ranks the same way he had slithered through the public school system; not by way of one school or unit, but by many. Using what has been described as the 'Flashman Technique', Masterson lied, cheated, stole, toadied, and brown-nosed his way through life. Animal cunning, a keen sense of personal survival, mitigated by a gargantuan deficiency in brain cells all combined to make him a danger to his men, the unit and himself.

Once his superiors along the rank structure saw that punishing him created more heartbreak for his punishers, they soon caught on that it was easier to promote him up and out of their areas of responsibility. He would arrive at a unit, settle in and then, with the minimum of time in rank attained, would be given a glowing report, a promotion, and a posting. Onward and upward he sailed until he hit the shoaling waters of the lieutenant colonel's promotion board. Members of the board, all colonels, and brigadier generals, stalled out in horror at the sheer thought of giving him a battalion. He was offered command of UARB or early retirement. Not expecting UARB to be a unit comprising four others, Masterson accepted. Under his command was the large captain mentioned earlier, Gregory Urquhart, who served as his second in command. In the office next to him was Lieutenant Louis Bryant. Both rejects from the cavalry, they banded together against Masterton's tyranny by justifying his actions as worthy of an Ordinance officer.

"Cannonballs and gunpowder! That's all he's good for," said Captain Urquhart.

Bryant agreed, "Quite. Lead in the head, no bang in his britches."

Unfortunately, they had demonstrated the acuity of those responsible for posting them to UARB by making these pronouncements within the hearing of Masterton. He retaliated by refusing to partner either of them in the bridge. When he played, he always took Smathers-Hughes as his partner. And despite Masterson's rotten play, Smathers-Hughes always won.

The staff sergeant was Jeremy Todd. His fraudulent dealings as a member of The Royal Army Pay Corps had never seen the witness stand of a court martial or even a summary trial. He had been accused on circumstantial evidence and the sneaking suspicion of his former commanding officer that Todd was smarter than he was. The Commanding Officer was more upset with himself that he had never thought of the scam first. In a fit of pique and greed, he had posted Staff Sergeant Todd in order to take the scheme over.

Captain Urquhart stared moodily at the pile of paperwork as it sat on his desk. "Same old crap. Same old analysis. Why do I bother?"

"Because, old chap, if you don't, then you might miss something frightfully important," said a voice from his doorway.

"Such as…?"

"Such as this," said Lieutenant Bryant, coming in and waving a shiny new file folder toward the Captain.

"And what is that? Some private soldier gone over the hill wearing nothing but his jammies?"

Lieutenant Bryant looked a bit like a cavalry officer, that is to say, he resembled a horse, leggy, long in the face and all teeth when he smiled. Lance Corporal Smathers-Hughes and Staff Sergeant Todd referred to Bryant and Urquhart as 'Abbot and Costello', but could never remember who was the fat one and who was the skinny one.

"Well, come in and give me the lowdown on the world's most exciting runaway," said Captain Urquhart.

The gangly lieutenant didn't move like a racehorse. In his patent leather cavalry boots, his gait was broken as if he were tottering about on high heels. He made it to the guest chair and toppled into it, tossing the file folder onto the pile in front of Captain Urquhart.

"This will chill your willies, Cap'n."

Captain Urquhart looked down at the folder as it settled on the huge pile of reports on absentee soldiers. "Oh, come on, Louis, can't you see that I have more than enough on my plate than to read another useless file?"

"Cap'n, I swear, this is not useless. In fact, it's so good that I didn't even pass it on to Major Importance before he left for the briefing."

"If it's so valuable, and you didn't get it to him, he'll skin you alive when he recovers from the shock of what Kennecott is going to do to him."

"Could be, but I've adjusted the time of arrival of this report as being after Masterson had left to go to lunch at his club. He'll be hanging off a cliff without the proverbial when a very rush copy of the report arrives on the Undersecretary's desk before he gets there. If Masterson had done his job and awaited for all reports to arrive and then trotted off to the briefing today as is directed, he'd be alright…"

"Are you telling me that this so very, very exciting report that you are waving in my face came in before he left?"

"It arrived an hour before he left. I took it, gave it a read and was going off to give it to him when he came into my horse stall and gave me shit for walking on the grass between our office and the parking lot. I shoved the report into my desk drawer and kept it there until he had buggered off."

"Loyalty, Louis, loyalty. Besides, you don't belong to an expensive club in London."

Masterson had left yesterday afternoon. He was able to get Staff Sergeant Todd to do up a false claim, for twenty percent of the take. Then Masterson had claimed for an overnight stop where rations and quarters were unavailable, thus gathering in the per diem as well..

The Captain, his curiosity piqued, reached for the file, opened it up and gave it a thumb through.

"Page twelve, Cap'n, sir. The bit about an Earl on the loose."

Bryant waited while Urquhart read through the file. As he waited, Urquhart read and by the time he had finished and looked up at Bryant, they were both smiling nastily.

"Luverly, as me dear old Mum used to say, Luverly, Louis. You Machiavellian donkey walloper, you," said Captain Urquhart.

"Ain't it the goods, old son?" said Bryant.

"That, Louis, my boy is the goods." Captain Urquhart stood up, put on his hat and said, "We'll stop in and tell Todd and Smathers-Hughes to forget the bridge game this afternoon. We're off to wash down this bit of news with a few drops of the old stuff."

CHAPTER 33

MASTERSON MEETS AN ULTIMATUM

As Bryant had prophesied, Masterson was indeed dangling, although it would be more accurate to say that while he was standing in front of Kennecott's desk, he was about to become the key ingredient in the soup du jour.

"Tell me, Major Masterton, why do I not find among your reports anything relating to the rocket I received from Undersecretary Nightingale earlier today? I have assumed that your office was in receipt of every absentee report in the country, correct?"

Major Masterson had no reply, even though he silently asked himself what the devil could old Kennecott be talking about. There had been no unusual report on absent troops up until the time that he had left the office for his club. There never was anything unusual in that damned forest of useless reports. That was why, when it was his turn to venture up to London, he left a day early and spent the time at his club, banging the snooker balls around and strutting through the lobby in his uniform.

"Nothing extraordinary, sir, no."

"What that suggests to me, Major, is that you have a limited understanding of the term 'extraordinary'. Would the report of an Earl being listed as absent when his regiment was tasked with overseas duty be classified according to your definition of nothing unusual as possibly commonplace or an everyday occurrence?"

"Absent in the face of deployment? Why that's desertion. The man should be shot!" said Masterson with a load of heat behind his tone.

"And the charge for not staying informed of such an act when it is the one and only task you are expected to be able to do?"

"Well, in that case, I'd say he's doubly damned, sir."

"Not him, you. That reference to not staying informed was a pointed comment directed at you."

Masterson saw a slight bump along his promotional highway, but not being bright enough to explain it away logically, decided to keep on with his denunciation of the Earl. Before doing that, he tried to sidestep the informed issue. He shrugged. "Probably a report that came in late from one of those overseas regiments, sir."

"How in the blue blazes can an overseas regiment be deploying for overseas duty, man? They're already over there."

"Over where, sir?"

"Who cares? You said that it was an overseas regiment that had turned in a late report."

"Yes, sir, very likely. They're always late with those reports, sir."

Kennecott was wise enough to see that Masterson would drag this around in a circle until one of them broke from the strain. "Never mind the overseas regiment. Why didn't you report that unusual incident?"

"Unusual, sir, the one about the Earl missing his overseas deployment? Yes, quite. I'm sure that we would have reported it tomorrow when the report arrived at the office."

"It's already been at your office. Someone by the name of Smathers-Hughes forwarded it to the Undersecretary, who then rather pointedly forwarded it to me amended with some viperish comments about me knowing or in this case not knowing my business. How do you explain that?"

"Well, sir, I have always thought that you did know your own business…"

"Not that. The reason why the thing ended up on the Undersecretary's desk, before you had seen it. Explain that!"

Masterson couldn't. No one was authorized to forward anything out of the office without his signature. This smelt of some devious plot concocted by that pair of donkey wallopers.

"Donkey wallopers…"

"Pardon me, Masterton? Donkey walloper? That's a derogatory term used by the infantry to describe cavalry? I served with the 21st Lancers, Empress of India's Royal Cavalry Regiment."

"…Yes, sir, it is. More of an in-joke in our shop. I was referring to the two officers I have back in the office. I expect they let Corporal Smathers-Hughes send that document to the Undersecretary. A mistake that I'll personally rectify on my return."

"Speaking of returns, be here when I return and read that report while I'm away." Kennecott got up from his chair and left the room.

Five minutes later he returned to find Masterson still deep in the report. "What do you find so interesting in that, Masterton? It strikes me that for someone whose job it is to keep on top of things of this nature, you're reading as if it's all new to you, eh?"

"Agreed, sir. This is new to me. I'm baffled by the idea that my shop had let me down badly in this matter. I'll be all over them like a buffalo stampede when I get back, you can count on that, sir."

"Yes, well, as you can see, my shop includes your shop, so you could say that my shop, meaning you, has let the side down badly. Do you imagine that if I were to come down on you like a buffalo stampede that it would have any effect on your future performance?

"I take your point, sir. Best to forgive and forget, what?" said Masterton, fully intending to whine out from under if possible. However, if one of those donkey wallopers or that over-achiever, Smathers-Hughes, come the 'forgive and forget' routine with me, he'll be on his way to wherever I can send him that is worse than where he's at now.

"Possibly, Masterton, possibly. For the time being, let's get back to this runaway Earl. What do you gather from this report?"

"Well, sir, according to the report, he's skipped the country."

"Where's he gone?"

"No intel on that, sir?"

"What the blazes is intel, Masterton?"

"Pardon, sir, it's a term we picked up from the Yanks, short for intelligence."

"It's damn dangerous to pick things up from the Yanks, Masterton. Forget using affected jargon. And to get back to the Earl of… what?"

"Says here The Earl of West Saxmundham and North Haselbury, sir, and to get back to the why of his fleeing National Service, it's a mystery, sir."

"First of all, why is an Earl dodging National Service? Surely he's too old to be called up. Why, he must be my age at least," said Kennecott.

"No intel…" Masterson caught the glare from Kennecott, stopped, then restarted, "There seems to be no file on him according to this report, sir… Very puzzling. No indication that his personnel record is available at his home unit."

"Curious, don't you think, Masterton?"

"Yes, sir."

"And what do you propose to do about it?"

"I'll check with his family, sir. Him being an Earl, there's bound to be a family seat or something. Although I've never heard of West Saxmundham and North Haselbury…."

"I have. Haselbury's in Suffolk, so I imagine that West Saxmundham and North Haselbury are close by."

"Excellent, sir. Top hole. I'll get right on it, sir."

"Good. See that you do. I want an answer that I can take to the Undersecretary at the close of day tomorrow."

Masterson turned to leave Kennecott's office. "One more thing, Major Masterton, at the same time you personally get the Earl situation sorted out, you will have an explanation as to why the Undersecretary received that message, why you didn't, and why I didn't. That will be all."

Masterson left, and as he drove back to the shop, he pondered the options open to him. First of all, he was sure that those two officers had set him up. They had somehow gotten Smathers-Hughes to send the Earl's report to the Undersecretary.

Masterson arrived back at his office to find the place deserted. He roamed the three little buildings that housed UARB and found no sign of life. He then realized that he had seen no cars parked in the various spots around the buildings. Looking at his watch, he saw that the time was only three-fifteen. Quitting time, if not for himself, at least for those under his command was four-thirty. He wandered into his own office and found on his normally tidy and empty desk a message. Scribbled in Smathers-Hughes' barely legible handwriting were the words,

Sir, Captain Urquhart and Lieutenant Bryant have gone to attend a Safety-At-Work seminar at Leicester. Staff Sergeant Todd had to go to the Camp Hospital for a check-up. I left at fifteen hundred to see the Camp quartermaster ref the muleskinner deal.
Yours Truly,
Corporal Rodney Smathers-Hughes

"Left to see the camp quartermaster reference the muleskinner deal? A bloody, jumped-up corporal who thinks he runs this place because he can type and play bridge? I'll have his bloody guts for garters!"

This was not quite an accurate description of Smathers-Hughes, the corporal clerk who pretty much kept them all out of jail. He had been condemned to a tour of duty under Masterson for the crime of beating his former Commanding Officer at the Brigade Racquetball Championships. A bad loser, his CO had demanded a stint in military prison and then a release back into civilian life. Someone higher up decided that a tour of duty under Masterson would be more rehabilitative and would give the offending Smathers-Hughes a better sense of place in the Army's hierarchy. Being a member of an influential and wealthy family and since he could type and make a decent pot of tea, he was kept on.

The muleskinner deal was supposed to have been a secret. Masterson and the quartermaster, Major Delaney, had been wheeling and dealing on how to turn the old muleskinner barrack block into an annex of the camp officers' mess. The current mess was three miles away in a far corner of the camp. The officers who regularly attended it were usually infantry types and reservists. Delaney, a Supply officer, wanted no part of them. Masterson liked the idea of being the PMC or president of the mess committee, even if the mess membership consisted of him and his two officers and Delaney with his three.

Masterson stormed around the office looking for information on reports and personnel files. He found a half empty bottle of Black Unicorn in Urquhart's wastebasket, hidden under some crumpled blank sheets of paper. In Bryant's out basket he found the remains of a ham and cheese sandwich. In Corporal Smathers-Hughes' office nothing had been left open; in baskets and out baskets locked away, filing cabinets held shut by huge padlocks. The keys to the filing cabinets were held by Smathers-Hughes because he was the security officer.

After ripping Smathers-Hughes' desk blotter into confetti, breaking all his pencils and stealing his prized Queen's coronation pen, Major Masterson went back to his quarters and spent the weekend sliding from a dark rage into an oblivious drunken coma.

CHAPTER 34

WE MEET CORPORAL RODNEY SMATHERS-HUGHES

Monday arrived on time to find all was quiet on the UARB front. Both Captain Urquhart and Lieutenant Bryant had arrived at the uncharacteristic and unholy time of zero seven hundred hours. Corporal Smathers-Hughes showed up at his usual time of ten or fifteen minutes after eight. He made no comment to the two officers about the state of his desk. He set about cleaning it up and putting on a pot of special roast coffee for himself. He made a pot of tea for the officers and put a pitcher of cold water on Staff Sergeant Todd's desk. Of Todd, there was no sign, but there never usually was until after tea break at ten.

At half past ten, Todd arrived, guzzled most of the contents of the water jug, burped, sat behind his desk and took off his boots. He put his arms on his desk to serve as a pillow and went to sleep.

At eleven-fifteen Todd was still sleeping at his desk, Smathers-Hughes was on the phone to his bookmaker, and Lieutenant Bryant had just wandered into Urquhart's office. He flopped into a large armchair at the side of Urquhart's desk. "No sign of our glorious leader, Cap'n? Think he's been incarcerated?"

"Seems a bit severe, a trip to the detention barracks for losing an Earl, don't you think, Louis?" said Urquhart with what was nearly a giggle. Since the cavalry never, ever, giggles, it could be said to be a toothy grin with a touch of a tooth grinding about it.

Bryant returned the non-giggle with a mouse-like chuckle which was barely manly enough to qualify for use in a cavalry officers' mess and said, "Betcha he ain't top holing anyone now, Captain."

At a quarter to twelve the front door burst open and in stalked Masterton. Staff Sergeant Todd uncharacteristically jumped to his feet, yelled, "Room, Attention!" and stood at attention. Across the room at his desk, Smathers-Hughes looked up but continued to talk on the phone. As Masterson stormed over toward his desk, Smathers-Hughes held up one finger to indicate that he would be finished shortly.

Masterton, still incensed over Friday's happening, and nursing a serious hangover, became engulfed in rage at his corporal's impertinence reached over the desk and snatched the telephone handset from an astonished Smathers-Hughes's hand. He flung it in the direction of the phone cradle, it banged into it, knocking the entire mechanism to the floor. It landed inches from Masterton's right foot and he lifted his shiny brogue and brought it down with a bang, scattering black chunks of phone across the room. Smathers-Hughes dropped the still hovering finger and shoved back on his wheeled chair to get himself out of range of his maddened boss.

"You better get that finger away from me, you little bastard! Get into my office now!"

Smathers-Hughes stood at least three inches taller than Masterton, and his parents had been married, but he felt that this was not the time to correct his superior on his choice of language.

"Yessir!"

The crash brought Urquhart and Bryant on the run, and they jammed themselves into the doorway of the orderly room to see what was going on. Masterson turned from Smathers-Hughes's desk and headed toward them. He rocketed a glare at the two officers and growled. "I'll deal with you two next. Don't go anywhere."

With that, he drove through the pair of them like a super tanker cutting through rotting Spring ice. Corporal Smathers-Hughes trailed behind, a tiny fishing dory in his wake.

Once in the office, Masterson flung his hat in the direction of the coat rack, it missed and landed in the waste basket. Smathers-Hughes deviated from his route and went to pick it up.

"Leave the fucking thing where it lays, Corporal."

"Yes, sir,"

And back in line he went to come up one pace from the front of Masterton's desk. Masterson plumped himself down in his chair on the other side while Smathers-Hughes thanked the small gods of his Celtic background that the desk was wide and sturdy. There was no telling what Masterson might do once his temper erupted. All members of UARB had seen Masterson lose his calm one afternoon and it had taken a lot of coaxing from Staff Sergeant Todd and some outright bribery from Smathers-Hughes to get the repair and renovation team out from the Engineers to replace all of the windows in the orderly Room.

Smathers-Hughes waited. Masterson fumed. Neither wanted to open the negotiations. Smathers-Hughes because he was in the dark as to Masterton's rage. Masterson because he thought that he could get Smathers-Hughes to sweat a bit. With no sweat appearing, and Smathers-Hughes looking ready to doze off, Masterson blinked first. "You're in big trouble, Corporal. Big, big trouble."

"Excuse me, sir?"

"No excuse me, sirs, today, Smathers-Hughes. Just explain why the fuck you ran off to the Undersecretary of Defence with that report."

"What report?"

"What report, sir."

"Yes, that's what I want to know."

"No, Smathers-Hughes, no. I was just pointing out that you neglected to say sir when you asked that question."

"What question, sir?"

"The one about the report."

"What report?"

"The one you didn't say sir to."

"Oh, that report, sir."

"Yes, that's the one, and now you've got it right."

"But, sir, I have no idea what you are talking about."

"C'mon, Corporal. What report? That's about the weakest denial I've ever heard."

"Not weak, sir, just accurate. I am truly at a loss."

"A loss? You'll be at more than a loss when you appear in the dock at your own court martial."

"Court martial? For what?"

"Smathers-Hughes, anyone would think that you have no idea what I'm talking about."

"That's true, sir. No idea at all."

"Pull the other one, Corporal. Do you mean to tell me you've never seen the Lost Earl Memo? That you never sent it to the Undersecretary. That you…" As he torqued up his anger, Masterson came out of his chair in a slow rise, placing his hands into fists and bracing the knuckles on the desk, he loomed toward the confused Smathers-Hughes. "You never withheld the memo and then made sure that I was kept in the dark about it? Is that your story?"

"Yes, that's my story, sir. Can you give me more of an idea what the Lost Earl Memo was all about?"

Masterson stopped to breathe. Smathers-Hughes was not stunned by this display, he stood there and enjoyed the exhibition.

Masterson gathered breath to go on, then on he went. This time about how useless Smathers-Hughes was to the Unit. As Masterson raved, he gradually rose up out from his chair, placing his knuckles on the desk he upped the glare to sunspot strength. Masterson was sweating from his anger, saliva flew from lips, papers from the desk. Smathers-Hughes said nothing, stood there and watched as Masterson wound himself up.

"Do you have anything at all to say, Smathers-Hughes? Anything to justify why you are such a waste of rations?"

His face was now inches from the Corporal's. Smathers-Hughes could see in Masterton's berserk eyes that there was a need for him to explain why he shouldn't have his rations cut off, to say something, anything that would keep Masterson on his own side of the desk. What could he say?

"Have I gotten through to you, Smathers-Hughes?"

"Yes, sir."

That answer seemed to settle him down. Masterson regained some of his calm, took another breath and said, "Good. Smathers-Hughes, good. You must understand, Corporal, that I do not usually fly off the handle like that. But in this case, Smathers-Hughes I am inclined to think that you have the potential to be a good soldier and it just pisses me off to see that wasted. Understand?"

"Yes, sir."

"Fine." Masterson straightened up and then sat back down.

"Yes, sir."

Masterson sighed then sagged back down into his chair. "Very well, Corporal. Here's the gist of the incident. A memo arrived at our shop advising us that a soldier, by the way, he's an Earl, had been reported absent without leave. It came in Thursday afternoon after I had departed for Mr. Kennecott's meeting. I arrived at the meeting Friday morning, and Kennecott had this memo. Someone…" Masterton's eyes glared in fury. He went on, "Someone by the name of Smathers-Hughes sent a copy to the Undersecretary. The Undersecretary, in turn, not understanding the memo, sent it to Kennecott requesting clarification. Kennecott, being as much in the dark suggested that I might have an answer. I arrived at Kennecott's office with no answers, and no knowledge, even though, according to the Undersecretary, the memo had come out of my shop."

"May I see the memo, sir? I might be able to help sort this all out."

"Sort it out? Smathers-Hughes, you are the entry port for all mail in and out of UARB. The mail arrives, you sort through it, then log it in and then you distribute it as per the addressees. Now, did you or did you not receive the mail last Thursday?"

"No, sir. I didn't."

"You didn't?" Masterton's amazement at this bare-faced lie purpled his cheeks and sent a red flush up toward his scalp. "But you always do. Of course, you did. There's no excuse for you not doing it. Damn it all," Masterson punctuated this outburst with a fist slam onto his desk. "You did the mail routine last Thursday, or else you're liable to be charged with negligence in the performance of your duty…" He stopped.

"However, I see your canny plan. You'd rather get in shit for not doing it than face a court martial for doing it, eh? Nice try, Smathers-Hughes. Nice try."

"That's not it, sir…"

"Don't interrupt me, Smathers-Hughes. Now, for the last time, did you receive the mail last Thursday?" Thinking that he had Smathers-Hughes where he wanted him, Masterson sank back into his chair and waited.

"No, sir, I didn't do the mail last Thursday. I couldn't have. I wasn't here."

"Not here? You're going to attempt that pathetic absent from place of parade excuse, are you?"

"No, sir, I was…"

"No. No. No." Masterson flung himself forward and waved his hands in the air in an attempt to silence Smathers-Hughes and keep him from dropping himself, as Masterson saw it, deeper and deeper into the shit.

"Corporal, please, stop it. Stop it this minute. Don't make it any worse for yourself."

You may think that Masterton's concern for Smathers-Hughes's well-being smacked of true compassion for another fellow being, but one part of Masterton's brain saw the shop minus Smathers-Hughes and Masterson minus a goodly sum due to Smathers-Hughes's financial wizardry. All he wanted to do was frighten Smathers-Hughes into a confession. From there he would extract a suitable punishment that did not include losing the illegal services of his clerk. But Smathers-Hughes was not to be deterred from his path of self-incrimination.

"Sir, please, sir, let me finish. I didn't do the mail last Thursday because I was not here on…"

"We've been over this, Corporal Smathers-Hughes. Now you're going to tell me you were absent without leave? That's worse, yet."

Smathers-Hughes felt that he was never going to get it out, so he flung his arms up into the air, and yelled "Sir!" and before Masterson could get over his shock, Smathers-Hughes flung out his reason for not being in the shop. "I didn't do the mail because you sent me into Leicester."

"I sent you into Leicester… During duty hours?"

Smathers-Hughes nodded.

"Whatever for? A serious medical problem? A compassionate reason perhaps?" Masterton's mind showed him a caring-for-the troops pose that no one but he had even envisioned. "Now, Smathers-Hughes, I'm not in the habit of letting my staff trudge off on sight-seeing excursions at her Majesty's expense. This better be good, Corporal. I hope you didn't take advantage of my better nature."

Smathers-Hughes was unaware that Masterson had a better nature and he felt that he should interrupt again before Masterson dug himself in too deep. "You sent me, sir, to pick up your car. You had taken it in for repairs. I was to give the mechanic a couple of boxes of army rations, a few jerry cans of fuel, and a case of duty free scotch that you had liberated from the officers' mess."

Smathers-Hughes managed to ignore the shift in Masterton's complexion from his usual pale-pinkness to the grape-purple-ness of a rich burgundy. Masterson swallowed a number of times and then gave out a weak, "Oh."

"Yes, sir, it would seem that if a memo came in when you say it did, and I was away from my duty at your direction and very likely committing a number of military offences, then it is you, with all due respect, who is in deep shyte, sir."

If one can stagger while sitting in a chair, Masterson did. He remembered very clearly now that he had ordered Smathers-Hughes to go and get his car and to pay for it with some of the black market goodies that Masterson had scrounged through his contacts in and around the camp. An inspiration shot through him. "Yes, I see, Corporal Smathers-Hughes. I see. You are suggesting, without saying anything out loud of course, that this opens the door to Captain Urquhart, or Lieutenant Bryant or even Staff Sergeant Todd as being the perpetrators of this heinous plot to cripple my career?"

Smathers-Hughes was not suggesting anything of the sort and thought that Masterson didn't need any outside assistance in derailing his own career. "No, sir, Maybe Captain Urquhart or Lieutenant Bryant, but not Staff Sergeant Todd. You gave me money for a taxi to get me into Leicester. I gave Staff Sergeant Todd half of it to drive me over."

Smathers-Hughes had no fear of reprisal over his confession. Masterson had more sins to account for, at least in this instance, and much more to lose if a threat-war between the two of them broke out. "And as for me sending that memo to the Undersecretary, the truth is, I didn't. And, I have no idea who did. A good guess, but no sure knowledge."

"Very well." Masterson didn't figure Smathers-Hughes for a liar. In fact, Masterton's thoughts on Smathers-Hughes were that the man was so full of venal sins that there was no room in his resume to include 'liar'.

"Then your good guess would be…?"

"As you mentioned a moment ago, sir."

"Yes. Fine, thank you, Corporal. That will be all."

Smathers-Hughes came to attention and said, "Alright, sir." He turned about and headed for the door. As he opened it, Masterson said to his back, "I don't suppose you'd consider splitting your half of that taxi fare, would you Corporal?"

Smathers-Hughes turned, shook his head. "I don't think so, sir."

"Yes, alright. Dismissed."

"And the court martial is off, sir?"

"I hope not, Corporal. All that has changed, it seems to me, is the name of the accused. On your way back to your desk, please ask Captain Urquhart and Lieutenant Bryant to see me immediately."

CHAPTER 35

MASTERSON MEETS THE FLOOR

A few minutes later the bulky Urquhart, shadowed by the skinny Bryant appeared in the door frame. Urquhart blundered in, and Masterson went for the throat via military protocol. "Excuse me, Captain Urquhart. I have no doubt that cavalrymen such as yourselves are quite accustomed to charging into battle, into dinner lines and even into your Commanding Officer's office without so much as a note from an accompanying bugler, but I would like to remind you…"

Masterson stopped talking long enough to shift his body so that he appeared to be peeking around the dense mass of Captain Urquhart's body to see Bryant. "Both of you. However, that is not how it is done here. In this office, as in the more refined units of the British Army, it is customary when responding to a summons from a superior officer to halt at the door, knock and while standing to attention, salute and await further direction. Let's try it again, shall we?" Masterson twirled a finger around in the air to indicate that the duo was to return to the doorway.

Captain Urquhart halted in mid-stride, threw up a nonchalant salute and resumed his forward movement.

"As you were, Captain Urquhart. As you were. From the start, if you don't mind."

Urquhart said, "Yes, sir." And turned himself around, banging into Bryant, who had been following in his wake. The two stood for seconds face-to-face. Urquhart rolled his eyes skyward and made the same gesture with his finger that Masterson had made at him. They both retreated back to the hallway. Once outside the office, Urquhart turned yet again and stood in the doorway at attention. He banged his feet on the wooden planking that served as a wall to wall carpet and shoved a more enthusiastic salute up as he sang out, "Captain Urquhart reporting as ordered, sir!"

A squeaky, "Lieutenant Bryant reporting as ordered, sir!" followed.

"Enter," Masterson said, and the two officers came forward, Captain Urquhart reached the desk and halted, while Lieutenant Bryant peeled off from the rear to end up on Urquhart's right side. Urquhart relaxed and slid into the position of stand at ease and then into the even more relaxed, stand easy position. Lieutenant Bryant followed his leader, but before he had gotten through the movement, Masterson bellowed at them, "Who told you to stand easy, Captain? Get back up to attention! You too, Lieutenant!"

Urquhart calmly said, "Yes, sir," as he returned to the position of attention. Bryant, startled midway through his shift from at ease to stand easy attempted to get back to attention. An arm, partly behind his back, wind milled forward to miss his side and flung itself forward too far and neatly caught Masterton's water jug, tipping it over in Masterton's direction. The flood gushed out like a desk top tsunami and headed toward Masterton's lap. Masterton, not really seeing the impending wall of water coming his way, suddenly realized that he was in danger of joining his desk accessories as flotsam and jetsam and leaped out of his chair. Too late, he was soaked from the waist down. Standing dripping, he glared at Bryant who managed a weak grin and an even weaker, "Sorry, sir."

Urquhart remained at attention, only his quivering belly indicating that he even knew what was going on. Masterton, shaking one leg and then the other had eyes only for Bryant and increased the wattage of his glare. As he flung himself skyward with a yelp, Masterton's chair headed backwards and stopped itself when in banged into the wall. As it did so, the only window in the entire building that opened, slammed shut, causing Masterson to flinch forward. The was silence as Masterson resumed his glaring at Bryant. Bryant stared at the wall behind Masterson and Urquhart stared straight ahead with no response to the banging window at all. They make cavalry officers out of stern stuff. Some of them. Bryant quivered in his cavalry boots. Masterton, ignoring his dampened thighs and other areas snapped back to his original plan and got on with his interrogation of Urquhart and Bryant.

He leaned one hand on his desk, putting it into a small puddle that had lingered.

"Shit!" He pulled his hand back and wiped it on his dry backside. He took his other hand and with his index finger pointed at Urquhart and said, "Shit!"

"Sir?" asked Urquhart. Keeping the finger pointed at Urquhart's bulk Masterson said, "I don't know what you've done..." He stopped. "No, I'll rephrase that. I do know what you've done. I don't know how you've done it." He shook his head as Urquhart began to reply. "No, no, Captain Urquhart, don't bother. I don't have any proof. But I do know that you did it. I just know it, deep in my water I know it."

Realizing that the reference to a liquid was redundant at this particular moment, he caromed his rage over toward Bryant. "As for you, Lieutenant, you're up to your eyeballs in this. You may have not done anything, but you sure as shit, know who did and what was done."

Masterton's finger shifted from Urquhart to bayonet Bryant's sternum. "You are, both of you, a pair of disloyal tools. You are a disgrace to the officer corps. To your respective regiments. You are a waste of good rations, you are a waste of desk space. A waste of skin and oxygen!" with his outburst over, Masterson slumped down and sank back in his chair. The chair, unaware that it was needed to catch a dampened officer's backside had remained tight against the wall. Masterson sat down. On the floor. Bryant gave a crumpled, only half caught snort. Urquhart's belly did the jellied-salad wiggle, but he controlled his facial muscles. Bryant and Urquhart stared at all of their Commanding Officer that they could see, which was his bald spot on the crown of his head. Time, as it does on occasions like these, lasted ten years for Masterson but sped by in milliseconds for Urquhart. Hoping to be able to stay so that he could see Masterton's face and enjoy his discomfort, he used reverse psychology. "Perhaps we could drop by later, sir?"

This tactic failed. Masterson grasped at the safety line inherent in Urquhart's statement. "Yes, good thinking, Captain. I'll see you both tomorrow."

Urquhart saluted Masterton's head, and this time he allowed himself a moon-faced smile. He turned and marched to the door. Bryant followed, saying as he reached the doorway. "I'll just close this for now, sir." Masterson sat on the floor for about five minutes and then he got up, picked up his hat from the floor where it had been sitting for most of the day. He opened his door quietly, looked out and seeing no one, he headed for the main entrance.

"Excuse me, sir?" said Smathers-Hughes as Masterson vainly slid past the orderly room doorway.

"Not now, Smathers-Hughes, I'll be back tomorrow morning." Knowing that Urquhart and Bryant could probably hear him, Masterson did not want to get into it with Smathers-Hughes at this moment, he guessed that Urquhart would innocently wander into the OR and Masterson couldn't face him at this time.

"But, sir, it's about the Earl, sir. It's really important."

Masterson gave up. Once Smathers-Hughes got it into his head that something was important, he hung on. And Masterson had been too quick off the mark more than once in shutting Smathers-Hughes down. "Very well, come into my office, but it has to be quick." They both went into the office and took their places, Masterson behind his desk. This time he checked his chair's location very carefully before he placed himself gingerly into it. Smathers-Hughes just plumped himself down and waited for what he saw as some strange chair occupying ritual to finish, then he began.

"Well, sir, since we last spoke, I have been doing some investigating. Staff Sergeant Todd told me that this Earl of West Saxmundham and North Haselbury was AWOL. According to my source, the Earl is missing due to one very simple reason."

"Oh, and according to this omnipotent source, what might that be?"

"He's dead."

"Dead?"

"Yes, sir, passed away about two months ago."

"And you are the only one who knows this?"

"Not exactly, sir, I imagine his family knows."

"Bah! I mean militarily."

"Oh, of course, sir. Well, you know, and of course, my source knows."

"No one else in the entire British Army?"

"Does appear that way, sir."

Masterson's felt that that was all he was going to get, but, relieved he had something, he dismissed Smathers-Hughes. Once alone, he called Kennecott and gave him the gist of what Smathers-Hughes had given him, but in this scenario, it was Masterson who had this wonderful source. Kennecott thanked him, but to Masterson it sounded insincere. No matter, he thought as he put down the phone, at least I'm off the hook for this mess. Masterson was so relieved to finish up with the Earl that he was almost gloating at his craftiness.

Kennecott's thank you was not insincere, it was merely a way to get Masterson off the phone and out of his own hair. Sincerity was not even on the docket as far as Kennecott was concerned.

Masterson's phone rang. It was Kennecott with plenty of sincerity

"Masterton, in reference to your recent, wonderful, news. I would suggest that the next time you get close to this wonderful, all-seeing, all-knowing source of yours..."

"Yes, sir?"

"Give him a swift kick in the goolies."

"The goolies? Pardon me, sir? "

"You heard me. A swiftie in the balls. That piece of so-called intel, as you so disgustingly phrase it, is deader than the Earl."

"I see. Old news, what?"

"Exactly. Now I'll give you something to take to this mystical fortune-teller of yours. Tell him…it is a him, isn't it?"

Masterson didn't know. He copped the news from Smathers-Hughes, stole the credit, and it blew up in his face. He took a guess. "A him, sir."

"Good, tell him thanks very much for the information about the Earl being dead. But, he's got a son who inherited the title. That particular version of the Earl is alive and kicking. Got that?"

Kennecott paused to catch Masterton's response but heard only choking. "Never mind, Masterton, never mind."

"Right, sir."

"Listen closely, Masterton. Get that elite team of incompetents rolling. The Earl's last known location is Winnipeg." Masterton's grasp of geography was quite simple. "Winnipeg? That's in North America, correct, sir?"

"Sort of? Masterton, sort of? It's actually the capital city of Manitoba, a province that is situated in Canada."

"Right, sir, and you want me to go there and find the runaway Earl?"

"No, send your be…" Kennecott was going to say send your best. He remembered that Masterton's best were the British Army's worst. "Belay that. Go yourself. Take whoever you need. But…"

"No problem, sir. I'll take the team, and we'll sort that Earl out. Top hole, no doubt."

Kennecott said, "All of them? Not necessary."

"We'll continue to do our jobs, while we are tracking the Earl, sir. We can do both and Canada is a big place."

"Your jobs, all of them, including yours, can be done by orangutans, and that's what I believe you've got working for you." Kennecott didn't mention that he thought that Masterson was the lead orangutan. "Well, Masterton, it's your job. You decide. And remember, you'll pay for it out of your own budget. I'm not giving you a penny more to track that loopy Earl."

"Yes, sir?"

"But remember that you've got seven days. And all expenses come out of your budget. If I don't get word that you have apprehended the Earl within that time frame, you may as well stay in Winnipeg."

Kennecott's plan was that Masterson would be lucky to find Winnipeg in seven days. One way or another, Kennecott would come out ahead. Either he'd have the missing Earl under lock and key, or if Masterson was unsuccessful, then the British Army would find itself short one major. If questioned, Kennecott would have preferred the latter.

CHAPTER 36

MASTERSON MEETS CANADA: IT'S A BIG COUNTRY

The next day Masterson dialled up Smathers-Hughes and invited him down for a chat.

"Sit down, Corporal." Smathers-Hughes sat and waited for Masterson to begin. With a bit of a tinge to his cheeks, Masterson began. "Corporal, I feel it is only right that I apologize for my loss of temper yesterday."

"Thank you, sir. Most appreciated."

"And I have something that belongs to you." Masterson handed over Smathers-Hughes' Coronation pen. I found this last Friday on the floor, must have rolled off your desk."

"Yes, thank you, sir. I had been looking for it."

Since Masterson had taken it out of the desk drawer and Smathers-Hughes had never ever used it, just kept it in the drawer, both knew that the pen had been taken, not found. Masterson looked a bit sheepish, but he could never admit to a corporal, especially a corporal such as Smathers-Hughes, that he had stooped so low as to steal a pen from a subordinate. Smathers-Hughes was just relieved to have the pen back.

He figured to get even somewhere else down the road. "Paybacks is paybacks." As he had heard Lieutenant Bryan saying.

"Smathers-Hughes, I am a bit disappointed in your source."

"Yes, sir. Me too, sir. He got back to me just now. The Earl is not dead. Or he is dead, but it's not him."

"Yes, interesting, Corporal. He's dead or not dead, but he's not him. Clever."

"Sorry, sir, but what I mean is that the Earl is dead, but his son now has the title. He's the one who is absent. He's the one the report is talking about."

Masterson smiled and played his trump card. "And you are about to tell me that the Earl, the young Earl is in Winnipeg, right?"

"Wrong, sir. I'm not. He's in…"

"No, Smathers-Hughes, I have it from a very reliable source that the Earl is in Canada, Winnipeg to be precise. That's the capital city of Manitoba, in case you didn't know."

"Yes, I did know, sir. But the Earl is not in Winnipeg."

"Smathers-Hughes, come, come. I can be magnanimous, it's perfectly acceptable for a corporal to be wrong now and again, even you."

"But I'm not wrong, sir. The Earl's in Oromocto."

"Oro-what-o? Is that a place? Oh, maybe it's a suburb of Winnipeg. After all, with a name like Winnipeg, why can't there be a suburb called Oro-what-ever you just said?"

"Sir, please, you're making a mistake. Oromocto is a city of its own."

"Okay, so maybe it's just outside of Winnipeg. That'd work, eh? Canada may be big, but I know my geography." The smug Major sat back and let the aura of awe that he felt was exuding from Smathers-Hughes at Masterson's sheer brilliance wash over him. He was dismayed when he realized that it was not a tidal wave, but more a ripple in a tea cup.

The Corporal, unaware of the lack of awe he was exhibiting, explained, "Oromocto is a city in New Brunswick, sir. About fifteen miles from Fredericton…"

"Ah, ah, gotcha, Smathers-Hughes. Gotcha! My Aunt Penelope comes from Fredericktown, and by the way, it's pronounced Frederick-town, not Fredericton. It's a small town in Ohio, which is in the United States." Masterson basked in the glow of supreme knowledge. Any minute now and the wave was going to break through Smathers-Hughes' know-it-all demeanour. With not even a damp toe, Smathers-Hughes ploughed on.

"I don't disagree, sir, Fredericktown is in Ohio, but Fredericton is in New Brunswick, Canada."

Masterson pushed his luck, he felt there was room for error here and that maybe, just maybe there was a Fredericton and it could have been in New Brunswick.

"Yes, fine, New Brunswick, just across the line from Manitoba, I believe, west of it, you know, towards the Pacific."

Anyone with a discerning gene in his vitals would have seen Smathers-Hughes' look of frustration. "No, sir, New Brunswick is in what is known as Atlantic Canada, it's lumped in as part of the Maritimes. It's east, way east of Manitoba."

"So, fine, it's east not west. Who cares?" Masterson saw a way to get out of this geographical who's who or where's where. "What does it have to do with us and our conversation?"

With things looking like they were getting back on track, Smathers-Hughes gave a sigh and said, "Oromocto is where the Earl is. He's in the army ."

Masterson half rose out of his chair to attack such an obvious statement, but, remembering his last foray into indignation, wisely remained seated. "Yes, of course he is. That's why we're getting his absence reports, remember, Smathers-Hughes?"

"Not our Army, sir, their Army."

"Who's they?"

"The Canucks, sir. He's a member of the Canadian Army."

"Non…" Masterson stopped. Smathers-Hughes was no fool. If the Earl was in Canada, why couldn't he be in the Canadian Army? Masterson was a fool, but around about now, he knew enough to let Smathers-Hughes explain. Once that was out of the way, Smathers-Hughes said, "So are we going to go to Canada to apprehend him?"

"No, we are not. I am. With my budget as small as it is, and with you lot gouging out great big chunks every month in the form of pay, in return for doing fuck all, I'll be lucky enough to get through to the end of the fiscal year."

Smathers-Hughes smiled. "Beg pardon, sir, but I think you need to know one little thing before you decide who goes and who doesn't."

"Corporal Smathers-Hughes, you cannot go, you run the OR. You are vital to this place. No, I'm sorry, but you must remain here and keep track of the rest of them for me."

"Okay, sir, but I know how to do this and still make some money for your budget."

"And that would be how?"

"Am I going to Canada, sir?"

Masterson began his chair rising ceremony, remembered and sat back down. "Look, Corporal, are you trying to blackmail me?"

"No, sir, I'm not. But if you take me, I'll let you in on a well-kept secret."

"And if I don't?"

"Then I guess it'll stay a secret a bit longer."

"And you say this secret will save me money?"

Smathers-Hughes shook his head. "No. it'll make you money."

Masterson gave it some thought. "Alright, if this little scheme of yours is a phony, I'll cancel your trip. As of me hearing this secret, you are going. So spill it."

"Fine, sir. See, when a file is opened on an absentee, and having a 'runner' such as the Earl being absent overseas qualifies, then the costs are all borne at the national level and are covered by the Home Office. If Mr. Kennecott sent his teams out more often, he'd actually save money, because the HO would pay the shot, including their wages while they are out of the country."

"And how do we make money?"

"We take three of us and claim for five."

"Brilliant, Smathers-Hughes, simply Top Hole."

"Thank you, sir, and by the way, what exactly does 'top hole' mean?"

Masterson looked thoughtful, or at least the contorted expression he assumed was meant to make him look thoughtful. Smathers-Hughes thought Masterson was about to be violently ill and was sorry he asked. "Not really, sure, Corporal. I know it does mean excellent, but where the term originated, I have no idea."

"Very well, sir, I'll get us sorted out for the trip shall I?"

"Yes, we'll take Captain Urquhart with us. Send in Lieutenant Bryant, I'll leave him in charge of the office and of Staff Sergeant Todd."

CHAPTER 37

MASTERSON MEETS OROMOCTO

Major Masterton, Captain Urquhart, and Corporal Smathers-Hughes arrived at the Montreal airport and waited for ten hours in the terminal for a connecting flight to Fredericton. On arrival there, they took a cab to Oromocto and found a motel a mile down the road from the front gates of Camp Gagetown. They spent the night there and the next morning found them dressed in their military best in what was laughingly referred to as, 'downtown' Oromocto. This was the Oromocto Shopping Centre. They had found a small café and had breakfast. While they were finishing up, Captain Urquhart asked Major Masterton, "Sir, we're here, and this is a big place, so what do we do now?"

Masterson looked at Smathers-Hughes. "Any further information from that source of yours on just where in Oromocto the Earl is likely to be?"

It's a bit of a shame that these intrepid kidnappers hadn't ran into me, I could have saved them a lot of work. However, we were not scheduled to meet until the parade from hell neared its conclusion. So instead, we have to make do with second hand information, which, I assure you, is accurate right down to Masterson's dialogue with the Mayor's mother.

Smathers-Hughes didn't have the right answer, but added a small clue. "No, sir, but he did say that right beside Oromocto was an army camp."

"Yes," said Urquhart. "I saw the sign when we came down here from the hotel. And if this camp is anything like one of ours, there's going to be a few thousand soldiers in it. We can't check them all."

"Quite right, Captain, so how do you suggest we handle this?"

Urquhart looked over at Smathers-Hughes. It was plain to see that he thought that Masterson should have had a plan before they got on the plane, not now. He was still miffed at having to ride with Smathers-Hughes in the back while Masterson had travelled first class on the plane. Urquhart sniffed the air, gave a shrug of his broad shoulders and said, "Why don't we go into the camp and see what's going on? We can wander around and get the lay of the land. Tell whoever's running the place that we're British exchange officers… well, not you Smathers-Hughes. Why don't you stay here and look around this shopping

230

centre of theirs? You know, pick up a few souvenirs of your trip to Canada, what?"

"Just a minute, Captain Urquhart, I'm in charge here, and I'll tell Corporal Smathers-Hughes what to do, not you."

"Very well then, sir, give him an order and while you're at it, why don't you tell me what to do as well?"

"Yes, alright then. I will." Masterson couldn't come up with a better plan than what Urquhart had laid out, so he said, "Captain Urquhart, take a taxi and go up to the camp and have a drive around, see what's up." Without waiting for Urquhart's response, Masterson turned to face Smathers-Hughes. "As for you Corporal, take a stroll around here and if you see any one in uniform, ask them if there are any British troops here, got it?"

"Yes, sir. And where will you be, sir?"

"I'll stay here and use this café as our overseas headquarters. Report back to me if either of you finds anything."

"And if we find nothing?" asked Urquhart. "Do we stay where we are?"

"Don't give me any of your smart-arse comments, Captain Urquhart, or I'll have you on the first plane home, thank you very much."

A period of silence ensued. The three of them took turns looking out the big window at Canada and wondering why they were really there. Smathers-Hughes got things going again.

"Excuse me, sir, but we are pretty sure that the Earl is in the Canadian Army, right?" Masterton, remembering Kennecott's speech about their valuable source, hesitated and then said carefully, in case Urquhart was taking mental notes of his conversation. "Possibly. The source is not infallible. But go on."

"Well, if he is in the Canadian Army and we are here on legitimate business, why can't we just go into the camp, visit the headquarters and ask to see him?"

Urquhart nodded. "Good idea, Corporal. Very good idea." He looked at Masterton. "Why don't we, Major?"

Masterson couldn't see any reason not to do that, except that it would take all the joy out of man-hunting. He wanted to sneak and peek and then grab the Earl when he least expected it and then bring him home in cuffs. "Well… it is a … good idea, Smathers-Hughes… a jolly good idea…"

"Top hole idea, sir?"

"Not quite Top Hole, because if the Earl has a contact in the camp orderly room he'll be warned and get on out of camp quick as mustard."

"Mmmm, yes, he'd then be absent without leave from two armies at once. A unique record, wouldn't you say," said Urquhart.

Masterson pondered this a while longer, then shook his head. "No… it's too risky. We need to locate him in a surreptitious manner. Close in on him while he's unaware that we're even here and then, wham!" Masterson brought his hand up as he spoke and then slammed his fist down onto the table with a crash. He had failed to look at the landing zone, and his fist hammered the cup and saucer in front of him. Pieces of china scattered across the room like buckshot. Urquhart caught one in the chest and grunted in surprise. A chunk of saucer headed toward Smathers-Hughes who ducked under the table as the shrapnel headed for parts unknown.

That was Urquhart's cue to get out. He got up and moving past the angry looking waitress, muttered, "Not me, Ma'am."

Smathers-Hughes stayed below the level of the table while Masterson tried to convince the waitress that the cup had self-destructed due to the heat from his tea.

"Shoddy workmanship, that cup, Madam. Probably made in China."

"Made from china, you mean. That'll be five dollars for the cup, three for the saucer and five more for chasing away my customers."

Masterson held up the handle of the teacup and said, "Here. Will this give me a discount?" The stern look that the large, forbidding, waitress gave him convinced Masterson to pay up without further negotiation. The moustache she was wearing reminded him of his Mother's upper lip, and he added ten dollars for the tip.

Smathers-Hughes said, "There goes our overseas headquarters, eh, sir? And did you see that chunk of teacup hit that soldier?"

"What soldier?"

"Guy in a kilt, coming out of the shitter, chunk hit him just above the eye. Bleeding like a stuck pig he was."

"Shitter? Really, Corporal. Is that any way to talk?"

"The bog, better, sir?" said Smathers-Hughes, thinking that the least Masterson could have done was go and check the casualty.

"Shut up, Corporal," said a still red-faced Masterton.

"Sorry, sir, just a comment."

"I've had enough of your bloody comments, Corporal Smathers-Hughes. Now fuck off on that souvenir trip Urquhart suggested. I'll be down at the far end of this shopping centre, by the taxi stand."

Smathers-Hughes left the café and began his tour. He wandered around and had finished his tour of the tiniest shopping plaza he had ever seen and was returning to the café when he saw a green Army bus stop at the end of the shopping centre near a bowling alley. He noticed that when they had gone in the restaurant for breakfast, there was nothing really happening down at that end of the mall, but now someone had decked out a few large poles with bunting and had stretched out between two light standards a large banner. As he waited to see who, if anyone, got off the bus, he moved to where he could read the sign. It read, 'Grand Opening, Oromocto's Finest Mall'. From what Smathers-Hughes had seen this was Oromocto's only shopping mall, and it was a sad thing in itself. He stood near what he thought was a cross between a war surplus store and a jewellery store, a large sign above the door read, 'Scully's'. He leaned against a pillar outside the store and watched a group of soldiers disembark from the bus. Then he saw them gaggle over to an empty part of the parking lot where a lance corporal yelled at them to form up in three ranks. Smathers-Hughes was close enough to hear the soldiers as they nonchalantly wandered into formation. The lance corporal didn't seem to mind, and then he yelled, "Smoke if ya got 'em!"

He pulled out a package from his sporran and lit up a cigarette. The boys, for that's all they were, stood in their three ranks, smoking and joking and tossing insults back and forth at one another. As they stood around, some of them tossing good-natured comments at the lance corporal, which he returned as good as he got, he suddenly stiffened and said, "Hey, we're missing a bunch of you lot. Who's not here?"

"The Squire, Ace Hornbook, Campbell, McGuffin, Levesque and …."

"And Foxy," someone else added.

Lance Corporal Anderson said, "So where the fuck are they?"

"Lieutenant Bowles came into the shack after breakfast and took them away."

"Where and why?"

"No idea, Lance Corporal."

Anderson looked the squad over. "Does anyone here know why the squad commander took those guys?"

Getting no answer he swore again and moved off to one side to await the squad sergeant's arrival.

Smathers-Hughes was about thirty feet from the group, and he saw that he could move up closer by going around a few parked cars and then realized that a part of the parking lot had been cordoned off. By staying behind the cordon, he was able to get right up behind the rear rank. Since they didn't seem to be too busy, he asked no one in general and everyone in particular, "Hey, lads, any of you British?"

A tall, skinny lad in the rear rank turned to face Smathers-Hughes. "Matta a fact, yep, the Squire is a limey."

"Is he an Earl?" asked Smathers-Hughes.

"An Earl? Yeah, I think so, or he's some kind of royalty, s'why we call 'im the Squire. He's outa Robinson Crusoe or something like that. Why?"

Smathers-Hughes didn't have an answer for that. He couldn't come out and say because we are here to kidnap him. "Oh, nothing, I thought I heard a British accent."

"You did, you heard yourself, pal, you're as limey as the Squire, aint'cha? An' besides, the Squire's not here yet."

A voice from the front of the platoon broke up the conversation. "Johnson, quit jawing with that limey squaddie and get back into place."

"Yes, Lance Corporal," said the soldier and he turned from Smathers-Hughes to face his front.

Smathers-Hughes stayed behind the platoon. As he stood there waiting, a sergeant clad in short sleeve order and kilt came over to the group. "Where's the piper?"

"He's in the restaurant taking a shit, Sarge," someone said from within the ranks.

"Well he better let it bake, we're on in five minutes."

"I've got his bagpipes, Sergeant," said Morgan.

"Excellent, Morgan, excellent. Can you play the fucking things?"

"No, Sergeant," said Morgan.

"Then who gives a shit about the pipes?"

Smathers-Hughes saw his chance. "Excuse me, Sergeant?" he said as he came around the flank of the platoon toward Clyde.

"What?" said Clyde as he turned to face the new voice. "Where the hell did you come from?"

"England, Sergeant. I'm on an exchange with Camp Headquarters."

He was cut off as another lance corporal came up to the sergeant. "Sergeant Clyde, Michaels won't be able to play. He's been taken to hospital with a broken arm and a bloody nose."

"What? How the hell did that happen? The damn fool only went for a shit?"

"Yes, but he got into an argument with some limey major in the restaurant. Seems the major had a fit in there and broke some china. Michaels was coming out of the shitter when he slipped on some spilled tea."

"And he broke his nose in the fall?"

"No, that happened after."

"After what, Duguay, c'mon, c'mon, don't make it a soap opera."

"Sorry, Sarge, but after he fell, he bitched at the major and the major gave him hell in return."

"How does that translate into a bloody nose? Don't tell me the major cracked him on the beak?"

"He got that from Lily, the waitress. She didn't like his language and hauled off and planted one on him."

"Well, shit! Now what do we do?"

CHAPTER 38

SERGEANT CLYDE MEETS SMATHERS-HUGHES

"Excuse me, Sergeant?"

Clyde turned to Smathers-Hughes again. "You've already said that. What the fuck do you want, Corporal. And unless you can play the agony bags, I don't have time for you."

"Matter of fact, Sergeant, that's what I wanted to tell you. I can play them. I spent three years with the Black Watch in Scotland, and I learned from their pipe major."

"And you think you can play…"

Another lance corporal appeared at Clyde's elbow. "Pardon me, Sergeant Clyde."

Sergeant Clyde turned to face the newcomer.

"What?"

"We've got time for a quick audition. But, even so, we're gonna have to go with the Corporal or go without music."

"You're right. Okay Corporal, give us Highland Laddie…you do know it, don't you?"

"Yes, Sergeant."

"Fine. Grab the pipes from Morgan and give us a short tune." Smathers-Hughes did as requested and despite being nervous, played Highland Laddie and then tossed in 'Black Bear' for good measure. The platoon applauded when Smathers-Hughes finished.

"Well, done, son. That was very good. Sorry I shouted at you a while back."

"No problem, Sergeant, and that's pretty much my repertoire, Sergeant."

"Won't matter to the crowd." He turned around and surveyed the parking lot. "What there is of it. My guess is that none of that bunch in the bleachers will recognize any pipe tunes. Just keep playing them, alternate whenever I give you the high sign."

Clyde turned to face the squad. "Right lads, here's a quick briefing. Now you all saw the chalkboard map, and we rehearsed this in the drill hall often enough…" He turned on his heel to where Lance Corporal Anderson was standing. "Lance Corporal Anderson, are you aware that we seem to be lacking the full complement of 1313 squad?"

"Yes, Sergeant. According to the lads, Lieutenant Bowles took the Squire, Hornbook, Campbell, McGuffin, Levesque and Foxworth on what he called a top secret errand. And before you even ask me, No, I don't know where or why. Neither does the rest of the squad, Sarge."

Clyde had endured a lot over these weeks with Bowles, and it was here that he began wishing that the Squire had left Bowles hanging on the death slide. He ground his teeth, spat and then shrugged his shoulders. "Okay, we go with what we've got. The squad commander will either arrive with the lads or he won't. As I was saying, you've seen the layout, and now you can see where we are in relation to the reviewing stand." Clyde paused to let the boys all turn and look at the shopping centre parking lot. "As you can see, we are in the southeast corner. The big shots and the reviewing stand are over in the northwest corner. We'll do a few warm up drill movements and when we get the signal, we'll march down toward the bowling alley, do a left wheel and come across the frontage of the shopping centre get in front of the reviewing stand and then do another left wheel so that we can come across in front of the reviewing stand and then the squad commander will order eyes right. We'll hold that movement for ten paces, and he'll give us the eyes front. We'll come up past the reviewing stand, do another wheel and then almost immediately another one to put us facing the reviewing stand. We'll halt, stand at ease and await the reviewing officer's inspection. That's pretty much it. Any Questions? I didn't think so."

Sergeant Clyde and a couple of the lance corporals chatted with Smathers-Hughes while they waited for the squad commander to arrive, or the reviewing stand to fill up with big wigs. A few minutes before ten hundred hours a roaring noise was heard from behind the squad. A few seconds later an APC, an M113, armoured personnel carrier roared into view.

Sergeant Clyde was the first to react. "My god! That's an APC! And if I'm not mistaken, the crew commander is Lieutenant Bowles."

The APC came shooting across the grass, tearing huge divots from the turf, spewing earth and gravel as it swung around to pull up alongside the squad. The noise was deafening, and Clyde made the cut across the throat signal to kill the engine. A moment later and the engine was shut down, and the rear hatch began to drop. Out from the back came the missing soldiers. They were all dressed in fighting order, cammed up with camouflage cream, wore leaves and branches in their steel helmet covers and looked very warlike. The remainder of the squad had been turned out in No 7C, Field Order, Summer with kilt, which was the walking out order for recruits and which they all called 'bush uniform'. Along with that, they wore the khaki balmorals, boots and puttees and their web belts.

Out from behind the soldiers came Lieutenant Bowles, dressed in his officer's version of Tee-dubs, or tropical worsted with a kilt. From behind he looked quite soldierly. Sergeant Clyde came up to him, saluted and said, "Good morning, sir. Are you planning to do something fancy with that APC and the cammed up troops?"

"Indeed, yes, Sergeant Clyde. Indeed, yes. It came to me yesterday. Since I had been the Top Dog's aide and had considerable pull." Pleased at being able to say this, Bowles smirked and then went on, "I just dropped in to the Armoured Corps lines and on behalf of the Top Dog requested this piece of kit for the day."

"And they gave it to you?"

"Certainly, Sergeant. They don't know me, but they know the name Sir Richard of Norbury."

They sure as shit don't know you. If they did, the closest you'd get to an APC would be under its tracks, thought Clyde. "Yes, sir, well, the driver can leave it parked here, and we can let the civvies wander through it after the parade. We sure don't have any plans for it other than that."

"Wrong-o, Sergeant Clyde. Did you think your old squad commander would let you down? We've got two things going for us. Number one, this excellent piece of kit. And number two, we've got me with a plan. What could be better, eh?"

What could be worse, you mean. We'll be lucky to be free men by sundown if that lunatic launches his plan. "Wellll…sir, we do have the plan in place, and it doesn't call for that."

"Flexibility, Sergeant Clyde. Remember your principles of war. Be flexible." Sergeant Clyde remembered that the last time Bowles had used the principles of war and specifically, flexibility, in his hearing. That had presented Toby and the squad with an opportunity to watch the squad truck explode on the rocket launcher range.

"Yes, sir. So what is the new plan?"

"The new plan, yes, very good, Sergeant. Glad to see that you are onside so quickly."

Clyde was not so much onside as he was frustrated. He wished that the regiment wouldn't send officers to The Depot to get trained. Better to send those who knew what they were doing and who understood that the squad sergeant was someone who it would wise to listen to.

"Here's what's going to happen, Sergeant Clyde," said Bowles.

No, what I'm about to hear is what should happen and what would happen if it did not include Bowles. What is going to happen is another unmitigated disaster. He liked the idea of using unmitigated. Lieutenant Colonel Dillingham had used it when he had spoken to The Depot RSM after the death slide incident. He gave a sigh and said, "Very well, sir."

"I'll ride up in the crew commander's hatch in the APC to the rear of the squad. You lead with the piper in front of you. Once you are in a position facing the reviewing stand, I'll bring the carrier up on your right flank…"

"And then…" Sergeant Clyde waited for the precise moment when the catastrophe would occur. It was going to occur, there was no doubt about it.

"And then, I'll send the signal and the driver will drop the ramp and the lads will storm out and run off to an angle and await further instructions."

Bowles did have the grace to blush at this. He was not going to tell his squad sergeant all of the details as he thought that Clyde might not go along with it. Clyde knew there was some element of the plan that he was not getting, but if it was as harmless as this, he could live with it. While Bowles and Clyde were conferring, the cammed up boys were over mixing in with the rest of the squad. Smathers-Hughes was backing up so that he was close to the right flank from where he would lead the parade. He was now placed where he could hear the lads all talking. As he stood there pretending to adjust the pipes, a cammed soldier came over to him and said, "Hello, I see that you're wearing a British uniform, but not a highland one, are you really a piper?"

The cammed gent was Toby, and he had wandered over to introduce himself to another Brit.

"Actually, I'm not. Your piper was taken off to the hospital with a broken arm after falling down. I volunteered to take his place because I can play the bagpipes. By the sound of your accent you're British, too, right?"

"Yes, Corporal, I am. My name is Toby Trelauney-Fitzgibboncrest and I live in Winnipeg." Toby was not going to go into all the details, especially when he didn't even know this man. And, after all, he was a corporal. Corporals were not those who one disclosed things to when still only a recruit. While the two of them stood there, Smathers-Hughes heard one of them yell out, "Hey, Squire, you gonna go into the bowling alley for another pair of those spiffy, free, shoes?"

Not understanding that, Smathers-Hughes paid it no attention, until the lad who he was talking to yelled back, "No, Offside, I'm not. Now that I know better, I'm going to have a pair made out of your hide once we get back to camp."

A few of the young soldiers laughed, and Offside shut up. Smathers-Hughes nearly laughed out loud. Masterson had sent him away to get him out of his way. Urquhart was busy in camp trying to track down the missing Earl. Smathers-Hughes, on his souvenir hunt, had walked up to him and spoken with him. It was so outrageous that he laughed out loud. Toby looked at him, but before they could continue, Clyde barked, "Right, sir, let's get this show on the road."

"Good-o, Sergeant Clyde. You get the troops formed up, and I'll get the carrier in behind them," yelled Bowles from up in the crew commander's hatch.

CHAPTER 39

CLYDE MEETS THE PARADE FROM HELL

The parade from hell, as Clyde liked to call it when telling it in the mess, began with the piper doing a very good job as he led the squad down toward the bowling alley. The squad came to within twenty yards of the sidewalk in front of the shopping centre, and Clyde gave the order, "Left wheeeeeellll!" and Smathers-Hughes wheeled around and headed down the long side of the shopping centre. As Clyde came up to the approximate spot where Smathers-Hughes had wheeled he followed suit and as he came around into the stretch he saw the reviewing stand and all the town's mucky-mucks.

As they came closer, he imagined where the disaster was going to come from. Standing peacefully chewing their cud, or whatever it is horses chew while waiting on humans, on either side of the reviewing stand were two horses. On the back of each were red-coated members of the Royal Canadian Mounted Police. Yes, if there's any dirty work at the crossroads, it'll be that damned APC scaring the shit out of them horses, he thought. Too late now, we just have to go into this praying. They made it to the next wheel and came around across the frontage of the reviewing stand. Clyde gave the "Eyes right!" and then the "Eyes front!" soon after he brought them around in another wheel and then another and the squad then came to a halt. A bit ragged, thought Clyde, but after all, they were recruits. As he stood the squad at ease, he gave a glance toward the horses. They were neighing softly and shaking their heads at the sound of the pipes but remained on duty. After all, they were Mounties.

Then the APC came along, and the horses began to dance in place, their riders a little unsure of how well their mounts were going to behave. Clyde watched them, ready in case they took off, to get out of their way. He and the squad were now positioned directly in front of the reviewing stand and the two horses. If they decided on a full frontal charge they were going to come straight at the squad and Clyde was in front of the squad. The APC did it's little trick and came up beside the squad, and all went well.

241

Bowles came down out of the hatch into the APC and then exited from the rear. He presented himself to the Mayor and then escorted the Mayor and his entourage along the ranks of the squad. The Mayor, the ex-batman of the ex-Depot Commandant, Lieutenant Colonel Dillingham displayed the usual pompous attitude of the inspecting officer, stopping along the ranks to ask this lad where he was from, this one how did he like the army and all the other irrelevant questions inspecting officers ask the troops who only want to get off the damned parade square, or in this case shopping centre parking lot.

Bowles led the Mayor back to the reviewing stand and returned to his place in the APC's hatch. The Mayor gave the usual, best parade I've ever seen speech told Bowles to carry on and then the shit hit the fan. From Clyde's vantage point, he could see nothing of the APC, as it was to his right. But the sound he heard as something flew through the air to land in front of the reviewing stand made him weak in the knees. The little pop that comes from a thrown smoke grenade as it ignites told him everything he didn't want to know. As bright yellow smoke billowed out from the small canister at the base of the reviewing stand's scaffolding, he couldn't think of a worse scenario. Lieutenant Bowles could. He tossed a thunderflash, a large firecracker used to simulate grenades, toward the reviewing stand and yelled, "Dismount left, dismount left!" The ramp lowered and out came the cammed up soldiers, yelling as if they were attacking the Alamo. They ran around the carrier and came up alongside Sergeant Clyde and went to ground. Not an easy thing to do when the ground is blacktop. As they flung themselves onto the pavement, they started firing blank rounds aimed between the reviewing stand and the squad.

Clyde said later, "I thought that Bowles had become more unbalanced that usual and decided that he had formed an assassination team to wipe out the Mayor of Oromocto and his council. At that point, I was sure Bowles had issued live ammo, and I hoped that a stray round would take me out of my misery."

The smoke, the thunderflash and the firing of six rifles was enough for the Mountie's horses. One did as Clyde expected and ran toward the squad. The other, probably because he was closer to the smoke and noise, tried to climb the reviewing stand steps. He succeeded in getting up the first few, but then staggered and got caught up in the bunting. Seeing that the high ground was not a feasible passage out of the fiery hell his rider had ridden him, he bucked to get rid of the rider and the bunting. Doing this on the wooden platform steps only caused him to bump up against the scaffolding corner post. As the poor horse, now only partially riderless, came crashing back down the steps, the reviewing stand collapsed, bringing the reviewing party down to earth faster than they had ever gone up. The horse got back to solid earth and headed back across the grassy slope behind the reviewing stand. As he got to the grass, he gave one more buck and the Mountie was launched into the air to crash on a softer landing zone than the occupants of the reviewing stand.

Smathers-Hughes had given up playing the bagpipes after the smoke grenade exploded. He watched the parade disintegrate into chaos. Major Masterson had come up to him and had gotten out the words, "What the bloody hell do you think you're doing, Corporalllllhhhh!" when he was hit from behind by the other terrified horse. This horse, with struggling rider, had dashed had toward the squad, missing Clyde by inches. In keeping with Mountie tradition, he got his man. The horse hadn't missed Masterton, catching him in the seat of his pants as he arrived on the scene to castigate Smathers-Hughes. Once past Masterson, the horse had only the squad to negotiate. The soldiers, quicker off the mark than Masterson or Clyde, just stepped to either side, and the horse ran through them and off toward the bowling alley.

Bowles had watched from the commander's cupola, and as the parade disintegrated into bedlam, he hauled himself out of the hatch, yelled at the driver, "Follow me!" and scrambled down the front of the carrier to the reviewing stand. The driver, half laughing and half stunned, followed.

By this time, Urquhart had returned from his trip into the camp with the knowledge that the elusive Earl was in the very place he had left. He had charged back by taxi to find that the shopping centre parking lot had become a battlefield. He was in time to see Masterson go ass-over-tea kettle and as he walked forward, Urquhart was laughing so hard his stomach hurt him. By the time he got to where Masterson was brushing himself off, and Smathers-Hughes was assisting, he heard Smathers-Hughes telling the luckless Major that the runaway Earl was right there on the scene.

"Sir, the Earl's that guy over there, the second from the left of those in camouflage."

Toby and the other camouflaged soldiers had dashed over to help dig civilians out of the wreckage that had once been a reviewing stand.

"We can grab him and get out of here. This place is a zoo. No one'll notice."

As he examined the war zone, Urquhart nodded, then said, "He's right, Major Masterton. We have the opportunity we need. Look, the APC driver is over helping with the reviewing stand people. The engine is running, and we are the closest to it. All we need to do is go over and grab that lad, I mean, the Earl and off we go."

Masterson stopped rubbing his bruised rear and looked over to where Toby was standing with the other combatants. "Who'll drive the APC?"

"I will. I'm qualified in a variety of tracked vehicles… shouldn't be too hard to drive this one."

"Are you sure, Captain Urquhart?"

"Not a problem. Qualified in a Centurion. Let's do it."

"Yes, why not. Top hole, Captain. Top hole."

"Just a sec, sir," said Smathers-Hughes.

"What now, Corporal? First, you go off gallivanting across Canada leading a parade, and now I suppose you're going to demonstrate your brilliance by offering us your thoughts, hey?"

Smathers-Hughes didn't think that strolling across five hundred yards of parking lot qualified as gallivanting across Canada. As well, he wanted to remind the Major that any half-wit could offer him better advice than what Masterson usually gave himself. "No, sir, I'm not. I wanted to suggest something."

Urquhart, well aware that Smathers-Hughes had pulled both UARB's and Masterson's chestnuts out of the fire more than once, supported any suggestions that Smathers-Hughes could come up with, said, "I think we should at least hear him out, sir."

Something in Urquhart's tone reminded Masterson that Smathers-Hughes was often right. "Go ahead, Corporal."

"Sir, the Earl is in the army, the Canadian Army, no less, but still he'll be accustomed to obeying officers, especially senior officers. I don't think we'll need to grab him. All we need to do is for you to go over and ask him if he's the Earl of West whatever…"

"West Saxmundham and North Haselbury," supplied Urquhart.

"Yes, and if he says yes, then ask him to step over near the armoured vehicle for a moment…"

"APC, Smathers-Hughes, not armoured vehicle. An armoured vehicle is a tank. This is an armoured personnel carrier," interrupted Urquhart. Deep inside, Urquhart was dyed cavalryman blue and was snobbish about it toward those who were any other colour, especially clerk olive drab.

"No matter, Captain Urquhart. We know what he means. Good idea, in theory, Smathers-Hughes, but I'm an officer, and you're a corporal. You do it and bring him back here.

Off Smathers-Hughes strode, leaving Urquhart to mumble, "It's important to be technically correct. I just wanted us to be accurate."

"No, problem, Captain," said Masterson as he watched Smathers-Hughes approach the Earl. Urquhart said, "I'm going to have a look at the controls and the driver's compartment. It's an interesting looking vehicle."

CHAPTER 40

THE MAYOR AND HIS MOM MEET BOWLES

As Masterson watched Smathers-Hughes approach the Earl, an elderly woman came up to him and said, "So can you tell me who on earth decided to have those poor terrified horses on a parade where there was going to be gunfire and smoke?"

"Why?"

"Why? So that I can submit a report, that's why. Somebody's got to."

"No need for you to stick your nose in things that don't concern you."

"What? Do you know who you're talking to?"

Masterson shrugged. He had no time for this. And if he had time, he wouldn't have wasted it with this crabby old woman."

"So, you don't know, and you're too thick-headed to admit it." It wasn't a question.

"Correct, Madam, I don't know, and I don't give a shit. Now buzz off."

Just then, Smathers-Hughes arrived at Toby's elbow. "Excuse me, soldier. May I have a few minutes of your time?"

Toby looked around to see the piper corporal standing beside him. "Yes, Corporal, I think so."

Masterson looked around, the place was starting to settle down. He didn't have much time.

But the woman wasn't finished. "Buzz off?"

"Let me put it another way, madam, go home. This party's over."

"I'm the mayor's mother, you jumped up little man. Besides, I was a war bride."

"Really, interesting, what war? The Hundred Year's War," said Masterson in a snotty tone.

"Why the very idea," said the Mayor's Mom. "I'll have you know…"

"Madam, you'll have me know nothing. Now you look like you survived the landslide, although you are probably all the better due to it, so get about your business and we'll be about ours." Masterson turned from her and said to Toby and Smathers-Hughes. "Follow me, lads."

Toby looked at the lady. "Sorry ma'am, he does outrank me. I have to go. I'm glad you are alright, goodbye."

"Thank you very much, young man," she said with a smile and then added, "You watch out for that Major, he's a sunnavabitch. I can tell."

"Yes, Ma'am."

Masterson turned to her and gave her his best shot. "Fuck off, lady, you and your fucking mayor son."

That did it for the exchange and Masterson led off around to the back of the APC with a puzzled Earl in tow. He marched up to the ramp of the carrier, stood aside and gestured to Toby to go inside. "Have a seat…er…er."

Toby entered the APC, sat down in the jump seat in the middle of the troop compartment. Masterson followed him in and sat on the right hand side bench. Smathers-Hughes came up the ramp and stood there at the top of it with his arms hanging from the roof of the APC, blocking any attempt to escape. Once he was settled, Masterson said, "I'm not sure how to address you. Are you an Earl or a soldier?"

"I'm both, sir, but the military people who outrank me address me as Private Trelauney-Fitzgibboncrest. Those of the same rank call me Squire. Every once in a while, Ox calls me 'Your Lordship, although he's called me Toby on rare occasions."

"Fine, I'll dispense with all the formalities and address you as Private."

"Okay, sir. Can you tell me what this is all about?"

"Yes, I can. It's quite simple, you know." Masterson nearly smiled in his delight. "What this is all about is that you, Your Lordship, are under arrest."

"Arrest?"

Toby started up. He looked over at Masterson and then to the rear of the carrier to see Smathers-Hughes drop his arms and brace himself for any dashing Toby might do in his direction. Toby looked up and saw the open hatch.

This hatch was yet another egress out of the APC. As Toby glanced at it, Urquhart could be heard in the silence, fiddling with the controls, the switches and swearing softly. Admittedly, he had driven a Centurion tank, but for about five minutes while under the strictest supervision of an Armoured Corps troop sergeant. The qualification that he boasted about gave him only enough knowledge to drive the tank out of danger, if and only if, everyone else in the tank was immobilized or dead. It was called emergency driving, and every officer in the Armoured Corps underwent the same training.

The APC or Armoured Personnel Carrier, also known as the M113 was an American vehicle and had been manufactured by a food machinery company called appropriately enough, FMC, which stood for Food Machinery Corporation. The vehicle that Toby and the kidnappers were occupying was a heavily armoured aluminum box on tank tracks. In the rear was the troop compartment, with seating for eleven soldiers. There were two benches for five men each, who sat huddled sideways in the back facing each other. Between the benches and in the middle of the compartment was the jump seat. In front of the crew compartment on the right hand side was the engine compartment and beside that on the left was the cramped space for the driver.

Directly behind the engine compartment and as a part of the main crew area was another jump seat where the commander could either sit or stand. Around the circular hatches of the driver and crew commander was a series of periscope-like windows, so they were able to operate with the hatches closed. Immediately behind the crew commander's hatch was a large rectangular hatch that could be used for getting stores and equipment in as well as permitting the troops to get in and out. They could also stand on the benches and look out this cargo hatch when the APC travelled in safe territory.

It was this hatch that Toby saw as his salvation. He didn't understand why he was being arrested by the British Army as represented by a British major and a corporal, but he decided that departure was the better part of valour. Toby sprang up, planted his feet on the jump seat he had just left and heaved himself out of the cargo hatch. Urquhart started the APC up.

Placing both hands on the outside part of the carrier Toby began to pull himself to freedom. At that very moment, Urquhart had discovered the ramp lever. Pulling on it, he turned in the driver's chair to see the ramp begin to rise. As it rose, the movement shifted Smathers-Hughes in toward the interior and at the same time he made a grab at Toby's legs. Urquhart, seeing that Toby was leaving the party too early, quit playing with the ramp and turned his body and attention to the controls. The controls were a pair of tiller bars that were connected to the drive trains of each track. Pulling on one would stop that track. Letting the other one go on moving, would turn the vehicle. Hauling back on both stopped the APC completely.

Urquhart stepped on the gas and then grabbed a tiller bar, heaving it backwards. The APC jumped forward a foot or two, then spun around to the right. Urquhart, startled by the rapid response to his actions, stepped on the brakes, which in this vehicle meant that he hauled back on both tiller bars. The APC stopped as abruptly as it had started. The occupants all reacted in the same manner; they were flung backwards. Then off to one side and them forward. After that, each behaved in a way that fit their own circumstances. Masterson banged his head on the jump seat post that ran from floor to ceiling. Smathers-Hughes spun around, clinging frantically to Toby's legs and then in the whiplash of the stop was tossed forward to end up in Masterson's lap. Toby, in mid-passage skywards, was dashed back first, since he was facing the rear of the vehicle when he jumped and then against the forward edge of the hatch, getting his wind knocked out of him and his escape plan.

As the APC leapt forward and then crashed to a halt then repeated steps one and two, Bowles was busy commenting to a confused and badly shaken Mayor, "Terrible, what? Isn't it, Your Mayorship? Seems a bit silly for the Mounties to be using horses that are nervous around gunfire. Think they'd have them better trained. Both Mounties are carrying guns, what if they had to use them?"

The Mayor, not fully back to normal, was busy pulling bunting off his person and hoping his heart was not going to explode out of his chest. He had planned to give this idiotic officer in front of him a damn good beating. Ex-Private, now Mayor Donaldson, had been on the battalion boxing team and he was sure he could still drive an uppercut or two into Bowles yapping face. Then the Mayor's Mom showed up.

"Reginald, there's a major over there who just told me to 'fuck off'. I demand that you speak to him."

The Mayor and Bowles turned to look at where she was pointing. "Over there, he's getting into that tank-thingy."

Bowles said, "Sorry to disappoint you, Madam, but…"

"I've had enough out of you lot, shut up. I wasn't even talking to you."

"I was only going to point out to you that that is not a tank, but rather, an APC, or to use its full name, an armoured personnel carrier."

"Reginald, shut this idiot up."

Which if Mom had waited a few minutes more before bothering the Mayor he would have done by now. Then the meaning of the woman's words managed to wiggle their way into Bowles' brain. "What did you say? A major in my APC? No, it couldn't be!"

"You calling my Mom a liar, whistlehead?"

"Pardon me, Mr. Mayor? A whistlehead? I am a Lieutenant."

"Right and so's a whistlehead."

"Oh, please, never mind that, I must get after that APC, it's driving away."

"Must be another officer driving, the ramp is only half up," said the Mayor.

Bowles ran off to catch up with his carrier. As he did, the Mayor's mom yelled, "You are too a whistlehead."

So after all that, the situation was this: the Mayor was consoling his Mom and wishing he could run after Bowles and punch his lights out. Toby was trying to get out by way of the ramp. Smathers-Hughes was struggling to get off Masterson's lap. Urquhart was working on getting the APC out of the parking lot without hitting any cars or the shopping centre itself. with his inadequate knowledge the operation was a stop and go process, but he was making some headway. The town council was gradually crawling out from under the wreckage of the bleachers. The squad was standing around enjoying the sights. Clyde was counting days to his retirement and trying to decide whether he should go AWOL or face the RSM, who he knew was going to blame Clyde for this debacle. And Bowles was running after the carrier, yelling.

CHAPTER 41

CLYDE'S JEEP MEETS AN APC

To further add confusion to the who's who of this shambles, for those of you still interested in keeping track of the characters, I, in my new role as Staff Sergeant Marvin Oxnard had just arrived in Sergeant Clyde's jeep. I had brought the jeep on Clyde's suggestion that it be used to drive Bowles back to his quarters after the parade. I drove slowly past the APC eyes wide open in amazement. My first thought was to ask Clyde if this was a normal shopping centre opening. As I cruised past the rear end of the carrier, it swerved around, its tail end swinging in toward the jeep. Quickly yanking the wheel to get clear, I then turned to yell at the driver. I could see Toby, half in and half out of the APC. He'd get up and nearly get a knee up on the outer edge of the carrier, then a head and a pair of arms would drag him back down. I could tell he was fighting and kicking at the person on the end of those arms. As the vehicle cut across in front of the jeep, I jammed on the brakes bringing the jeep to a rapid halt. As it crossed my line, I found myself staring right into Toby's eyes. I was stunned. This couldn't be happening. Toby recovered first. "Ox, Ox, I'm being arrested! Help!"

I thought it looked more like a kidnapping but felt that that point could be argued later. Foot off the brake, I stepped on the gas, down-clutched and yanked hard on the steering wheel in a racing turn that got me in behind the APC. Halfway through the turn and out of the corner of my eye, I saw what looked like Lieutenant Bowles charging toward us.

As I pulled jeep tight in behind the APC, I could see Toby struggling. Thinking that he was going to get hurt if he fell off, I pulled the jeep back out and around, then goosed the gas pedal and roared off to get ahead of the APC. Once ahead of it, I drove over to the exit. With nearly a hundred yards between the jeep and the APC, I slammed on the jeep's brakes and spun the jeep around so that it ended up facing the APC. I had blocked off the escape route and hoped the APC driver would stop rather than plough through the jeep and myself. My reasoning was that the driver would have to come to a near stop to turn around and that would give Toby an opportunity to disembark.

If the driver did keep on coming, the jeep was not going to slow it down a lot, so I de-jeeped rapidly. Placing myself in front of the jeep and unwisely thinking that I could stop the APC, I put up a hand in a grand gesture to halt it.

The APC was closing in rapidly when Urquhart realized that he was going to jellify what appeared to be a British staff sergeant standing in front of a Canadian jeep. He hauled back on the tiller bars, and the carrier skidded through three inches of asphalt to come to rest five feet in front of me. I didn't wait, but ran up to the stopped carrier and yelled toward the opening where I had last seen Toby.

Urquhart didn't have the knowledge to put the APC in reverse, so he just sat there. The force of the sudden stop flung Smathers-Hughes back onto Masterson's lap. Toby lost his grip on the top edge of the ramp and fell back into the carrier. Once the vehicle settled, he got up and pulled himself up onto the top of the carrier then jumped just in time to be caught by me.

I straightened Toby up and said, "Are you alright, Your Lordship?"

"Yes, fine, but these lunatics arrested me and then, all of a sudden, kidnapped me."

From inside the carrier, Masterson yelled, "Urquhart, it's too late. He's gone. Get us out of here, now!"

"But…Major?"

"No fucking buts, get this thing moving. Now, damn it. That's an order, Urquhart! Move it!"

"Yes, sir," Urquhart yelled back and released the tiller bars. He stepped on the gas. The APC, now minus one Earl, roared forward, smashing through Clyde's jeep as it did so.

Toby and I stood there watching as the carrier climbed over a bicycle rack, crashed a newspaper box, clipped the side of a milk truck, banging it into the side of the bowling alley then disappeared past Oromocto's sole roundabout. As we stared in mutual disbelief at the carnage surrounding us, Bowles arrived.

"You, Private, what were you doing? That's my APC. What have you done with it?"

"Nothing, sir. Some Brits stole it. They tried to kidnap me."

"Kidnapped? Brits? You? What on earth for?"

"I don't know."

"Possibly a kidnap plot by a gang masquerading as British soldiers," I said.

"Fine. A gang to steal a lousy private? Excuse me, Private, just a comment. Come on, Staff Sergeant. You can't fool me. Steal a lousy private? Your pardon again, Private. Why they'd be better off stealing me. My family's got nearly a million dollars in real estate. Now, I'd be a bargain for kidnappers."

"Not compared to this lousy Private, Lieutenant. Private Trelauney-Fitzgibboncrest's family is fairly well off, but he's got five million himself. Pounds, not dollars."

Clyde arrived with the rest of the squad. It was interesting to note that he didn't even ask Bowles to explain the situation. "Marvin, what that hell's going on?"

"We believe it was at kidnap attempt on the Earl, Sergeant Clyde."

"Yeah, he's got millions," added Bowles.

"But they got away?"

"Yes, they did. Went up and over the hill."

"And took my jeep as well?"

"No…we were lucky on that, J.P.." I used Clyde's nickname in an attempt to get him ready for the news. "There's your jeep, over there." I pointed at a pile of crushed metal and shredded canvas.

Sergeant Clyde told me we were invited to a little after work session with Lieutenant Colonel Smith and the RSM. Initially, I was concerned about me being in uniform, a British uniform, at that, and me demobilized years ago. When I mentioned this to Clyde, he told me the idea of bringing me into the squad had come from the RSM. While we were explaining the situation and, for that matter, gathering more information, the phone rang in Colonel Smith's office.

Once he knew who it was, Colonel Smith put the conversation on speaker, after first telling us not to make a sound. It was Lieutenant Colonel Schultzberger calling from the First Battalion. "Good evening, Smitty, wasn't sure if you'd still be working after all the fun you depot guys had this morning at the shopping centre. After all, it is a Saturday."

"Very, funny, Jackrabbit. In fact, it's almost as funny as me RTU'ing Bowles. Guess where he goes?"

"Now, Smitty, I'm sure there's no need for such harsh action. How can I help?"

"Good, I thought you might want to cooperate. First of all, I cancelled the next two day's dog and pony shows at the shopping centre."

"Good plan. I don't blame you. Just for the record can you summarize your official After Action Report?"

"Easily. It's embedded in my brain. At the end of the day, The Depot is out one jeep, three hundred rounds of blank ammunition, one smoke grenade, yellow, and one thunderflash; all pyrotechnics that had been intended for squad training. To show for it, I am now in hock for one reviewing stand. One newspaper box, a bicycle rack, one hundred and fifty gallons of milk, sixty gallons of ice cream…"

"What flavours?" asked Jackrabbit.

"You wanna hear the rest of it, or do you want me to bring Bowles over now?"

"Sorry, couldn't resist."

"For your information, assorted varieties, twelve gallons of sour cream, forty pounds of cottage cheese, destroyed left rear fender on a delivery vehicle, rebuild corner of bowling alley, fifteen yards of asphalt, plus wages to repair the parking lot, five civilian suits, three civilian dresses, two hats, a pair of high heels, and fifteen dollars in nerve tonic for the Mayor's mother."

Smitty took a breath and Jackrabbit said, "Wow, that's gonna cost you a pile."

"We did avoid a lawsuit because we were able to explain away that bunch of Brits as a gang who were going to rob the Oromocto bank. And tried to grab one of the boys as a hostage. Not a problem, though… The way I see it, Jackrabbit, it's worth it just to send Bowles back to you."

"Now, wait a minute, Smitty. I thought you weren't going to do that. Didn't you just agree to keep him?"

"That was before I tallied up my losses."

"How about a bribe, then? I'll chip in half of your expenses…"

"And replace the ammo and the jeep?"

"Ammo, yes. Jeep, no."

"He'll be reporting in at dawn tomorrow."

"Good God, you drive a hard bargain, Smitty. And after all I've done for you."

"Yes, I'm glad you reminded me. You got me promoted, but with the promotion came the job at The Depot. I was on vacation, remember, until you began manipulating the Canadian Army?"

"True. Alright, a jeep."

"And, you take the wrecked one and write it off in training?"

Jackrabbit, that user of men, knew when he was being used and he nodded to himself. "Fine, you win. All of that. But you keep Bowles."

"Roger that, Jackrabbit. Now aren't you glad you called me to chuck shit at me?"

Lieutenant Colonel Schultzberger hung up without replying then scribbled a note on his field message pad to have the battalion transport officer get the jeep issue sorted out. He hadn't finished when the phone rang.

"Jackrabbit, I forgot, one more thing."

"No, Smitty, not a chance…"

"Dawn, Jackrabbit."

"Smitty, leave me alone."

"Dawn it is, then."

"No, wait…"

"This is just a small favour, Jackrabbit and it was going to be something that we had talked about earlier."

"Fine. Give."

"We sent a couple of squads to your battalion for the brigade concentration, right?"

"Right. One of them with a lieutenant who has an unpronounceable name."

"Correct, Featherstonehaugh. Don't look at his name tag when you speak to him. See the name in your mind as Fanshaw. Otherwise, it'll drive you crazy."

"Okay, and the favour?"

"Originally, it was planned that Bowles was to take his squad to the concentration. That was the way Dillingham had arranged it. I changed it. I thought that Bowles could do less damage at a shopping centre opening than with a squad in the field…" He paused to let that vision cross Jackrabbit's mind then added the final touch. "In your battalion, I might add."

"Imagine that, eh, Smitty? Destroying a Mall opening with one little lieutenant. And as for keeping that clown out of my battalion, I do appreciate that, Smitty."

"Yeah, well, now I need to send him and his squad. I have to get them out of sight for a while."

"Summary Investigation?"

"No, a Board of Inquiry."

"Yeah," Jackrabbit said. "Makes sense. This is too big, and I'll bet the Camp Commander wants to control the fallout."

"Yes, and as he told me, there's no way he's prepared to let me do a unit summary investigation where I can minimize the damage and lay off the blame."

"And the kidnapping?"

"Based on statements from everyone else, that is, everyone other than Bowles, that seems to be true. It was an attempt on Toby that coincidentally, was launched at the same time as Bowles destroyed the mall opening. I've put together a statement from Sergeant Clyde, his corporals and signed it off as being from Bowles. No way I want him appearing in front of an adversarial Board of Inquiry."

"And, so I inherit him?"

"Can you suggest another place to hide him?"

There was silence on Jackrabbit's end. Finally, taking in a gallon of air, Schultzberger said, "Very well, Smitty. Since you had intended to assist me by keeping him out of my hair. I'll assist you by getting him in my hair."

"Thanks, Jackrabbit. I won't say you won't regret it, because no matter what we do, short of assassination, Bowles will make us both regret it. Cheers, Jackrabbit."

"You know, Smitty, you're becoming more like me every day. Goodnight."

CHAPTER 42

SMATHERS-HUGHES MEETS THE BOYS

Meanwhile, back at the motel, the gang re-grouped. Masterton was not happy with his team. "We should have gotten that damned Earl and gotten away."

"Where the hell did that staff sergeant come from?" asked Corporal Smathers-Hughes.

"Who cares, he was there, and he put paid to our little excursion," answered Urquhart.

"Well, they know we're after him now. It's going to be a bit tougher to get him away."

Masterton sniffed. "No, Smathers-Hughes, it's not. We are now going to do this my way. We have done the nice, walk over and ask him to come with me shit and it failed miserably."

"You have another plan, do you, sir?" asked Urquhart.

"Of course, Captain Urquhart. I was trained to have a back-up plan. You know that proverb that says, 'No battle plan survives contact with the enemy.' With that in mind, I have another plan. Now, before I disseminate it, did you gather any other intel that may prove useful?"

Urquhart thought about it. He had had a light lunch at an Armoured Corps officers' mess and had dined at the expense of the mess due to the generosity of the PMC. The talk was all about a brigade concentration and an in-progress Escape and Evasion exercise.

When he had finished, Masterson said, "When does the brigade concentration begin?"

"It has already begun," said Urquhart.

"Good, then the camp is now probably quite empty. We should be able to track the Earl down and grab him with little or no opposition. Here's the plan."

Smathers-Hughes thought that if that little military proverb were true, then Masterton's next plan was going to go for a shit, too. He still figured that if they went in the front gate, and explained to the Camp Commander what this was all about, they would get it settled. He looked at Masterton. Masterton saw him looking and looked back. "Well, Corporal, do you have a plan?"

Smathers-Hughes decided against telling Masterton what he thought, he'd only get blamed when it failed as well. He had been on the verge of adding his proverb to the mix; the soundest tactics are the opinion of the most senior officer present; unless of course, they lead to defeat. He shook his head.

Masterson, usually on top of such insubordinate gestures, but this time wanting only to demonstrate his brilliance, ignored the lack of military servitude that expected a 'No, sir' as opposed to an impertinent shake of the melon. He pushed on. "I thought so. Alright. First of all, we need to get a Canadian uniform. We need to find some out of the way place and wait for a soldier to come along and then we'll toss a blanket over his head and douse him with chloroform. Once he's out cold, we'll take the uniform and off we go."

Smathers-Hughes saw all kinds of problems with this scheme. Where were they going to get chloroform? What if the soldier was bigger than them and overpowered them before they could douse him? And did they need a specific size of soldier? Who was destined to wear the uniform and for what?

He left these alone and decided that Urquhart would have to step in or else they would go with this batty idea. Urquhart didn't disappoint him. He asked those questions and added an easier solution.

"Sounds good, sir, however, getting someone else involved will bring the MPs out after whoever attacked the soldier. We are in a bit of a spot right now because of that shopping centre thing. Why don't we track down a war surplus store and buy a uniform? That way, we'll get the size we want without any added danger."

Masterton tried to look thoughtful. He succeeded in making Urquhart and Smathers-Hughes think he was ill. Inside, Masterton was seething. No matter what idea he came up with, there was always opposition. Did Montgomery or Patton have these problems? I'll bet that William the Conqueror didn't get any objections during his Battle of Hastings briefing to his knights. If he did, that was one less Norman knight in the orders group.

The one aspect of Masterson's plan that appealed to Smathers-Hughes was where a corporal was to go to the CMSR Junior Ranks Club and see what he could pick up in the way of information about the camp, the Recruit Depot and even the Earl. The club was officially known as the St. Andrews Club; the troops called it Andy's. With him being the only corporal on strength, he didn't even need to volunteer.

A browse through the phone book came up with a small military surplus store down the highway in the opposite direction from the town. Dressed in civilian clothes, he walked to it, and there purchased boots, pants and a combat shirt in his size.

Changed into the unmarked uniform, Smathers-Hughes' ordered a beer from the bartender and was surprised to find that it cost ten cents a glass. Masterson had given him ten dollars for expenses. He ordered another one. He saw four soldiers at a table in the corner and walked over to sit near them. He knew this was an infantryman's club and he knew his uniform had no badges. From a pamphlet about the camp he had learned that there was an entire brigade stationed in Gagetown. He decided to be from the Service Battalion, a clerk of course. What to do about the missing shoulder titles and cap badge was solved for him. At the next table, one of the soldiers said, "I'm off tomorrow on that Brigade Escape and Evasion exercise."

"Sounds like fun. How long is it?"

"Report to the exercise area at noon. Get into the uniforms they give us. No markings of any kind. Then we are taken to a briefing area, given hard rations, a compass, and a map. Then they take us out by deuce and a half, with the sides and back all covered up. We have three days to get to a safe area."

"Where to?"

"Dunno, they take us out and drop us off, and we head out to the area on the map."

"So, you don't know where you are, but you do know where you have to go, right?"

"Right."

"Sounds terrible. I heard they torture you if you get caught."

"Yer get brainwashed, too."

"So who's the enemy force?"

"Someone said it's the Van Doos."

"Oh, boy, if they get you, you are well and truly fucked."

As he drank the beer, which was surprisingly good, Smathers-Hughes decided he was an escapee from the escape and evasion training.

Then gold mine!

One of the lads said, "I gotta get going. I'm bushed. I got tomorrow off, then on Monday I have to pick up a squad from The Depot and deliver them to the battalion bivouac site by 0880 hours."

"From The Depot? I thought we'd gotten all of those rookies we were gonna get?"

"Roger that, except this is the bunch that fucked up the shopping centre the other day."

The soldiers all started laughing. One said, "I'd have loved to have seen that."

"Me too, their lieutenant steals an APC and drives it into the side of the shopping centre."

"Yeah, and they fired on the mayor while he was on the reviewing stand."

"He's an exercise-CMSR, too."

"But what about them other guys?"

Oh, Oh, here it comes, that's us, thought Smathers-Hughes.

"Other guys?"

"Yes, supposedly there was a gang of kidnappers out to grab some limey recruit."

"Yep, he's a cousin to the Queen or something."

"And what happened with that?"

Smathers-Hughes decided to bring an element of truth into the conversation. "Pardon me, fellas."

Fellas sounded like proper Canadian talk he thought. They all stopped and looked at him.

"You're not in the CMSR, are you?" said one.

"No, I'm not. I'm with the Service Battalion."

Then another soldier, probably the brightest one, helped out. "I'll bet you're on that escape and evasion exercise, right?"

"That's right," said Smathers-Hughes.

"And I hope you guys won't blow the whistle on me. I'm hiding out here until dark."

"Brilliant, hide out in the club. What a great idea. Stewie, you'd better give this a shot. When you get turned loose, head for the club."

"Yeah, great idea."

"Thanks," said Smathers-Hughes. "But what I wanted to tell you is that I was at that parade."

"Really? And what was the real scoop?"

"Well, to begin with, the lieutenant only borrowed the APC and the driver. And the royalty chap is an Earl and no cousin to the Queen. As for the kidnappers…"

Smathers-Hughes decided to help his own cause here. "The police report said that they had left town."

"Chaps…and that accent. You a limey, too?" said bright boy again.

"Yeah, seems like Gagetown is overrun with them all,"

"Limeys and Van Doos, you mean."

Which brought a laugh from all of them again.

"Well, yes, I am British. I came to Canada about three years ago with my parents. After school, I joined the army, and I'm a clerk."

That seemed to satisfy them, so Smathers-Hughes took a gamble. "Look, I've lost my map. I got chased the other night. I was busy looking for some high feature and had my map and compass out. Then a patrol came by, and I had to run for it. Dropped the map and compass. I ran away and travelled across the country. I ended up over by the recreation centre. I needed to find a map because I had a rough idea of where the finish line is. Can any of you help me?"

"Sure," said the one who was going to drive Bowles' squad to the field. He took a map from his combat pants pocket and coming over to Smathers-Hughes table he spread it out.

"See, here's the camp, we're over here."

The map was no real help, but it did give him a start point. "You said that you're driving the group out to the field, where are they going?"

The bright one looked at him from over at his own table. "Why do you need to know that? Not one of the kidnapper's gang are you?"

No…" Smathers-Hughes felt a panic attack and swallowed, then said quickly, "No, not at all. It's just that after seeing them in action, I want to be a long, long, way, away from them."

"I don't blame you," said map boy.

"You goin' alone with them recruits?" asked another soldier it.

"Nope, taking Johnson. We'll head over to transport for 0630 hours. We'll each take a deuce and a half. Johnson has to go to the officers' quarters to pick up the lieutenant."

"I'll bet it's the same dopey lieutenant who nearly killed the Adjutant in a car crash a couple of months ago."

"Could be, anyway, I'm taking them to the battalion bivouac area. And he pointed to an area on the map. It looked like it was twenty or thirty miles to

Smathers-Hughes who memorized that point and then slid his finger down along the training area. "If I remember correctly, my finish line is down here."

When Smathers-Hughes left the club, it was getting dark. He had had a half a dozen beers with the soldiers and had even bought a couple of rounds.

Nice bunch of lads, he thought, even if they were infantry, colonial infantry at that. Despite being pretty well pickled, he was pretty sure he could find the main gate and then go on to locate the motel, but as he cut across the grassed meridian, he stumbled over a solitary bike leaning forlornly against a slender maple tree. Gashing himself on the shins as he tumbled, he shoved an arm out and grabbed the tree. Realizing that the bike was not locked up, it was the work of a moment for him to climb aboard and head off at a gallop. Luckily for him, the gate guards were too busy with their night lunch of sandwiches to be paying attention as a wobbly cyclist cleared camp lines, hell-bent for the Bide-a-Wee-While Motor Hotel.

CHAPTER 43

SMATHERS-HUGHES MEETS THE MORNING, BUT TARDILY

On arrival at the hotel, Smathers-Hughes left the bike against the wall beside his room and without bothering to report in to Masterson, went straight to bed. He was awakened at 0830 hours by a banging on his door. He arrived at the offending door still dressed, although the spot on his left leg where the bike had attacked him had bled leaving a blackened oval on his new combat pants. He opened the door to a too bright morning where even the sparrow's song was too loud. Compared to the birds' soft warble, Masterson's voice was the crack of doom.

"Where the bloody hell have you been, Corporal?"

"Good morning, sir. I've got good news."

"Good news, it had better be marvellous news, seeing that you've been gone for days."

Smathers-Hughes made a brief attempt at counting the hours since he had departed the Bide-a-While homestead, gave up after three and contented himself with betting Masterson was wrong on the day issue, although he had to admit that he was willing to take either end of the bet; it was just one of those mornings. Asking Masterson what day it actually was, was tantamount to admitting he didn't know, so he ignored it.

"Come in, sir, I'll just be a minute," Smathers-Hughes said.

"Never mind, Corporal. Get yourself cleaned up and meet us at the coffee shop across the road in twenty minutes."

"Yes, sir."

Masterson stormed off. Urquhart's moon face popped into the doorway and he said, "Hope it was worth it, Laddie-buck. And I hope you've got some prime intel, as his Nibs would say."

He left. Smathers-Hughes had a quick shave and shower and threw on his own uniform and headed off to find Masterson.

An hour later, after of bowl of oatmeal, two eggs, bacon, toast, fried potatoes, and three cups of coffee, Smathers-Hughes had been de-briefed by Masterson and Urquhart.

Masterson said to Urquhart, "Alright, Captain, summarize what we've got."

"Very well sir, here's a thumbnail of the events. The Earl and his bunch are departing for parts that Smathers-Hughes can possibly locate on a map. It is estimated that said parts are approximately a long, long, way, away. We are on foot, although one of us has his own mode of transport; namely a bike. Next, we have a pretty sure bet that we will be able to find the dopey lieutenant who turned a small parade into something along the lines of Pearl Harbour, minus the ships. From these points, we can develop a rudimentary plan."

"We can?" said Masterson. "I mean, we can. Yes, indeed we can. Can you suggest just what's on your mind, Captain Urquhart and we'll see if it meshes with mine?"

Smathers-Hughes, deciding that three cups of coffee were a good start, guzzled another thinking that any plan will mesh with Masterson's because any plan of his would be a blank slate. Urquhart looked over at Masterson, who was now doodling on his paper place mat. Then Urquhart looked over at Smathers-Hughes and nodded with a grin that told the corporal that he thought Masterson's plan was nothing more than a bag of air as well. Then Urquhart came clean with his plan.

"We need to get into the officers' quarters and have a chat with that subbie."

Masterson interrupted. "By subbie, I'm assuming you mean subaltern. Please don't go coarse on us because we are in a foreign nation."

"Very well, Major, the subaltern. Someone else in our group needs to pedal his arse…himself to a car rental agency at the airport and rent us a vehicle."

The someone who pedals his arse, coarse or not, will be the corporal, won't it, thought Smathers-Hughes?

"Anything else, Captain?" asked Masterson as his doodle of a cat became a doodle of an ink blot.

"Yes, sir, we will need a decent map of the training area and the roads leading into and out of the camps training area."

Masterson looked over at Smathers-Hughes who seemed to have stopped listening and was asking the cute waitress if he could have an order of toast and jam. She'd giggled. "You've got a good appetite, soldier." Then she hurried away.

Smathers-Hughes thought briefly of his UK sweetie and then put her from his mind. *She's not here, so I can love the one who is.*

"Smathers-Hughes, if you don't mind?"

"No, sir. What was that again?"

"I said, do you have anything to add?"

"One thing, sir, Captain Urquhart has got a good idea here, and I understand where he's going with it."

Which is more than can be said for you, Major Masterson, Urquhart thought as he sat back sipping his Earl Grey tea: with a lemon slice.

"Yes, then be so good as to tell us where you think he's going with it."

"Well, my guess is that we take any information we get from that Lieutenant, get into the car along with the map and find the closest civilian entry gate to the battalion bivouac area. Then we'll get a line on the Earl and snatch him, head back to the car and make for the nearest train station."

"Yes, good show, up to a point, Corporal. But a train will not get us to England. You may have forgotten that little pond that is known as the Atlantic Ocean." Masterson's chuckle at his own wit sounded like a starved raccoon trapped inside a tin garbage can.

"No, sir," said Smathers-Hughes. "I hadn't forgotten. It's just that with only one decent-sized airport in this country, it'll be watched as soon as the Earl's absence is noticed. From my memory of the map, we'll be at least two hours away, and by then there'll be roadblocks and the airport will be shut down tighter than a Scottish ram's arse hole."

Urquhart laughed, Masterson turned purple. "Really, Corporal. Language."

"Sorry, sir, seemed appropriate."

Silence hung around the coffee shop, broken only by Smathers-Hughes chomping on crisp toast and washing it down with slurps of coffee. Finally, just to crack that silence a little, Urquhart spoke up, "Sir, why don't you give us your plan now?"

"Very well," said Masterson after a moment's thought. "It's like this. Number one, Captain Urquhart will go to that transient officers' quarters and locate the lieutenant. Number two, Corporal Smathers-Hughes will go and track down a map, a railway schedule and some stores that will enable us to stay out and live in the field for a day or two. Number three, I'll go to the airport and rent a vehicle."

The silence slunk back in, and was broken again by Urquhart, "You'll pedal a bike to the rental agency at the airport, sir?"

"No, Captain, much too undignified for a major to travel by way of a bicycle. I'll get a taxi."

Once the different plans have been tossed about until it all had become Masterson's brilliant creation, the meeting broke up. Urquhart headed off to the camp by way of the main highway and from there in through the main gate. Masterson telephoned for a taxi and waited at Bide-a-Whatever. Smathers-Hughes, fully recovered and with another ten dollars in his pocket, set out on the bicycle to get the maps and the train schedule. As he left the diner, the cute waitress was standing beside the door.

"My name's Annette. Here's my phone number." She handed him a folded note.

He thanked her, said, "My friends call me Rod." At least, the boys I met in the club called me Rod. He took out his wallet and put the folded note in it. "I'll call you," he said and set off to follow his plan.

His plan, not divulged to Masterson was to get his tasks out of the way quickly so that he could return to Andy's Club for a fix-me-up beer or two.

CHAPTER 44

URQUHART MEETS WITH SUCCESS

As he cycled to the main gate, he saw a number of places through the trees that lined the road and guarded the camp. He assumed quite rightly that those were shortcuts carved through the woods by soldiers heading to and from camp to the married quarters across the highway. On the off chance that one might indeed be a shortcut for himself, Smathers-Hughes turned into the next one he came to. It brought him out in a complex surrounded by trees. A narrow ribbon of road ran down from the array of buildings laid out in a fan shape. From the look of them, they came in threes. A dorm-like building, an out building and one other that he guessed was a mess. In fact, Smathers-Hughes had come across the officers' lines, a place privates and corporals avoided unless on duty. As he cycled out onto the main stretch of road running from the main gate, he came across a perspiring Urquhart. He stopped his bike, saluted and said, "Good morning, sir, we meet again."

Urquhart pulled up to a stop, ignored the salute and pulled a large khaki coloured handkerchief from his trouser pocket. After a wipe of his forehead and face he said, "How the devil did you get here so quickly, you blarsted pimple?"

"I took a shortcut."

Smathers-Hughes straddled the bike and half-turned in the direction he had come. He pointed to a break in the tree line.

"Head off through that gap in the trees, sir. You come out just down from the motel."

"Thanks, all this trotting around on the hind legs is tedious."

He gave himself another wipe and said, "So, where to now? Back to that club, I'm figuring."

Smathers-Hughes had mentally solved both map and schedule problems in one swoop while pretending great interest in Masterson's lecture on behaviour and frugality. Now he needed to put his scheme into play.

"Not quite, sir, first off to the movements building. I'm sure that whatever they call it, it will have lots of info for those posted in and out of the camp.

After that, I'm guessing they'll have a range scheduling office. I'll bet they'll have a camp map for me."

"Yes, it's back over there. I passed it yesterday. They call it Range Control."

"Thanks, sir, I'll see you back at the Bide-a-Wallop later. Good luck with that subbie, he's a looney."

"Yes, I'd gathered that from that abominable display of soldiering he demonstrated at that shopping centre."

Smathers-Hughes laughed and said, "Catch you later, sir, as the Canucks say. I'll be up at the corporals' and privates' club helping cement Anglo-Canadian relations."

Smathers-Hughes saluted again, re-mounted his rusty steed and headed off. Urquhart gave a perfunctory waved he classified as a salute and trudged on.

Since I'm both participant and narrator, I am able to leave Smathers-Hughes with the comment that he did achieve his ends, even getting a free beer from the bartender, who's bike it was and move on through this appalling mess of a story. The free beer came because Smathers-Hughes was seen returning the bike and quickly inventing a tale of finding it up in the officer's lines and was bringing it back.

As for Masterson, even he had no major difficulties in getting a car. His sole credit card was looked at with deep suspicion, but one phone call to the head office assured that clerk that Lloyds of London was an actual company that issued legitimate credit cards.

Toby and the squad were dashing to and fro from The Depot stores and the QM stores to gather equipment or replace lost items and then packing, so they can be dispensed with in these few words.

We can now return to Urquhart's meeting with Bowles. As he walked on deeper and deeper into Officer country, he came upon a large sign that detailed a map of the lines. Off by itself was the transient officers' quarters. Smathers-Hughes hadn't seen this sign as on its reverse was only an exhortation to drive carefully. It was expected that any officer leaving the lines knew where he was coming from but likely would need a reminder to drive safely. Urquhart made it to the transient officers' quarters without cardiac arrest and entered the dormitory-style building.

"Excuse me, soldier," said Urquhart as he walked in through the lobby.

"Yes, sir?" replied the soldier. He was dressed in short sleeve order, bush trousers, and an armlet that identified him as belonging to the Royal Canadian Dragoons.

"I see by your armlet that you are a trooper, correct?"

"Yes sir, Trooper Robinson, I'm Lieutenant Porter's batman, but he's loaned me out to a visiting Strathcona lieutenant."

"Are you familiar with the infantry lieutenant who was involved in that dust-up at the shopping centre?"

Trooper Robinson grinned, a move that stopped his features from totally resembling a weasel with a robin's egg in its paws. "His name is Lieutenant Bowles, sir. Fine show from what I heard."

"Yes, it was, I saw it. I'm from Queen Victoria's Thirty-Third Horse Guards, and I wonder if this Lieutenant Bowles has a batman?"

Again the grin, only wider, the weasel likeness disappeared entirely. "He ain't got one, sir. He's had three. They all quit. The last one was threatened with a spot of digger time, but he said go ahead, I'll take it."

"Digger time? You mean extra duties in the garden?"

"No, sir, Digger time is jail. I think your lot call it the Glass House."

"Ah, yes, I understand. So this Lieutenant Bowles, would he be around at this time of day?"

"Yes, sir, upstairs about midway down the corridor. I think his door's open. Packing for the field I understand. They got shut down on the dog and pony show at the mall and are now being sent off to the brigade concentration. Leaving later on today, unless he's already gone by way of the back door."

Urquhart made his way upstairs and down the dingy, poorly-lit corridor. It seemed like home to him. Urquhart had spent a military lifetime moving into an out of quarters like these, some bordering on sumptuous, others that would make a slum-dweller cringe. This place appeared to fit somewhere in the middle. Hearing some kind of anguished keening or exclamations of pain coming from the open doorway he headed for it and stopped at the entrance.

It was Lieutenant Bowles' room. And the proprietor was busy stuffing equipment into a rucksack that was propped up on the bed. While stuffing, Bowles was giving his all to make a regimental song unrecognizable. Bowles was half dressed in combat pants, boots, and white tee shirt. Around his neck on the chain were his dog tags. A combat shirt was hung over the back of a chair jammed into the leg space of a small, chipped and scarred desk of burgundy painted wood.

Urquhart knocked gently on the door. Bowles carried on bellowing something like, "The claymored clans broke from the woods, Redcoats fled in disarray."

Urquhart knocked harder and said in a loud voice, "Lieutenant?"

Nothing happened, other than verse two. Then, turning to pick up a waterproof poncho from the floor, Bowles caught sight of the figure shadowing his doorway. He shrieked. Urquhart jumped. Bowles stared.

"Sorry to startle you, Lieutenant."

"Not at all, sir. Not startled, just have super-developed reflexes."

The man's an idiot. But oh well, we've got Masterson, the Canucks have Bowles. We'll be lucky to get his room number out of him. May as well test him on that, thought Urquhart.

"Is this room two one four?"

"Er…not sure. It's my room. That's for sure, or else why would I be in it?"

"True – ah, yes, here's your room number, up on the door. Yes, two one four. And then you must be Lieutenant Bowles?"

"Well, I know that for sure. Ha. Quite funny, don't you think? Fellow lives in a room for nearly three months and doesn't know his room number."

"Yes, hilarious. Anyway, my name is Captain Urquhart. I'm with the armoured contingent here in camp. I am here to observe infantry and armoured cooperation during a practical exercise."

"Righto. And I'm the infantry portion, am I? First CMSR to be more specific. Thirteen platoon, D Company, to be exact. And I would be pleased to cooperate with you, sir."

"Good. Although there's not a lot of cooperation required. I'm what we call a free runner. Travel on my own and observe activities as I see fit. I've been told your platoon was going to the field soon and I wondered if you knew what kind of training your platoon will be exposed to?"

"None, whatsoever. Jackrabbit is busy getting orders from the Brigadier. He'll pass those on to his own O group."

"Jackrabbit?"

"Our commanding officer, Lieutenant Colonel 'Jackrabbit' John Schultzberger. He got the name in Korea as a young lieutenant doing recce patrol work. Not sure of the story. He's also called the Old Man."

"But not to his face, I imagine."

"Quite. To his face, we sir him."

"And you are privy the CO's O group?"

"No, My company commander, Major O'Connor is. He'll attend the CO's O group and then call his own O group. I'll attend that."

"Yes, of course. Very similar to how we do things."

So similar, Urquhart thought that you bloody bunch of colonials stole the system from us.

"Yes," said Bowles. "I understand you Brits do a lot of things our way."

Urquhart bit his tongue. "Do you know where you will be bivouacked?"

"Certainly. I do know that much. Wouldn't know how to get there otherwise, eh? Anyway, here, I'll show you." And from his combat trouser pocket, he pulled out a map, unfolded it and said, "We're out there near Blissville."

Seeing the word Blissville on the lower left quadrant of the map, Urquhart pointed it out to Bowles who were searching grid square by grid square and was still running his fingers across the squares occupied by camp headquarters in the north.

"Jolly good, sir. You must be very familiar with Camp Gagetown."

"Nope. Just lucky, the name caught my eye."

"I see."

Urquhart folded the map up and placed it on the desk and said, "Thank you. And could you point out the Armoured Corps officers' mess from this window?"

"Yes, of course, but not from this window. Come on. We'll go the end of the building, and I can show you from there."

Bowles headed for the door. Urquhart made as if follow him and then turned back, grabbed the map and it was the task of seconds to get the map stuffed inside his tunic.

Once clear of Bowles, whom he left at the window, promising to look him up in the field, Urquhart went down the stairs at the opposite end from where he'd come in. He reached the main floor and saw a small room with three washing machines and three dryers all rattling along, clothing buttons banging inside drums, water sloshing down into the sink and the groaning of overworked machinery accompanying it all.

Urquhart dashed inside, yanked a dryer door open, pulled out armfuls of clothing and jammed it all into a large duffle bag that was lying on the floor. Seconds later, he was out the door. Once safely ensconced back in the motel, his sense of duty told him to conserve energy: he took a nap.

That evening, in Masterson's room, it was decided that since they now had a camp map, a railway schedule and Bowles' map of his whereabouts, there was no need to rush into things. A train was scheduled to run from St. John to the south, north to Riviere-du-Loup nightly, stopping at Fredericton Junction at approximately 0300 hundred hours each morning so any day would work. Urquhart, fond of his creature comforts like most soldiers, persuaded Masterson that they needed a trip back to the War Surplus store or a camping store to outfit themselves for what looked like an extended stay in the field. They even, at Masterson's insistence and later on in this tale, to Urquhart's relief, each carried a small bottle of chloroform to put the Earl under, if necessary.

CHAPTER 45

SMATHERS-HUGHES MEETS UP WITH HIS SUPERIORS, FINALLY

In spite of Bowles' assistance, Lance Corporal Steele and myself got the squad, now re-named Thirteen platoon, D Company, down to the battalion bivouac site without incident. He let Bowles navigate from the recruit quarters down Highway 7 to Finnegan's Hill, where, once off the beaten track, he directed the driver himself. The platoon travelled in two deuce and a half trucks, but once settled in, they received one APC, three, three quarter ton trucks and one deuce and a half with five drivers from battalion transport. Sergeant Clyde took the squad's regular three quarter ton truck for supplies, telling us he'd see us at the bivouac site.

The platoon was put into four ten man tents in D Company's lines. Bowles was finally ensconced with his peers in D Company officer territory and located well away from the rabble. Sergeant Clyde, as befitted his rank, was partially de-rabbleized by being shoved into a tent in the sergeants' mess area with two other senior NCOs between the high and mighty and the aforementioned rabble. That left the lancejacks: one per tent to maintain law and order. They were immersed to their collective necks in rabble, but they did have the consolation of being able to escape after each day's training to the corporals' mess tent and mingle with the rest of the battalion's one and two stripers.

A day later, after a late, but enjoyable breakfast, The FURG, the Fearless Undercover Recovery Group, as Masterson had christened them, set out in the rental van to follow the route Thirteen platoon had taken. Urquhart had muttered to Smathers-Hughes as they loaded the vehicle that FURG stood for, 'Fucked Up Really Good. Smathers-Hughes couldn't have agreed more, but being a lowly corporal, he contented himself with a smile.

Urquhart, wearing what he was pretty sure was Trooper Robinson's uniform, which was a bit snug under the arms and around the belly, drove the van.

The atmosphere inside the van, on such a beaut of a morning, was definitely matey. Masterson was confident that they were going to get in, get out and get home effortlessly with the Earl in tow. Urquhart was positively joyous at how he had scammed the uniforms, had had a great night at the mess and was especially pleased that his hangover had been unable to catch up with him. Smathers-Hughes, riding in the back of the van, was half-dozing, half-observing Canada's beauty and half-hoping to get in a bit of visiting with Annette before there they returned to England. They sped southwards, traveling through scraggly fir, scattered maples and other species of arboreal items that Smathers-Hughes didn't know the names of. It was a pleasant day in New Brunswick. The birds were singing, "Oh Canada" at least the ones that knew the words. The others hummed in bird-ese. Insects did what their instincts told them to do, and all was well in the world.

Masterson's cup of neighbourly-ness was sufficiently running over that he treated them all to hamburgers and chips at a service station where they fuelled up the vehicle, loaded some water into a jerry can and then set off again.

According to the map, and Masterson, who was navigating, they soon reached the gate. Due to the Brigade exercise, a sentry was on duty at the gate, and he refused them admittance. Even Masterson's avowal that they were official visitors to the brigade from the British Army meant nothing to the skinny, pimple-faced private standing guard.

"I'm sure everything is all okay, sir. But I have my orders."

"But…"

"Sorry, sir. I'd rather get in shit from the Commanding Officer for not letting you in and doing my job, then to face my CSM for letting you in."

"CSM?"

"Company sergeant-major, sir," said Corporal Smathers-Hughes, the resident know-it-all.

The private did have a suggestion. "If you need to get in to see the Brigadier, then you can drive down about half a mile." He pointed further south. "Just around the bend is a small rest stop with toilets and parking spaces. You can go in from there on foot."

"On foot? How far? Look, son, I'm not infantry like you. I'm a tanker. You savvy?" said Urquhart.

"Yes, sir, but if you want to get in…"

"Understood and appreciate the assistance," said Smathers-Hughes. "And on foot, we go to …?"

"Cross a meadow with a small creek in it should be pretty dry this time of the year. All in all, it's almost a thousand yards until you hit this road again. At a big-dog leg. You can't miss it."

Urquhart even gave it one more try, knowing full well that Masterson would travel across Canada on foot in a blizzard to get the Earl. He was not looking forward to a long trek on foot. It made no difference to the sentry. They headed back out onto Highway 660 and then turned south. Once established at the new site, Urquhart shut off the ignition and said, "What's next, sir?"

Masterson was studying the map. After a moment he looked around to ensure that every one of the FURG was awaiting his direction.

"Here's the plan," he said. "Captain Urquhart and I'll go off on a recce. Smathers-Hughes, you'll stay with the van." He looked at his watch. "It's now nearly fourteen hundred hours. We'll be back no later than…"

"Seventeen hundred?" supplied Urquhart.

Masterson said, "Alright, seventeen hundred. But I'm sure it won't take us that long."

He turned and set off into the interior of Camp Gagetown. Urquhart picked up a chocolate bar and a can of pop. As he prepared to follow his fearless leader, he said to Smathers-Hughes, "If we're lucky, we'll be back a day or two after the plane leaves for Blighty, with you on it, Corporal." He winked, sighed, gave a roll of his eyes heavenward and trudged off behind Masterson.

Smathers-Hughes smiled and agreed with Urquhart. He ducked around the van into a small copse and took a leak. As he did so, he thought of the worst case scenario for himself and how close he thought Masterson would come to it. To that disaster he was sure was coming, he added an image of an utterly stupid move that Masterson would throw into the mix. This unknown calamity would further jeopardize the entire expedition. With that settled on as the worst possible outcome, he grabbed a bag of potato chips and a pop, climbed in behind the steering wheel and settled in for a snack and then a nap.

As he wiggled into a comfortable position, he noticed the map lying on the passenger side of the van on the floor. Masterson must have thought he was shoving it into his pocket. He waited for them to discover their loss and sat contentedly gobbling chips and guzzling pop. After ten minutes he played guess how long before they got back. At two thirty he gave up. Masterson was too far gone on his wanderings now to admit that he even needed the map. Smathers-Hughes dozed off, thinking that sometimes a corporal's life is to be preferred over a commissioned officer's.

Smathers-Hughes woke up. He looked at his watch; six thirty or 1830 Army time: an hour and a half past Masterson's deadline. He had been asleep for nearly four hours. It was nearly time to panic, but since he wasn't lost and had his orders, he knew that Masterson would be doing enough panicking for the three of them. He picked up the map and gave it a going over. He found where the gate guard had been and where he suggested they go. But on the map were all kinds of symbols and boundary markings. Lieutenant Bowles' map had the complete battalion concentration area and a number of other places drawn in with grease pencil. Studying the map carefully, Smathers-Hughes saw that there had been no need to go the route that the guard had specified. Further to the south, there was a track or small road that led to a fire guard that ran due north to intersect the road that the battalion was using as its in-route and that the sentry had been so enthusiastically protecting. Forty minutes later and with no sign of the intrepid duo, and nothing else to do, Smathers-Hughes started the van and drove off further south to find that road. He wasn't sure what he was going to find, but he did offer his conscience the balm that he was on a rescue mission.

Driving along he came to the path and turned off the main road. As he travelled slowly along, he wondered how he was going to help by rambling across the camp's training area in a civilian van. He had gone about a half a mile when he came to a gulley. The sandbagged culvert across the road was too small to be called a bridge, but he was able to see that the stream that ran through it was not that deep. As he went up the slight ravine on the far side, he heard voices yelling at him. Smathers-Hughes remembered that he was in enemy country and that there were all kinds of military exercises going on. He recalled what those Van Doos, whoever they were, did to their prisoners and stepped on the gas. Through the gathering gloom of approaching dusk, he thought he could make out one of them gaining on him. He tromped on the pedal and zipped away.

The chasing man stopped, cursed and waited until the other man caught up to him.

"Goddamit, it was Smathers-Hughes! He got away!"

Urquhart, breathing hard couldn't answer. He had heard the sound of a vehicle as they lay inside a small copse of trees. Smathers-Hughes' last few hours had flown past while he snored in dreamland. Urquhart's last few hours had taken an eternity to pass by. He had followed Masterson through the thickets, through an innocent pastoral field that hid a nasty swamp. Plunging into a pothole in the water meadow had cost him his chocolate bar, soaked him up to his armpits and filled his boots full of water. Squishing along behind Masterson he asked to have a look at the map. Masterson, realizing that he had left the map in the van, made a huge production of searching his pockets to come up empty. "Must have lost it when traversing that bog back there, old chap. No matter, we're still heading in the right direction. I'm navigating by the sun."

Is the stupid bugger aware that the sun is whipping across the sky at a million miles an hour? he thought. Urquhart hadn't cried since he was nine years old and was traveling on the train away from his home, friends and parents en route to a prestigious, but legendary concentration-camp-style public school. This time it was the van disappearing away from him that brought him nearly to tears. He was chilled, hungry, footsore and fed up to the teeth with, "Just around the next bend," or "Just over this rise."

Masterson, full of his own despair, felt it was incumbent on himself to deliver the morale boosts. "We shall continue on in the direction of the van. Maybe it will turn around and come back. When it does, I'll charge Smathers-Hughes with disobedience of a lawful command."

That idiotic comment almost drove Urquhart to do murder. He refrained from physical assault and made do with a verbal one. "He's looking for us. Using his bloody initiative, instead of hunkering down in that parking lot waiting for you to guide us back. There is no way in hell you were going to find him. You're lost. You've been that way since you got out of the van. You're not going to charge him with anything. In fact, Major, if he does come back this way, you will bow down and worship him. So will I."

"I say, Captain Urquhart, you go too far…" Masterson turned to head down the trail toward the hill which the van had disappeared over and muttered, "Point taken, there is some truth in what you say. But not bowing to a corporal." Masterson shuddered. "No. No bowing."

As they cleared the crest, the sun dropped behind a large stand of willows. While the air was still warm, Urquhart shivered, in anticipation of a long, cold night in a strange country with nothing to keep him warm but the hot air of his superior officer. A disembodied voice shot out from the left hand side of the track, starting Masterson into prayer and Urquhart into a more secular brand of epithet.

"Excuse me, sirs, but it really is you. What a jolly piece of luck."

Out of the gloom came Smathers-Hughes. "I got out fast when I heard voices. Once I was sure I was out of sight I hid the van. Then doubled back to confirm that it was you or some enemy patrol."

"Good man, Smathers-Hughes."

"Anyway, I'll see you both later."

He turned back toward the fire guard as Urquhart said, "Where the bloody hell are you going? Where's the van?"

"Second question first, I believe, Captain. The van is about two hundred yards down this fire guard. The answer to the first question, I'm going back to the van, getting in and driving it back to the spot where I was told to wait. Then I'm going to wait for you both to come back. I do not want to be charged with disobedience of a lawful. See you both back there."

Urquhart scrambled to Smathers-Hughes side yelling, "No! No! It's alright. There'll be no charges."

Smathers-Hughes looked at Masterson. He nodded. Smathers-Hughes said, "Very well, I'll get the van."

Urquhart said, "In fact, the Major wants to thank you for coming out and finding us, don't you Major?"

Masterson wasn't that thrilled, although he too, was glad the mad trek through this nightmarish countryside was over with. "Yes, Corporal. Our thanks for making an effort. It is well appreciated."

Smathers-Hughes, mollified, led the two battle-weary officers to the van. Once they were all aboard, he said, "Looking at the map, sir, I see that there is a small trail running very close to where Lieutenant Bowles' squad is going to be bivouacked. We can put the van in under the trees and set up the tent well away from the training area, but still be close to the Earl."

Masterson had had enough of maps for the day. He could have cared less about trails, small or otherwise. All he wanted was a hot shower, a gallon of scotch and a decent meal, one served by his club that offered up brown soup and melt-in-your-mouth plaice.

"Yes, good idea, Corporal. Carry on."

Five minutes later Smathers-Hughes was humming softly to himself while he listened to Masterson and Urquhart battle it out in a snoring contest. He decided to let the two of them rest while he got them into the safe bivouac site near the CMSR battalion lines.

CHAPTER 46

THIRTEEN PLATOON MEETS
THE ROAD

Training for Thirteen platoon had to be condensed. In order to permit the recruits to participate in a brigade exercise, there was a lot of catching-up to do. With all the stops pulled out of their training in order to enable them to meet the challenge of working with the battalion during the concentration, the boys were busier than ever. Days started a bit earlier, although how a day that begins at five thirty can start any earlier was beyond thinking. Long slogs to and from the rifle range, on foot to toughen them up, survival rations for lunch and rehearsals of section tactics during the noon meal hour began to get to Toby and his comrades.

On Wednesday, the day after FURG had managed to infiltrate the area of the battalion bivouac site, Thirteen platoon, had an inhuman day of advance-to-contact section and platoon assaults. Inhuman barely covers it. Due to having competent platoon commanders, the rest of D Company only had it brutal. One can only feel for Sergeant Clyde and his Corporals, faced with a full day of Bowles in a command position during a series of mini-wars. Their leader, filled with a fearless sense of idiocy, led them through right flankings, left flankings and full frontal attacks in ways that made World War I look like a day at the beach. Three times they were overrun because Bowles refused to attack but waited for a counterattack.

"Sir," yelled Clyde during one platoon assault. "We do not wait for a counterattack when the coy is advancing. We are the attackers!"

"Ha, exactly what the enemy are waiting for, Sergeant." After that third disaster, the Company Commander, Major O'Connor, placed Thirteen platoon in reserve and left them there until the final attack. By this time, the recruits, having done three times as much as the rest of the company due to Bowles unique take on land warfare, were bordering on exhaustion.

During the subsequent route march back, a mere fifteen miles in the heat of the afternoon, not surprisingly, one of the lads went berserk.

Alphonse Morgan spun out and with a cry that would have chilled the soul of a Viking berserker high on Kentucky moonshine, he charged at his platoon commander. Lieutenant Bowles was running alongside the platoon, his whiny, squeaky, tinny voice, keeping up a steady patter of John Wayne-like drivel that lost any motivational appeal short of urging the hearers to commit hari-kari on the speaker.

Morgan had been situated in one of the rear files. As he spun out of his place in the ranks to get a shot at Bowles, he accidentally banged into Offside McGuffin. Offside, who had been traveling in front of him, unceremoniously butted up against Toby, the man in front of him. The domino effect kicked in, and the snake of bumped recruits toppled toward the front of the line, it ended with the right marker, Stuffy Stouffer. Stuffy, having no one to break his fall, scrambled, danced for balance and then tumbled into the dust and gravel of the road.

All Bowles saw was Stuffy suffering an apparent bout of narcolepsy while in the middle of a platoon run. Bowles gave a leap in an effort to catch the falling object. This saved him from Morgan's grab. Toby recovered quickly and reached out to snag Morgan by the back of his webbing and yanked him backward. Morgan's fingers missed their opportunity of grasping Bowles' by the slimmest of whiskers.

Sergeant Clyde, dog-trotting nonchalantly at the rear of the column, called a halt and the mass of recruits jumbled itself to a standstill. Morgan, frothing words from his mouth, struggled with Toby and begged to be let loose. Bowles, now looking down at the hapless Stuffy, turned to see what the commotion was about. He saw Morgan being grappled by Toby; Clyde moving up swiftly from the rear; Lance Corporal Jason Steele drifting through the halted platoon ranks from the other side where he had been keeping up morale by telling jokes as he ran. Lance Corporal Steele was a marathon runner, to him, these short little runs of ten or fifteen miles in hundred degree weather were like Sunday strolls along the boulevard.

Morgan stopped wiggling and suddenly sagged in Toby's grip. His yells of anger turned into sobs. "That voice, that fucking, cat-screeching, fucking voice constantly at us to 'Keep smiling, keep smiling, every step taken is one less step to take. Every step taken is one less step to take. Every step taken is one less step to take. Keep smiling...ARRRGGGHHHH!"

Toby released him slowly, and Morgan melted into a sobbing puddle of dust, perspiration, and olive drab combat clothing. In a low voice, he said, "He makes me crazy. Damn you, I have to throttle him."

As if reminded of his original mission, the idea of throttling Bowles resurrected Morgan's spirit, and he climbed back up, a grubby phoenix arising from out of the road grime and his own sweat.

As Lance Corporal Steele put the arm on Morgan, Toby, turning to McGuffin, said quietly, "He's correct on that. If it wasn't against Army regs, I'd have had a finger or two on our shitheaded lieutenant's windpipe long before this."

"Now, now, Squire," said Lance Corporal Steele with a wink. "No talk of mutiny out here on the Lawfield Corridor. This ain't the Bounty and he ain't Captain Bligh."

While in Steele's grip, Morgan quieted back down. Bowles walked back to where Morgan, now a silent lump squatting on one knee, suffered in silence. With no recruits joining him, Morgan seemed to see the futility of further resistance. His earlier outcry, no doubt intended to raise the fiery cross of recruit rebellion, had fallen on deaf ears. Bowles came up to him and said, "What appears to be the problem, soldier? You don't fall out from this platoon. We march or die."

Sergeant Clyde, standing a few paces from the two of them muttered to Lance Corporal Steele, "He's got that right. If the Squire hadn't put the glommers on Morgan, we'd be viewing a dead-in-the-ditch lieutenant."

"Yes," replied Steele. "Darn shame that we have to say well done, Squire, quick thinking on your part saved the lieutenant's life. When we should be saying, 'You idiot, why'd you stop Morgan?'"

Clyde grunted his agreement and then walked out into the middle of the road. He waved back in the direction from where they had come, and the deuce and a half that had been traveling about five hundred yards behind them began to roll towards them.

"Get Morgan on board the deuce, Jason, have the driver run the kid to the battalion aid station to see if he's got sunstroke or has gone loopy and needs further care. I think he'll be okay and I don't think he's nuts…" Clyde lowered his voice, "After all, he only did what we all want to do, eh?"

"Right, Sarge, couldn't agree more." Steele turned to Morgan. "Alright, son, on your feet, we'll just take a ride into camp."

CHAPTER 47

URQUHART MEETS THE D COMPANY SUBBIES

Going bonkers in the heat of a Gagetown summer seemed to be an activity fast approaching cult-like status. Three days later, back in the illegal hide of FURG, all of the members were close to requiring head doctor appointments. To Masterson, this episode in his military career had taken on a resemblance to the movie, 'The Desert Rats', without the sand. All that was missing was Rommel's tanks banging away at them. Urquhart was feeling the pressure of Masterson's over-attentive-ness toward what he deemed supervision of the lower ranks in every aspect of their communal living. The constant eye upon him, recording right down to the number of sheets of toilet paper used per man, per day, per wipe, was tempting Urquhart, even though he was unaware of the existence of the recruit and his shenanigans, to pull a 'Morgan'.

Smathers-Hughes had held his own in the battle against boredom and bugs, but, at least twenty times a day, he had come close to going over the hill. The irony of someone going AWOL while on an expedition to collar an AWOL-ee wrung a grin out of him each time and was all that was necessary to bring his mind back above the plimsoll line that divided the sane from the insane.

The FURG had been on the qui-vivre for seventy-two hour now. Tempers were running high, body odour even higher, and mutinous thoughts were at their highest. On the other hand, food stocks were low, expectations of success even lower and faith in Masterson as even a nominal leader was at its lowest.

To top it off, they had not even come close to a situation where the Earl could be grabbed easily and without arousing the brigade. Somehow, both Thirteen platoon and FURG, as well as the rest of the brigade, got through it all without any serious loss of life. Although is there any other kind of loss? The days passed, Thirteen platoon continued training. Morgan was supposedly rehabilitated by the medicos although the platoon staff hoped for another breakdown, and did their best to ensure that when the day heated up that the

Squire was nowhere near his lieutenant. Through it all, no opportunity presented itself to FURG for the big grab.

Finally, Masterson agreed to let Urquhart go into the squad lines and speak with Bowles. Urquhart had been after this arrangement from the first night, but Masterson wanted to sit back, watch and then dart in and grab the unsuspecting Earl. With all patience exhausted, Masterson gave in.

Back at FURG headquarters, Masterson and Smathers-Hughes were waiting for the return of their secret agent, Captain Urquhart. Then, with Smathers-Hughes reduced to playing crib with Masterson, Urquhart returned, grinning like a white picket fence in the moonlight.

"Yes, I've got something. I've got the lot," said Urquhart as he paraded triumphantly back from his visit to Bowles bivouac area.

"You got the lot? You mean you've got the Earl?" said Smathers-Hughes.

"No, Rodney. Not quite that good."

During their internment in the wilds of Camp Gagetown, Captain Urquhart had taken to calling Corporal Smathers-Hughes by his Christian name.

Masterson said to the two of them. "Alright, settle down, both of you. Let's remember this is a military operation. We'll go to the tent, and I'll hold an O group where Captain Urquhart can give us a briefing."

Defiantly slouching, they trooped along behind Masterson. Masterson went through the by now slightly ridiculous process of assigning seats on three tree stumps, placing the map in the centre and then announcing in a deep voice, "Orders."

Urquhart looked at Smathers-Hughes. Smathers-Hughes grimaced while Urquhart rolled his eyes. Even these actions were now an established part of Masterson's O groups.

"You have the floor, Captain Urquhart," Masterson said.

"Thank you, sir. The squad, now known as Thirteen platoon is readying to move. D Company is readying to move. The battalion is readying to move, and some elements of the brigade are already on the move. The brigade exercise is starting to kick in. All unit training has ceased. The units will use today and part of tomorrow to do clean up and get re-supplied for the final exercise. The CMSR, I can never remember their full name…"

Smathers-Hughes spoke up, "The Caledonia and Musquodoboit Scottish Regiment, sir."

"Thank you, Corporal," said Urquhart with all the seriousness of a mortician receiving a delivery. "As the knowledgeable corporal has so neatly put it… The First Battalion, The Caledonia and Musquodoboit Scottish Regiment, are part of a combat team that will defend the western half of Camp Gagetown against their traditional enemies known as The Phantasians."

"Very good," said Masterson. "Go on."

"D Company will defend the furthest southern boundary of the exercise area. Lieutenant Bowles' platoon will be the southernmost platoon of D Company. They are tasked to do a fighting patrol along the west bank of the Nerepis river from here to the Lyons Bridge. During which the platoon will ensure that there are no enemy layback patrols of the retreating Phantasian Army in hiding. If they locate any, they will destroy them or capture them. Once they've done the sweep and ended up at Lyons bridge, the platoon will man a road block here, and put in a bridge demolition guard on Lyons bridge."

"Excellent, Captain. And I'm sure a perfect opportunity to snatch the wayward Earl will present itself to us. But where on earth did you get such detailed information, Captain? I was not aware that Bowles would be able to provide that kind of intel, or even understand it."

"Correct, sir, none of this came from Bowles. He shares a tent with another platoon commander by the name of Lieutenant Alexander. When I showed up there, Bowles was out, and as the lieutenant phrased it, he was causing his sergeant grief, irritating the lance corporals, and generally fucking around with the platoon's ability to get ready for the exercise."

"And that prompted him to give you their tactical plan?"

"Not yet, sir, I'm coming to that. I said that I was going to be attached to Bowles platoon as a ready-reserve with a squadron of Centurions. I was to be held back behind Bowles' position and that I was to liaise with him on the details."

"Ah, excellent thinking, Captain. No wonder I sent you on this mission," said Masterson.

Urquhart ignored that comment. "Then another couple of lieutenant's arrived with some beer. We were introduced by Lieutenant Alexander and then I just happened to haul out my last bottle of Famous Grouse."

"You got them drunk? Appalling behaviour, Captain."

So much for being the wonder boy Masterson had selected for this mission, thought Urquhart.

"Not at all, sir. These were civilized subbies… I mean subalterns. I merely offered them a touch of the old country and asked how long they thought Bowles might be."

"Yes," said Smathers-Hughes. "You had already figured out that you had not fallen into a local branch of 'Bowles for King'?"

"On the button, Rodney. The button. Once we settled in, with our drinks and cosy seats, Lieutenant Alexander said that I was wasting my time in the hope that Bowles would come up with anything slightly useable. We had refills all round, and then the three of them treated me to as fine a detailed briefing as the one Sitting Bull gave to Crazy Horse on the night before Custer's Last Stand."

"Very good, Captain." Masterson turned to Smathers-Hughes. "Any questions, Corporal?"

"Just one, sir. Captain, will that platoon be responsible for the blowing of the bridge?"

"Oh, please, Corporal. This is an exercise. They won't be doing any explosives in this kind of training."

"Beg pardon, sir," interrupted Urquhart. "Generally, in an exercise of this kind, a nominal explosion would be touched off near the bridge. To maintain realism, of course."

Masterson verbally about-turned. "Of course. That's what I meant."

Smathers-Hughes stood up and said, "And they are actually planning to let that lieutenant use demolitions? I'm not going anywhere near that platoon until this is all over. Slam me into jail. I am not, definitely not, going anywhere near that lieutenant if he's handling plastic explosives."

"I understand, Corporal," said Urquhart. "But fear not. An Engineer section is supposed to link up with Bowles' platoon a few hours prior to the bridge being blown up. They'll do the demolitions. If all works well, by the time the platoon has arrived at the bridge demolition guard site, the Engineers will have set up the explosives to blow a crater a hundred yards or so from the bridge."

"So now we wait, correct, Major?" asked Smathers-Hughes.

"Indeed. We observe and when they move out, we follow. Until then, we wait."

It could be a long wait. All brigade exercises start off slow and aside from a few minor feuds between small sub-units, remain that way for the duration. A brigade begins training at its lowest sub-unit level, for the infantry that was the section. They did refresher training in section tactics, fieldcraft, camouflage, and concealment. This phase was toughest on the troops. They've got lance corporals, corporals, sergeants, staff sergeants, second lieutenants, lieutenants, captains, and majors all haranguing them. platoon training pushes the microscopic eye a little further back and a layer or two of micromanagement is shifted from the soldiers onto the section commanders. With company level training the emphasis moves higher by applying pressure to the lieutenants. At the battalion level, the heat is aimed at the company commanders. Until, finally, at the rarefied heights of the brigade, it is the battalion and regimental commanders who appear in the Brigadier's cross-hairs. As the emphasis slides up the rank structure, action slows down. By brigade exercise time, the knowledgeable private knows that his section might have to do a rapid bug out from the bivouac, accelerate past the start line to get moving but that once in place, he'll have a slack time of it. Experience has taught him that the Brigadier cannot get involved at the two man fire-trench level when he's supposed to be juggling battalions of infantry, regiments of artillery and squadrons of the armoured corps around the battlefield.

CHAPTER 48

BOWLES MEETS A BDG OR WAS THAT A DBG OR A GDB?

In the battalion command post or CP, Lieutenant Colonel Jackrabbit Schultzberger had finished his O group with his company commanders. As they were all leaving the tent and Jackrabbit was making his way to the huge coffee pot at the back of the command post tent, he noticed Major Jimmy O'Connor hanging back, obviously waiting to see him.

"The O group is the time for questions, Jimmy, you have more?" A slight smile signalled that he was well aware of Major O'Connor's reason for being there after the O group.

"Well, sir, unless I have marked my map wrong…"

"You haven't, Jimmy. You haven't," the smile expanded as a grinning Jackrabbit shook his large head.

"Alright, then, sir, if that's the case, that bridge demolition guard at Lyons Bridge, I'd say that technically, it's out of bounds of the exercise area."

"Technically, my fanny, Jimmy. It's definitely out of bounds, and you are very correct in your interpretation. However, you have your three regular platoons, and they'll all be in play to the north, right?"

"Yes, sir… ah." Major O'Connor caught on. Jackrabbit knew he would. It was why he gave Bowles to him in the first place. Everyone in the battalion knew of Bowles. No company commander in the battalion or for that matter the regiment was unaware of the nightmare of the Bowles clan.

"Rest assured, Bowles won't come within sight of an enemy of any description. If an enemy stumbles on Bowles, I hope to heaven that he's said his own prayers. Bowles is safe where he is, and it lets you get on with running your show. That flank I put you on is critical. We cannot let them do an end around run on us. I have complete faith in you."

"Thank you, sir. Very well, I see the wisdom of your plan."

"Not so much wisdom as experience and a hope that God will keep Bowles out of the picture and that the enemy force commander will play by the rules. Good luck, Jimmy."

If Jackrabbit had considered his comment on commanders playing by the rules, he would have noticed he wasn't being as honest as he hoped his enemy counterpart was going to be. It was up to Bowles to discover the rampant duplicity amongst senior officers on both sides of the battleground.

Major O'Connor returned to D Company lines and passed the word for an O Group at 1800 hours that evening.

He held his O group in the D Company mess tent. In attendance were the headquarters group comprised of the company second in command, Captain Mike Sloan; Company Sergeant-Major, WO II, Jeff Partz; company quartermaster, Staff Sergeant Haggerty; and the company signaller, Sergeant Miles. Along with these worthies were the four rifle platoon lieutenants: Ten platoon had Lieutenant John Alexander; Eleven platoon's boss was Peter Christopher; Twelve platoon were led by Keith Stokeley. Of course, Thirteen platoon had our hero, Artie Bowles.

After interviewing Bowles upon his arrival at the concentration area, and now thinking about Jackrabbit's scheme, Major O'Conner had no qualms about deploying Bowles safely out of the exercise area. He had been concerned over denying the young soldiers exercise training but shelved his conscience by telling it that they were just beginning their careers. They would sit out most of this exercise, but there would be many more to come.

The company second-in-command arranged the O group attendees and then called them to attention when the Company Commander walked in from under the tent flap. O'Connor positioned himself in front of the seated group and christened the ground on the map board placed on a six foot table.

"As you can see, we are to deploy along the Nerepis River and Lawfield Road as the battalion's and brigade's right flank. Ten platoon…"

"Sir."

"You'll be located in this area, use the high ground and put your headquarters on a reverse slope to the west."

"Roger, sir."

"Eleven platoon, Mr. Christopher, from that cart track north of ten platoon's left flank up through approximately six or seven hundred yards; the ground will dictate, but have at least one trench covering that track."

"Yes, sir."

"Mr. Stokeley, I want Twelve platoon to site on this track as your right boundary and cover the same amount of ground to here."

"Right, sir. No problem."

Major O'Connor clear his throat. The exercise boundary was clearly marked and he hoped that his next lieutenant wouldn't notice that he was going to be playing out of bounds.

"Mr. Bowles?"

"Yes, sir!"

"Mr. Bowles, you will be responsible for the southernmost corner of the exercise area. You will be conducting a BDG on Lyons Bridge, a roadblock on the crossroads here and a mini BDG on Wood Mills Ford Bridge. There may be friendly engineers in the area who will blow the bridge if the Brigadier deems it necessary."

"Roger, sir, a BDG and a roadblock. Wow! That's pretty impressive."

"Yes, now if you will permit me, I'll give orders."

"Oh, yes, jolly good, sir."

O'Connor, now that he had outlined the patrols' areas of responsibility, gave a standard set of orders. He issued orders in a well-rehearsed and deliberate manner that left no one in the dark except for Bowles. Three lieutenants diligently wrote their notes and looked wise or as wise as twenty-year-olds could look. The fourth lieutenant looked as he usually did, which was stunned. Catching a glimpse of that moon-faced map, O'Connor wondered how much information was soaking in. Bowles took few notes. Instead, he dwelt on the meaning of BDG.

At the end of his orders, Major O'Connor, asked for questions. The three Lieutenants each asked a couple for clarification purposes. Lieutenant Bowles when asked, said, "Yes, sir, only one question."

"Go on."

"Well, sir, what's a BDG?"

"It's a Bridge Demolition Guard. You have conducted one in training haven't you?"

"Oh, yes, a BDG. Brilliant. Yes. No problem, just a tad confused over those initials."

"Good, anything else?"

"No, sir, good to go. No sweat, sir, fighting patrol and a BDG."

"And a roadblock," said Lieutenant Stokeley sitting next to him.

"Orders end. That's it, Gents. Good luck and have fun."

As the tent emptied, O'Connor looked at his deputy. "Well, Mike, how do you think it's going to go?"

"One question, sir, who is Lieutenant Bowles' platoon sergeant?"

"Sergeant Clyde, from The Depot, used to be in A Company."

"Okay, yes, I know him. Good man. Probably save the platoon from anything totally embarrassing. Although my guess here is that he'll be sacrificed along with his promotion due to exposure to that nitwit, sir."

"Ah, there's the rub, Mike. That same infection may spread through the company and the battalion."

"And we haven't been inoculated, eh, sir?"

Orders at company level are generally what will be done in a general sense. The specific details of how it was to be done being mapped out by the people on the receiving end. Bowles should have gone back to his tent and sat down and expanded on Major O'Connor's orders to him. Instead, he went back to his tent and took a nap. Thankfully, Lieutenant Alexander of ten platoon had taken him to the O group early, and Bowles had had a chance to accurately and completely mark his map.

Sergeant Clyde found Bowles asleep when he came to the tent to discover why Bowles was not at the platoon O group.

Bowles, awakened from a sound sleep by Sergeant Clyde, sprang up with a yelp.

Clyde said, "Good day, sir, you're half an hour late for your own O group. Do you remember telling me to assemble the platoon at this time?"

Bowles, sitting half up on his cot, nodded. Then his tongue returned from dreamland. "Yes, Sergeant, yes. I'll be right there. Must have dropped off while writing orders. Yes, give me ten minutes. Off you go and get the lads organized."

"They're already organized, sir. They've been sitting on their organized fannies for the past three quarters of an hour."

"Yes, very well,… you do know what had a GDB is, don't you? We're gonna do one for the Major."

GDB, thought Clyde. The closest thing I can figure out, it means God Damned Bowles, and while I can imagine Major O'Connor hoping for that, I don't think that's the definition Bowles is looking for.

"No, sir, can't say as a do. Sounds familiar. Any clues come with it?"

"Well,…, yes, it's about a bridge. We're going to guard it."

Sergeant Clyde saw the light. "Ah, it all comes clear now, sir. I think you mean BDG- a Bridge Demolition Guard? Is that what you're referring to you?"

"Yes, very good, Sergeant, can't fool you. BDG. Yes, funny, how you get those letters mixed up, isn't it?"

As he was speaking, Bowles was putting on his boots and rearranging his uniform. Sergeant Clyde, in order to refrain from applying the FTM, or Full Throttle Manoeuvre on Bowles as he struggled up with his webbing, left the tent in disgust.

During what passed for his orders-giving session, Bowles neglected to pass on the intel about the Engineers coming to link up with the platoon at the bridge. As for the actual O group, we can skip it. It confused Clyde and myself, baffled the lance corporals and bored the shit out of the recruits, who weren't interested anyway. Once that part was over, Clyde made what sense he could of Bowles' gibberish, had a quick word with the corporals, and then he headed off to where he knew he'd get more intelligent orders; even though he knew it would hit him in the wallet.

He made straight for the sergeants' mess, taking me with him. There we found the sergeants from Ten, Eleven, and Twelve platoons and pumped them for what we could get, while they, in turn, pumped us for the beer they could get. Since their respective lieutenants had not passed on anything about Thirteen platoon, we only got crumbs in exchange for liquid gold. Luckily, the company signals sergeant, Jeremiah Miles trotted in and gave us a lot more. Because he needed to see the entire company picture, Miles was able to fill Clyde in on the some of the missing points. But Miles drank gin by the barrel, so Clyde and I paid dearly for this intelligence briefing.

Since the platoon was not due out of the bivouac until the next morning, Clyde had the time to dig our corporals out of their mess and hold his own version of an O Group. Denying Lance Corporals Steele, Anderson, Caruthers and Duguay their last night in the mess for the next few days seemed to him to be cruel and unusual punishment, so he signed for a case of beer from our mess, and we took it with us to his O Group. It was at that meeting that Clyde undid all the damage that Bowles had inflicted on his subordinates.

CHAPTER 49

BOWLES MEETS THE ENEMY

The next evening, with a clearer understanding of what was required of the platoon the NCOs got them all sorted out. Without wasting breath explaining to Bowles what he was doing, Clyde left me and Lance Corporal Duguay at the road block with Duguay's section. I agreed to stay as a reserve section as long as J.P. promised to give me the whole story of Bowles fighting patrol. He said he wouldn't dream of keeping the coming disaster a secret and that it would most likely mean he and I would drink for free in the sergeants' mess for life. And he kept his promise, which is why I am able to relate the details here. What he didn't know, I got from Toby.

Lieutenant Bowles, thinking he had the entire platoon with him, set off full of piss and vinegar. In single file, with two scouts out in front of him, Bowles led them away from their start point. Clyde, being the patrol second in command, was at the rear, ensuring they didn't lose anyone.

They hadn't gone ten yards when he charged up to the head of the column. "Lieutenant Bowles, we're going in the wrong direction."

Bowles stopped, shone his red filtered flashlight on his compass. "You may think so, Sergeant, but we are doing this to bamboozle the enemy. They won't be expecting us from this direction."

"Going in this direction, we'll have to walk completely around the world to even find the enemy."

After a long silence, Bowles said, "On reflection, Sergeant, you are probably right. We don't have that kind of time, do we?"

"No, sir, we don't. I've been in this area quite a bit, why don't I get us to the edge of the enemy area. From there you can lead us."

Bowles agreed, and the patrol turned about and set off again. Clyde turned the show over to Bowles after showing him their location on his own map and their objective. Then he decided to just tag along and hope for the best. His thinking in this was that when Bowles got them totally lost, it wouldn't matter to the overall scope of the exercise and if they couldn't find the enemy, hopefully, the enemy couldn't find Thirteen platoon.

Two hours later Clyde had become thoroughly discouraged. Bowles was surprisingly enough, stumbling along in roughly the right direction. Maybe they could make a difference in the war game. He passed the word up the patrol to call a halt. When they halted, he moved up to talk to Bowles. "Sir, this is taking us quite a ways from the bridge. We need to get in closer, or even go back and come down the other bank."

"Nonsense, Sergeant, we're still following the river. And as Sherlock Holmes would say, 'Elementary, my dear Watson', it has to lead to Lyons Bridge."

Clyde, being smarter than he looked and more knowledgeable about Sherlock than Bowles, was going to comment that Conan Doyle's character never uttered that famous phrase, at least in the books. It came later in a theatre presentation of Sherlock Holmes. He let it slide, hopes of holding an intelligent conversation with his squad commander, now platoon commander had evaporated in the first days of meeting him.

"Yes, sir, I agree, but we are taking far too long to get to the bridge. We may miss an enemy formation moving through it, and then we would be on the wrong side, and they would hold the bridge."

"Well, Sergeant, if you hadn't stopped us, we'd be well along by now, eh?" said Bowles giving his head a shake as if to say, 'some sergeants'.

Clyde nodded in defeat and gestured for the patrol to continue when Bowles held up a hand. He looked around in the gathering moonlight. "Actually, Sergeant, it is quite beneficial that you called a halt. This is a perfect occasion for what my old instructors called a teaching opportunity."

"What? Here? Now?"

"Exactly, Sergeant. Right here, right now. Perfect and it'll take but a moment. Gather them round, Sergeant."

"But sir, as you said, we've no time to waste."

"A waste, Sergeant? Not so. The lads'll love it. Besides, I've been pushing them a trifle hard. Even with all the training we've done lately, they're not as fit as me."

If there was one thing Bowles was, it was fit. He had the stamina of a Tyrannosaurus Rex chasing a Neanderthal for his supper, the T-Rex's supper, not the caveman's. It was unfortunate that he had not been given a more balanced make-up, with a bit more smarts to even things up with his physical side.

Clyde tried one more time. "Sir, we're in enemy territory."

"No need to fear, Sergeant Clyde, at this stage of the game, those Johnnies are all locked up in their sleeping bags or sitting around their campfires swapping tales of derring-do. I've seen it all before." He waved his arm airily as if he had been in the thick of it all with Patton, Attila, and Richard the Lion-Hearted instead of experiencing his first major exercise.

Clyde obeyed, and the patrol all closed in on the stalwart warrior. "Look around you, boys."

"At what? It's fucking pitch black out here," whispered McGuffin to Toby at the edge of the group. Being the Getaway man Toby was the last man in the patrol. In front of him travelled the second-in-command, who in this case was Sergeant Clyde. Directly in front of him was McGuffin, quite proud of being selected as fire team number two's second in Command. Clyde had gone forward to confer with Bowles and was now near him. Toby and McGuffin were still at the rear, Toby sitting on a stump, McGuffin leaning with one hand on the same stump.

"Steady, Offside, use your night vision. The moon is coming up, it'll be like daylight here in a minute."

Bowles went on, "We're standing in what I would call a perfect ambush site."

"Makes you wonder why we're standing anywhere near it then, doesn't it, Squire?"

"It does that indeed, Mr. Tactics, so listen to the great man."

Bowles pointed off to the east. "There's a high feature where an enemy force could open fire on us."

"They probably soon will if that bloody lunatic keeps jabbering so loud," said Clyde to Lance Corporal Anderson.

"Yeah. If this was a cowboy movie, just about now John Wayne would say, 'I don't like it. It's too quiet.'"

"And then all the Indians in the world would drop on them and kick the living shit out of them," added Clyde.

"To our front, we have a small stream. It wouldn't stop us, but it would add to the general confusion if we came under fire. And over to the west is the river. Anyone who dove in to escape would be cut to ribbons while trying to swim away."

"Too fucking cold for me, I'd stay here and surrender," said McGuffin.

"I wouldn't let you. If we were ambushed, I'd drag your sorry ass away with me," replied Toby.

Clyde said, "Fuck this, I've gotta try and stop that moron." He moved out toward Bowles and said, "Sir, we're doing this on the wrong side of an ambush. We hafta get outta here."

"One moment, Sergeant Clyde. You wouldn't deny me my place in the sun would you?"

"No, sir." Clyde stepped back and shifted in close to Anderson. "It'll be a place in paraflare heaven if he takes too much longer."

Bowles finished up with, "Yes, remember this moment, men. We are here in a perfect ambush site."

A red flare jumped into the sky as he spoke. It startled Bowles enough for him yelp. He recovered quickly and said, "Probably a signal of some kind."

Clyde immediately yelled, "Fucking right it's a signal. We're gonna be…"

His words were drowned out by small arms fire that erupted from the hillside Bowles had pointed out. At the same time, parachute flares, launched at the red signal, pop-popped above the helpless patrol bringing the surrounding area into day time brightness.

Toby leaped to his feet as McGuffin shouted, "Well done, like daylight here in a minute, you said."

Clyde yelled again, "Disperse, back up and head for the last RV. Run!"

As he screamed orders, Clyde unslung his SMG and began firing. Lance Corporal Anderson did the same, and as he did he yelled toward Clyde, "All the fucking Indians in the world!"

Then he ran forward toward the stream, yelling "Follow me!"

Bowles stood in the light, a tall, skinny figure, with a wide open mouth and glazed eyes.

Toby spun back and grabbed at the sputtering McGuffin, saying, "C'mon, we're leaving."

A few of the recruits turned to follow Toby. They too had been on the furthest edge of the patrol's formation and were closest to the escape zone. Off they sped as the firing continued. Toby reached the edge of the tree line when a figure, pretending to be a large, leafy bush, sprang up in his path. "Halt. You're my prisoner!"

Toby, still pulling and dragging a protesting McGuffin stopped, but as he did so, he used his body as a fulcrum and levered Offside around and straight into the centre of the talking tree. It went over backwards, McGuffin on top.

Toby took off again, pausing to grab McGuffin by his back web straps. Pulling him along, they shifted out of the light and into the concealing night. A weak voice floated back to them. "I had you. You can't do that."

As the trotted along, a breathless Toby gasped. "Who cares?...We did... I'm not ...going to be... a POW."

"He's...he's...," an equally out of breath McGuffin said, "He's right... you can't do that. I mean use me as a human bowling ball."

"Tell me later... For now, let's get under cover... and be quiet. They may chase us. In... here."

Toby left the trail and led McGuffin into a small thicket. Once inside they both knelt down and caught their breath. Toby thought about what to do next. They had no map, no plan and no idea where they were. McGuffin helped him out.

"Squire," he whispered. "We're lost."

"Not really," said Toby once his heart rate gave its approval for the vocal chords to get back to work. "We know that we are between two bridges. We know that we're on the east side of the river."

"We know something else, Squire."

"What's that?"

"We're on the wrong side."

"Yes... shhh..."

The sound of whispering voices reached into their hiding place.

"He's out here somewhere."

"So, why did we run? We shoulda just stayed put. Now we're fucked."

"You can always go back, asshole. But not me. I'm with the Squire... And Clyde, for that matter, he said run. We're loose. We need to get back to the road block."

"And then?"

"And then Ox'll look after us."

"It's Stuffy and that prick, Agnew," whispered McGuffin. Toby stood up and said in a low voice, "Hey, over here, Stuffy. And, Agnew, shut the fuck up."

The sound of someone muttering came closer as did the rustling of the branches. "Bossy, Brit-shit."

"I heard that, Agnew. We'll discuss it later," Toby said as four recruits came into the tiny clearing in the undergrowth. A few minutes later, two more recruits wandered by and were hauled into Toby's lair. The next set of rustlings were nearly their undoing. At the last second, Toby stopped McGuffin from calling out. They lay in silence while the enemy patrol passed by.

As Toby and his crew watched from the safety of their thicket, the enemy force captain led his patrol along the track toward the bridge.

Toby gave them five minutes and said, "Let's go. We'll tag along behind them. I'll bet they're on their way to that first bridge. The one our guys were left behind to defend. Ox is going to need our help. He's got what, ten guys? This bunch is at least thirty strong.

Agnew said, "Who made you boss, Limey?"

"No one, I was talking to Offside. He's with me, and that's what we're gonna do. You take your bunch and go wherever you want."

"Fuck off, Agnew, you're lucky you got this far without walking into a tree," said Offside.

"Now, steady, Offside, steady. We don't need to get violent about this. C'mon, let's go."

"Just a sec, Squire," said Stuffy. "I'm not part of his bunch."

"Me neither," said Craig Montana.

"Or me," said Eddie Leduc. "We all ran this way 'cos you did."

"It appears to me, Agnew, that you're on your own. We're with the Squire."

Agnew muttered under his breath about being put in with a group of jerks, but said, "Fine. Seems I'm outvoted. Go ahead. I'll agree to let you lead us."

"Very well, if you're with me, then I'm the boss, alright?"

No one objected. Toby went on, "How about it, Agnew, we've got the makings of a small section here. Want to be second-in-command?"

Agnew, shocked at this offer was silent, then he said, "Right, since we are alone out here, a proper command and control system needs to be in place. I'm in."

"Let's go then," said Toby and led the group out of the thicket. Once out on the trail, he put them in single file, Agnew at the rear.

"Eddie, you're our best man in the bush. You'll be our scout. We'll only use you, the rest of us couldn't be as quiet as you if we wore pillows on our feet. Stay about ten, fifteen yards in front. Go slow and stop often. We're in no hurry. Alright?"

"Sure, Squire," said Eddie Leduc, a boy who had spent his formative years as a runner for a bootlegging operation in a little hunting and fishing community just outside of Sudbury in Northern Ontario.

"We're going to follow them to the bridge and then we'll get across and re-join Ox and his section, right?" asked Eddie.

"Yes, although, since I don't know what these guys are going to do at the bridge, we'll hold up once we make sure we're there."

Eddie headed off, and after a minute Toby followed. They travelled slowly, with Eddie taking frequent halts to ensure that he didn't walk in on a halted enemy force five times their size. As the night wore on the boys began to get tired. They had been on the go with adrenaline pumping since early afternoon. They hadn't eaten since sixteen hundred hours, and we're getting hungry as well.

As they travelled along in the wake of the enemy, Eddie suddenly appeared in front of Toby.

"What the...shit, Eddie, you scared the..."

"Shhh." Eddie got in closer where Toby could see his finger on his lips. Then Eddie moved in even closer and whispered, "There's someone out in front of us, coming this way. Sounds like he's lost. May be one of ours or one of theirs."

"On the trail?"

"On the trail, most of the time, I think, but he's blundering around, and every once in a while I can hear him."

"Okay, you take McGuffin and get on the far side, we'll lie low here. If it's only one guy you can jump him or let him come through to us."

Eddie ghosted away in the night, a not as silent Offside following him. Toby shifted back and gave the others the word and then they all went to ground. As they lay there, Toby tried to pick up any noise. He heard nothing. Then the sounds of bushes rustling, twigs snapping so loud that Chingachgook, the last of the Mohicans, if he had made that kind of a racket, would have turned burgundy in embarrassment. Then came a voice, loud in the night, which Toby had no trouble hearing.

"I say!"

"Shit! Gerofmee, Offside."

"Sorry."

"You are? Why did you jump me then?"

"Not you, I mean Eddie."

"Shut up, you're our prisoner."

"Bloody hell!"

Toby got up, thinking that it was time to break up the give and take show, Eddie called out softly, "Hey, Squire, we got him."

"Yeah, so I hear. Wait there...Let's go, guys, we got us a prisoner."

"No, you haven't. Let me up, you bloody colonial."

These words reached Toby very clearly, and he realized that the boys had snagged a Brit. When they reached them, he saw that McGuffin and Eddie were sitting on the ground, backs against a tree with the prisoner between them.

As the rest of the group gathered around them, Toby said, "We'll take him with us. Now listen, whoever you are, we do not have a lot of time to screw around with you. I want you to follow behind me, and we can talk as we go. Alright?"

"Fine, just keep those two oafs away from me."

"Eddie, go on back on point. Agnew…"

"Squire?"

"Take the lead of the section. I'll be in the rear for a while. No questions? Good, let's go, we may have lost that patrol."

With that, the section headed out again. As they marched along, Toby and Smathers-Hughes answered one another's questions. Smathers-Hughes realized that Toby or the Earl had not gone AWOL and that there had to have been a mix-up at the paperwork level back in England. He told Toby of the FURG and all the tribulations they had suffered under Masterson. In the telling, a lot of it was very funny, and both Toby and Smathers-Hughes had a few low laughs as they went along. Toby gave Smathers-Hughes the idea of what they were doing on the brigade exercise and what his group was planning to do.

Smathers-Hughes told Toby that Masterson and Urquhart were somewhere back at the road block hoping to get a line on the Earl so that they could chloroform him and kidnap him back to England. "I'd been on watch a few yards from your bivouac when I heard you all getting ready to go. I didn't know how long before you left, so I couldn't go back and pass the word. I just followed along behind you."

"You were with us when we were ambushed?" asked Toby.

"Sort of. I was way back, and then all the shooting happened. I just stayed down and waited."

"And followed them?"

"Yes, it was that or wander around in the wood forever."

"And then you were grabbed by us."

"Yep, as you colonials say, and here I am."

CHAPTER 50

JACKRABBIT MEETS WITH BAD NEWS

Once again your erstwhile narrator is faced with divergent narratives. I have myself and Lance Corporal Duguay and his section back at the main road block. We have Masterson and Urquhart was circling the wagons like hungry vultures awaiting the opportunity to chloroform the Earl. Added to that, there was Toby and his remnants along with the turncoat Corporal, Smathers-Hughes, busy on a recruit retreat from Moscow. There is now Lieutenant Bowles added to the mix and roaming the wilds of Camp Gagetown as a prisoner of a large enemy fighting patrol. Not to mention a brigade of approximately five thousand troops rampaging around in a grown up version of cowboys and Indians. It's wonder they didn't all run into one another. And to top it off we had Lieutenant Colonel Jackrabbit Schultzberger popping in and out unannounced. All of his story came to me from his adjutant after the exercise.

Jackrabbit was sitting in his CP that evening when his sharp ears caught mention of Thirteen platoon being ambushed.

"They were hit where?"

"You want the grid, sir?"

"No, I don't. Just tell me."

"It seems to be on the east bank of the Nerepis River on the trail."

You said east bank? And you're sure that's the correct grid ?"

"Zero, niner, six... four, six, four... yes, sir, that's what they sent us."

"They?"

"D Company's command post, sir. Seems the platoon signaller got off a contact report to their CP before he was put in the bag."

Jackrabbit said a bad word. Then added, "I hope he scrambled his radio frequency before he was grabbed."

"The CP radio operator said the duty signaller who was on the air at the time the platoon was hit, got a warning off and seconds later the patrol went off the air."

"So we're not sure, but it could mean the company's frequency has not been compromised."

"Yes, sir, and a new message said that Sunray, D Company issued a frequency change."

Sunray was Major O'Connor. We do not have the time or space and you probably don't have the inclination to wander through the arcane arts of the Canadian Army's voice procedure system, so I'll skip it.

"Good. Excellent. I knew Major O'Connor wouldn't let us down. However, show me where it's all happening on the map."

Jackrabbit went over with the duty officer, and they were shown the grid where the ambush had occurred.

"Hmmm... Zero, niner, six. Well, if it was zero, eight, six, that would put Bowles a thousand yards to the west, that's nowhere near where he was supposed to be."

"Yes sir, sir but even zero, niner, six, puts him where he shouldn't be, right?"

"Correct, Ron, my guess is the idiot crossed the river. He was told the patrol would travel on the west bank, and not to cross the river, at all."

Jackrabbit sat down on a bench. His batman brought him a canteen cup of coffee. Jackrabbit thanked him, sipped and said to no one in particular. "So, Bowles is in the bag, and the exercise is only hours old. Maybe I should have just sent him directly toward the enemy heartland. Oh well, same result. He can't do any more damage." Jackrabbit left the CP for his own trailer. He needed to think through the second phase of the exercise, and he didn't need to be hearing anything further about Bowles.

At that point in the exercise, Bowles was tagging along behind the enemy force captain. The members of his platoon who had not been umpire-killed brought up the rear. They were tied by their hands and to one another.

The enemy captain's plan was to take the POWs to a pick up site where vehicles would meet them and haul the POWs away. Bowles was permitted his freedom because he was an officer and the Captain felt he was harmless. As the enemy force approached the Wood Mills Ford bridge, the captain said to Bowles, "You know you were well out of bounds when we hit you, don't you? I have recorded an official protest with the senior umpire."

Bowles gave it as much thought as he could while trying to avoid walking into any trees and then replied, "I did think that I was a bit off course, but it was not intentional."

Bowles didn't twig to the fact that if he and his platoon had been ambushed in an out of bounds area, then the ambushers were also out of bounds. In fact, the enemy force captain was annoyed that his little deception had been discovered, although by accident and by an apparent idiot. His battalion commander had sent him out of bounds deliberately in order to roll up Jackrabbit's right flank and end the exercise with an overwhelming victory. Now the captain could only hope to capture the bridges in time for the armoured regiment to use them. He needed to travel fast to get back into bounds and still capture the two bridges.

Back at the road block, I had set most of the reserve section on the west side, the friendly side, of the bridge. I had ten recruits, one corporal, the driver and myself to man a road block at the crossroads and a smaller bridge demolition guard on Wood Mills Ford Bridge. I placed two men on each side of the bridge approximately thirty yards back where they could see the entire bridge. They were at an angle to one another so that they wouldn't be shooting at one another across the road. I put two more men with the section automatic weapon back fifty yards more, dead in the centre of the road. They were in a vulnerable position if any vehicles got over the bridge and bore down on them, but I had briefed them on a variety of anticipated scenarios.

"Lads, you're likely to face a fighting patrol of about platoon strength. If they come, it will be with a scout or two in front. The scouts will leapfrog one another across the bridge then travel on about twenty yards. They will then signal all clear. You have got to keep an eye on both of them. Let them get across and signal. Give them a bit more time to let the patrol get almost to our side of the bridge and then shoot the scouts immediately, then fire off the flares. The automatic weapons team will wait until they can see the trip flares."

"But, Staff Sergeant, those flares are on the other end of the bridge. The scouts will set them off even before they get on it," said one of the machine gun team.

"No, we haven't set them up on trip wires. Cords are loose and go all way back to the flankers. One of you will yank on the wires as soon as you're sure that both scouts have come across and are on our side of the bridge and the patrol is fully on the bridge. Doesn't matter if a few of them are on our side. When the flares go off, it's instinctive to turn and face where the flares came from. That'll cost anyone looking their night vision. The light from the flares will also backlight the patrol and all of you will be able to see a lot of silhouettes on the bridge."

The boys grinned at me and Nelson said, "Fish in a barrel, eh, Staff Sergeant?"

"Right, Lad. But the key is keeping quiet and being patient. Don't get jumpy when you see the scouts. Depending on how good they are, they could get across without you seeing or hearing them. The patrol will probably not be all that quiet, a patrol will make some noise, no matter how good it is. And if you're hit while I'm up at the road block, I'll muster a counterattack squad, and we'll come running."

I checked the trip flares and strings, put the teams in place, told them I would be back in an hour and not to shoot me on my return, then left.

CHAPTER 51

THE ENEMY PATROL MEETS OX'S LADS

It had gotten fully dark, and a half-moon had begun to peek over a tree line when Nelson on the left flank saw a flicker of movement on their end of the bridge. But he wasn't sure. It seems to be a darker blob shifting against a not-so-dark background. He gave Clements a gentle nudge and whispered, "I think I saw something."

Clements replied, "Yes, you did, see, just at the edge of the bridge at the far railing, he's squatting."

As Clements spoke, another dark figure blurred his way past the first.

"They're both across. Shall I?" asked the nervous Clements.

"No. See if you can see either of them signal in some way."

The first dark blob of stood up. He turned, and Clements saw the quick flash of a red light. Then one of the figures said, "All clear, Johnny. That patrol commander didn't leave anyone to protect this bridge."

The other figure moved back and then as the moon came higher up, Nelson saw both figures stand up and relax. He could even make out the dull gleam of their weapons. SMGs, he thought to himself. Then a noise like a group of people trying to be quiet came to Nelson's ears.

"Now Nelse?" said Clements, almost peeing himself in his excitement.

Nelson, a little calmer said, "Wait. Ox said patience. Better to let them get fully on the bridge... Wait, wait, Clem... take up the slack on the strings, but don't pull too hard..."

"Okay, I'm ready."

"Pull!" said Nelson. His rifle already up in the aim, he fired two quick shots as Clements yanked on the strings. The night lit up on the left bank of the bridge, and almost simultaneously the right side flankers' flares burst into white fire. Then all six men of my ambush opened fire on the pile of bodies making themselves busy in either dropping onto the heavy wooden planking of the bridge, running back toward the flares or running forward off the bridge. The patrol had closed up and on the red signal had come onto the bridge in two files. From the vantage point of the machine gun team, it was indeed, fish in a barrel.

Bowles and the captain were nearly across to our side of the bridge. When the flares went off, Bowles jumped and gave out of little scream.

"Shut up, asshole," said the captain as he dragged Bowles by the arm and flung the both of them off the edge of the bridge into a ditch on the left side.

Here, hold this." He had pulled a small shoulder pack off his back and thrust it at Bowles.

"Stay here and be quiet."

He jumped up and yelled, "Enemy to the front, charge!"

The captain knew the bridge was a death trap and going backwards was just as much an abattoir, so he charged the frontal guns. Staying down in cover with Bowles was probably the safest thing he could do, but the captain needed to save as many of his men as he could. When hit in an ambush, wisdom says charge! He charged!

Just when it looked like he was going to be able to rally a small counterattacking force, Lance Corporal Duguay arrived with a reserve of three and mopped them up.

To make the poor enemy force Captain think that God had gotten him confused with Job, Toby and his crew arrived to slam the final door shut on our trap. The enemy soldiers who had elected to return to their homeland via the bridge ran into a concentrated wall of fire from a direction that should have been safe. Five minutes later it was over. The flares had died out into little candle-light burnings. The umpires then called an exercise halt to assess casualties on both sides.

The umpire staff, a major, two lieutenants and a sergeant were traveling near the rear of the enemy force. Once the firing began the major ran forward to where the scouts were, in order to get a good view of the impending carnage. He was able to see exactly how well we had set our trap.

Bowles had stayed put, and he had stayed quiet. He lay in the ditch wondering what to do. In a night now illuminated solely by the moon, he had no idea where he was or what was going on. His only experience in an umpired exercise had occurred about ninety minutes ago when he had been umpired out as at POW. The umpire major walked over and stood in the middle of the road. Bowles was ten yards away in deep cover. He stayed there, stunned. He heard the major say, "You're dead, Captain. Good effort, but the ambush was even more effective than your own."

"Understood, sir. I'll just get my pack."

"No, Captain, afraid not, you're dead. You can sit where you are. Put the tag on your uniform. Your pack will be returned once the area has been swept and all casualties and POWs accounted for."

"But, sir, it's just over there.

"And it will be staying there for the next little while. Sorry, stand or sit still in that spot."

Bowles realized that the pack the captain was referring to was the one in his possession. He nearly stood up to say, "Here it is, sir," when another voice said, "Where's that Friendly Force patrol leader?"

"No idea, Sergeant Matheson," said the voice that sounded like the major's. "Maybe he cut and run when the firing started."

"I suppose so. And we'll let him go, sir?"

"Yes, if he was smart enough to make a break for it, good for him."

The enemy force captain, now a disgruntled dead person offered his opinion. "Personally, it was my impression that he was as thick as two planks. I'll bet that he's lying doggo around here somewhere and if you call his name, he'll bounce up yelling, "Right here, sir."

The sergeant laughed. Bowles thought it was pretty funny too and was just about to laugh when the major said, "What was his name, anyway?"

"Bowles, sir, Lieutenant Bowles, he's in the CMSR."

Then Bowles realized that he was the one they had been talking about. He slid backwards down the slope to where the ditch ran into the river. He crawled backwards into the river up to his knees before he felt the cold water. Then he turned, changed his crawl for a squat and duck-walked into the river. Once it got up to his neck, Bowles swam over to the other side, climbed out and headed into the trees.

CHAPTER 52

TOBY'S GROUP MEETS A FLEEING ENEMY

I had left Toby and his gang traveling behind the enemy force patrol. We catch up with them as Eddie came back to re-join the main body to report. He called a halt then whispered to Toby, "You can see part of the bridge uprights from just ahead, at least it looks like wooden girders in the moonlight."

"Probably it. Any sign of the enemy patrol?"

"Nothing. I'm not sure, but I get the feeling they've stopped and are checking the bridge out."

"Yes, they'll be looking to see if any of our guys are on the bridge. Good job, Eddie. I'm going to pull back a bit so I can talk without being heard by anyone. Will you stay here and act as a sentry?"

"No problem, Squire."

Toby went back with the rest of them, and they settled in a tight circle. As Toby began to give them a briefing, two shots interrupted his little speech. As Toby spoke, he was suddenly able to see the faces of the boys flicker in front of him.

"Flares," said McGuffin.

"Ours, likely," someone else said, but anything else was drowned out by the sudden bursts of automatic weapons.

Toby said loudly, "That'll be the enemy running into Ox's ambush."

"Quite a night for ambushes, eh, boys?" said Stuffy.

"Well, Squire?" said Agnew.

"I think the enemy have been hit as they went across the bridge. Sounds like they're being shot to hell. I'd say it was payback time. We're going to come up behind them and give them merry hell."

"Actually, Squire, we'll either give them merry hell, as you call it, or we'll get merry hell. We could very well run into another ambush," said Agnew.

"Yes, there is that," replied Toby.

"Shut up, Aggie," said Offside. "Squire says we go, we go. Don't like it, stay behind."

Toby led off at a brisk walk through the last part of the tree line. The rough and ready section followed, ready to throw themselves into the fray. Once out in the open, there was sufficient moonlight for them to shift into a rapid trot and soon they were on the road leading to the bridge. Nearing the bridge, Toby yelled for extended line, and they all fanned out and broke into a charge. Charging right at them from the bridge were four of the now fleeing enemy. Toby's section opened fire, and as they ran through the enemy where the flares were starting to burnout, an umpire jumped up from the edge of the bridge and yelled, "Okay! Cease fire! Cease fire!"

Toby halted the section, and they gathered around the umpire who turned out to be a lieutenant. "Good show, lads. Amazing display. I am totally in awe."

"Why's that, sir?" ask McGuffin.

"Your fire discipline and presence of mind. Correct me if I'm wrong, but aren't you guys fresh out of The Depot?"

"Still in The Depot, sir. But we do have some excellent NCOs."

The lieutenant noted that there was no mention of the officer, but he realized that Toby was obeying the old dictum of nothing nice to say, say nothing.

"Yes, I'm sure you do. So, tell me, who's plan was it to have a four way ambush?"

At first, Toby said nothing, he hadn't the faintest idea what the officer was talking about. Then he figured it out. Ox must have sent a counterattack team down to help out when the firing broke out. "Well, sir, we're not really part of this. We were ambushed down below and ran away."

"Part of Lieutenant Bowles' fighting patrol?"

"Yes, sir. We ran off and re-grouped and then while we were hiding in the bush, the enemy patrol went past."

"We just tagged along behind them," said Stuffy.

"Yeah, we didn't want to miss this clambake," added McGuffin.

"And so when the firing broke out, where were you all?"

"Back about fifty yards or so in the tree line. We were just waiting to see when it was clear to cross the bridge and report to Ox, I mean Staff Sergeant Oxnard, sir," said Toby.

"And who decided to do the Charge of the Light Brigade?"

Agnew, standing behind McGuffin, spoke up, "That was the Squire's idea. He figured we'd either be a cut-off group or we'd get massacred. We should have stayed in the bushes, eh, sir?"

"No, not at all. What this Squire or whoever…"

"Just Squire, sir. It's a nickname. I'm Private Trelauney-Fitzgibboncrest."

"I can see why they call you Squire. It's a whole lot easier on the tongue. Nonetheless, it took a lot of guts and initiative to charge down here and help your comrades." He turned to face the group. "You are all to be commended and I want you all to stay here until my Sergeant comes along to take your names. I'm going to have you all written up. Good show all round."

As soon as he had wandered away to complete whatever umpirely duties umpire lieutenants have after a battle, McGuffin gave Agnew a sharp elbow in the belly. He oofed, as was natural and then a sergeant showed up to write their names down. He came over to where Toby, Offside, and Smathers-Hughes were standing. By this time the moon had risen high enough that it was more like daylight. The Sergeant looked at the three of them and noticed that Smathers-Hughes was not carrying a weapon. "Where's your rifle, son?"

Smathers-Hughes had been thinking of the Earl Kidnapping Plot and not paying a whole lot of attention to what was going on around him. "At home, Sergeant," he said absently.

"At home? You left your weapon at home? On a brigade exercise? Where's home? Main camp?"

"No, Sergeant, it's…"

"No? Where then? Petawawa? Wainwright?"

Smathers-Hughes, knowing nothing of those Canadian Camps, shook his head. "Well, where then? Suffield? Look, what's your trade? You wear no insignia."

Smathers-Hughes could answer that one. "I'm a clerk, Sergeant. But in the British Army, it's pronounced, 'clark'.

"What's a clark?"

Toby, who had been chatting with Offside and Eddie, suddenly got involved with the Smathers-Hughes and Sergeant Umpire debate. "He's a clerk, Sergeant."

"So… from Camp Borden then?"

"No, Sergeant, Aldershot," said Smathers-Hughes.

"Aldershot? It's closed. All the units from there are now based in Camp Gagetown."

Toby broke in again, "Aldershot, England, Sergeant. He's a non-combatant. Here on exchange duty."

"Alright then, carry on. I won't need your name. What's yours?" he said to Toby. Toby told him and when the Sergeant moved on for fresh names, Toby, still in the middle of the bridge, walked over to the edge.

"Psst, Offside, come here, quick."

"What's up?"

"Over there, just about three quarters of the way across and heading for the far side. Someone is swimming. I'll bet it's one of the enemy."

"Want me to shoot him?" McGuffin raised his rifle. "Got 'em in my sights, say the word."

"No, I don't think so. The umpire did call a cease fire. Maybe this is how they play it. Take a timeout after every attack to assess casualties and do a body count."

"'Spose so, but I have a feeling I shoulda popped him. He might be the escaping general, and we'd win the war if I shot him." Offside lowered his weapon. "No matter, whoever he is, I'd bet the CO would have thanked me if I had shot him."

"You're a bloodthirsty little wretch, Offside. He's out in the water, harmless to both sides. How can he affect the war? Leave him be."

A few hours later Toby would have cause to remember this discussion and wish he had let Offside empty a magazine at the runaway soldier.

CHAPTER 53

URQUHART THINKS HE MEETS THE EARL

While the enemy force was moving toward the bridge, Toby shepherding his lambs behind them, I was in relaxed mode back near Thirteen platoon's vehicle park talking with Lance Corporal Duguay and Private Draper, the battalion transport driver who had been attached to us for the duration. "Lance Corporal Duguay, would you go down and see how they're doing at the bridge? I'm going to take Private Draper and do a walk around the vehicle park. We'll meet you back here in about half an hour, alright?"

"Sure thing, Staff," replied Lance Corporal Duguay. "I need to get the lay of the land anyway. I'll visit the road block, too and make sure they're ready to act as a counterattack or a reserve force."

"Excellent idea, Lance Corporal Duguay. I believe that Recruit Adair is the nominal commander. A sharp cookie in my estimation."

"Yes, he is that. I'll see you later, Staff."

"Cheerio to you and would you please come with me, Private Draper?"

"Right, Staff."

In the tree line approximately twenty yards away a large bush breathed a sigh of relief and then rustled around. Out of it stepped Urquhart.

"Careful, man, he'll see you," came the panicky whisper from Masterson.

"Relax, Major. Thank God those two have finally separated."

"Quite. If Smathers-Hughes had been here, we could have jumped all three of them an hour ago. As it is, we are pushing things, time-wise."

"You did tell the lad to go around the other way and try and locate the Earl, sir."

A petulant mutter of agreement came from the bush and Urquhart refused to respond. At that time, unknown to me, the two of them had been skulking in the underbrush for some time after hearing my English accent. Since mine was the only British accent they had heard, they took it for granted that I was the Earl. I had been on the scene of the mall opening, I was wearing a British uniform and since they had not checked any details on the age of the Earl, assumed that I was Toby. Now it was dark, the last time they had run across the Earl, he had been painted up, wearing a steel helmet, his webbing stuffed with branches. An honest mistake.

"If we let them get a bit farther down from the road block, we can be sure no sounds will reach the recruits," said Masterson.

"Fine. But if this is done right, all the noise they'll be making will be snoring. He said they were going to do a check on the vehicles, if we creep up closer, we'll get a chance to leap out and chloroform them both before they know what hit them."

Draper and I made our rounds, chatting as we went. We had finished a sweep of the vehicles and had come back to the main track and the junction with the little road. As we walked back toward the road block area, the sound of small arms fire disturbed the peace of the evening.

"The bridge. Someone's attacking the bridge. Come on, Draper."

I picked up the pace into a fast walk, Draper scurrying along trying to keep up without running. We cleared the hill's crest and from there could see the glow from the flares on the bridge.

"We're about a thousand yards from the bridge. Too late to run down there, we'll probably get shot. Lance Corporal Duguay knows what to do. We had better stay here. If the enemy gets through, we have to hope the bridge section has at least cut their numbers down. And then add another hope that Lance Corporal Duguay and his counterattack force can finish them off."

"So why wouldn't we want to go down to where he is, Staff?"

"It's too dark to see clearly, we can get shot by the enemy, the bridge crew or Duguay's section. If we stay here, we command the high ground, and if the enemy scatters, we're likely to get one or two stumbling onto the vehicles and making away with one of them."

"Right, Staff. We can also see down to the road block and pretty much back to the vehicles from here."

Here was the precise spot where Urquhart had suggested that he and Major Masterson lay in wait for the Earl.

Safe in their hideaway, Captain Urquhart said, "I'll tackle the Earl, Major. You can handle that little pipsqueak."

"Yes, of course."

Masterson was relieved that he didn't have to handle the burly Earl. Urquhart fished the cotton batten and the small bottle of chloroform from his pockets and made ready the sleeping potion. Masterson fumbled with his, dropping the bottle cap as he sloshed chloroform on his hands, the cotton batten, his uniform and the ground.

As the astringent odour reached Urquhart's nostrils, he said, "Be careful with that stuff, sir. It's potent."

"Yes, good. I'm ready," replied Masterson, hoping that his hands would dry off quickly. He had already given himself a good dose of self-medication and was feeling a bit woozy.

While they had been getting ready, the small arms fire had stopped.

At that moment, I was out in the road about twenty paces from my potential assailants. I said to Draper, "Maybe it's over." Then another round of gunfire echoed over the river valley.

"Oops, too soon. Must be the Corporal and his counterattack team," I said. That was when I was hit from behind. A large hand went across my mouth and nose as I stumbled forward from the force of the charge. Getting the wind knocked out of my lungs, I immediately responded by inhaling a bushel of air. This air found its way past the cotton that had been crammed in my mouth and up my nose, only to pick up in passing a good dose of chloroform. As I sank to the ground, I attempted to short struggle and then collapsed as the chloroform took effect.

When Urquhart left the safety of the trees, Masterson followed. He was a couple of paces behind him when Urquhart crashed into me. Draper turned to see what was happening to the staff sergeant when a dark irregular shape moved across his peripheral vision. The shape, tottering toward him suddenly stumbled as it tripped over one of my legs. The form managed to stay upright and continued on toward the young private. Draper had had some warning, and he sprang to attack the oncoming Masterson. While not in my league when it came to hand to hand ability or burliness, he was no slouch when it came to street fighting. He landed on top of Masterson, bringing him to the ground in a heap. As Masterson fell, he landed on the handful of chloroformed cotton batten. As he snuffled the frothy mess in his face, Masterson began to succumb. He too, had had the wind blown from his body and like me, he drew in a large amount of the Gagetown night air, complete with a burst of chloroform. It was Masterson's last waking breath for a while.

Urquhart lowered the now comatose imitation Earl halfway to the ground and turned to see how his accomplice was doing.

By this time said accomplice was doing nothing more dangerous than dreaming. Draper, a bit confused at the ease in which he had dispatched one foe, turned on one knee to search for another. But his next opponent was not Masterson. Seeing that Masterson had failed to perform even to his usual low standard, Urquhart lunged at Draper, as that fine young soldier was climbing to his feet. Draper got off a loud yell then bang! He was down again. Urquhart dosed him with sleepy juice and stood up slowly and with a satisfied smile on his face, said, "And another one bites the dust". His glance travelled from body to body, his head shaking in disappointment as his eyes came to rest on his Commanding Officer deep in slumber. "Why would I expect anything different?"

CHAPTER 54

MORGAN MEETS URQUHART

Back at the battalion CP, Jackrabbit was in his trailer when the night's serenity was broken an hour and a half after he had heard of Bowles' self-inflicted ambush. He was busy with bridge demolition and counter attack timings when a knock on the door brought him to the present.

"Yes?"

"Duty officer, sir, Lieutenant Jameson. Captain Taylor said you would be interested in the latest from Thirteen platoon."

Jackrabbit hesitated. It had been his understanding that Thirteen platoon no longer existed unless it was in the depths of an enemy POW compound. The last thing he wanted was the latest from Bowles. He gave a growl. But he was interested.

"Pardon, sir?"

"Nothing, Lieutenant. I'll be right there."

Five minutes later, Jackrabbit strode into the CP and over to where Captain Taylor, his Intelligence Officer, was standing talking with one of his Intelligence operators or Int Ops.

"Thanks, Sergeant Simon, that's it for now."

Jackrabbit nodded and said, "Evening, Sergeant Simon." as the Sergeant went out past him. Jackrabbit's batman handed him a coffee and left. Jackrabbit, after a long sip, said, "Alright, Tony, let's have it. I suppose we've been captured and Bowles is now the Commander of the Phantasian Armed Forces."

Tony Taylor laughed. "Not quite, sir. But remarkably prescient. It appears that the enemy fighting patrol that ambushed Bowles headed for Wood Mills Ford Bridge and was, in turn, ambushed on that bridge by the roadblock section that Bowles had left behind. Wiped out. According to the Intsum from D Company's CP, anyone not killed was captured."

"It couldn't be Bowles, though, wasn't he with the enemy force as a prisoner?"

"Possibly, or he was umpired out as killed. We have no confirmed report as his radio went off the air at the time of the ambush on his fighting patrol and we have had no word since."

"Right, so who's getting reports back to D Company?"

"We believe that it's someone from the force at the road block. It has to be a recruit as the voice procedure is sketchy and we sometimes lose them completely."

"Which was more than we got when Bowles was ramrodding that outfit," replied Jackrabbit. He wondered about Bowles leaving a reserve force back at the road block. He shook his head thinking, no, gotta be Clyde's doing.

"At least whoever's running things now is awake."

Which could not be said for the bunch back at Sleepy-Hollow-on-the-Ridge. Captain Urquhart stood surrounded by three people who were all in a state of unconsciousness during which their voluntary functions were suspended. In other words, they were unhelpfully dormant. He heard, between the soft whistles from Masterson, the manly snores from the Ox, who he thought of as the Earl, and the peaceful, lullaby-like noises from Draper, the valley below turn silent once again and he figured that he had a bit of time to spare before someone came looking for the driver and the Earl.

He took off back down the smaller trail until he spied the vehicle park. Looking them over, he selected a three-quarter ton truck as his getaway car. Hopping in, and reviewing the controls and gear shift arrangement by the light from his pocket flashlight, he saw that aside from the truck having its steering wheel on the wrong side that it was drive-able. He hopped out and shifted around to the driver's side and got back in. Starting it up and suffering through a series of sharp lurches forward coupled with sudden stops, he bounced back down to the wilderness bedroom of Masterson, the Earl, and Draper.

Getting out and leaving the engine running, he half-dragged, half-carried the Earl over to the back of the three-quarter, dropped him, dropped the tailgate, picked up the Earl, then grunted him onto the tailgate of the truck box. While he had him in that position, Urquhart found his baling twine and tied the Earl's hands and feet. He ripped a chunk of the Earl's shirt sleeve and using that with some twine fashioned a gag for him. Then he shoved him in to the back. He repeated the dragging and loading process with Masterson. It was only with great reluctance that he refrained from tying him up and gagging him. Once the tailgate was back in position, he then dragged Draper over into a small bush, kicked some loose leaves over him and headed back toward the truck. Panting with the effort, heart racing, he came close to cardiac arrest when out of the night came a challenge, "Hey, what's going on?"

It was our old friend, Alphonse Morgan, he of berserker fame. With the bridge secure, Lance Corporal Duguay had sent a runner back to find me and give him a situation report, or as the army calls it, a sitrep. Urquhart, his heart still leaping in his shirt like a BC salmon in the rapids, jumped around. Not five yards from him stood a camouflage painted gargoyle, complete with rifle.

Urquhart was aware that the above-mentioned rifle's muzzle was wavering none too confidently in his direction.

"Put that weapon down. Can't you see that I'm an officer?"

"No, I can't…sir?" replied Morgan, covering his bets. What he could see was a rather large, possibly fat, breathing-heavy, sweating-copiously, man in a too-tight uniform without any markings of any kind, preparing to get into a three-quarter ton truck. As he said that, Urquhart remembered Trooper Robinson's uniform. And to be honest, he thought, I'd be the first to admit that at this point in time, if I were looking in a mirror, I would have to say the image looking back would not be overly officer-like.

"My apologies, old chap. Of course you can't see that, can you? Forgot myself there for a second. I'm incognito."

Morgan, as we have seen, was not a soldier whose mental armament included a fully loaded rifle. In fact, if you had been the camp psychologist who had recently re-evaluated Morgan, you would have been considered charitable if you had given him the grading of ten cartridges in his twenty-round magazine sized brain.

Morgan ran the word across his lips and then gave an enlightened grin. "You're in disguise, eh, sir?" It never occurred to him to challenge Urquhart's self-proclaimed commissioned status.

"Yes, that's right, smart fellow. I'm in the Armoured Corps, and I'm out on a recce." As he spoke, Urquhart manoeuvred himself toward the driver's door. He had driven out of the vehicle park, turned left and headed along the slight downhill slope to the body pick up place and stopped close to where the Earl had been lying. This had placed the vehicle nose first toward the bridge. "Can you tell me if I can turn around anywhere close down the hill?"

"Yes, sir, just go on a little way further, and you'll come to a crossroads."

"Thanks very much, good bye."

"Goodbye, sir," said Morgan, excited by meeting an undercover spy.

Urquhart climbed in and headed off toward the crossroads. What Morgan had failed to tell Urquhart was that the remainder of Thirteen platoon was manning the crossroads. Breathing a sigh of relief at the truck moving off without any grinding of gears of jumping, Urquhart set a course for the crossroads. As he approached, he was met by another soldier, this one, too, was pointing his rifle at Urquhart. Behind him, faint in the moonlight, Urquhart saw more soldiers. He shifted into a higher gear, or tried to. The Canadian Army was notorious for having insisted that the three-quarter ton truck manufacturers make the shift from second to third nearly impossible unless the driver was double jointed at both the elbow and the shoulder. Ninety percent of the candidates of a driver-wheeled training course fail because they cannot learn how to do that ingenious shift.

Urquhart couldn't do it either. What he could do, as he gave up grinding the gears, was to slam the transmission back into first and stamp on the gas. The vehicle leaped forward like a deer taking a cattle fence. The sentry managed to dart to one side. As the truck bore down on the improvised barrier, those not busy hurling themselves out of the way of the angry truck, opened fire. Urquhart crashed the barrier into toothpicks and then found himself on a steep slope that cut into the hillside; there was no turning back here. Shouts from the rear encouraged him, and he made another attempt at getting into third. A near dislocation of the right shoulder convinced him that second gear was just as good and he returned his concentration to the road. Suddenly he arrived at the site of the automatic gun group in the centre of the road. He ran over the C2, the big brother of the FNC1 that the Canadian Army carried as its primary infantry weapon, crushing the folding bipod and collapsing the thirty round magazine into the receiver group. The C2 gunner, Recruit Joseph Forde, without concern for the weapon, cleared ten yards in his escape. The truck powered on, leaving the troops behind puzzled over what appeared to be one of their own vehicles leaving the field of battle, but heading toward enemy lines.

From there it was a short hop to the bridge. As shouts of confusion and yells of fright and anger mixed in the night air, Urquhart and his unconscious cargo left the scene and were absorbed by the trees and what was left of the night.

The truck tore down the road, Urquhart not sure where he was going, but just as unsure of where he had been, slowed for a turn in the road. After a glance into the rear view mirror showed him no light or flashes of gunfire, he brought the vehicle to a standstill. As he paused to re-group his thoughts, Urquhart wondered what to do next. He leaned forward on the steering wheel and brought his head down on his hands. As he sat there considering popping into the back and strangling Masterson, a tap came at the driver's window.

Dazed at the idea that such an empty looking piece of Canadian wasteland such as Camp Gagetown could be so full of irritating people; he turned to face yet another intruder. With a start, he pulled himself back from the window as he confronted a dripping wet nightmare. He forgave himself the little shriek that escaped and stared in horror at the apparition that stood outside the cab of his truck. He caught himself, rolled the window down an inch and managed a weak question, "Yes?"

"Can I get a ride?"

"What?"

"I said could I get a ride?"

"I heard you."

"Then why did you say what for?"

"I didn't say what for, I said what."

Getting the urge to check to see if Masterson had somehow gotten out of the back and gone for a shower with his clothes on, Urquhart said, "Who are you?"

"I'm... I say, well done."

"What for?"

"Ah-hah, there. You did say what for."

"Yes, but I wanted to know what you said well done for."

"I didn't say well done for. I said well done."

"And I said, what for?"

"But you said you didn't."

With the urge to check on Masterson's whereabouts edging toward a compulsion, Urquhart thought that he had better put an end to this. "Do you know where you are?"

Bowles looked in at Urquhart, the face was extremely familiar, but he didn't think that he'd met a truck driver who looked so frayed and stressed.

"Do you have a map?" asked Urquhart.

"A map? No, mine was confiscated when I was taken prisoner."

Both officers had enlightenment deposited in their brain cases at the same time.

"I say!" squeaked Bowles.

"Lieutenant Bowles," said Urquhart.

"Yes, it's me."

"Go around to the other side and get in."

Bowles did so. As he made to go around the rear of the vehicle, Urquhart shouted, "No, go around the front." He didn't want Bowles to catch a glimpse of his sleeping beauties. Bowles obeyed, stopping himself in his tracks, doing an about turn and coming around via the hood of the vehicle. As he manoeuvred, Urquhart pondered on what his story was going to be. He wasn't sure if the old liaison officer trick would hold up. He needn't have worried. With Bowles there was never any danger of him analysing anything.

Opening the door, tossing in the pack and then following it in, Bowles said, "Bit of luck finding you out here, Captain. I've had a merry chase tonight."

"Yes, by the looks of it, you've been for a paddle."

"A paddle? You mean boating?"

"No, for a swim, my little joke, ha, ha."

All his dealings with Bowles flashed through his mind. *I could easily chloroform this idiot, take him and Masterson out and over to a thicket and strangle them both. Oh, joy! No, I need to get back to England. And with the Earl in my possession, that's now a given.* Reluctantly pushing aside all thoughts of vengeance, Urquhart said, "Do you have any idea where we are?"

"No, sir, I don't, but this road does head away from the bridge that has been attacked."

"Then we'll head the way the truck is pointing and trust to luck."

"Very good, sir, but I hope we can get back to my platoon before dawn. I need to meet up with some Engineers who are going to blow another bridge to stop an enemy force from coming in from the south."

Urquhart drove on, he was pretty sure that Bowles had no idea where south was, and wanted to avoid any more Masterson-like dialogues. Five minutes later, Urquhart's luck ran out. As they swung around a tight corner, they found the road closed. It was not a flimsy barrier such as Bowles' men had put up. Being a centurion tank, this one had a bit of stopping power. Urquhart had been glancing at Bowles in a vain attempt to see if he was a total idiot, he brought his eyes back to the road and his foot to the brake pedal. The three-quarter slammed to a stop fifteen yards in front of the tank. A tanker, propped up on the glacis plate, stared in amazement as Urquhart flipped the truck into reverse and backed up rapidly. They skeetered backwards, veering right, then left as he tried to steer to the rear in the night on a gravel road that seemed to slip out from under the tires.

"See any kind of side road?" he yelled at Bowles.

"Yes, we just passed one, to the right, but I don't know where it goes."

"We didn't know where this fucking road was going either, and it turned into a tank…"

The truck stopped as Urquhart jammed the brakes on. He glanced back down the road. It didn't seem like the tank was chasing them.

"Yes, I see it, hang on."

Too bad the pair in the back can't hang on, they are going to be pretty bruised up when then get out of here. If we get out of here, Urquhart thought.

They travelled along the barely recognizable track. As he drove, Urquhart fiddled with the controls. "Do you know anything about this vehicle, Lieutenant?"

"It's a three-quarter ton truck, I think it was first used in Korea, we used it as a section vehicle until the army issued APCs. Yes, if I'm not mistaken, it was used in the Korean War. Before that, there was the… I forget which, but I do know that during the…"

Urquhart tuned him out, thinking, Oh, bloody hell, I asked for it. Now I'm going to be treated to a history lesson conducted by a man more suited to be emptying dustbins. Not that I've got anything against dustmen since Uncle Alf was one.

Bowles rattled on. To himself, Urquhart sang the chorus of, 'My Old Man's a Dustmen' as he drove with one hand and played with the truck's various switches with the other. Suddenly the world went black. Once the shock of being plunged into darkness in the middle of a country filled with trees to ram into and ravines in which to dive down at twenty miles per hour passed, Urquhart realized that the truck could still be seen through some form of illumination emanating from the truck.

"Oh, good idea, sir. Those headlights were sure to give us away. Make targets out of us. We'll be much safer with cat's eyes."

"Cat's eyes?"

"Yes, we call that kind of truck lighting cat's eyes. Used when in an operational environment." Bowles tittered, Urquhart shuddered. He had learned days ago in his conversations with the lieutenant that his tittering was a signal that Bowles had found something humorous. His passenger went on, "And we are certainly in an operational environment, eh, sir?"

"Yes, indeed, extremely operational…" Urquhart ran out of words as the truck ran out of road. "What? A dead end? Can't be?" he stopped the vehicle. "It would be nice to have a map, wouldn't it, Lieutenant" without waiting for an answer, he carried on, "I'm going to go on a bit further. Maybe an aberration…"

Like you and Masterson, Urquhart thought as he downshifted into first gear and then ploughed on slowly. Five minutes later and with the road maintaining its state of invisibility he accepted that there was no road on the immediate horizon and said so.

"But if we turn back, we'll be blown up by that tank," said Bowles.

"We are not at war, and I don't think those tanks are going to be using live ammo on an exercise, Lieutenant."

"Quite, sir. So we could turn back, right?"

"We could. We're not, Bucko. Not a bleeding chance," replied Urquhart, grinding teeth and gears as he dropped the shift into bull low. "Not a fucking chance. This is a fucking-cross-fucking-country-fucking-three- fucking-quarter-fucking-ton-fucking-truck. We're taking the fucking thing across the fucking country. Hang fucking on."

Bowles hung fucking on. The tone of suppressed frustration, not so unsuppressed fury, mingled with Urquhart's determined emphasis on nasty profanity spoke volumes to that faint spark of intelligence flickering in his head. Bowles was not going to challenge Urquhart in any way.

The fucking-three-fucking-quarter-fucking-truck struggled across-fucking-country at a pace that made travel by turtleback appear supersonic. Based on Urquhart's knowledge of Camp Gagetown and Bowles vow of silence as he rode with a suspected madman, we can be assured that the fucking three-quarter will spend nearly as much time in the fucking wilderness as fucking Moses did. We can now safely seek out another set of players in the Brigade exercise. Granted the field of champions has diminished slightly, what with Masterson, me, and Draper sleeping it off, Jackrabbit imitating us in his trailer, and the enemy force captain and crew rendered hors de combat.

CHAPTER 55

TOBY MEETS FURG

At the road block site, Lance Corporal Duguay was the ranking member of Thirteen platoon. He did a fast recce of his bridge team, road block party and the vehicle park sentry only to come up short in his body count by one driver and one staff sergeant.

"Squire?"

"Corporal?"

"You've been wandering around, seen anything of Staff Sergeant Oxnard and the driver?"

"Nothing, Corporal. He was down here?"

"No, I left them up at the vehicle park."

Toby and his section Duguay detailed off as the ready reserve and sent them up to the vehicle park to grab some rations from the trucks and hopefully get a hot meal inside themselves before the next assault.

Smathers-Hughes, not having anything better to do, tagged along. Once at the vehicle park, McGuffin and Eddie got water boiling on a camp stove set up behind one of the deuces, while Toby pumped Smathers-Hughes for information on their plot to kidnap an Earl.

"Well, your Lordship…"

"Skip that. In fact, you're a corporal, and I'm only a private. Call me Toby or Squire, either is acceptable."

"Very well, as the pompous Major Masterson would say, I'll bow to conventional wisdom and address you as Squire. And I think I know where your staff sergeant has gone." Smathers-Hughes stopped. "He's that British staff sergeant, right?"

"Yes."

Smathers-Hughes gave out a chuckle. "In my opinion and I admit it's only a guess, I think Major Masterson and his un-able second in command have grabbed the Staff Sergeant in the assumption that he is you."

"You guys were the ones at the Mall opening?"

"Yes, and that's what confuses me. I thought that both the Major and the Captain had seen enough of you to identify you while you were in the APC…"

"You were the one on the ramp, grabbing me."

"Correct, and no hard feelings, your … Squire-ship?"

"None," Toby laughed. "It was worth it to see that carrier demolish Sergeant Clyde's jeep and the bike rack."

Smathers-Hughes grinned back in the dull moonlight, agreed and went on, "Now Captain Urquhart is really the silent force in FURG …"

"Furg? Are you choking?"

"No, FURG is short for, 'Fearless Undercover Recovery Group, but Urquhart says it means, 'Fucked Up Really Good."

"And Urquhart is the brains behind FURG?"

"To the extent FURG has any brains at all, it's him and me," replied Smathers-Hughes modestly. "And it's likely that Urquhart didn't get a good look at you. Most of the time he was trying to drive the APC."

"And I was cammed up with face paint and trees in my helmet."

"Yes, so I think that Urquhart picked Staff Sergeant Oxnard out in the dark based solely on his accent and Masterson just followed along."

"So," said Toby. "Ox has been kidnapped…no, Ox-napped?"

"Yes. And if I'm not mistaken, they're heading to a place called Fredericton Junction, where we are supposed to catch a train out of the area. We'll then get to an airport and go home."

"Do you think they're the ones who crashed the road block?" Toby asked as McGuffin came over with a couple of heated tins of food. He handed one to each of them. "Careful, cans are hot. Here's a couple of spoons and some crackers."

McGuffin left them alone and then Lance Corporal Duguay showed up. "Good, get some food into yourselves. As for that three-quarter that ran the road block, it seems to have been one of ours. Unless Staff Sergeant Oxnard and Draper took it. But they wouldn't have crashed us. My thinking is that the two of them have been taken prisoner and the three-quarter was the escape vehicle."

As he was talking, Duguay took a long, slender package of waxed paper out of his pocket and unwrapped a huge chunk of sausage. "Horse cock. Lots of protein and fat to keep you warm."

"Horse cock?" said Smathers-Hughes.

"Farmer's sausage. Who are you?" Duguay asked, noticing Smathers-Hughes' presence for the first time. "One of the enemy?"

Toby, between mouthfuls of Jambalaya, gave Duguay a brief sitrep.

"So, Staff Sergeant Oxnard has been snatched by a couple of Brits? Him'n Draper?"

"Who's Draper?" asked Smathers-Hughes.

"He's a driver, and he's missing as well."

Toby had an idea. "Corporal Smathers-Hughes, didn't you say that you all came here in a civvy van? I'll bet the gang took the three-quarter and are now heading for the van. They'll have changed vehicles. If we go there, we'll be able to get the three-quarter."

"I don't think so. The van is over that way, and the truck went off in the opposite direction. They'll be nowhere near the van."

"But if we get to the van we'll be able to intercept them when they come back."

"Maybe… If they get back," said Smathers-Hughes.

"So here's my plan, Corporal Duguay. I'll take Corporal Smathers-Hughes, and we'll stake out the van."

"Well…"

"Look, Corporal, you don't really need me, and anyway, officially I'm on that patrol with Lieutenant Bowles. How about it? It could be a feather in your cap if we catch the truck thieves."

"Yeah, and there's a chance that I'll get a whole lot of feathers from Sergeant Clyde. Along with a bucket of tar to go with it. Shit… go ahead. Go on, get outta here."

"Thanks, Corporal Duguay."

"Here," he dug his map out of his combat trouser pocket and handed it to Toby. "This may help. If you do get totally lost, fire three shots and wait five minutes and then do it again. We'll come and get you."

"We won't get lost, Corporal."

Toby put his webbing back on, slung his rifle over one shoulder and as they left the vehicle park, he grabbed a couple of apples and two small milk containers and said to McGuffin, "Keep an eye on my helmet, Offside. I'll be back in half an hour."

Smathers-Hughes was no Eddie, but he was no Bowles, either. They found the van after twenty minutes of searching. There was no sign of any visitors.

"I told them both that the keys were under the front seat." Smathers-Hughes opened the driver's door, climbed in and sat down. He reached under the seat and pulled out a key ring.

"I'd say they haven't been here."

"Wonder if they'll be very long. They must have figured out that they went in the wrong direction."

"Knowing the Major's skills or lack of them in navigation and map using, I'd say they're out there on the enemy side, well and truly lost."

Toby looked at his watch. "It's been five hours or so since our patrol set out. Ox was okay when we left. If they're in the three-quarter and they're looking for this place, maybe they are blundering about, still looking."

"Or…"

"Yes," said Toby. "They've been captured."

Smathers-Hughes said, "I'd say… just a sec…" He leaned over and fished a provincial highway map out from between the seats. "Hop in the passenger side and leave the door open so the light stays on, Squire."

Toby did so, and Smathers-Hughes opened up his map. "Do you know approximately where we are?"

Toby took a turn at the map producing routine and hauled Duguay's map out, looked it over and said, "Yes, in here. On this track. See, the Corporal's marked the road block and Lyons Bridge. That's the bridge where we should be right now. Oh well, that's Lieutenant Bowles' problem."

"I see, look, up there on the upper left. That's where we are going to get the train. And we've got to go from….. down here to there."

"Wow, that's a long way to go." Toby's eyes went back to the military map. "Just a sec, Corporal, what if they're out there, still lost and still trying to get out of the training area?"

"And so?"

"And so, if we went here," Toby pointed at a junction. "Morrison Road and Highway 7."

"And I say again, and so?"

"We could wait for them."

"Squire, do you have any idea of the odds involved in us intercepting one little army truck in a country the size of Canada? Besides, your Corporal is expecting you back soon. We may wait all night, or what's left of it."

"Yes… it's a long shot as Offside would say, but it's all we've got, and I've got to get Ox back."

"We don't know that they've even got him."

"But you do think they do, don't you, Corporal?"

There was silence as Smathers-Hughes considered the evidence. Toby didn't wait for an answer. "I've got to get Ox back."

"I heard you the first time, I'm thinking."

"He's my gentleman's gentleman. His family's worked and lived with our family for generations."

"Maybe he saw his chance and ran away to gain his freedom."

"Very funny. Anyway, are you game?"

"And suppose, just suppose, as we pull up at the intersection and the truck is sitting there waiting for us. What do we do?"

"Simple, we'll get Ox back. Once you all get back together at the train station, you can explain why I'm in the Canadian Army and then you can all go home."

"Simple, alright. But let's give it a go. I have had it with this bloody country. Bugs, cold nights, and fucking trees everywhere you look." Smathers-Hughes looked Toby in the eye. "You're on, Squire."

So off the pair of them went on what Smathers-Hughes thought was the longest-long-shot-wildest-wild-goose chase of all time.

CHAPTER 56

THE WILD GOOSE MEETS WITH SUCCESS

As Toby and Smathers-Hughes were debating the merit of going to the potential cut-off site, Captain Urquhart and Bowles were chugging along at two miles per hour, tops. Suddenly, they cut a trail.

"We don't know where it leads, so my guess is that a right turn will take us back toward where we have come from, but that going left will at least take us into a new frontier."

Urquhart had guessed correctly; five hundred yards farther on, they hit another intersection, this one with a real road. And again Urquhart guessed correctly, he turned right. "We went left the first time, so now we'll try a right turn."

On the new road, he was able to travel faster, but he was soon outrunning the cat's eye lighting.

"Fuck it. We're alone out here, or we aren't. Out here we call no one friend."

He stopped and then played with the switches until the headlights lit up the countryside. "Excellent. Well, Lieutenant, as they say in your neck of the wood, let's make tracks."

He gunned the engine, and the truck sped off. Urquhart had mastered first and second gear while traipsing across country. He left it in second, remembering his troubles with third gear. Five minutes later they came to Lyons Bridge. Two hours later, after successfully traversing miles of Lawfield Road, crossing Crozier bridge and coming across Highway 7, Urquhart heard a voice from the rear. He looked over at Bowles to see the lieutenant nodding in his seat. They passed a sign saying Oromocto that had an arrow pointing in the direction they were traveling.

Now he knew they were heading north and he knew that Fredericton Junction was north and west of Camp Gagetown. He pressed on.

Toby and Smathers-Hughes had been at the intersection of Morrison Road and Highway 7 for a long time. Toby had jammed his bayonet into a

328

link in the length of chain that held the gate lock. He couldn't get the lock off, so he attacked the chain. Once he had it arranged to his satisfaction, he gave the bayonet handle a wicked butt-stroke with his rifle. The bayonet fell to the ground. In the van's headlights, he could see that the link had been spread slightly. Four more repetitions of that manoeuvre and the link gave up the ghost. Once through the gate, they parked the van on the other, south side, of the Highway, so that the windshield gave them a good view of the oncoming traffic heading north.

Since Highway 7 was a civilian highway that lanced through the training area, there was a certain amount of vehicle movement through the night. When a pair of headlights hove into view, Smathers-Hughes started the van, and they got ready to turn and chase the three-quarter. They had now done this for six large farm trucks, two tankers, one milk truck, seven passenger cars, one of which was a Corvette. Before Smathers-Hughes had the key turned in the ignition, the Corvette had flashed past them.

"Definitely not them," said Toby as they settled back to chat and tell one another their life stories. At each sighting and subsequent disappointing outcome, their level of exuberance and optimism dwindled, until Smathers-Hughes finally said, "Squire, this is hopeless. We have to face it. We've missed them, they've been captured, or they're still out there lost."

Toby agreed, "I suppose so. And by looking at the map, I see that they could have driven right across the training area and exited on the east side, driven up around the Camp Gagetown boundary and headed toward Fredericton Junction without even coming close to this location. We may as well head back."

Smathers-Hughes started the vehicle and drove it slowly back across the Highway and into Morrison Road. He got past the still open gate when Toby said, "I'd better close that thing, but I'll just hang the chain on it."

"Fine. I'll keep the engine running."

Toby got the heavy gate back in place and was wrapping the chain around it when headlights showed in the distance. He squatted in the long grass beside the gate and waited for them to pass. Smathers-Hughes caught the flash of light and turned off the van's lights and engine. Neither of them felt that the oncoming vehicle was their long shot arriving in the nick of time, but neither wanted to advertise their presence. The lights came closer.

The occupants of the vehicle closing in on Toby and Smathers-Hughes were an assorted lot. The driver was a plump, no, to be honest, overweight captain in the British Army's Armoured Corps. The passenger beside him was a dopey lieutenant, fast asleep and dreaming of a world where nightmares vanished when you woke up and didn't pester you when you were awake. In the rear of the three-quarter was a wide-awake, very angry, very hog-tied gentleman's gentleman serving on temporary duty as a staff sergeant in the service of Her Majesty's Canadian Army. Positioned beside him, and appropriately enough propped with his back toward Bowles, and also awake, was Major Masterson, Commanding Officer of UARB. Ox may have been raging, but Masterson was experiencing chloroform withdrawal and severe motion sickness. As the vehicle approached the gated intersection where Toby and Smathers-Hughes waited, Ox began drumming his heels on the truck floor. Masterson sat there wishing the truck would stop so he could get out and throw up. Ox drummed his heels. Urquhart looked at Bowles. Bowles slept on. Masterson made a futile attempt to kick Ox to make him stop. Ox grunted through his gag. Masterson choked back bile.

Bowles came awake. "What's that noise. Is the truck breaking down?"

"No, it's one of the E and E guys we've got in the back. He's come awake."

As the banging became louder, so did Bowles. "Captain, what's an E and E guy?"

"Escape and Evasion. Part of the exercise. I caught two of them and was able to subdue them. Now it looks like we'll have to pull over and sort them out." As he spoke, Urquhart slowed the truck and then cruised it to a stop fifty yards past Toby's hideout.

Bowles said, "What are you going to do?"

"I'm not going to do anything, you are. Here…" Urquhart fumbled in his combat shirt pocket for the last of the cotton batten and the bottle of chloroform. Finally getting it free from the magazine pouch on which the bottle had snagged. He handed them over to Bowles. "Get out and drop the tailgate. Then pour a little of the chloroform onto the cotton batten, and then jump inside and gas them both."

"I say!" Bowles was outraged. "No, sorry, sir. I couldn't do that. Hardly Geneva Convention, Captain."

"Fuck the sodding Geneva Convention. You're only going to knock them out temporarily. They're legit POWs. And I'm fucking ordering you to fucking well do it, understand?"

Bowles understood that he was debating with a red-eyed, rabid, wolf. He didn't want a reappearance of the Urquhart that had ranted on about the fucking truck going across the fucking country. He nodded, gulped and said, "Yes, sir."

He got out of the truck, the enemy force captain's pack getting caught up on the door handle.

"Here, gimme that!"

Bowles handed it over. He closed the truck door and set out for the back. Urquhart watched for him to come up in the rear view mirror. He planned to let Bowles put the Earl and Masterson back to sleep, then when Bowles was returning to the cab, Urquhart was going to squeal away leaving the dopey lieutenant to his fate. Bowles placed the bottle in his pocket and undid the chain hooks on either side of the tailgate. It came down with a bang. He took the bottle out, opened it and splashed a good amount everywhere, then put both the cotton and the bottle on the edge of the truck box.

"Sorry, chaps, orders is orders. Just playing the game, understand."

Hearing that voice coming out of the night, I gave my head a shake. Bowles? Here? Well, at least he would now be freed. But what was Bowles rabbiting on about? Playing the game and being sorry?

Masterson, ready to find relief outside the truck, struggled up, shoving me back full length on the floor. Trussed like a helpless hog, I promised severe retribution once my bonds were loosened. All I could do now was roll around, like a piece of flotsam or a lump of jetsam tossed by the storm. Bowles jumped up, one hand holding the cotton batten, the other latching onto the bench seating and levered himself into the truck. As he did, Masterson managed to regain his feet, head ducked due to the low ceiling. As he made it semi-upright, his gorge rose in his throat. Bowles' head hit him amidships and his stomach contents, propelled from the external pressure, streamed out over Bowles' hunched back. As the river of last night's partially digested dinner deposited itself down Bowles' backside, Masterson was flung backwards to land on my legs. I yelled another deadly promise through the damned gag. Bowles landed on top of Masterson. Being re-squashed, I renewed my promise, tossing in threats of removing Bowles' organs by hand. In the jumble of arms and legs, torsos and hands, Bowles managed to stuff the cotton into Masterson's now empty mouth, the overflow of the chloroformed cotton jammed itself into Masterson's nostrils. My indecipherable promise and Bowles' garbled apology were soon mixed with Masterson's relaxed breathing. One down, one to go, Bowles thought.

Back at the gate, Toby realized that in playing dice with the interception theory, he had rolled a seven with one dice. He yelled at Smathers-Hughes to turn the van around. Smathers-Hughes, looking out the window saw the outline of a truck at about the same time. He turned the key and revved the engine. Toby downed tools and took off toward the three-quarter. A quick glance showed Smathers-Hughes that there was no convenient turning point. He shifted into reverse and crashed backwards through the gate.

Urquhart saw lights appear in his mirror. He didn't know who it was, but for him, any lights meant an enemy of some kind. He yelled at Bowles to gas the other one as he started to put the truck in gear. Bowles was finally upright, holding onto the wooden cross pieces of the canvas-topped frame. He half turned and saw the lights. Not understanding Urquhart's yells, he pulled himself along to the rear and was out of the truck and running around to haul open the passenger door. He was halfway in when Urquhart took off. Toby was twenty yards away by this time and gaining on them, screaming, "Hang on, Ox, I'm coming!"

Smathers-Hughes backed out too fast onto the Highway, and his left front tire dropped into the ditch. Urquhart pressed the gas pedal and tried to shift into that misbegotten third gear. The truck rebelled yet again. The sudden hiccup in motion served to swing Bowles fully into the cab, the door slamming shut behind him.

Urquhart said, "Fuck it!" and got it back into second, then floored it again, just in time to evade Toby's grab at a hanging canvas strap. The truck escaped by the skin of its paint job. Toby, regaining his balance, gave up and turned to see his van rocking back and forth as Smathers-Hughes alternately shifted into reverse and then into forward. Toby, still breathing hard, jogged back to the truck. He slowed to a walk as he neared the van and it suddenly popped out of the ditch. "Get in," yelled Smathers-Hughes.

Toby broke into a run, and once he was aboard, Smathers-Hughes launched the van into a rapid following pace. "It was them, wasn't it?"

"Yes," panted Toby. And waved to indicate that he needed time to catch his breath. Smathers-Hughes let him rest as he set sail in the direction of the gradually dimming taillights. The chase was on.

In the lead vehicle, the stench gradually crept up from Bowles' back and the now soggy seat back cover.

"Shit! You stink. What the fuck did you do, Lieutenant?"

"Nothing, sir. One of those guys in the back was coming out when I was jumping in. We banged into each other, and he threw up on me."

Had to be Masterson, thought Urquhart. "Was one of them still tied up?"

"I don't know. There seemed to be one on the floor, but we fell on him. I did get the puker, though." He looked down at his hand. In the faint glow of the dashboard light, it appeared sticky. He wiped it on his pant leg. As he did that, Urquhart again attempted the third gear shuffle with the same result.

"What's the matter with this fucking truck?" he got the lever into neutral and no further.

"Ah, I see you've run into the shifting problem that strikes many amateur drivers."

"If you call me an amateur again, I'll backhand you so hard you'll think it came from God, Lieutenant."

Not wanting to experience a backhander from God, Bowles said meekly, "Yes, sir. Let go and see if I can shift it from here."

"Never mind. I'll stay in second, thank you very fucking much."

He glanced into the rear view mirror and saw the weak shine of headlights. He didn't know if it was that vehicle back at their last stop, but he couldn't get caught this close to home.

"Alright, Lieutenant, give it a shot. When I say now, that means I've stepped on the clutch. Got it?"

Bowles immediately grabbed the gear shift and gave it a dreadful grind.

"Not yet, you idiot. When I say now."

Bowles did it again, and Urquhart realized that as far as the moronic lieutenant was concerned, saying when I say now meant that he had already said it. He sighed and said, "Fucking now!" as he stepped on the clutch. Bowles did nothing.

"What the fuck? Are you deaf? I said now."

"You said, fucking now."

"Fucking, bloody hell!" Urquhart waited a five count. "Now."

Bowles gave the lever a wiggle and a shove and the stick slipped into third like it was on automatic.

Bowles tittered. "An old trick a driving instructor showed me. It seems that the angle of the driver's arm puts the lever at an awkward angle and it grinds. When the passenger does it, the angle changes. It's a manufacturer's defect. Most drivers get the hang of it after a while."

"Fine. Fucking fine. And shifting to fucking fourth gear? Do I need to climb out of the cab and kick the gear shift with my right leg while humming the Bridge on the River Kwai?

Bowles giggled. "No, sir. Fourth is easy, just slip the clutch in and pull back on the stick."

Urquhart did, and for once Bowles was right. The truck's engine whined at a lower pitch and the vehicle smoothly accelerated.

CHAPTER 57

URQUHART MEETS BOTH FRUSTRATION AND EXASPERATION

While Urquhart and Bowles had been playing, Toby and Smathers-Hughes had gained on them but were still a mile and a half behind. As the hydro poles whizzed past the three-quarter, Urquhart's stomach reminded him with a hearty growl that it had been ignored for too long. Then he remembered Bowles' pack.

"Got any food in your pack, Lieutenant?"

"Yes, sir."

"Good, let's have some then, I'm starved. Get it out."

"I can't, sir."

"Why not? All you have to do is reach into it and drag out the grub."

"My pack is back at the road block, sir."

"Your pack is on the floor of the truck, Lieutenant. Or is that a cat you've been lugging around all night? So open it up and get out the food."

Bowles picked up the pack. "This. No, sir, this is not my pack."

"You stole it? Well done. Didn't think you had it in you."

"No sir."

Urquhart sighed. He would rather attempt communications with a chimp than with Bowles. "So for God's sake, where did you get it?"

"It belongs to a captain in the fighting patrol that ambushed us. He told me to hang on to it. So I did."

"What's in it?"

"I don't know, I've never looked. It doesn't belong to me."

"Where is he now?"

"He was designated an umpire-casualty. Last I saw of him he was sitting on the bridge."

"Then he won't need whatever's in the pack. Open it up."

"Is that an order, sir?"

"If that's what it takes, yes."

"Very well, but it is another man's property."

"And that fucking other man is not here. Open it."

Bowles did so. In the pack were two slightly squished bananas, a more than slightly squished ham sandwich, two chocolate bars, melded together, but edible, a map and the captain's field message pad. Bowles hauled the items out one a time, announcing what each was.

"Give me half of the sandwich, or all of it, if your conscience won't let you eat it or else you're Jewish."

"You can have it all. I don't want any of it, that's stealing."

"No, it's not, it's foraging. You never heard to the victor go the spoils?"

"Who's Victor?"

"Victor who… Oh, shit! Shut the fuck up, you…" said Urquhart as he ripped the sandwich out of Bowles' hand and with one hand on the wheel, quickly unwrapped the sandwich with his teeth. As he chewed noisily, he stopped in mid-chew. "A map?" The sandwich caught in his throat. He choked, got it clear and then swallowed. "Did you say a map?"

"Yes, sir."

"Do you mean to tell me that we have been wandering around like lost bloody babes in the woods and you had a map with you all this time…"

"Yes, sir. But it's not mine."

"So you told me. What's a field message pad?"

"This, it's a notebook for NCOs and officers. We write down notes and orders."

"Might have been useful a few hours ago, along with the bloody map. Now… I'd rather have a banana."

The entire sandwich had disappeared in a few bites. Urquhart did some more pocket diving and pulled out a flashlight. "Here's an electric torch, take a dekko at that map. We need to find out where we are."

Urquhart glanced at his rear view mirror. It looked like the vehicle behind them was gaining on them.

"Where are we going? What are we going to do with those guys in the back?"

"None of your business. It's exercise Top Secret. I can't tell you… look a sign, we're getting close to a place called Geary. See that on the map?"

Urquhart risked a look at the map now spread out on Bowles' legs. He saw Bowles' finger moving along the top of the map. "No, more…Lieutenant…go down to the lower left hand of the map. We can't be that far north."

The reflection of the lights from behind caught Urquhart's eyes, blinding him momentarily. He shook his head, moved the rear view mirror slightly and then stepped on the gas, but he was already in top gear, and the pedal had hit the metal. A horn boomed out at them. Bowles dropped the light and the cab went dark as a semi-trailer going at a tremendous pace, pulled out and passed them as if they had stopped.

Bowles said, "Wow, a biggie."

"Pick up the torch."

"Yes, sir." But he did nothing, and the cab stayed in darkness.

Then in a tiny voice, like he was awaiting a backhander from God, said, "What's a torch?"

"What's a torch? Are you an idiot? It's that thing you just threw on the floor."

Bowles had no idea that torch was British for flashlight.

"I didn't throw anything on the floor."

Urquhart took his eyes off the road for a second, saw that the torch was shining away on Bowles' feet.

"It's on the floor."

"Right, sir, the torch is on the floor. Must be beside the flashlight."

"Bloody fucking hell. The flashlight is the torch."

There was silence. Urquhart took another glance. Bowles was sitting there.

"Lieutenant, pick the damn thing up."

Bowles fumbled around and then said, "Got it." And there was light in the cab again. Urquhart saw nothing in the mirror, so he flipped the vehicle into a lower gear, then another and gradually brought it to a stop on the shoulder of the road. "Let me see that map."

There was silence in the cab for a few seconds.

"Hold the bloody light still."

"Yes, sir."

After a minute, Urquhart said, "Yes, there we are. We need to swing over that way. We'll take a turn here, and that should lose whoever's following us."

Bowles looked out the rear window. "There's no one there, sir."

"Yes, there is. I don't know how far back they are, but they're out there, and they won't quit. Let's go."

Before he started up again, Urquhart rolled his window down. Then off they went. Urquhart had Bowles do the shift thing, and then he got it into fourth gear, and they sped down the highway. After another length of silence and speed, Urquhart said, "Good God, man, you absolutely stink. If I had to sit beside you much longer, I'd vomit, too."

"Sorry, sir, but it's not me."

"I know. I know. But it's sickening just the same."

Urquhart rolled his window down and a minute later started slowing again. "There's the sign."

The truck made the turn; on they went, dragging their prize escapee closer to England with every rotation of the tires. Seeing no lights in the rear, Urquhart relaxed. He got Bowles to do the trick with the stick shift, but this time it was not so smooth. Grinding noises erupted from under the hood, so Urquhart took control and rammed it back into second.

"Not a problem, Lieutenant, it's a gravel road, and we're making good time." As he spoke, lights glared into his eyes from the rear view mirror.

His tone of voice returned to Neanderthal mode. "Shit. Fucking, bloody shit! I thought we'd lost them."

He very nearly had. Toby and Smathers-Hughes had zoomed along, and as they sped past the turn off, Smathers-Hughes had caught a glimpse of brake lights to the left. He jammed on the brakes as they whipped past the corner, got it slowed, turned and back the other way.

The runaway three-quarter came to a stop sign. "Hoy! This is it. We go right here and then it's clear sailing for about ten miles to the station. Roll your window down. We need air."

"It's cold in here with your window down, sir, couldn't you roll it up?"

"No, you stink. Roll yours down. Look in that guy's pack, maybe there's a sweater you can borrow. He seems like a well-prepared boyo."

Bowles thought that was a great idea, and he was only borrowing it. With one hand he struggled with the open map, fighting with as if it were alive: and losing. With the other hand, he fumbled around on the floor for the pack.

"Lights! They're on us!" shouted Urquhart. "Get ready to shift for me. We need speed."

At this time, as we take a short leave of absence of Urquhart and Bowles riding in first class, with Masterson and I napping in tourist class, Urquhart is yelling, "Now!" Bowles was losing both the battle of the map and the war with the pack. The shoulder strap, now an octopus, wrapped itself around the gear shift, which Urquhart had released for Bowles to grab. Behind them, Toby and Smathers-Hughes were in sight and closing. The three-quarter's transmission sat idly in neutral as the three-quarter sped toward a hairpin turn on the gravelled, one lane road. Five miles from Fredericton Junction, the two vehicles were galloping along toward where Appleby met the Adjutant in the not-so-distant past.

CHAPTER 58

APPLEBY MEETS BOWLES YET AGAIN

Do you remember Appleby? We had not heard from our gentleman farmer in this epistle for some time. We knew that he had become an associate member of the CMSR officers' mess. What was new was that he had turned the running of the farm over to an experienced deputy and then had turned professional as a taster of single malt scotch.

As well, one of the toys purchased from the windfall he had toppled into from the seat of his combine harvester was a brand new jaguar XKE. Silver body with a black canvas convertible roof, the XKE could do a hundred on a twisty gravel road while the driver held the steering wheel loosely in one hand while the other hand anchored a bottle of scotch. When that previous non-social meeting with the Adjutant and Bowles had occurred, he had been returning from his local pub. Tonight he was going the other way. He was still returning from a pub, but since his elevation, by virtue of wealth, into the agricultural elite, he had been compelled by his daughter, Tuesday, to find a more sophisticated watering hole. The one Tuesday selected for him was in the other direction from his farm. Fate, not finished with him by a long road, placed him in Urquhart's path.

"Looks like they're slowing down, Corporal. Go faster," said Toby.

"Yeah, sure. In a van I don't trust, on a road I don't know. I'm the driver, not you," replied Smathers-Hughes.

The three-quarter disappeared around a corner.

"Don't lose him now!"

"Settle down, Squire. We're on their trail, and we do know where they are headed. Relax."

We had left Urquhart and his truck entering a sharp curve. We now re-convene inside that stinking cab as Urquhart is fighting to free the gear shift from the pack strap and Bowles is being defeated by a large uncooperative map of Gagetown. No eyes are on the road, which suddenly side-stepped to the right. Coursing along like its namesake in hunting mode, the Jaguar was entering the hairpin from the other end. Urquhart's eyes transferred themselves back to the windshield in time to be blinded by the rapidly encroaching high beams of Appleby's silver bullet. Appleby, fortunately for himself this crash, was not concentrating on opening a bottle with this teeth. This time he was adjusting the radio, hoping to find something other than pig futures, wheat prices and commercial messages for farm implements.

Urquhart, his night vision gone for a burton, as the English say, screamed, "Look out!"

Bowles, now encased in his paper shroud was looking close up at the fine details of roads, bridges, rivers, towns and other topographical delights when his wallpapered head met up with a suddenly stopped windshield. Rebounding from the bang he crumpled and slid to the floor. Urquhart, his body jammed in behind the wheel, had Trooper Robinson's shirt buttons embedded in his tummy as he lost consciousness. In the back, the super-cargo fared much better. Me, being tied and Masterson as relaxed as sleep can relax one, had nothing to brace themselves against and with no forecast of the impending crash bounced around a couple of times before re-assuming their pre-crash positions. I had been able to get a two-legged kick in at Masterson while we were at the apex of our launch.

On the other end of the business meeting, Appleby, his head coming up as the lights of the three-quarter advertised oncoming traffic, was hurled through the canvas top and instantly retired from radio disc-jockeying. He hung over his now shattered windshield.

As they tore around the corner and came onto the scene of vehicular carnage, Smathers-Hughes hammered both feet on the brakes. Toby yelled, and the van skidded to a near halt, then banged gently into the rear of the three-quarter. Toby was out and peeking into the truck box before Smathers-Hughes had turned off the engine. Before the van's headlights went out he saw dark silhouettes on the floor, heard grunting noises and climbed in.

Smathers-Hughes went to the front of the vehicle, looked through the driver's open window to see Urquhart's motionless form. He leaned in and found a wrist. Using his old Boy Scout First Aid skills, he determined that Urquhart was still occupying breathing space on planet Earth. Toby by this time had found, mainly by tripping over them, two bodies.

"Corporal, back here, people."

Smathers-Hughes dropped Urquhart's arm and went back to the van. He backed it up and left it running. With the van lights on, he and Toby were able to drag me and Masterson to the edge of the truck box. Toby produced his pocket knife and cut me loose. Smathers-Hughes checked Masterson and found him unhurt and asleep. He smelled the vestiges of chloroform and guessed that Urquhart had done it to maintain his own sanity. After massaging my ankles and legs, I clambered down to the ground and by balancing against the truck's superstructure, leaned and waited for the pins and needles of returning circulation to go away. I assured a worried Toby that I was fine.

Toby and Smathers-Hughes then went off to see who else was involved. Smathers-Hughes opened the truck's passenger door and Bowles, still gift-wrapped in his map, tumbled out. The enemy force commander's field message pad landed on the gravel beside Bowles' carcass. Smathers-Hughes picked it up and handed it to Toby, who placed it in his pocket and then began to unwrap his platoon commander. Once that was done, he let Bowles drop to the ground and retrieved the field message pad. He held it up to catch the van's headlights and saw that it belonged to Captain George Whalen. He slipped it back into his pocket and said, "We had better check on that civvy vehicle."

As they climbed over the now severely compressed hood of the XKE, Appleby opened his eyes and struggled to stand. His feet dangled in the air, his torso overlapped the windshield, and he was going nowhere.

"Hep… Hep… Hep me."

"Hang on, sir, we're coming," said Toby. Smathers-Hughes reached for the driver's door handle, opened the door, and both door and handle fell at his feet. Jumping onto the driver's seat, he grabbed hold of Appleby's belt from the rear and heaved. Appleby returned to his seat, which at that moment was being occupied by Smathers-Hughes. He promptly fell down, and Appleby landed on him. Toby had a laugh and then helped Appleby out of the car. Once clear of the wreckage, Appleby groaned at the sight of his car. "Less than six month old, boys. Army bought it for me."

"Maybe the army 'll buy you a new one," said Toby. He had heard rumours, who hadn't, of the crash and Bowles involvement in it. He said, "We're going to take you home. You can call the police from there."

Toby, Appleby, and I jammed into the front of the three-quarter, which aside from a few cosmetic dings and scratches was unhurt. Bowles was deposited, minus his map, in the back. Then the three of us loaded Masterson and Urquhart into Smathers-Hughes' van. Toby and Smathers-Hughes said goodbye. Toby telling Smathers-Hughes that he would give him a good hour or more to get away from the crash site, before reporting it.

Toby, Appleby and I arrived…Oops, Bowles, too, at the Appleby Estate. Aside from learning by doing, as Urquhart had done, how things in the cab of a three-quarter were arranged, Toby had had no trouble driving a stick shift. Stored in a warehouse back in England was a car he owned, an old Austin, whose transmission design was not dissimilar from the three-quarter's and had been tougher to manipulate.

By this time, Appleby's alcohol level had diminished to half-pissed, which seemed to be his normal operating procedure and he had recovered from the accident. They parked between a BMW and a Chevy half ton, both shiny and new. I gestured toward the vehicles as they headed toward the house. "From the army, Mr. Appleby?"

Appleby laughed and said, "That's right. Now look up at the second floor."

They stood ten yards from the house and waited. A light came on in an upstairs window, a figure silhouetted itself, was gone, and then lights tracked the figures progress through the house. A porch light came on, and the front door opened.

"I don't know who you are, but if you're looking for Josiah, he's not here."

Appleby muttered, "She means me."

"We're not looking for him, Ma'am, we're bringing him home."

"Well don't bother me with him. If he's in a coma, drag him over to the barn and heave his drunken carcass into the hay and get out of here."

"He's been in an accident, Ma'am."

CHAPTER 59

MRS. PRENDERGAST
MEETS AN EARL

"The man's an accident all by himself," She said, with no sign of sympathy.

"I'm alright, Mrs. Prendergast. Nothing's broke." Lowering his voice to what he considered a whisper, Appleby said, "Mrs. Prendergast, my housekeeper. Cranky old bitch if she doesn't get her eight hours. I'll deal with her."

"No, you won't, Josiah Appleby. You'll thank these gentlemen and then you'll come inside and get to bed."

"Can't, Mrs. Prendergast. Need to feed these guys and take a look at the one in the back." He jerked a thumb behind him, nearly poking me in the eye. "C'mon in, soldier boys," he said as he limped up the steps and into the house.

As he went by the housekeeper, she said, "You are a disgrace, Josiah. A disgrace. What would you poor old wife think?"

"Being as she's been dead going on twenty years, can't think she'd care one way or another. Now that we've discussed my shortcomings…"

"Or just started," said Mrs. Prendergast.

"That too, how about you rustle up some ham and eggs for these gents?"

"Very well. You are my employer." The housekeeper followed Appleby in and then in came Toby and I behind her.

As they wended their way to the kitchen, what Appleby had said sunk into Mrs. Prendergast's consciousness. "What, a body in the back of the truck? You've gone and killed someone, you old fool? Have you called the police?"

"No one's dead, Mrs. P. he's out cold from the crash."

They continued down a long hallway past a set of stairs that led to the second floor. White trim, and pale blue walls, where handsome pictures of the outdoors of Canada hung in two rows down the length of the hall. They went in past what looked like a parlour, then entered a large kitchen and dining room combination. This part of the house had begun life as a barn that Appleby's great grandfather had built. Strong enough to withstand the entire Mexican

Army of General Santa Ana, it had been converted by Appleby prior to his marriage, when he had inherited the farm.

He had built the rest of the house onto the barn, gutted and refurbished it by himself. It was now the centrepiece of the property. Large, open-spaced with high rafters, the original beams crisscrossed and were used to house the heads of all varieties of once inattentive game, now uncaring animal heads. Toby came in and stared at the animal heads. His father's, now his, estate at home held some Indian and Asian game heads, but Toby had sighted one that he had never seen before, at least in the realm of taxidermy, but was quite common in farmer's fields. Toby gave me a nudge. "Look, he's got a cow's head up there next to that deer."

Appleby, a few steps in front of them chuckled and said, "No, lad, an Elk, not a deer."

"And," I added. "Not actually a cow, rather a Holstein-Friesian; a male, two years old is my guess."

Appleby looked at me in amazement. "Bang on, soldier boy. Bang on. My first head. The bull belonged to Old Man Reeves. Found that sunnavabitch helping himself to one our Black Angus cows. Guess he thought he'd wandered into a harem. I took him out with one shot while he was giving it furiously to Molly-O, our prize winning milker."

Appleby laughed at the memory. "If you gotta go, I guess that's the way to go."

"Josiah, that is a filthy tale and a filthy trophy. It should have been burned years ago," said Mrs. Prendergast as she scurried around rattling pots and pans. After settling them around a large wooden table, the housekeeper got them all cups of coffee, slamming a steaming cup in front of Appleby. She said, "You need this the most." And returned to her cooking.

As they sat there sipping the coffee, I said, "Thank you very much, Mrs. Prendergast. This is wonderful coffee."

"You're welcome, sir," she said and kept cooking.

Toby remembered the field message pad that Smathers-Hughes had given him. That was quite a coup, for a recruit to have his own field message pad. They were on issue to lance corporals and above, only a crafty private would know how to get one.

"This is great. Hardly used at all. Thank you, Captain Whalen, whoever you are." He browsed through it, coming across training notes, supply lists and other junk. Then he got to a page that had written across the top, 'Brigade Orders'. It was dated two days ago.

"Listen to this, Ox. It's a set of orders for this exercise, some of it refers to today."

"Or yesterday, possibly, since tomorrow is now today, I fear."

"Yes, this is the guy who attacked us on that patrol and who we nabbed on the bridge."

"Yes, he didn't fare too well on that second venture, did he?"

"No, we blasted him and his troops into smithereens."

I stood up. "Let me know how it turns out. I had forgotten our luckless lieutenant."

I departed just as Appleby said something about draining a snake. The housekeeper hissed at him, and Toby delved deeper into Whalen's orders. He came upon a list of timings and then spoke loudly, "Shit!"

Mrs. Prendergast said, "Pardon?"

"Oh, sorry, Ma'am. Terribly sorry. I've been too long in a world of guys who swear with every second word."

"Josiah, you mean?"

"Him, too, I guess, but this field message pad has dynamite information in it."

"I have no idea what you said, young man, but you sound excited."

"I am. It's to do with an exercise back in Camp Gagetown, Ma'am. Big stuff, enemy plans."

"Enemy plans?" said Appleby and myself as we appeared at different doorways. I had re-appeared through the original door from the hallway, Appleby from a door way that hid a bathroom. As we resumed sitting, once again picking up our coffee cups, Toby said, "Ox, we've gotta get back. They're gonna attack that bridge we were supposed to be guarding. That was the task of the owner of this book. He was supposed to be taking and holding three bridges in our area in order to let some tanks and infantry come across. They are due to launch an attack across the bridges, then swing around and up through our company and battalion."

"Yes, they'll do that attack and then try to roll up our flanks. If a group can catch the edge of an enemy formation, it is usually the end of that battle in favour of the flanking attacker. And by the sound of it, we have very little opposition in place."

"Opposition, nothing. Bowles never made it to the first bridge, and the one we've got now only has what's left of our platoon."

"You are correct, your Lordship, we do indeed have to get back. We need to find that Engineer group and get them to blow the bridges ahead of time."

I looked at my watch. "It'll be close, Toby. We are at least an hour away from the platoon."

Mrs. Prendergast came over with two huge platters of eggs, ham, beans, and fried potatoes. "Here you go, gentlemen, and do not think of running out to that silly war game of yours before both of those plates are empty."

I looked at Toby and Toby looked at his plate. Toby said, "There are priorities, and there are priorities, Ox." He picked up a knife and fork and dug in.

"I quite agree, your lordship," I said as I too began to get the meal into me. A few minutes later, Mrs. Prendergast brought Appleby his plate and then sat down at the table with them. She sat there sipping a coffee and beaming as Toby and I heaped praises on her cooking; Appleby just gobbled. Toby finished first. As I mopped up the last of his eggs, he thanked the housekeeper again.

Appleby spoke up as a figure loomed in the door way. "Well, I'll be damned!"

"Yes, and soon, hopefully," said Mrs. Prendergast. Appleby fork in hand, mouth full had half risen from his chair. "It's, it's … you know. The fella who saved my life."

"Hello again, Mr. Appleby. How did I get here?"

At that point in time neither Toby or I were in the know about the finer details and were not aware that Bowles had done anything but cause the accident.

Appleby pointed his fork at Toby and me. "These two brought you here. You were out like a light."

Toby said, "We are just finishing up, sir. We have learned of an enemy plan, and we need to get back right away."

"But, this gentleman needs to eat, "said Mrs. Prendergast as she rose from her seat to get back on duty. I took another look at my watch, "I'm sorry to say, sir, that we are on a deadline. Time is short." I turned to Mrs. Prendergast. "Thank you, Mrs. Prendergast, for an absolutely delicious meal. It was truly memorable."

"Oh…thank you."

"Yes, Mrs. Prendergast, it was marvellous," added Toby as he got up from the table.

"Hey, fellas, why don't you both head out in the army truck now. Me and… forgotten your name soldier boy?"

"Lieutenant Bowles," said Toby.

"Yes, right. Lieutenant Bowles. He can stay and eat. I'll run him down in my truck. Where are you headed?"

"Lyons Bridge. But it's a long way from here."

"Yes, it is. Over by Boone's Mountain. I know that area inside out. I've done a fair bit of poaching over that way. Why, I'll probably get him there before you do."

I thought that if Bowles never arrived at all, it would be a good thing for both the Army and Thirteen platoon.

Bowles said, "Excellent. And as I can smell your good lady's cooking, I'd love to stay. Been eating out of tins these past few days."

"Ain't my good lady. That's Mrs. Prendergast."

"Well, this is the first time that Josiah and I have agreed on anything. I am certainly not his good lady. Now you sit down here, you poor man. I won't be but a few minutes."

And that was that. Toby and I went on out, Appleby followed to say goodbye. The two of us piled into the three-quarter, Toby at the wheel. I waved to Appleby, and we went back to the war.

On the drive back, I suggested that we get back to the road block, pick up as many recruits as could fit into the three-quarter and head to the bridge.

Toby agreed, after all, I was a staff sergeant, and he knew that I knew the game.

CHAPTER 60

FOXHOUNDS MEET HOLDFAST

"There's no one around. Are we on time? Are you sure this is the right bridge?"

"Yes, yes and yes. Now get off it. This is where we are supposed to be."

"There's no one around. You said there'd be a platoon of infantry here to do a bridge demolition guard. We hang around, and we're gonna get put in the bag. There's only two of us, you know."

"Jesus H. Christ, Sutton, I've told you over and over, number one, we're in the right place. Number two, there was supposed to be an infantry platoon and lastly and most importantly, number three, we left camp together. We got into the truck together. There was no one else in it. We didn't pick any one up, and we have travelled about thirty miles with only us in the cab, so, yes, I am fully aware that there is only fucking two of us. Sheesh."

"No need to get excited, Paulie."

"You continually state the obvious, Neill. And by the way, since we are out on an exercise, how about we use our proper ranks."

"Oh, my, so sorry, Big shot Staff Sergeant. Yes, Mr. Big shot Staff Sergeant. I do know that now I'm stating the obvious, I can see your rank badge, it tells me, even in this moonlight, that you are a big shot Staff Sergeant."

"No need to get testy, Neill. It's for the exercise."

"Well I'm on exercise, too, so I'd appreciate it if you would address me by my rank as well."

Staff Sergeant Paulie Kessler sighed. "Sure, Private Sutton, I'll do that. Now, Private Sutton, stay here in the vehicle. I'm gonna take a leak."

"Yes, Staff Sergeant Kessler."

The commander of the Engineer demolition team walked away from the truck and did his duty. On his return, Private Sutton asked him, "How long we gonna stay here, Paulie... I mean, Staff Sergeant?"

"I don't know. The bridge demolition guard commander was going to give me a briefing..." Kessler stopped talking. He realized that he had told Sutton all this at least twice already and he didn't want the private to accuse him of stating the obvious. As they sat on the front bumper without talking, the low whine of a deuce and a half traveling in bull low fractured the silence.

"Maybe that's them, Paulie."

Kessler didn't bother to correct him on the rank thing. "Maybe. You get in the truck and be ready to start her up and get out of here. I'm gonna go meet them. I'll flash twice with red for all clear."

"But red means danger. How can it mean all clear?"

"It can mean anything I fucking want it to mean. Especially since it's the only fucking colour filter I've got."

"Okay, okay. And how many if it's not clear?"

"If it's not fucking clear, you'll hear a whole lot of fucking shooting, for fuck's sake."

Kessler moved off toward the sound of the approaching truck. He nearly got caught, and it was only because he stepped quickly back off the track and into a small copse that the scouts didn't shoot him. Whoever's running this show has got his shit together, even if he can't tell time, he thought. Scouts out ahead a long way. But I beat them. His smile died on his lips as the barrel of a rifle was stuck in his back.

"Halt. Hands up or I'll shoot." Kessler let his submachine gun dangle from the neck sling and slowly raised his hands. Scouts out on the flanks, too, he thought.

"Hey, Squire," said the voice from behind in a barely audible whisper. "Got us a POW."

"Bring him in. We got his truck too," a louder yell came back.

Wow, this guy is good. But if he's so good, why is he so late?

"Out you go. Get on the track and don't let your hands drop."

"Aren't you going to ask me for the password?"

"Nope. Don't know it. Didn't get passed down at the O group. Just head back to your vehicle. We can get it sorted out there."

Kessler was growing more puzzled as they walked. No brigade password, yet all the super-stealth of a pro. What the fuck is going on here?

As they arrived at the truck, Kessler could see Sutton standing out beside the truck.

"You can drop your hands, Staff. We're on the same side. Good show, Eddie," said a soldier standing near Sutton.

Toby and I had made better time on the return than Urquhart had made on the way out. But a hundred yards short of the vehicle park, the three-quarter ran out of gas.

Toby and I walked the rest of the way in and found Lance Corporal Duguay and the now revived, but grimy Draper at the road block. I explained the situation to them. Lance Corporal Duguay quickly threw together a section and a half, loaded them on a truck. I directed Lance Corporal Duguay to remain at the road block while we drove to the other bridge.

With Draper driving, and myself in the cab, I led them to Lyons Bridge. Four hundred yards from where Kessler and Sutton were waiting, I directed Draper off the main trail and down a track that paralleled it. We stopped, and I unloaded the lads. No way we were going to drive innocently into an ambush. I put Toby and McGuffin out front and Eddie and Stuffy on the right flank and Steele and Vaughan on the left. There were three more that I left on the truck. I gave the scouts a minute or so to get out in front and then we followed.

When the deuce pulled up at Kessler' three-quarter, Staff Sergeant Kessler and I had a quick chat, and a plan was made.

"According to war game protocol, Staff Sergeant Oxnard, we will place charges within fifty yards of the bridge to be blown. Aside from the placement, and the size of the charges, the rest is done as per wartime."

"I see, and you will use electronic means to detonate the charges?"

"No, we will use safety fuse and detonation cord. Safety fuse runs slow, and a two or three foot length will give you ample time to get safely away."

"And detonation cord?"

Kessler laughed. "Det cord, it goes like a fart through a greyhound. Once it hits that cord, it's gone."

"Right, so my people will be safe if they are a minimum of a hundred yards from either charge?"

"Yes, no problem. But just in case, have them dig in a bit."

Kessler and Sutton went off to prepare the demolition charges, while I took Toby, Eddie and McGuffin over the bridge for a recce. As they walked, Toby said, "Excuse me, Staff..."

Now back in the military environment, Earl and gentleman's gentleman put on their military game faces.

"Yes, Private Trelauney-Fitzgibboncrest?" Although I realized that I did go overboard with the Private Trelauney-Fitzgibboncrest at times. Toby wished he would call him Squire, but I was, pardon the expression, a Jeeves on propriety when necessary. We had finished the recce and were coming back up from the bridge when Toby asked me, "Staff, we're changing the timings that came down from D Company, right?"

"Sort of, they probably came down from brigade. Bridges do not normally get blown without being part of a brigade fire plan."

So if we had a radio, we could call D Company's CP and let them know what's goin' on."

"Yes, we could. If we had a radio. As it is, Lieutenant Bowles took three radios with him on patrol. They were either captured or have gone missing."

"The ones at the road block and at the other bridge are okay, aren't they, Staff?" asked McGuffin.

"No, one got crushed when that three-quarter crashed the bridge. We had to leave the last one with Lance Corporal Duguay."

"So he's going to pass on the new timings, is he?"

"All being well, he's already done so, but we were in a poor radio reception area. There's no guarantee."

"Well, Squire, if any tanks come charging over the hill, we'll have to get out of the way."

Suddenly Toby realized that he could see Ox, McGuffin, and Eddie quite clearly.

"It's dawn. Boy, that has got to have been one of the longest nights of my life."

"Yes, and if we're going to be hit, it'll be very soon. If there are any real exercise activities scheduled to happen here, either from the enemy point of view or ours, then this place will be swarming with umpires just before it starts. So, get your section, Trelauney-Fitzgibboncrest and place them on our side of the bridge about here."

Here, was off to one side of the road that led over the bridge and in a small clearing that had a good field of fire.

"One other thing…"

"Yes, Staff?"

"Dig in."

"Dig in?"

"Yes, the Engineers are going to blow a pair of charges, one on either side of the bridge. You're section will be close to both sites. There should be no problems, but you might get showered with debris and falling rock. Best not to take chances."

"Yes, Staff."

"Any other questions?"

"No, Staff, we'll be fine."

"Roger, Private Trelauney-Fitzgibboncrest, I'll head back and put our reserve force in place. Hopefully, Lance Corporal Duguay has gotten through to D Company."

I got up to leave when Toby said, "Just a sec, Ox, I mean Staff. Those demolition guys, won't they have a radio?"

"Excellent thinking, Squire, I mean Private Trelauney-Fitzgibboncrest. Let's go and find out."

They did, and then Toby was on the air to the Engineer headquarters. With Toby's limited knowledge of radio/telephone procedure, Staff Sergeant Kessler had to explain to him that over the air, appointment titles were used to disguise the level of command of a unit, so he had to use Foxhounds for the Infantry and that Holdfast was the appointment title for the Engineers. "But, surely the enemy would know, that, Staff?"

"Yes, they might know that it's the infantry and the engineers, but they do not know if it is an infantry section or a battalion, an Engineer squadron or just me and my explosives wizard, Sutton."

"Right, thanks." With that, Toby got onto the Holdfast net and requested that their current situation be passed on to the regular brigade net.

CHAPTER 61

DAVIS MEETS THE COLONEL AGAIN

Back at the battalion CP, Jackrabbit Schultzberger was up and around, getting in the way of the MFC, the Mortar Fire Controller and his staff, the intelligence cell, the Sigs Officer and the radio operators and anyone else who had a real job within the CP. He blundered around, generally feeling jumpy. A man of action, Jackrabbit couldn't sit still this far back from the front. A signaller found him doodling with grease pencils on the back of the map board.

"Sir,"

"Yes, Davis, what is it? Has it come to this? That a lonely Private, in the Signal Corps no less, has come to chide me for doodling?"

Davis looked bewildered. "No, sir, the duty officer said to get you. He'd received a strange message from the brigade net that originated with the Engineers."

"Okay, carry on." Jackrabbit put down the grease pencil, gave a half-hearted wipe with the palm of his hand on his doodle, got his hand covered in blue and green grease stains and said, "Fuck it."

He went over to the CP area and found Major Colin Bradshaw, the Deputy Commanding Officer, and the duty officer, Captain Brian Wilson, in council.

"What's up, gents?" Jackrabbit asked, wiping his hand on his own backside.

The DCO said, "Message from the bridge demolition guard at Lyons bridge, sir."

"Lyons Bridge? Isn't that where Bowles was bagged last night? If so, we don't have anyone there. Do they confirm?

"Yes and no."

"There's an explanation just about to fall from your lips, isn't there, Colin?"

The DCO smiled. "Of course, sir. The message is that the bridge demolition guard has two section strength Foxhounds and one section of Holdfast in place at Lyons Bridge. Charges set to blow at 0545 hours."

"I see what you mean about yes and no. The information is partly right, and the timings are dead wrong. Who the hell are those Foxhounds? What about any authentication?"

"The Holdfast net is satisfied that the transmission is from their people and the group out there at the bridge do authenticate as Engineers. So up their net is alright. Then down from them to us, it's also okay. No one knows who the infantry are."

Jackrabbit looked at both officers then said to the duty officer, "What does D Company say about this?"

"They have nothing from Thirteen platoon after the reserve team on the road block stopped that assault on the Mountain Bridge."

"Is there anything more, Colin, from anyone at Brigade for the advancement of the demolition?"

"No, sir."

Jackrabbit went back to the coffee pot and pondered. He had lost his desire to doodle, and his stomach had already had an overdose of coffee.

"Sir?" Davis was on him again.

"Over here, Davis."

As the young soldier approached Jackrabbit, he said, "Son, is your only task to haunt me until I crack up?"

"No, sir, the duty officer, sir."

"Oh, he wants you to haunt me until I crack up?"

"No, sir."

"Never mind, son, just the ramblings of an old man in the pre-dawn before the attack."

"Yes, sir."

The two returned to the CP, and this time the duty officer said, "Message from D Company's mortar rep. This is from the MFC."

"Yes?"

"Sir, D Company's Fire Control Centre reported armoured movement in front of the three forward platoons."

"Got a grid?"

"Yes, sir, it's here," the duty officer pointed to the map where an enemy armoured regiment had two squadrons already listed as being in place.

"They moved in there approximately twenty hours ago, sir. Suddenly we get word that they're pulling back."

"Pulling back?"

"Yes, sir."

"Do we have a land line in and up to D Company's CP? I don't want to talk to OC Delta on the radio. For all we know that frequency has been compromised."

"Yes, sir, although it's intermittent. We have had a line crew out that way three times in the last twelve hours. Either enemy patrols have been cutting the wire or our vehicles have been chopping it up."

Jackrabbit looked at Captain Wilson. "My money's on Bowles cutting it up."

"Pardon, sir?"

Jackrabbit waved it away. "A passing thought. We'll go with the landline if it's still up now. Get Major O'Connor on it for me."

A few minutes later Jackrabbit was speaking to Major O'Connor. "Jimmy, what's the last you have on Bowles?"

"Bowles? He was captured early last night, sir."

"Hang on a sec, Jimmy."

Jackrabbit turned to the duty officer and asked, "Did a list come down from the umpire net with Bowles name on it?"

The duty officer went off to review the POW list. While Jackrabbit waited, he said to O'Connor, "I may be imagining things, but I have this weird feeling that that Goddamned Bowles has been resurrected."

"I was wondering why a lieutenant was a concern to my Battalion Commander at this stage of the exercise. A resurrection, that's grounds for concern, sir."

"Very funny, Jimmy, and I'll laugh back in the mess. Hang on."

The duty officer came back shaking his head. "Seems he was on one list as being captured. Then on the next list he had been removed. A typo possibly. Also, due to the confusion when that enemy patrol was attacked and ripped apart on the bridge, a number of our soldiers who had been captured when that patrol ambushed Bowles, just went back to re-join whoever Bowles left at the bridge."

Jackrabbit laughed. "Bowles men just ran away and got back into the war without anyone noticing?"

"Wonderful. A lot of initiative coming out of that platoon, none of it from Bowles, but he's creating some very good soldiers… probably out of pure self-preservation." Jackrabbit paused, chewed at his upper lip and then said, "And, that's not a typo, Brian, that Bowles name isn't on the list. That's a sign from God."

He returned to the phone. "Jimmy, still there? Good. Look, Bowles is on the loose... What? I don't know. Just a hunch."

"Yes, sir."

"Put all your anti-tank assets on your southernmost flank."

"Thirteen platoon's flank, sir?"

"No, your next most southern. I've got a real bad feeling the enemy are not playing by the rules. I think General Vachon is running an end around on us, an armoured one."

Major O'Connor said, "Sounds like you think he might be popping out of bounds and then back in again, Colonel?" There was laughter in his voice.

"Again, I commend your sense of humour, Jimmy. But I was doing it for self-preservation, mine and yours. Okay, get your anti-armour over on the high feature overlooking Merrit Road."

"Roger, sir and if you're correct, and I think you are, can we have mortar support on call?"

"You'll be the number one priority."

Jackrabbit hung up. He didn't know what was going on, but he would bet the remaining part of his pension that it involved Bowles. Colin Bradshaw came over to his boss with two cups of coffee and handed one to Jackrabbit. "Touch it up, sir?" Colin said as he pulled out a hip flask.

"Thanks, Colin, damnedest thing, ain't it?"

"Yes, it is, sir." Colin stopped speaking and looked at Lieutenant Colonel Schultzberger. "Imagine, a General sending his troops out of bounds to score a shallow victory over us. The rotten bastard."

"Yeah, yeah, Colin, I've already had it from O'Connor, give it a rest. We, I mean me, did it only to keep Bowles out of play, not to do anything for the war effort. Bowles," Jackrabbit shook his head. "The man's a fucking Jonah! He's the worst possible enemy to whichever force he's attached to. First of all, he gets his platoon decimated. Then we annihilate an enemy fighting patrol. As it happens, Bowles was with both of them."

"Definitely a Jonah, sir," said Colin. "He's also our best bet to finish off the Cold War, if only there was some way to get him to defect."

CHAPTER 62

BOWLES MEETS MORGAN AGAIN

I got the bridge demolition guard set up and then went over to check on the Engineers. Kessler took me on a walk about to see the set-up, saying, "We have the ravine here, and one charge is down there. It's marked with a strip of mine tape so we can see it if it turns out to be a dud."

"You one said charge, there's more?"

"Two. I'll man this one, and Private Sutton will be on the other one. He's over on the other side of the road, and his charge is down in that gulley, about 80 yards away."

"That's correct. On a long fuse as I told you earlier. The set-up is the same, a four minute fuse and a foot of det cord, which will burn in less than a couple of seconds."

"And both set for the same time?"

"Correct."

"It's C4, isn't it?" I asked.

"Yes, but they may go off one after another, or at the same time. Depends on the atmospherics and how damp or dry one length of fuse is compared to the other. No matter, the difference will be minor. Piece of cake."

Which was what Bowles was eating as he sat beside Appleby in the new Chevy truck. "Mmm, love that chocolate cake. Boy, Mr. Appleby, your wife sure can cook."

"She's not my wife. She's my sister. She lives with me and my daughter, Tuesday. Say, are you married?"

"No, I'm still free and foot fancy loose."

"You mean footloose and fancy free?"

"Oh, yes, I suppose so."

"Maybe you should meet Tuesday. She's a lovely girl. Too bad you guys came so late at night. We'll get together again after this is over, alright?"

"Sounds fine to me. You want that piece of cake?"

"No, thanks, you have it. I'll have a slug of this." And Appleby pulled out a new bottle of scotch. "Want a shot, chocolate cake goes with scotch." He laughed. "Matter of fact, there's damn little that scotch doesn't go with, here," he held out the bottle to Bowles.

"No thanks, Mr. Appleby. And by the way, you're drinking and driving. That's against the law, you know."

"Damn right. We'll I've survived four head ons, two of them involving you. Being pissed at the time of impact probably saved my life each time."

Even Bowles was smart enough to see the fallacy in Appleby's argument, although he wouldn't have recognized the term fallacy if it had been sitting between the two of them. He said nothing, sat tight, while Appleby got tighter, eyes on the road as the night drifted into day.

Appleby made a few turns, crossed a number of trails and then said, "There's the bridge over there, Lieutenant. I won't go any closer, 'cos you soldier boys are playing war. S'long."

Appleby had brought Bowles to within three hundred yards of the junction of Lawfield Road and Olinville Road. Bowles got out and headed toward the bridge. He left the road and ducked into the tree line, heading to where he could just see a part of the bridge's superstructure as a darkened silhouette against the slowly dawning sky. He managed thirty yards through the dense undergrowth when he was intercepted. One of my sentries, and who was it who hauled Bowles over? You guessed it, our old chum Alphonse Morgan. Lance Corporal Duguay had not wanted him at the road block, so he planted him on me. I hadn't learned that Morgan was with me until they had all dismounted from the deuce. I didn't want him anywhere near explosives, so Morgan had been placed in the area that was least likely to see enemy action.

"Halt, who goes where?"

Bowles stopped, heart racing. The shock of the challenge made him stop instantly, but also made him choke on the last of the chocolate cake. The challenge sounded right, yet he knew it was wrong. Coughing his air passages clear, he said, "I beg your pardon. Don't I know you?"

"Yes, sir. It's Private Morgan. I'm in your platoon."

"Then why are you challenging me? And it's not, 'Halt, who goes where?', it's stop. You there, say password."

"I don't think so, sir. I'm very sure it is halt."

Bowles, now that his fright had gone, and being full of great food, felt beneficent toward his fellow man, even if it was only a private. "Well, maybe so. Say it again."

"Halt, who goes where?"

"No, not that bit. After halt, if halt's correct say the password."

"I don't know the password."

"Why not?"

"The Corporal told us that was the part you left out during the Order group, sir."

"Oh, well, it's Coleman lantern." For the first time in his life, Bowles had stumbled across someone lower on the brain chain than himself. "Never mind. What did you say your name was?"

"Sir? What my name was? It's the same as it is now, sir."

"Yes, of course it is. I'll speak to you later. May I pass?"

"You didn't say the password."

Bowles beneficence had dribbled away. "Oh, for heaven's sake, 'Coleman'."

"And the rest of it?"

"...Huh?"

Off in the distance came the low growl of Centurion tanks on the prowl.

"Look, Private..."

"Morgan, sir."

"Morgan, the password is Coleman Lantern."

"Correct, sir, advance one and be recognized."

"I'm only one."

"Yes, sir."

"So can I advance?"

"I suppose so, I don't know what is next. So come ahead."

Bowles came forward and said, "Anything happening? I hear APCs or tanks."

"Yes, sir, according to Staff Sergeant Oxnard we're blowing the bridge at any minute."

"Blowing the bridge? And what if those tanks need to cross it?"

"That's why we're blowing it, sir, they're the enemy."

Seeing that this was a perfect time to conduct a teaching opportunity, Bowles said, "You do know that this bridge will not really be blown, Morgan. It's all simulated."

"Oh, so they won't blow anything up?"

"Of course not. Camp Gagetown is the property of the Queen. All that will happen is that a simulated charge, like a big firecracker will be set off on the bridge."

"So now one really blows anything up?"

"'Course not. Don't be ridiculous. We can't have a lot of Engineers running around blowing up bridges. It's all simulated. Nothing but a big firecracker. And after it goes off, the umpire staff won't let anyone use the bridge for the rest of the exercise."

"Why not, sir? It'll still be there, won't it?"

"Yes, it will… they're getting louder."

And closer, sir," said Morgan glad to provide a service to his platoon commander who had taken time out to explain simulated explosions to him.

"They're coming this way, I think, sir."

"Coming this way? Good Golly. I'd better get down there and make sure the GBD is on top of things."

"I think it's called a DBG, sir," said Morgan.

"Fat lot you know, Morgan. You didn't even know the password."

Bowles headed in toward the bridge. As he scrambled along through the bushes and trees, he went down a small ravine and past a fuse smoking its way toward the C4 charge.

He cluck-clucked out loud as he saw the charge. "Ah, hah, a bridge demolition simulated charge. Oh, that's it. Morgan was wrong. It's a BDG bridge demolition guard."

Bowles went closer to the charge. "Why did these silly Engineers put it here. It's supposed to be on the bridge."

He followed the slow-burning fuse to its end and saw the plastic explosive sitting out on the ground. "Someone's going to be in big trouble when this goes off. Especially if those tanks get here and the bridge isn't blown."

Bowles picked up the plastic charge. "Still got a long way to go. And they placed it in the wrong spot. I'll fix things and save the Engineers from embarrassment."

Balancing it in one hand, Bowles clambered up the side of the small ravine. One would imagine that with Bowles' poorly defined level of skill at traveling through the bush, he would stumble, trip or just fall over a log. At the very least, knowing the man's track record for creating disaster, we should expect that the fuse would have been plucked from the charge long before he reached level ground. And examining that track record closely, that would have been the way to bet. But as we have seen, this story is one of long shots. He was up and on the bridge road, without anything catching on his clothing or his webbing. The fuse remained tightly embedded in the plastic explosive, instead of sputtering impotently on the ground. As he broke cover and began his march along the road to the bridge, Toby, from his vantage point back at his half-dug trench saw quite clearly that a lunatic had picked up the explosive and was now lugging it onto Lyons Bridge. A slight breeze thinned the river's morning mist, and Toby saw that it was not a lunatic, but his platoon commander. Although to the trained eye, the difference was negligible. Toby threw off his helmet, dropped his rifle and dashed forward yelling, "No sir! Toss it in the river!"

CHAPTER 63

TOBY NEARLY MEETS HIS MAKER

Bowles was on a mission, and he heard nothing but tanks roaring down on his platoon's position. He reached the middle of Lyons Bridge. It was a historic wooden memorial to the semi-legendary Wilf Lyons of Lower Gagetown. With only minor repairs, the bridge had survived eighty-five winters. The record for summers would terminate at eighty-four.

Toby made the edge of the bridge and stopped. He yelled again, "Toss it in the river!" as he pointed at the charge. Bowles, hearing Toby but faintly and interpreting the pointed finger to indicate the other side, turned to look. A Centurion tank crashed through some hardy pines trees, turning fifty year old trees into a million toothpicks. Bowles dropped the charge and beat it off the bridge as the tank screamed toward the other end of the bridge. Another tank appeared to its left, then another off to the right, following closely. They all swung into a single file as they hit the road.

Bowles darted past Toby yelling, "Tanks!"

Toby took a few seconds to estimate the distance to the explosive package and swivelled back to chase his Lieutenant. Bowles was fast disappearing up the road.

Ten yards from Toby, feeling safe, Bowles stopped and turned back to watch the fireworks.

"No, sir, keep going," yelled Toby, closing in on his squad commander. Reaching him, Toby threw his arms around Bowles, forcing him back further. A line-backer pouncing on an unprotected quarterback.

"I say… Nothing to be alarmed about, it's only a giant fire…"

Toby had taken three steps with Bowles in his grasp when the fuse burnt to the det cord. He managed a further quarter step before the flame reached the detonator. The explosion came ripping past his ears before his foot had made it to the ground on the fourth step.

As Toby flew through the air, a chunk of eighty-four and a half year old timber bounced off his helmet-less head and smacked him just behind the left ear. He crumpled into the ditch beside the road.

Bowls, having Toby's body shielding him from the main blast and its accompanying debris, was torn out of Toby's grip and tossed rearward to land near Toby's trench. He was startled to see Offside staring up at him with eyes stretched wide enough to engulf a small country. Still in motion, Bowles tumbled in on top of little McGuffin. The charge, not content with disintegrating the upper timbers, also ripped the floor board planking up and cracked the cross beams. The lead tank, fifty-two tons of steel incapable of stopping on a dime, plunked straight down, nose first, into the soft muddy riverbed and stood upright, back end leaning against the bridge's pilings.

The tank behind it slowed as best the driver could manage, but it skidded to the jagged edge and the toppled forward to bang forcibly on the tail end of the first tank. The third tank crashed into the second and created a gigantic traffic jam on the far side.

Jackrabbit's bad feeling had come to pass. Shocked umpires leaped out from wherever shocked umpires leap, yelling "Cease fire!"

The war was over for Thirteen platoon.

When Toby came to in the camp hospital, twelve hours later, he said that it felt as if God had picked him up in one hand and flung him down the Grand Canyon. Urquhart would have described it as the perfect backhander from God. Both accounts would work.

I was at the hospital when Toby came out of his coma. I told him that Bowles had been commended for saving Toby's life during an unfortunate ammunition accident. I hated to break it to him, especially the part of the story where Bowles had fearlessly risked life and limb to rescue a private soldier of his from certain death while preventing tanks from storming through a section defensive position sited wrongly by a staff sergeant. And in doing all this magic, Bowles had prevented an enemy force from wiping out his Company in a surprise attack.

The origin of the tale could be traced to Jackrabbit. Seems, that on hearing of the debacle, he had said to his Deputy, "This is so improbable, I'll bet Bowles is the hero." Bowles, within hearing, decided that if his CO had said it, that was how he was going to report it.

To top it off, the Brigadier even lauded Bowles for calling in mortar fire on his own position at the bridge once it had been blown. No one was going to contradict the Brigadier, even when it was learned that Bowles wasn't within a hundred yards of a radio.

Sergeant Clyde, along with some of Thirteen platoon, now happily renamed 1313 squad, and safely ensconced back behind The Depot walls, paid a visit to Toby in the camp hospital.

That same evening Lieutenant Colonel Smith and Jackrabbit met up in the officers' mess.

"Ten days and he's out of my Depot," said Smitty.

"Smitty, after all I've done for you."

"Cheers, Jackrabbit, he's gonna be back in your battalion."

CHAPTER 64

WILL JACKRABBIT MEET CAPTAIN BOWLES?

Four days after the brigade exercise ended, Jackrabbit was sitting at this desk savouring a decent cup of coffee and not worrying about mosquitoes, rain or baking heat. He always enjoyed coming off an exercise, and he did admit that he liked setting off on one. As he sat there, rummaging around in the mound of paper that had accumulated in his in basket while he had been away, the RSM knocked on the door frame and came to attention in the door way.

"Good morning, RSM, how may I help you?"

RSM Dixon came in, stopped in front of Jackrabbit's desk and handed him a piece of paper. "If it's alright with you, sir, I'd like to go on leave, ASAP, sir, and would appreciate the leave pass being effective immediately."

Jackrabbit took the leave pass and looked up at his RSM. "Nothing serious, Mr. Dixon. I trust?"

"No, sir. I just feel the need to head out for a bit. Six weeks of living in each other's pockets gets the nerves on edge. Kinda strained, if you know what I mean."

Jackrabbit had no idea what he meant. Dixon had no nerves. There was something up.

"I see, very well. But I can give you five days off like the rest of the battalion's getting and you need only use up nine days of your annual leave allocation."

"No, thank you, sir, I'll take the full two weeks as annual. I'll still let it overlap the brigade time off period so that I'm really only away from the battalion for nine days."

Now Jackrabbit was really suspicious. Something was definitely up. RSM Dixon was too much the old soldier to give up five days of free time. So, if the RSM was in retreat, what was moving in the battalion that he had missed? He had heard nothing at coffee break in the officers' mess. Not that that meant anything. The Officers usually apprehended the rumour wind when it was leaving camp as a gentle breeze. The sergeants' mess intercepted rumours at the hurricane level, and even the junior ranks club caught it at fierce gale altitude. He nodded, signed the pass, returned it to the RSM who came back up to attention, saluted and said, "Thank you, sir, see you in two." He turned and marched out.

Lieutenant Colonel Schultzberger sat back in his chair, his morning in tatters, his once tasty coffee now a scowling cup returning his glare. His first thought was that Bowles was back. He shoved the suddenly stale coffee to the far edge of his desk and dialled Smitty at The Depot.

"Morning, David," he said when Smitty answered.

"Morning, Jackrabbit, and forgive me for being suspicious, but what do you want?"

"You know me well, David, but not that well. I don't want anything."

"Nothing?"

"Well... the answer to one question."

"Oh, I see. And I suppose the question is will I take Bowles for another six month tour of duty at The Depot? My answer is no. A large no, at that. A definite no and that is final."

"Amazing. See you don't know me that well. That was not the question. The question is, is Bowles still at The Depot?"

"Of course. At least he's supposed to be. Is that all?"

"Yes, thank you, Smitty, see you later."

Jackrabbit hung up the phone. Yes, even with Smitty's reassurance, something was in the wind, and it was rolling up its sleeves in preparation to roll in with some dirty deeds at the crossroads.

He sat and pondered a bit then called out, "Captain Wavell?"

His adjutant, who we had met during Appleby's first automobile intervention, yelled out, "Coming, sir."

Seconds later, he dashed into Jackrabbit's office only to be met with the command, "Get the DCO and the QMSI, both of them right away."

"Yes, sir." A few minutes later and the two of them were standing at ease in Jackrabbit's office. When Captain Wavell asked if he should stay, Jackrabbit said, "No." Then as Wavell turned to go, Jackrabbit changed his mind. "Belay that, Adjutant, stay. Who knows? Maybe four heads are better than three." Jackrabbit had just remembered that in his position as the Adjutant, Wavell had a vast array of nosy, muck-raking, like-minded unit adjutants who when not making trouble for the soldiers, were collecting, analysing, embellishing and gossip-mongering amongst themselves.

Three of this four person committee you have met. The fourth, WO II Peterson, who as QMSI, or Quartermaster Senior Instructor, was RSM Dixon's deputy.

"Gentlemen, take a seat, but hopefully, this will be a very short meeting. I need you all to offer responses in the negative."

The Adjutant made a noise like a question being swallowed, bit his lip as the CO glanced his way and then went on, "First a bit of background. The RSM has gone on leave. My signature on the leave pass wasn't dry before he made a rapid retreat from camp."

"Curious, sir. Tres curious," said Colin, the battalion's second-in-command.

"Yes, it is, and it becomes... what that's term?"

"Curiouser and curiouser, sir?" tossed in the QMSI.

"Yes, Q, Curiouser and curiouser. And to add to it, he passed up the five days the Brigade Commander's authorized for all units."

"He what? Sorry, sir. That's just not him," said the Q.

"Agreed. Not him at all."

"Pardon me, sir, It may not be the RSM's usual routine, but I believe I know why Mr. Dixon has scarpered, sir," said the Adjutant.

"There, you see," said Jackrabbit. "I knew the Adjutant's pipeline would see us through. Give, Adjutant, give."

"Very well, sir, although I have been sworn to secrecy..."

"Bullshit, Wavell, if this is out of that leper colony you call the Camp Gagetown Adjutant's Mutual Support Society, it's just advanced knowledge. Spit it out," said Colin, half-rising from his chair.

"Easy, DCO, easy, I'm sure that Captain Wavell is bound by loyalty to the regiment more than to any ad hoc group."

"Yes, there is that," said Colin, settling back into his chair. "And... I'm sure that the good Captain understands just who writes his performance appraisal," he added, taking up his cup and saucer and having a satisfying slurp. As DCO, it was Colin's job to write up the Adjutant's personnel evaluation report.

The Adjutant took a breath, looked at the DCO and then to the CO. "Well, sir, I have it on good authority that the Brigadier is going to announce a special parade to honour Lieutenant Bowles."

"He must be out of his mind!" said Colin.

"No fucking way!" said the QMSI, and added, "Beg pardon, sir."

The man who called down mortar fire on his own troops took it a bit calmer. "No apologies necessary, Q. I think that is the appropriate comment at this moment. What in heaven's name is he doing that for?"

"So, Adjutant," said Colin. "What the devil is Bowles getting a brigade parade for?"

"Not exactly a brigade parade, sir…" Wavell hesitated.

"Go on, Adjutant."

"Yes, sir."

Silence.

"A little louder, Adjutant, we didn't hear that."

"It's to be your parade, sir, with the Brigadier as reviewing officer. He intends to bestow a Brigade Commendation on Lieutenant Bowles."

"A Brigade Commendation? This gets worser and worser, instead of curiouser and curiouser. And I'm the one to be seen as publicly endorsing that empty-headed, half-fucked fool's actions?" said Jackrabbit. "No wonder the RSM went on leave. He knew of this."

The QMSI said, "He didn't pass it on to me, sir…the sonofabitch."

"To be sure," said Colin and with a wry smile toward the CO said, "I wonder if the Commanding Officer can spare me for the next two weeks?"

"No, the Commanding Officer cannot," said Jackrabbit. "What the Commanding Officer wants is to be surrounded by loyal and committed officers."

The room grew quiet as Jackrabbit sank into thought. Then he shifted forward and slammed a huge fist onto his desk. "That sonofabitch! To paraphrase the Q. he knew! That disloyal, scheming son of a bitch! He knew!"

Jackrabbit looked around at his three astonished subordinates. Jackrabbit shook his head, took a deep breath, exhaled and took in another breath. "Pardon me, gents, but you must remember that if I was able to call in mortar fire on that conniving weasel while in Korea, I'm sure that it is perfectly acceptable to call him names now."

Colin looked over at Jackrabbit, a smile on his face.

"And as for you, Major Colin Bradshaw, you can wipe that shit-eating grin off your ugly mug…"

Bradshaw's smile shifted into a large chuckle and then outright laughter. Jackrabbit threw his hands in the air and joined him. So did Quartermaster Senior Instructor Peterson. Only Captain Wavell, whose sense of humour was an inch thick and half as wide, stood there in disbelief. His austere sense of duty, coupled with his predisposition for martinet-cy prevented him from seeing the joke.

As the laughter subsided, a gentle rap, rap on the door frame caught their attention. "Would it be permissible for a conniving weasel, disloyal, scheming son of a bitch to join in the merriment?"

RSM Michael Peter Hector Dixon stood in the doorway.

"Yes, very good of you to join us, Mr. Dixon. How was your leave?"

"I beg the CO's pardon. I reacted impulsively. I apologize." Dixon held up his leave pass and tore it in two.

"No apology, necessary, Mr. Dixon. Every one of us here has been influenced by the presence of Lieutenant Bowles in amongst us. I'm sure that if we had thought of it first, Captain Wavell would have been legging it for the main gate with me and the CO in hot pursuit," said the DCO.

"Well, gentlemen, let's have a quick run through on the prelims to holding a parade. In order to permit myself a little spleen-venting, I'll run us all through the background." No one contradicted him because that was not what junior officers did to commanding officers.

"We begin with an idiot appearing in the battalion's area of responsibility and we end up with said same idiot appearing as the guest of honour on a battalion parade. He's fucked things up four ways from Friday and if he is to be recognized for anything it should be as Canada's contribution to military disasters."

Jackrabbit paused, took a sip of his now very cold coffee and the Adjutant added, "Too true, sir, too true."

Jackrabbit smiled at Wavell and the memory of Lieutenant Bowles' arrival at Camp Gagetown. "Yes, Adjutant, your initial meeting with Bowles in an admirable example of the depth of the stupidity in which he's been dipped in. And now, after nearly killing recruits under his command, destroying a historic bridge, a number of not so new tanks..."

"Tanks we can easily forget about," said the DCO with the infantryman's contempt for the Armoured Corps.

"Yes, but we must also remember the thousands of dollars burned up, blown up, ran over, all in the name of Lieutenant Bowles. And what happens to this knucklehead? The God dammed fool gets a parade in front of the Brigadier."

A knock on the partly closed door interrupted him. All heads swivelled around to see who would dare invade the CO's lair. Lieutenant Donald Karlsen, the Assistant Adjutant, stood firm in the collective glare of the battalion's big-wigs.

The Adjutant, seeing his assistant, sprang up and yelled, "Karlsen, this had better be good. Damn good!"

"Unfortunately, sir, it is bad, damn bad."

"Not a problem, Donnie," said Jackrabbit, with a calming glance at his Adjutant, who was notorious for his despotic attitude toward subordinates and his infuriating brown-nosing toward his superiors.

"We are not in the habit of shooting the messenger, Donnie, Come in and share this catastrophe."

Lieutenant Karlsen saluted and came in. "I just got this from Lieutenant Colonel Smith. With you all in conference, he called me."

"Yes, Donnie, good, now relax and tell us of this calamity."

"There's going to be a brigade parade for Lieutenant Bowles, sir."

"We already know that, Karlsen," snapped Captain Wavell. "And it's a First Battalion parade, not brigade."

"Yes, quite true, Donnie, we were aware of that fact," said Jackrabbit.

"Yes, sir, Colonel Smith did think that rumour had trickled out by now."

"Appears to have flooded out to certain individuals as opposed to the trickle that took it's time getting to me," said Jackrabbit, with an eye to the RSM, who, on catching the eye, returned it and threw in a grunt as a bonus.

"There is another part of the Bowles parade that has not been so well-distributed, sir. Colonel Smith is pretty sure that the very latest is still a secret known to only a few."

"Yes, Lieutenant, and if you don't get on with it, it'll remain a secret within these walls," said Colin, but not unkindly. Wavell gave a low snarl. Jackrabbit nodded. Karlsen took a breath, as if unsure of the CO's statement on the future of messengers. Expelling a truck load of air with his words, Lieutenant Karlsen finally got it out, "The Brigadier is promoting Bowles to captain on that parade, sir."

Jackrabbit deflated like a machine-gunned air mattress. As his breath leaked out, he muttered, "Captain...Captain Bowles..."

AFTERWORD

"What? Are those Canucks crazy?" yelled someone from out of the crowd. Goody had advertised that this was to be the club's final afternoon for the adventures of Toby and Bowles. The place was packed and I didn't recognize the voice. Goody did. "Heathcliffe-Dupont, that'll be enough!"

Over the rumbled mutterings about decorum, Goody went on. "Please, Gents, remember where we are."

"He may be overly loud," said Martindale, but he's got a point."

I stood up. "From your viewpoint, Squiffy, that may be true."

"Even from Jackrabbits point of view," said Nelson Graves, who had been with us since Day One. "They're making him a captain!"

"Not on, old boy, not on at all," groused the Crotchety-One, a retired Lieutenant-General who we kept around to provide the Club with a touch of class.

I was pleased that so many had taken to my telling of Toby's exploits. They'd begun to associate themselves with Toby, Jackrabbit and even Colonel Smith. But I didn't want to incite a mutiny amongst my own ranks.

We had been at it now for several weekends and the gathering had increased with each Sunday. The committee had been overjoyed that the once ghost-town atmosphere of a Sunday afternoon had turned into a cross between a gold rush and a carnival. Of course, all the gold had flooded into the club's coffers not mine.

"I agree completely with you that the decision to promote Lieutenant Bowles was not a wise move."

Groans, sprinkled with comments about lunacy, gross stupidity and foolhardiness fell about my ears as I stood there. I let them finish and when the room had quieted, I said, "You must remember that an army, any army is not always able to do the smartest thing. The Brigadier acted on what he was told, not the full story. Bowles' actions from a birds eye view, could have appeared to border on the heroic whereas we all know it was closer to being imbecilic."

Goody stirred and stood beside me. "No matter, the outcome was as Ox, our patient story-teller has stated. With that, I would like the members to put their hands together to show Mr. Marvin Oxnard our appreciation."

As one the crowd, those seated first joining the ranks of the already standing, gave me a gratifying ovation. It swelled, paused and then took off again. With no regard for club rules or decorum, loud cheers thundered along with the applause. I held up my hands to quiet them. They ignored me. By this time, I had to confess, my gentleman's gentleman façade had crumbled into a huge teeth-exposing grin.

I turned, moved to the sideboard behind me. Reaching into one of the three large cardboard containers I took out two books and held up one in each hand. "My publisher…"

I had to stop. No one was hearing me over the renewed clapping. They had recognized that I was holding up copies of Greatcoats On! Greatcoats Off!. Finally the tumult ceased. "My publisher, toy Soldier Press has graciously provided the membership with two hundred copies of my book." They roared their endorsement. I passed one copy to Goody and handed the other to someone who had charged up to me.

Later that evening I mentioned to Toby that I spent nearly two hours signing books. Over dinner, which a generous club committee had paid for, Goody said, "Ox, no one's picked up on it yet, but your story…" he had a faint grin on his face.

"Incomplete?" I inquired.

"To say the least and to quote Squiffy Martindale, "You left us hanging.""

I nodded as I cut off a piece roast beef, carefully dabbed a spot of horseradish on it, then forked it into my mouth. After chewing and swallowing, I took my wine glass and held it high. "To Captain Arthur Victor Llewellyn Bowles… who's military exploits during peacetime are as catastrophic as the rest of his family's adventures during wartime."

Goody stood up with his wine glass and said, "To the successful continuation of Bowles' military career. And for that matter, Toby's too."

ABOUT THE AUTHOR

Jim Miller is a retired Canadian Army officer with over forty years' service who is now writing full time. Now a published author, he served in the Canadian Armed Forces for over forty years, moving through the ranks from private to warrant officer and then taking his commission. He worked with the Canadian Rangers and retired as a captain. He has a BA in history and philosophy from University of Manitoba and an MA from Royal Roads University. Married to Bev, they have two children, Camille and Michael.

Made in the USA
Charleston, SC
26 December 2016